SECRET FRONTIER

TOM DYNE

CYBERMECH PRESS

Published by Cybermech Press
Cover design by Vanesa Garkova

ISBN 978-1-7333047-0-2 (paperback)
ISBN 978-1-7333047-1-9 (ebook)

Library of Congress Number: 2019915031

First Edition: October 2019

10 9 8 7 6 5 4 3 2 1

Printed in the United States of America

SECRET FRONTIER

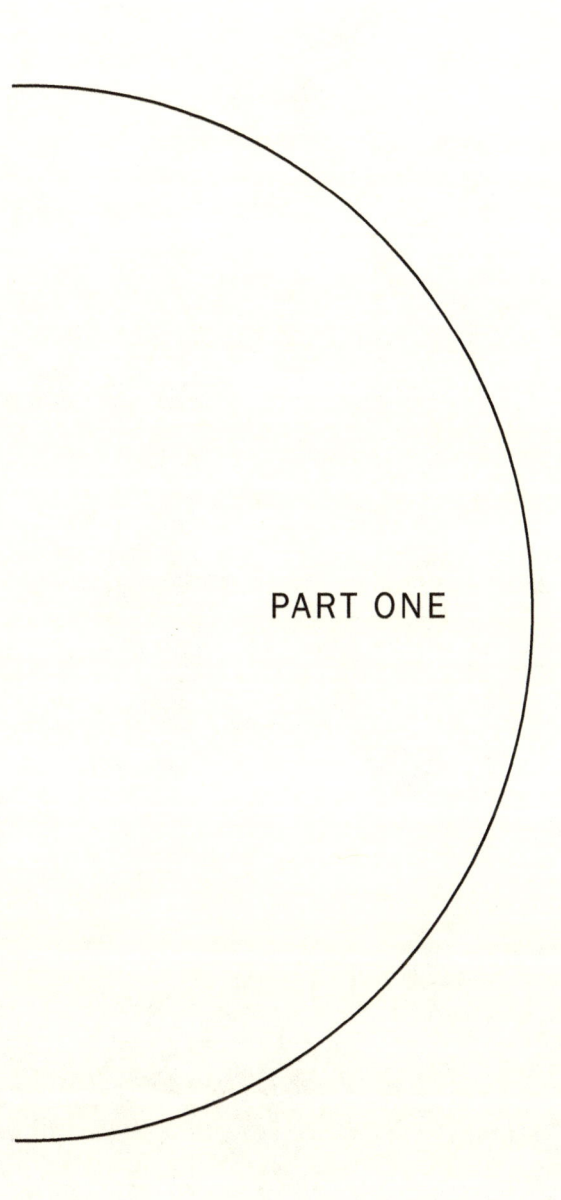

PART ONE

— 1 —

STACKED DECK

"Do you consider the outcome a curse or a blessing?" the shrink asked. I was embarrassed by my suicide attempt because I'd failed. So I lied about my reasons. I said I was a loner who'd left a trail of broken relationships—a girlfriend here, a man there, a best friend. But I didn't talk about the betrayals in my life. The shrink bought it—was pleased even—and left my hospital room looking satisfied. I didn't know his questions were an evaluation, but looking back, I see what it was—the first of many hints I'd been taken against my will. I wasn't the only person who could be cold and hard.

I tried to take my life because I was in a looping, pathetic dream without hope and because I had no power to change it. What I told him was close to the truth. The real reason I did it was to reclaim control.

Day in and day out, I'd crawled into my cubicle at Banadane Systems, just to come home to funnel nutrients into my body and engage my pleasure centers on VR_World. Every day was a repeat of the last, like a robot whose value was measured by how many computation cycles it output. To convince myself I was still free, I wrote code exploits while on the clock—nothing sinister, just harmless hacks into government servers for kicks, like erasing medical debts for military vets chosen at random or fast-tracking housing vouchers for kids who were wards of the state as I'd once been. But my small-time rebellions couldn't shake the feeling I was owned.

So I jumped twelve stories from the Thomas Jefferson Bridge.

Before hitting the water, I remember a voice saying *are you sure?* and seeing a blinding flash. Only to wake up to being controlled by others again without even knowing it. There was a difference now, though I didn't understand it: I wanted to live, but why?

The next thing I knew, I was lying in this cramped bed in a room decked out in instrumentation. There were no needles or wires in me, yet readouts of my vitals floated on what appeared to be holographic panels. One holopanel displayed my genetic profile, with accurate representations of my black walnut hair and hazel eyes. I didn't remember emergency rooms being this way, though who knew what advances were borne from our back-to-back Unification Wars of the last three decades. The room shook for a few seconds and tossed me side to side—like I said, strange place.

A blinking message demanded my attention: *WELCOME TO YOUR NEW LIFE.* Curious, I reached over, and when my fingertips passed through the holoscreen, the message dissolved into the next. *Congratulations on passing our selection process. Starting today, M2057-BLG-197, your old life—*

A nurse barged in, and the holopanel scattered into a jumble of dots. She was a middle-aged woman with blonde, curly hair and light green eyes. She drew her lips into a tight line, and her eyes darted around the room, like she was checking for danger. Her arms trembled at her sides, and she proceeded to open and close drawers hidden in the walls. Was she looking for something?

"Darin," she said my name in the most angelic voice, "you need to hide. Right now." She reached down to touch a spot on the wall by the foot of my bed. A spacious compartment slid open to reveal syringes, cotton swabs, and medicine bottles packed end on end. She cleared the contents to one side in a violent sweep. "In here. Hurry." There was kindness in her eyes, an expression I hadn't seen directed at me in a while. "We worked so hard to save you. It can't all have been for nothing."

I was too hazy to protest when she shoved me into the tight space.

4

My knees were folded against my chest. She tapped the wall with a palm, and the compartment door—made of a glossy, semi-transparent material that concealed me well enough—slid down shut.

A moment later, two bulky shadows entered the room. The men advanced upon her. She struggled with the pair. Strident crashes rang in my ears and rattled me. *I need to help her.* But my body wouldn't listen. *No, not again.* I'd been brought back to life to be useless again.

The last time I heard the nurse's voice was her blood-curdling scream. When her body hit the floor, the odor of burnt flesh filled my nostrils and turned my stomach. Why was this happening?

The two men turned to speak to one another. A gruff voice said, "Geoff, what did I tell you? High oxygen environment. Your dot blaster is a last resort. Start a fire, and we'll burn up along with our haul."

Dot blasters? They continued using more terms I didn't recognize.

The other man, Geoff, said, "She pissed me off running like she did...figured she was trying to trigger a silent alarm."

"No more deviating from our clients' instructions. Shock batons from here on out. Understood?"

"Roger." There was rustling like a gun being holstered.

How would these thugs profit from holding up a hospital? This poor nurse's only mistake was caring for a wretch like me. It brought back memories of the day when the rickety wooden gate of my foster home closed behind me, and like so many kids, I felt like defective goods abandoned by the roadside. Now, her children would live through years of loneliness and neglect like I had, all because these animals justified hurting others to earn a living. If I only had the power to do something...

I furrowed my brow. For a fleeting moment, her voice was inside my head: *"You remind me of my son. He will be okay without me, won't he?"* My brain fog sent me reeling—was I hallucinating from the meds?

One of the men, the gruff voice, exited the room, but Geoff

remained near my hiding place. Something crackled like a walkie-talkie. *Click.* "Boss. Over."

Click. "Geoff, what now? Why haven't you come back? We got the rest of this bird to lock down."

Click. "Boss, this bed is still warm."

Click. The walkie-talkie crackled again. "What? Do you think we missed a passenger?"

There was my cue. I searched the compartment in which I lay hidden. Nice, a syringe. I peered over my other shoulder, half-expecting to find a bottle of chloroform. No dice. Making do, I gripped the long, nasty needle in a balled fist.

Click. "Find out who the nurse was looking after, Geoff. No witnesses."

"As long as we make off with this bird in one piece, we'll be set for life, right?"

"For all the people we had to nix, we better be."

Before Geoff clicked his walkie-talkie to say, "Over," I tapped the cabinet door. It slid up and open without a sound. The nurse's body was lying in a pool of blood, and standing next to her, an arm's length from my face, was the bottom half of a man dressed in camo fatigues and black combat boots.

I swung my arm out and plunged the syringe into the back of his knee. The needle slid into his flesh like a knife into butter, and the momentum carried me into a roll out from my hiding place and into a crouch. Only in my dreams could I be so smooth.

Geoff let out a grunt and looked down. I met startled gray eyes and a face concealed by a balaclava. What did he have in his right hand? It reminded me of a policeman's baton, except sparks arced across its cylindrical head. Mesmerizing.

When I moved to stand up, he swung the weapon downward and struck me square in the chest. My body lit up like a tacky Halloween decoration.

The wonderful thing about adrenaline was it sobered the mind in an instant: I wasn't dreaming. This fight was real. The heat radiating from my assailant's weapon registered, but the strike itself didn't. Thank you, morphine, or whatever painkiller they had me on.

My opponent was as taken aback by my non-compliance as I was. He swung his arm wide and out for another strike. A voice in my head passed by in a jumble, like a train horn muffled as it entered a tunnel. *"No way he's got the guts for a proper counter..."* And then the voice was gone.

He reached the height of his swing and paused for the shock baton to charge up.

When the deck was stacked against me, my go-to choice was the most reckless one. I sprang up and clapped both hands over the baton's electrified end, fingers interlocked. Unbearable searing pain coursed through my hands this time. Light leaked out from the gaps between my fingers and flooded the room.

When it was over, the masked intruder lay beside the nurse. It'd all happened so fast. I placed two fingers against her neck first, then his. She didn't have a pulse, and neither did he.

The poor woman was kind to me, and this was how she was repaid. Senseless acts like these made me lose it. In my short life, I'd seen evil men ascend to fame and glory, the well-heeled steal from the masses without consequence, and patriots imprisoned for speaking their conscience. The news reported on these events every day, but when I looked around, I saw a world that shrugged and accepted injustice as the norm.

I wouldn't accept it—not this time. My chest was heaving, and my hands ached. It'd been so long since I felt anything at all that I didn't want it to stop.

Geoff's walkie-talkie went off. *Crackle*: "All units report to the main hold." In the background, there was frightened screaming.

— 2 —

HUNTER

I found my old clothes left folded by my bedside and rushed to pull on joggers and a light jacket. When I stepped out into the hallway, it dawned on me that I hadn't been staying in a hospital. The floors were made of bolted sheet metal, and circular port windows lined the hallway. I peered out into the dark nothingness of night. How long had I been out if they'd gotten me onto a plane?

My brain fog lifted—the dull, burning in my chest sped up the process. I remembered the men had spoken of a major payday. They were hijacking this plane for ransom. Did it even make sense to do that in this day and age?

I examined the weapons I'd stripped from Geoff. The shock baton betrayed no power source and collapsed into a cylinder small enough to fit in my palm. Then there was the dot blaster, a gun made of a pearl-white material as lightweight as plastic. Hold on, what was I even doing?

At least I wouldn't spend my last moments as part of another heartless transaction. I would get back at these animals.

I passed by the port windows and sidled up to the door at the end of the hallway. The door had been left ajar, and when I peered in, I understood what their ringleader meant by the "main hold." There were passengers, but they weren't seated in neat aisles the way I'd expected. Instead, men and women sat strapped into harnesses on opposite sides, facing each other across a wide, bare floor

8

as in a warehouse. They were dressed like civilians—like me—but it seemed we were on a military cargo jet.

I caught my breath when I spotted what was in the middle of the hold. A pile of bodies lay scattered in a morbid line. Standing around the corpses were more masked hijackers. I counted ten in total. They wore the same camo-green fatigues and oil-sheen combat boots as Geoff had and carried white guns like the one tucked to my side. They pushed forward a middle-aged man dressed in khakis and a T-shirt. They clubbed him with their batons until the electric shocks no longer elicited groans. He was probably dead, and he joined the other bodies crumpled on the floor.

What kind of hijackers killed off their hostages? Dead people made for poor ransom negotiations.

A young girl, maybe a teenager, was next up for the chopping block. Her long, raven-colored hair covered half her face, and the checkered pattern of her skirt stood out among the carnage around her. The other passengers watched, distraught, as she was struck behind the neck. She cried out, and her head hung down facing the white laces of her red sneakers. She fell to her knees.

One of the masked men stepped forward and struck her again, and again. Her screams cut through the silence. She fell to the metallic floor. She was going to die, suffering and alone, while others stood by and did nothing—and I was just as guilty.

I pulled back into the corridor and leaned against the wall, clenching my fists inside my pockets. Disgusting. Human beings were disgusting. Those murderers had already squandered their lives, and now they would rob her of hers. This wasn't a hostage situation—it was a mass execution.

The masked man raised the shock baton for one final blow, his hand held aloft while it charged back up.

I palmed the gun at my hip. Stepping through the door and into the open, I squeezed the trigger. Out from the muzzle came beams of what I could only describe as pure light. I blinked twice, perplexed; what kind of gun did *that*? Not like I used it to my advantage—I missed by a mile, and the light beams splashed the bulkhead in ear-piercing, explosive bursts. Oh, right, high oxygen environment.

Angry faces swung toward me in unison. Hostages and hijackers alike gawked at me as if I were off my rocker. So what? It *did* distract them from killing the girl. I wasn't going to stop, regardless of the danger to the plane. I held the trigger in and unloaded.

One of the masked men unholstered his dot blaster, leveled it at me, and fired. A beam hit above and to my immediate right. Before I could blink, the hold was plunged into darkness. Had we damaged the wiring?

Our shots arced through the cabin and lit it up like a strobe. I pulled my arms up to shield my face by reflex. Heat from the rounds radiated near me. My stomach twisted as if it might fall out. I lurched off my feet and conked my noggin on the bulkhead above. It was absolute chaos.

When the floodlights flickered back on, it was as if gravity had gone on vacation. Except for those strapped in, the rest of us—the hijackers, hostages, and I—were floating through the air like a scattered deck of cards. Was the plane in a nosedive? Maybe I'd overdone it this time, but at least I'd take these murderers down with me. For men who killed without a second thought, their faces held the terrified grimaces of people attached to living.

I squinted and made out a spherical object. It was constructed of polished chrome and was the size of a medicine ball. The sphere bounded in from the far back before levitating straight up into the hold's vertical center. It opened in half to emit a maddening screech followed by an overwhelming array of lights. I was now blind, deaf, and incapacitated in midair, a fetus helpless in the womb.

My eyesight washed back into view. Four armed guards—no, four soldiers dressed in some sort of alabaster-white body armor—swept into the hold. One soldier marched across the sheet metal deck toward us; two trotted perpendicular to each side wall counter to the laws of physics; and the fourth soldier walked on the ceiling, upside-down from my perspective. They stopped to form a diamond-shaped cordon around the hijackers massed together in midair. Five more soldiers, all wearing the same power armor, rushed in next. They took up positions staggered among the first group and together encircled the hijackers in three-dimensional space.

The newcomers steadied rifles—the weapons reminded me of harpoon cannons—and fired in unison. From their muzzles sprang forth ropes with weights attached to the ends. The bolas spiraled out and wrapped themselves around the hijackers' bodies. The soldier standing upside-down on the ceiling raised his gauntleted arm and pushed a button on his wrist console like he was checking the time. The immobilized enemies dropped like lead. They slammed into the metallic floor with a low-pitched *thud* so heavy it made me wince. The threat had been neutralized.

I survived, but my old life as I knew it had ended.

◐ ◑

I was standing back on solid ground. The ringing in my ears subsided, but I was still trying to piece together what'd gone down.

"Eleven intruders in total," one of the soldiers said to me. He told me their squad was called Charlie Company. The name "Byron Colbee" blinked onto the dog tag affixed to his suit's breastplate. "We found one of their accomplices in the medical bay. Were you responsible for the kill, Rook?"

I didn't know why he was calling me a rookie, but I gave an

absent-minded nod anyway. I was too busy staring at his armored boots and working out how he had walked on the ceiling.

Byron said, "Gravity boots—it's just a nickname—they get the job done all right. Join Charlie Company, and you'll get your own pair one day."

Gravity boots...Charlie Company...he talked like these things were familiar to me.

"Your diversion was what we needed. It gave us a window for a flashbang and caught them off guard."

So our saviors were officially military.

He leaned over to his squadmate and said, "Though who knows what those fools were thinking. The tech they smuggled in is obsolete next to our Omnisuits. And where were they planning on going once they landed?"

His teammate hollered in acknowledgment, and they touched gloves. Byron turned back to me. "Doesn't matter who starts the fight, Charlie Company finishes it."

Light filtered in through the port windows then, and I gazed out, hoping for the sunrise of a new day. Only then did it click.

I wasn't aboard a plane. Not the regular kind anyway.

Outside the spacecraft, stars twinkled across the infinite universe. The light wasn't coming from the sun. It was coming from our landing zone. The surface below was a rocky gray, devoid of distinguishing features save one: a massive crater. Spanning the crater's open top was a gargantuan dome. The structure was formed from interlocking panels shaped like hexagons.

"They love to put on a show for the newcomers," he said with a grin. "Once they switch the Holosky Projectors back on, it'll appear to be another boring crater. But it wouldn't make for a proper welcome, would it?"

As we descended, I could make out compact pods, oblong cylinders lying on their sides and spaced out in neat sectors. Were those buildings inside? I traced paths and roads—were those people walking down below?

Byron slapped me on the back so hard I almost jumped. "Rook, welcome to life on the Lunar Colony!"

The Moon? It was impossible for me to accept. How could there be a city here? A shiver shot through me like an electric current. I'd given up—wished for a chance to start over—and now...

The first time I laid eyes on the Lunar Colony, a beacon of light among the vast reaches of space, I was held transfixed in wonder and awe. It was like anything was possible going forward. Would my life be different this time around?

— 3 —

NETWORK

"Freeze the video. There." Hurston Segerstrom carried a wild-eyed expression like he had hooked a big one. Once engaged, he wouldn't let up until his suspicions were satisfied. He hadn't always been this way, but things changed after the incident so many years ago. "Ladies and gents, do you see it?" Seger turned to his staffers in the newsroom and gestured with open arms toward the jumbo holoscreen. He swung to point with two fingers, and a lick of his pale blond hair fell on his forehead.

His staff reporters exchanged glances with one another. He guessed they were deciding whose turn it was to take the bait. He could tell they were exhausted from poring through the footage taken from the recent spacecraft hijacking. They'd cross-referenced the identities of the masked members of the cell. Hell, they'd even completed background checks on every single passenger on board.

"No volunteers? Whatever shall I do?" He was aware his worn tweed blazer and loosened tie didn't fit the part, but he loved to pretend he was on stage delivering a Shakespearean soliloquy. After a search consuming his newsroom around the clock, no leads panned out. The hijackers all hailed from Earth, but that was it. They were part of a resistance group against the One World movement—in reality, just disaffected young men looking for an excuse to score. He wasn't satisfied with this explanation. The profit motive—selling the ship's technology on Earth's black market—didn't account for a whole lot. How'd these nobodies know about the spacecraft? And how'd they obtain knockoffs of weapon tech available only to those on the Lunar Colony?

The last bit bothered him the most because contact with Earth was the highest of crimes. It was considered a treasonous act and one worthy of execution. It was taboo for lunar colonists to even joke about it. And to keep angels honest, the AlloSym Firewall blocked all data packets from leaving the Colony or coming in from Earth.

His reporters had scrambled to determine if the Colony's presence on the Moon had been let out of the bag. But for mainstream media back on Earth, Tuesday was another slow news cycle. If anything, the pop star Minetto V3 and the details of her latest sordid affair occupied the masses. Then there were the standard segments affiliates aired—on racial tensions, socioeconomic conflict, mass shootings—all which distracted the populace from the few who pulled the strings. It was business as usual.

Next, Seger ordered a review of Charlie Company, the elite military squad revered by Colony citizens. The home team had retaken the spacecraft and defended the Colony's interests yet again. Although the skyjackers hadn't known Lunar Defense Force soldiers *always* escorted shipments from Earth, it was standard operating procedure. Nothing out of the ordinary there, either.

And the passengers? Loners. Suiciders with no family and nothing to lose—the usual crop shipped up once every decade or so to supplement population growth. Many Transplants couldn't adapt at the outset, and many burned out in the first few months. Their survival rate was abysmal, but this chain of events was an even less auspicious beginning than usual.

He predicted the attackers' motives would never be determined conclusively. If this cell operated like most paramilitary outfits on Earth, they would sneak cyanide capsules to prevent interrogation. If not, they faced a military tribunal, which maintained a zero-tolerance policy for threatening the Colony's classified status. Did any naive soul doubt the outcome? A swift conviction followed by execution and cremation.

The rescue had generated a high-ratings news day on the Colony, but he predicted the details would be forgotten in a week. A morbid and unresolved segment was not what he needed to turn his outfit into a household name.

"Mr. Director, sir," a young woman said, her voice strained, "what are we supposed to be looking for?" Lauren was seated a few rows back among the staffers. Her head peeked over her console. Good kid. She'd been working here for a little over a month, and she was already following the script.

From his position at the front next to the jumbo holoscreen, he gestured around him in his typical showman's fanfare with his hands open. "Our new star."

"Star for what?" Lauren propped her chin up against her fist.

"For what our public demands. They don't know they want it yet, but they will when we broadcast it into every home."

A freeze frame of one of the spacecraft's passengers, Darin Armacite, was plastered on the jumbo holoscreen and repeated across the staffer's consoles. The still depicted his light jacket open while he loosed those wild first shots. Security cameras had recorded the seconds before the gunmen returned fire, moments before the lights blacked out and Charlie Company swept in.

"Sir," she said, "he managed to prevent a hostage's death, but he pretty much bumbled around and made loud noises. His actions endangered the ship and could've killed everyone. He's another forced migrant—ninety percent of the people we bring in don't make it past the first year up here. I don't see how he'll be any different."

Seger nodded, reminded yet again how negatively public sentiment toward Transplants had swung. Ever since Selene, the first child born on lunar soil, a distinction began to form between natives and imports. Now that most were native-born, would relations ever recover?

He aimed the pointer at the jumbo holoscreen and clicked forward a frame, and then backward one step again. In the first frame, a man wearing a balaclava aimed a dot blaster at Darin. The next frame captured beams mid-flight and Darin shielding his face. Another click forward: darkness when the cabin lights cut out. "Now, watch carefully." He cycled through the same frames twice more.

His reporters were at full attention. He had a reputation for being melodramatic and entertaining delusions of grandeur, but nobody could deny his eye for ratings. He'd built the first lunar news network from the ground up, squeezing out revenue from a populace naysayers claimed was too self-sufficient to be sold on anything.

"There. Follow this shot's trajectory." He looped the footage once more. "It was headed for a direct hit to Darin's chest." He clicked to the next frame. "But in a fraction of a second, the beam missed. That's impossible, ladies and gents. No one noticed because the artificial gravity shut off and unleashed pandemonium." He cycled the frames one final time, and paused before delivering his bombshell: "You're looking at someone who's supposed to be dead."

OVERSIMPLIFICATION

I sat under the shade of an oak tree and squinted at the city streets below through digital lens binoculars. I'd been told by the government clerk when she signed it over to me to do nothing but "observe and integrate" for the first few weeks. It was probably in hopes we wouldn't snap, having gone from a suicide to a hostage situation in tight quarters and ending with new lives as Transplants. People-watching reminded me of the loneliness I'd known when I'd hacked into computers to find out how others lived and how much trouble I'd gotten into as a teenager for it.

What'd become my favorite spot, a short hike up to a grassy knoll, rewarded me with a panoramic view of the Lunar Colony. A cool breeze blew by, and the sky looked like an old master had painted the heavens in red and orange hues. If I hadn't been told it was projected onto the dome as part of an artificial weather system, I'd have forgotten I was on the Moon.

Zoomed out, I could tell the Colony was a hyper-planned city arranged into concentric rings. In the center sat City Hall, the seat of the lunar government and the office of President Keane.

In the ring surrounding the political center, I counted more than ten villages. A "village" was local terminology for residential sectors—Turtlepin, Dreotta, Amiden, and others where citizens lived. Roads radiated outward from City Hall in a spoke-like design. The roads sliced the sectors into wedges of a cheese wheel and marked the village boundaries. I found it hard to believe the residential ring alone used to *be* the entirety of the Colony—until the population grew past the First Demarcation and triggered procedures for expansion. Then came the drilling and moving of defense lines.

It reminded me of my first week in Turtlepin Village, and I frowned. I'd walked past cylindrical pod homes with the curved roofs I'd seen during our descent. The first people I encountered on the street, a young couple dressed in iridescent, form-hugging clothing, glanced sidelong at me in fear. They checked back often to make sure I wasn't following them. Later on, I passed by a family with a toddler—they clutched their son and carried him away in a frantic rush. Even back on Earth, I never could figure out why others were unnerved by my presence. But I wasn't going to change how others saw me, so I shrugged it off and moved on.

I opened my eyes and adjusted my binoculars. I moved out to the wider concentric ring surrounding the pod homes. The Industrial Band, or I-Band, housed the Colony's factories and other office buildings. Citizens moved to the villages closest to the I-Band where they worked—it was a pretty clever way of making a live pie-chart. I learned this let city planners visualize resource distribution and logistical needs as the sectors shifted.

But less obvious to me was how the I-Band allotted space for its military bases. They were slotted between a random warehouse or factory here and there, so I couldn't figure out what portion they took up. Odd, considering how everything else was laid out in a grid.

The last two rings went unused. The Expansion Ring (or X-Ring, as most called it) contained undeveloped land for the Colony to grow into. And the outermost Buffer Deadzone was a barren sliver touching the Colony's dome barrier.

I put my binoculars down on the short grasses beside me. Despite a cold reception from my new neighbors, my first week here was what I needed. I breathed in air redolent of pine trees and was born anew. My worries evaporated, along with real or imagined obligations, and the funk hanging over me—a downward spiral of rumination—flitted away into the Holosky.

It'd given me time to reflect on my previous relationships and why they'd all started as whirlwind romances before failing catastrophically. Was love only meant to trick us into passing along DNA? If so, then I dreaded what it meant: love and heartbreak were two parts of a petty game—a capture-the-flag I didn't want to play. But before I could entangle myself further, I was distracted by a commotion.

Honking. And lots of it. I scanned the residential band with my binoculars and honed in on the source: an elderly man sprawled across the intersection of Saite Avenue and First Street. His groceries were scattered beside a brown paper bag next to a spot on the asphalt glinting in the sun. He must have slipped and fallen. The hovercraft were raring to go, but this old man had done the unthinkable and blocked their path. They laid on their horns while he struggled to rise to his feet. His hand clutched his back, and pain was written on his face.

I adjusted my digital lens to focus on the instigator. It was a hoverbike rider. He sported a crew top like one of the soldiers on base. *Honk Honk Honk.* A shape blurred into my field of view—I swung back to the old man and his groceries to find a new figure standing there.

It was a plain, young woman with pale skin. She stooped down and helped the old man back onto his feet. The riders laid on their horns again. But she spun around to confront the pack, and the noise stopped dead. She collected his groceries and stacked them back into his brown paper bag. For a moment, the silence made me think time had stood still. But once she guided him across the street, reality resumed pace, and hovercraft zoomed by.

She turned to leave. Nothing stood out about her, not even her walk. Too bad; without something distinct, it was a kind act I'd soon forget. For Adam and Eve were not cast out of Eden but had destroyed paradise from within—which was my long way of saying, I wanted to remember something good so I wouldn't be in darkness.

I was grateful when an alert came in and disrupted the onset of one of my moods. I looked down at the wristcom wrapped around my forearm. I was also assigned this device—villagers used it to contact each other and handle household needs—to help me adjust. A holomessage appeared to float in front of me. It said to "report in." Playtime was over, but I was intrigued by what my new life had in store for me. I packed up and headed back into town.

◑ ◐

I arrived at the military base and checked in at the front desk by giving a retina scan. Our assembly room resembled a hangar of sorts, with tin beams intersecting multiple stories overhead. The space was tall and wide enough to accommodate multiple cargo ships or a few thousand soldiers standing in formation. The generals standing at the front—a row of walking epaulets and service ribbons—faced the rest of us seated in folding chairs. The more grizzled commanders sat in the first row, and the veterans sat in the second. And so the hierarchy went, from the rookies to the prospective recruits in the back where I sat.

One of the generals, the flat-top in the middle, called us to order. He droned on about squadron redistribution, something about synergizing capabilities in the field. I was trying to pay attention, but I was distracted by motion in my peripheral vision.

Some said coincidences signified nothing—-strangers find out they shared the same birthday, or two friends call each other at the exact same time—scatter a deck of cards enough times, and the Queen of Hearts would appear face up on the pile. To avoid sounding batty, I pretended to agree with the logicians. But their oscilloscopes and spectrometers measured only what we knew to look for. So I kept an open mind.

Out of the corner of my eye, I saw someone approach the clerk's desk out in the hallway. It was a young woman. Her untied hair hung down the back of her mechanic's overalls. I wrote her off as dull at first—yet another who accepted the system as it was rather than rock the boat. But my curiosity got the best of me, so I strained to listen in.

"Tera Arkwright...I submitted a petition last week to collect your defective transistors...You can? What a wonderful world."

Who'd put in such a weird request? I leaned out to get a good look and almost toppled out of my folding chair—she was the one I'd seen through my binoculars, the one from the intersection.

Later that night, my wristcom beeped with more notifications. I lifted my forearm to read the holomessage: *All Transplants must report to their designated base at 0800 hours.* It hinted if I didn't comply, I'd be escorted. The Lunar Defense Forces wanted me to come in for an intake physical. I doubt anyone bought the excuse, especially after I met Dr. Lunik.

I arrived at base early the next morning. I was led into a room where I was subjected to a battery of tests: vision, reflexes, and more genetic screening. The assistants left, and I sat on the examination bed, waiting. Then the door swung wide open, and a physician waltzed in. He was past retirement age, with hair almost as white as his lab coat, and was preoccupied with a handheld device resembling a glass clipboard. A security badge was clipped to his pocket: *Dr. Lunik.*

He spoke to me without looking up, "According to our test results, you've been adjusting to our artificial gravity and simulated atmosphere marvelously." He scribbled some notes onto his digital clipboard. "It's unexpected, given your condition back on Earth." He still didn't make eye contact and appeared to be having a whimsical moment in his head.

"What was my condition back on Earth?" I asked.

"Dead." He clapped his hands and chuckled before looking up at me. "Cremated, to be precise. You see, no one inquires about ashes—your 'death' was recorded as yet another suicide. And if you were gainfully employed, you'll be replaced within a week. Modern efficiency for our modern times."

I didn't see the humor. "So I was chosen because no one would care if I went missing..." It was less a question and more of a realization.

"Who'd notice the disappearance of someone never truly alive in the first place?" He had a point.

"Where do Transplants like me go from here?" I asked. I started to wonder if the way I'd been left alone so far had been meant to disarm me. Since arriving, I'd been given free run of the town. Meals were credited anywhere I wanted to eat, and not once was I asked to report to anyone...until now. It was like winning a paid vacation from a sweepstakes mailer and waiting to find out what the scam was.

Dr. Lunik held up a syringe filled with an apricot-colored liquid and flicked the tube to remove air bubbles.

"A test subject, huh?"

"Deem yourself a worthy specimen? High opinion of oneself, have we?" His smile now appeared less friendly than on first impression. He was like an android straining to emulate human facial expressions. "No, it'd be a waste given the significant expense to ship you up."

His reasoning made sense to me, so he was probably telling the truth. But it didn't ease how I felt about the needle in his hand.

He grabbed my arm.

I pulled away on reflex. "Hold on. I never agreed to this. What's with the orange gunk?"

"Relax. It's a cocktail to help you acclimate. Most Transplants don't survive the first month up here. Imagine a goldfish dumped into a new bowl of water. The shock of your new surroundings—cosmic radiation putting you at risk for heart disease if you absorb enough to hit the Millisievert Redline—puts the odds against you. We're giving you a fighting chance." He reached for my arm again.

Yeah, I needed to get out of here. I knocked his hand away and leapt to my feet. I bolted for the door and scrambled out into the hallway—and found myself caught between two hulking aides. They were dressed in blue scrubs and reminded me of the orderlies found in lunatic asylums of old. One advanced on my left while the other came from my right. They overpowered me with ease and forced me back inside. My wrists and ankles were then shackled to the examination bed with magnetic restraints.

Dr. Lunik continued right where we left off as if nothing untoward had happened. "This orange gunk, as you call it, is a physio-supplement." He stabbed the needle into my bicep and depressed the plunger. The orange cocktail emptied into my arm. "If you were a fast runner before, you could gain some pep in your stride. If you've an abundance of short-twitch muscle fibers, you may find yourself stronger. These are oversimplifications, but you get the idea."

I looked at him out of the corner of my eye. I was sure he wasn't telling me everything.

"Don't look so skeptical. It'll only boost your natural aptitudes

slightly—it's not a revolution in medical science—not yet anyway."
He laughed to himself.

I wondered if he ever considered whether his laugh sounded
unnatural. I didn't get to ask him because I was interrupted by
a wave of euphoria. My mind was reeling, and his voice sounded
like a hand saw cutting into steel. It shifted gears, and my mind
spun into a merry-go-round of paranoia I couldn't get off. I was
going into convulsions; my chest heaved up, but my arms were
pinned to the bed. In between gasps for air, I managed to whisper,
"What did you do to me?"

He tapped his flat-panel clipboard a few times. His thin lips
spread into a sly smirk. "Oh, I'm sure you'll figure it out soon
enough."

— 5 —

SOCIAL CONTRACT

Whatever experimental compound that was, it hit like a truck. I slumped away from the base, woozy and delirious. The clinical staff hadn't even let me rest. "Too many appointments today to spare a bed," they said. But then again, what medical standards could be enforced on a Colony most Earthers didn't even know existed?

What was home, and where was it again? My eyes strained against the artificial sunlight as I squinted down the barren back-road I'd stumbled onto. Plumes of sand-brown dust kicked up in the distance. The source came closer and into focus: a *Xay*-class hovercraft, a vehicle used by military personnel at the base. It was a beefier, military-grade version of the civilian hoverbike, and it reminded me of a quad for climbing sand dunes or a compact version of the original lunar rover—well, except there were no wheels to speak of. It floated on a cushion of air, which was useful since leveled roads were a luxury. As the rider drew closer, I made out nine more traveling behind him.

The squadron approached in V-formation. The soldiers were straddled atop their hoverquads and exposed to the outside terrain. Charlie Company. I recognized their standard issue Omnisuits, gravity boots, and full helmets. The sun reflected off the embossed insignia—a black and white half-moon—on their transparent faceplates.

They pulled up beside me in a whirl of dust. The soldier in front dismounted his hoverquad first—their squad leader, I assumed—and extended a gauntleted hand. I shook it in greeting, even as my glance tracked to the dot blaster and shock baton tucked into his brown rigger's belt.

"Darin, right?" he asked. "Welcome to Moon Base Zero." He broke into a good-natured grin to acknowledge how outlandish it must've sounded to me. His squad members dismounted in unison and leaned against their vehicles. Their hoverquads were plated in pearl white like their armor but had black detailing on corners and grooves. Some soldiers removed their helmets to stare off into the simulated clear blue sky.

I nodded at his greeting—I always felt like there was an invisible wall between me and others, so I chose silence whenever I could.

"I'm Commander Tarsus, CO of the most decorated military squadron in the LDF. Central HQ informed me you completed intake today."

It wasn't a question, so I didn't answer. He was a full head taller than me, so I had to look up to meet his eyes in his dry, creased face. His shotgun slug of a head was waxed to a sheen and bolted onto a muscular frame.

He didn't like how I didn't answer. Few people were so friendly with me at the start, so I was waiting for the hammer to fall. He took the lead. "I've come here to ask what role you'll play in the history we're forging here."

"My role?" I wasn't planning on answering but my voice leaked out in a slur. It was like the ground was moving, so I put my arms out to steady myself. "I mean, nothing here makes sense. First off, how are there people up here? How am I moving around like I'm strolling down Broadway?" I was uninhibited but didn't know why.

"Boys," he spoke with a drawl and tilted his head back to his crew, "we've got a live one." They hooted and hollered. "You sure get riled up, Rook. Come on now, I'm sure you already got it figured out. The Space Race. A treasury's worth of national resources invested, the technological research, the risk—you believe we would've done it for no return on capital? You ever thunk it strange how in the decades after, there were no pictures, no missions, no news at all, from Earth's natural satellite and closest landmass? One of humanity's greatest milestones, and poof, forget about it?"

My mind was racing to make connections.

"Rook, we never left!" He raised his arms to indicate everything surrounding us. "Do you think we, who settled new frontiers from coast-to-coast and engaged in military conquest after conquest, would claim a territory so vast it's considered a lost planet by some, and then say, 'Nah, leave it'—does that pass the smell test to you?"

The more I thought about it, the more obvious it was in hindsight. The supposed defunding of space agencies, the proclamations of how nothing could be gained from further lunar exploration—it was like discovering a gold mine but convincing everyone else there was nothing there of value.

"He's connecting the dots. Boys, this one may be a thinker," he said to the hoots and hollers of the rest of his squad. This squad commander—he made me feel good about myself and put me in my place at the same time.

"But it's still impossible," I said. "You have hydroponic collectors, beam weapons, and technology orders of magnitude ahead of the research I've read about on Earth."

He whistled. "Now I'm impressed. You're right. The miracle is not how the human race first achieved flight and then landed on the Moon sixty years later. Or even how we've staked a claim up here for two centuries since." The other Charlie Company soldiers were yawning at this point like they'd heard this summary before. "The first man on the Moon—his audio broadcast back to Earth was edited, shall we say, for public consumption." He was hedging what he said next. "We were not the first to arrive. In the full recordings, the astronauts reported discovering an abandoned site. It confirmed we were not alone."

I had to let it sink in. In my opinion, a conspiracy theorist was someone with abundant skepticism. When I studied history, I was never satisfied with the explanations of why nations were so eager to surrender sovereignty to the United World Government. The world hurtled into globalization flailing and screaming—damn the consequences, precipitated by neither catastrophe nor threat. "Was the discovery responsible for...all of this?"

"Affirmative, Rook. Subsequent forays were undertaken in secret. The relics we recovered were reverse-engineered and then innovated upon." He adjusted the gauntlet on his right hand and began to list them off. "Quantum computing, the Aegis tech responsible for our Colony dome, Luxpane photovoltaics, our dot blasters—what you see before you came from there."

The UWG's expenditures spiraled out of control every year to the public's disbelief—now I understood why: they'd been funneling resources into black budget projects to establish a foothold up here. And the torrent of propaganda to settle Mars, which with current engine designs would take two years of space travel no human would survive—it was a distant goal to divert attention from Earth's nearest neighbor. I touched a hand to my cheek, working hard to think over the buzzing that'd started in my head. More facts didn't add up. "But how has the Colony remained hidden for so long?"

"The Moon completes its own revolution as it orbits the Earth," he traced a gloved finger through the air in a circle. "We hide on the side never facing Earth and its prying telescopes. Even if probes swung by, our Holosky Projector shows an empty crater. We don't use radio frequencies or even share common data protocols with Earth, ensuring no one picks up on our transmissions."

I doubted people could be entrusted to keep a secret forever. "But what if someone from the Colony leaves?"

"Easy. No one here leaves. Period." For a moment, the Commander's face was tinged with a menacing glow, but he recovered. "If nosy Earthers dig too close to the truth—no need to snuff them out and draw attention to ourselves—we can paint them as nuts in your mass media. When it comes to the Moon, Earthers cannot distinguish between fact and fabrication anyhow. Because the two overlap."

He was spot on. People dismissed things if they clashed with the established narrative. I used to believe—naive as I was—it came from ignorance. But I didn't give others enough credit where it was due. It was more comforting—maybe smarter—to play along with the charade. Otherwise, we'd have to admit the institutions we supported also deceived us on the regular. If there was ham on the dinner table and endless VR_World amusements available, why make waves?

I processed what Commander Tarsus had told me (and how I'd be here permanently). "I assume you didn't come all this way to give me a history lesson."

He flashed a charismatic smile. "Damn straight, Rook. Our Colony advances at breakneck speeds, but it's not through luck. Everyone—and I mean *everyone*—here contributes. In your case, you get to start over, with your sins forgiven and your worries left in the past."

"Are you asking what work I can take on? I guess I could pitch in with your computer systems. I'm fluent in programming languages like Quartz, R##, and—"

The other soldiers roused and burst into laughter. He waved for the ruckus to die down. "You have to understand—the children born here pick those up in primary school. They compile their own operating-system kernels for lunch. You'd be a dinosaur."

My face got hot. I mean, I wasn't looking to be a cog in a machine again, but I was proud of my programming abilities.

He rested an armored glove on my shoulder. "Look, I saw what you did on your trip up. We all did. Without training, you neutralized one hostile and disrupted a terrorist cell. Your death wish aside, Rook, you saved a lot of people. And up here, survival is king." He continued, "Moon Base Zero is humanity's first defensive layer. We need to be prepared for threats *out there*. You've got potential. We could mold it and put it to good use."

"Guys like me who have no family and nothing to lose, right?"

He deflected. "I'm extending you an invitation to the most respected squad in the LDF. You won't be a nobody anymore."

"And if I don't want to?"

His jovial demeanor vanished in a heartbeat. "Most Transplants don't make it past the first month. Life's harsh up here. Everyone contributes."

I narrowed my eyes, and my hand balled into a fist. "I get it. I'm only wanted as long as I'm useful, right?" I'd been given a second chance and didn't want to use it this way. Don't get me wrong, I liked those films and games like everyone else, but after a while, their invitations began to feel disconcerting. It was as if someone wanted me to be okay with it, almost as if I were being primed if the need ever arose. And every year, when the government garnished my wages to fund yet another war—they never called it war, though—I'd shrugged my shoulders and gone along with it. But now I'd started over, and I wanted to try doing things in a different way.

"In return, all your needs will be taken care of. This is our version of the social contract, Rook. It's the foundation of human civilization."

Become part of a system which was heartless and made me broken the way I was? I said, "Sorry, but no thanks. I'll find another way to help out."

He didn't like my answer. Such was the case for someone I imagined was accustomed to always getting his way. "A lifetime of service has shown me there are two kinds of people: those who protect the weak, and those who—on the ship up here, didn't you hide while a nurse was butchered?"

A fire shot up through me, and I swear I almost swung at him. Instead, I glared at him through gritted teeth.

He turned to leave. He and the other soldiers donned their helmets and mounted their hoverquads. Before they took off, two soldiers broke from the pack and walked over to me. I read the names "Lt. Victoria Haron" and "Sgt. Hugh Ambrose III" on their dog tag displays.

Ambrose said, "We've been receiving unusual reports. Soon, you may be involved, whether you like it or not. Think about it." He gave a casual salute. I glanced over at Victoria. She rolled her eyes at me and looked bemused.

The pair rejoined the rest of Charlie Company. The crew revved their engines. Their hoverquads lifted off the ground and spewed dust at me before taking off. I covered my face with a sleeve and coughed. The whole production made me lightheaded again.

— 6 —

TERA ARKWRIGHT

Tera Arkwright scooped the amber resin into her containment jar. She pushed down on the vacuum-seal latch, and the container hissed shut. Almost enough to call it a day. Enough for her botany experiments and maybe even enough for a separate blueprint she'd been preparing for the mini-fabricator. She stood up and stretched her slender arms to the sky before reaching behind her head and checking if her long hair was still tucked into a bun.

She took in a vista of flat wasteland, undeveloped X-Ring lands far from village pod homes, where few dared venture. All around her was the faint aroma of soil. Although protected overhead by the Colony's dome, these lands sat unused aside from the occasional farming study. Eventually, they'd become home to a new village, but it'd take three more decades in the current plan.

Enough of a break, Tera—time to get back on task.

It'd been a fruitful but painstaking day out in the terrain between the Daedalus and Icarus craters. At first, the detector she'd fabricated led her to a breadcrumb trail which was iffy at best. The path teased her along the way, a fleck of amber resin here and there before it led to usable samples. She had to keep moving to collect it all because their distinctive heat signatures blinked before disappearing again. She hadn't perfected the device—or her other inventions for that matter—so the readouts only meant the resin was somewhere nearby.

The dome's self-contained ecosystem had begun to surprise her with its dynamic nature. on her quest for raw materials for experiments and inventions, she'd never come across anything like the amber. Were the new arboreal species people planted—loblolly pine, sycamore, redwood, dragonwort, and sweetgum trees—responsible for the amber's emergence, or had it always been native to the lunar surface?

Her first encounter with the mysterious substance was fresh after a meteor shower had pounded the lunar surface. In the eerie twilight that followed, she'd set out on one of her impromptu scavenging runs. In lands near the Aitken Basin, she'd spotted a glowing light suspended in air. When she reached the source, she discovered a yellow-orange glob perched atop a lone hawthorn tree. It was the only vegetation in the middle of nowhere.

She brought the resin home for analysis, but its molecules matched nothing in the reference databases of either terran or lunar origin. She ran more tests that suggested the resin could promote seed germination. Now to fine tune her hypothesis, she was out on the hunt for a larger sample. What if she were on the verge of discovering a new method for terraformation? She became giddy at the thought.

But she had looped around a few times and still couldn't locate the cluster her detector promised. Her wristcom beeped, and she pushed a button to play the alert. A hologram appeared, an animation of the real sun setting outside the Colony dome: "Nokto Cycle commencing." Night on the Moon was something she didn't mess around with; even with the dome's artificial climate, roaming without protection meant hypothermia and death. This lesson had been drilled into her throughout early education—kids were fed an urban legend about the tragic "Tanner Party" who hadn't returned in time. Cautionary tales didn't deter teenagers from using the danger for their rites of passage, nor did it stop people from unsavory activities when police became lax—but the difference was they wore insulated suits, and she hadn't packed the proper gear. Calculated risks were one thing, but she didn't believe in recklessness.

She was distracted when her detector flashed. It located a cluster—all right!

But then she caught her breath misting in the cold air. Maybe it was best to bookmark the coordinates and come back tomorrow. Would the cluster still be there? Whenever she returned, the resin had vanished. It was either a volatile compound, or the lunar government was collecting it as she suspected. She imagined men in black trench coats scouring the outskirts of town, magnifying glasses to the ground, sticky gold in their hands. A chortle escaped and almost broke into a laugh. *Wait—the sun. Focus, Tera!*

Nothing could stop her now that she was in brighter spirits. She trudged, gear pack bouncing, toward the signature's locus. There. The bottom of the mini-crater up ahead—wasn't it the kind of place treasures were hidden?

She wished this was one of those rare times the Colony shut artificial gravity off, so she could leap in. Instead, she turned her back to the crater, lowered herself over its lip, and slid down the side. At the bottom, it glowed before her like in a dream. The amber resin sat atop a hawthorn sapling, a situation almost identical to the first time she'd laid eyes on it.

Almost identical. Except a body was lying on the ground next to it, like somebody had fallen in. It was a young man with short, dark hair.

She slipped her gear pack off and rushed over. She rolled him over. His face—sharp and sullen features drawn tight—seemed familiar. Then it hit her. He was the Earther who made Channel One news with his ill-advised attempt to stop the hostage-takers. Someone who didn't respect survival like that didn't deserve to last up here for long.

But she couldn't help herself. She cradled his head in her lap and placed an ear near his face. *Please be alive.* His faint breath grazed her cheek. It was still warm, and more importantly, still there.

◑ ◑

I wish I could say the first time I met Tera was a biblical event involving harps and trumpets, but in reality, it sounded more like an air horn.

I bolted upright. Where was I? What was making that awful racket? I stared into the face of an unassuming young woman. Her thin eyebrows were level and a shade lighter than her golden-brown hair. She had a generous forehead, smooth and unwritten like a blank slate. Her eyes were cold and detached, but the pull on her cheeks made it look like she was trying not to laugh.

"Hm...I made this device for self-defense," she said. "But maybe I should refit it as an alarm clock instead." She laughed. "The most abrasive frequencies played at discordant intervals—you should've seen the look on your face! Who could've guessed it'd work so well?" She brushed sun-bleached bangs away from her face and typed something on her holopad computer.

She wasn't a Transplant, though I didn't know how I could tell. It wasn't her airy frame alone. Maybe it was her face: her plain features weren't hardened like the urbanites I'd known on Earth. Plain wasn't a fair description—it was more like I couldn't divine her motivations. I was disoriented, and shrill sounds were still bouncing around in my head's echo chamber. Her lips moved, but I didn't catch the rest. "What?" I asked.

"I said, mister, what were you doing out in the X-Ring yesterday? Hoping to become another statistic, it appears."

"Brutal." I smiled, maybe for the first time since I arrived, maybe for the first time in as long as I could remember. My vision was still hazy. I scanned the dimly lit room. It was filled with spare circuit boards, sketchbooks, and potted plants stacked along the floors and desk surfaces. A bipedal automaton the size of a fire hydrant lay cut open on the table, its circuitry on display like a human cadaver's innards. This place was organized chaos.

"Last thing I remember," I said, "I was walking back to my cot in the barracks. I remember feeling dizzy, and that's about it."

"Well, mister, you ought to know night here is a two-week-long affair. Two weeks by Earth standards—we still use the same calendar and time—though it doesn't make a lot of sense other than to keep us in tune with the rest of humanity. By the way, Tera Arkwright, pleased to meet you."

"Darin Armacite. I go by Darin. I mean, same." God, why was I so awkward? My eyes adjusted. Metal instruments lay on the table beside me. Multiple holoscreens on every wall scrolled neon green text against black backgrounds. Wires spilled out of every nook and cranny. "Am I in a lab? You're not going to inject me with experimental gunk, are you?"

She laughed. "Do all Earthers jump to such preposterous conclusions? This pod is my home. These machines are my pet projects."

"What's with all the plants?" I asked.

"You could call them everybody's pet project. Ecological terraforming. The Lunar Colony expands based our germination rate. Shrubs, trees, and bacteria maintain our carbon and other nutrient cycles."

She paused at the puzzled expression on my face—I was thinking about what it would take to create self-sustaining cycles inside the Colony dome; it was nothing short of magic. "Is that what you were doing out there?"

Her complexion took on a hint of rose. "I wasn't out skipping around like Johnny Appleseed, if it's what you were thinking."

"Not at all." I was holding back a grin.

She held up a clear cylindrical container resembling a coffee thermos. "I was out gathering samples."

The jar contained something viscous which shimmered between various hues of yellow and orange. The substance was like iridescent sap.

She said, "I discovered this amber resin inside the Colony last year. It's aromatic, like a flowering fruit, but its properties are unlike anything I've ever encountered."

"What's so special about it? It looks like honey to me."

"It's a mish-mash of improbability. In solid form, it has a density similar to water's. My tools could not reach its ignition temperature, though I suspect it may be as high as magnesium's. When dissolved, the resin takes on the properties of a superconductor." She was animated and almost on the verge of shouting. "I combined the resin with everything I could think of to see if I could get a reaction."

"And? Don't keep me in suspense."

"When I coat seeds with the resin before planting them, the seeds are almost guaranteed to sprout. And when they do, they do so twice as fast. I see you've already deduced the importance. A terraforming catalyst? It'd be a scientific breakthrough." She seemed like was trying to slow herself down. She was about to say more, but she hesitated.

So I said, "But?"

She turned away from the bed, sat down at the console against the wall, and clacked away on the keyboard. A topographic map—a three-dimensional hologram—appeared above us. "These purple markers represent the clusters I've collected over the last standard Earth year. As you can see, the quantities are insignificant. Far too small to impact the Colony's global germination rate."

I pushed my hand through the holographic map to see its colors on my hand. "So why go treasure hunting?"

"Don't you want to know what else it can do? What other scientific fields it could revolutionize?" She jumped up from her task chair and came at me by passing through the hologram. "And most important of all, where did it come from?" When she was passionate about something, she lit up the room.

"Were you searching for the resin when you found me?"

"Affirmative, stranger. Though I fear the cluster I located is long gone by now. It was either secure my haul or let you die from hypothermia." She looked me dead in the eyes with a serious expression on her face. "Tough call, I know."

Her deadpan—who could tell if she was joking? My mental fog cleared up. I put two and two together of where I'd seen her before. She was the one I'd spied helping an elderly man to his feet, and later, at City Hall, she was the person I'd overheard making a request for transistors.

I didn't know why, but I wanted to do right by her. "Let me go back and collect the cluster for you."

I must have said something inappropriate because she shot me a guarded look. "Why? Because you think you owe me something?" Her eyes became stern and her shoulders tightened up. "Forget it. No deal, random Earth dude."

Now, I'd be the first to admit I didn't understand women, or Moon-folk for that matter. Throw the two together, and I didn't know what I'd done wrong. I played it off. "No, I thought it'd be fun. I haven't accomplished much since settling in up here."

She studied my face for a moment. I stared back into pale green eyes spiked with orange—eyes that challenged me—but I was never one to flinch first. Her expression relaxed, and she turned away before saying, "Okay. I'll buy that." She smiled.

And in a flash, she rushed over to a storage bin in the corner.

She leaned over and rummaged through its contents. After finding what she was looking for, she spun back around and tossed an object my way.

I caught the device in a clumsy lunge. It looked like some sort of high-tech flashlight used for cave-diving.

She said, "I fabricated this device to pick up on the resin's light and heat signatures. My detector relies on the same principles as Gravdar does. Quantum-entangled atomic clocks measure gravitational fluctuations."

I held the trapezoidal bar in my hand like a bat. Quantum-entangled atomic clocks. Sure, whatever that meant.

"Yesterday's coordinates are bookmarked," she said. "They should lead you back to the resin, if it's still there."

She had neglected to mention—as I discovered about her other gadgets later on—that her detector often malfunctioned.

7

PROGRAMS THAT RETURN '0'

What was it like, to seek something not knowing what it was? What was it like, to not know what I needed until I'd found it?

My quest for the resin led me back to the barren X-Ring lands where Tera had stumbled upon my unconscious body. However, I was starting to wonder whether the coordinates were accurate. When I was out cold, she had attached anti-grav pods to my body and pushed me back to her homepod, so it wasn't like I could recognize my surroundings. Worse, because it was "night time" on the Colony, the artificial sky had been turned off. The area was only visible because of stars overhead and the occasional light fixture, stories above on the dome.

But at least I was outfitted for the cold this time. I was dressed head to toe in insulated gear. In front of me lay unforgiving desert. There were no military bases, no pod homes, nor even roads here. A scattering of shrubs indicated early success with eco-engineering, but she said villagers wouldn't live in this part of the dome until these efforts matured.

A *thump* came from the device in my hand. Tera's resin finder. It was essentially a makeshift motherboard wired to a holoprojector. And it functioned like an odd combination between a metal detector and a global positioning system. It produced a holoscreen which tracked my coordinates along with nearby heat signatures. It ceased *thumping*, blinking green to indicate I'd reached my destination.

I stood in the stillness of the night. Ahead of me lay a flat plain of gray sand and patches of soil, a level surface pocketed with small craters. She said she'd found me lying beneath a tree with twin branches, but when I peeked into the nearest crater, I found only pebbles. I walked to the next mini-crater and the next—they were all empty.

There was one thing I couldn't stand, and it was making promises but coming up short. I considered myself a failure in many respects: I'd been a wage slave; I couldn't hold down meaningful relationships; even my own neighbors were unnerved by the way I looked—or was it the look in my eyes? But there was always one thing I took pride in. At least I was a man of my word. It was the one thing I held onto as true and kept me sane all those years I felt so alien to my own kind.

I wouldn't accept returning to her empty-handed. I'd never say, "Sorry, can't help you," like every other blank and unfeeling face I'd met, of those who made excuses to avoid trying in the first place. I was guilty of many things—but I'd never be a program that always returned "0" regardless of the input.

I worked to calm myself before I entered one of my moods again. It was a loop that built upon itself until I blew up and did things I regretted later. Perhaps it was for the best I was alone out here.

When I took a deep breath, the frosty air stung my nose. During the Moon's night cycle—a fortnight during which Nokto Cycle policies went into effect—the temperature dropped 10 degrees every 24 hours. Even with the dome's homeostatic dampeners, it was blisteringly cold. The air carried the crispness of a snowy day and was quiet to match, save for the faint hum of the dome's heating systems. I reached into the pockets of my insulated suit and palmed the heat-orbs Tera had prepared for me.

Back to finding the resin. I waved the detector around, but its holoscreen dissolved. I frowned. She did warn me of the dangers of going out during a Nokto Cycle—electronics went on the fritz when they were needed most. I grabbed the trapezoidal bar with both hands and shook the device. When its holoscreen flickered back on, a yellow blip appeared where none had been earlier. The heat signature was tiny, much too small to be the cluster I was searching for. But Tera had said: *The resin creates a trail. Follow the minor strands, and they'll lead you to a cluster.*

A buzzing swarmed the back of my skull, like an insect had gotten into my head and was gnawing on my brain stem. It'd been happening more and more whenever I daydreamed too long or got into one of my moods. The throbbing had begun after my visit to Dr. Lunik—was it a side effect?

I shook it off and trudged to the signature's coordinates. In plain sight, lying on the rocky ground, was the amber. Up close, it was a sap-like substance the size of a coin. After many passes of my hand through the loam soil, I managed to scoop up the resin without it slipping between my gloved fingers. I hit the button to vacuum-seal the containment jar, and when I checked back with the detector, I noted the coordinates had been off by roughly twenty paces.

A new fleck appeared on the detector nearby. When I arrived at the target coordinates, I found another small handful of amber. The pattern repeated, and in following the trail, I lost track of time and also where I was in relation to Turtlepin Village. No man's land was a frigid sea of gravel and sand.

The resin fragments I found grew larger in increments as she'd promised, but I'd only filled a quarter of the containment jar. She'd mentioned one of her pet projects needing resin for its "next stage of evolution"—whatever that meant—so I wanted to return with a full container.

There! A yellow signature, a sizeable one this time, blinked on. Jackpot.

I focused my eyes on the ground while approaching, taking extra care not to trip into any craters. However, once the signature appeared centered, the detector's holoscreen fizzled out. Great, it'd gone bonkers again.

Puzzled, I glanced back up at my surroundings. I still think back to the day I found what'd been missing my entire life.

◐ ◑

The abandoned manor before me was much larger than the pod homes I'd seen in Tera's village. Its construction looked like an older design; it wasn't efficient and compact, and its crumbling roof was a traditional gable instead of a curved hemisphere. Rubble was rubble in the end—there was nothing special about eventuality—except the resin trail disappeared here, and I'd not found the cluster I'd been promised.

Why'd the detector lead me to the middle of nowhere, and why was there a home here at all? The ruins reminded me of a Roman bust split down the middle by lightning. Although its arched entrance sat in shambles and its second story had collapsed, its walls still held the once-proud structure up. I imagined the place in its former glory, idyllic like a country estate back on Earth.

I was jolted back to reality when something pelted my visor. Then another drop hit before it began to sprinkle. Impossible. Rain? In preparation for twenty-four hours in the Expansion Ring, I'd stuffed my gear pack to the brim: anti-grav orbs, insta-rations, and even an emergency transmitter in case I got lost. What I hadn't planned for was rain. The Moon harbored no atmosphere except for inside the dome—had the Colony already managed to sustain a water cycle? The drizzle turned into a torrential downpour and drenched my suit.

My disbelief soon gave way to Tera's warnings about hypothermia. For the two Earth weeks the Moon went through night, most businesses closed early. Most people stayed cooped up inside their heated pod homes while they waited for the sun's return—until they were certain the solar collectors had enough reserves for the next nightfall. On the frontier, death was too common to tempt the fates.

There was no shelter anywhere else, and a voice in my head was saying, *Go inside.*

I ducked under the manor's collapsed archway. The double door entrance was still functional—though worse for wear—and swung inwards with a creak. I stepped into the vestibule and found shelter from the storm. It was dark, but ambient light (and rain) filtered in from the destroyed upper landing.

I needed to find a wing of the home with an intact ceiling. I wound my way down the hall, and at the far end, entered a room. I closed its door behind me and took a quick look around. Damaged holoscreen projectors lined the walls. Some books still sat on shelves, their pages frayed at the edges or covers worn off, while other tomes lay scattered across the faded maroon carpet. *Frontier Politics, Quantum Field Induction, Strategic Warfare, A New Corporatism*, and so on—a serious collection. This must've been the study.

I imagined what it would have been like to spend a carefree childhood here. The study still gave off the feelings of warmth and comfort I was only familiar with from how others described home. A pleasant patter came from the rain against the skylight overhead.

It couldn't rain much longer—I was hard-pressed to believe the Colony had introduced much water into the dome's ecosystem. To pass the time, I went to poke around. I tapped my wristcom to activate the lamp on my visor.

And there it was, surrounded by fine tapestries, as if it had always been there: the amber resin. It was resting on top of a sapling which had sprouted between the cracks in the floorboards and torn throw rugs.

I knelt down and trained my visor's light onto the sapling. I worked to harvest the cluster so as to preserve every drop. But in the end, the cluster was immense and overflowed my containment jar. After worrying I'd never find enough, I needed to leave some behind.

I was still on my hands and knees when something straight ahead caught my eye. A glow was coming from under one of the bookshelves. The object was tucked deep into the recesses, and I'd never have found it had it not been for the resin.

I put the containment jar aside and crawled over. Under the bottom shelf was a spherical canister. As I drew closer, its metallic hull began to emit slow, intermittent flashes. I reached over and dislodged it from its hiding place.

I played with the object in my hands and touched its cool surface. Its indicator lights began to blink faster. Much too fast. In a fit of paranoia, I hurled the sphere at an oil painting across the room and dropped to the floor.

The sphere opened mid-flight and bathed the room in white light. For a brief second, I could see every detail of the study as clear as day—the ottoman, the candelabra, the fireplace—almost as if I'd been transported back in time.

And right then, someone called out my name.

"Got your attention, have I?"

When the light dimmed, I made out a faint silhouette. My eyes adjusted, and I was startled to see another person in the study. He appeared to be wearing military formal dress, a black-blue collared jacket with three buttons down each side. His special forces beret was marked by a half-moon insignia which reminded me of the uniforms worn by Charlie Company. "As you may have surmised, your genetic fingerprint triggered this module. Now when I look upon you myself, I confirm a legitimate activation."

I didn't believe in much of anything, let alone ghosts. "Do I know you?"

"Yes and no. You and I haven't met in person. However, we share a common lineage," the gentleman said.

I understood half of what he'd said. Strike that, none of it made sense. He had a stern expression on his face, and the sides of his crew cut had grayed to salt and pepper. Standing with broad shoulders squared, his posture was ramrod straight like a support beam.

"Who or what are you?"

He took a long pull of breath, as if he were puffing a cigar. "I am Captain Cyril Armacite, or at least, the best approximation of him. I am your ancestor four generations removed."

I performed some mental arithmetic. "You mean, you're my great-grandfather? You could've just said that."

"This is accurate," Cyril said.

"It's unlikely, don't you think? No offense, but if it were true, you'd be dead. And best-case scenario, you'd be pulling close to a hundred and twenty."

"Your assumptions are valid."

"So when you say 'best approximation,' you mean..."

"I have been compiled from historical records, audio-video feeds, and personal accounts. My source code was comprehensive—perhaps unprecedented."

"A computer program," I said.

"Simulacrum is more apt." He adjusted his beret. "I am a live simulation of who Captain Cyril may have been."

"But how could you be up here, on the Lunar Colony?"

"Tease out the possible scenarios, and you will come to the only logical conclusion."

He was right, but I didn't want to face it—wasn't ready to face it.

He stepped into the light, arms folded across his barrel chest. "Yes, come to terms with your heritage. The Moon was, and still is, your home."

◑ ◐

"Calculations to the present time indicate you were the first generation of Armacite sent to Earth," the Simulacrum said. "For you to be the one to activate me was not anticipated. However, my directive remains the same."

"What directive?" I asked. "Who built you, Cyril?"

"The generation prior to yours created me, to be awoken upon contact with a member of the ancestral line. However, those plans did not include you, the first generation removed from the Lunar Colony." He appeared to clasp at a cigar that didn't exist in his virtual recreation.

"My folks created you?" All those years wondering why I was out of sync from others...all those years wondering who my parents were, where they'd lived, coming back to the same question of why my life had to be the way it was. And this Simulacrum... it hadn't even been meant for me. "Did they leave me a letter or a message?"

Silence.

"Simulacrum, respond," I commanded. My patience wore thin, and I was in a nasty mood.

"Compiled into my kernel is an advanced artificial intelligence meta-package. It catalogues information sourced from multiple databases and updates itself upon connection to a wide area network. As to your query, I have found no relevant data with which to respond."

"Right, a software routine, as if you were what I needed in my life," I said, as if he could understand. "I find out where I'm from, and it's an empty shell. Why am I not surprised?"

No response.

"Do you know what it was like? I suffered, alone, with nothing to my name and not even family I could call home. And this dumb ghost script is all that's left of my so-called heritage?" My hopes were an ark dashed against the rocks.

He idled there adjusting his green beret and collared vest-jacket. "We do not have much time left. My power reserves are minimal, and you have been off the grid for too long. We cannot be seen together."

"Then hurry up and fulfill your grand directive." There was a dry taste in my mouth.

He cleared his throat. "Your residency on Earth was by design. You were sent there to restart the family line after our ancestral home was left in ruins and our lives destroyed."

"So, you were activated to tell me how it went down? You know there are easier ways to deliver a message."

"No." His eyes were darkened by shadows. "I'm here to help you get revenge."

8

LUNAR CHANNEL ONE

Hurston Segerstrom studied the twenty holoscreens tiled in front of him. His news station had never been more abuzz than it'd been in the last week. Reports poured in on covert military exercises. A backlog of anonymous tips from Colony citizens needed to be followed up on. And then there was his new star from Earth: Darin Armacite. The stress from the workload made him look like a chain-smoker in a bespoke suit.

He turned around to address his staffers. They were seated among the rows of the newsroom, their glowing consoles reflected in his gray irises. He asked, "So Darin turned down enlistment terms from Charlie Company?"

"Video from our Sky-Eye drone confirms it," an aide said. "We followed him out after his intake physical."

Another staffer added, "After the life he's had, you'd think he'd take a contract known for its generous bonuses."

Seger took a moment to weigh his reporters' comments. "It's not the most noteworthy thing here. You've all buried the lede." In his experience, Charlie Company was the vanguard of Moon Base Zero, sent on the move before major policy announcements. Of course, during those formative stages, the government warned him how published reports should refer to "military advisors" rather than deployed troops—no need to alarm the public. As a consequence, Lunar Channel One's reporters often followed the squad's movements in search of a story. "Isn't it strange to you that an elite group like Charlie Company would be so eager to draft someone untrained and untested?"

"What could it signify?" Lauren asked.

Good, the staffers were playing along the way he liked. "A scoop sits right under our noses, girls and boys. The tides of history are shifting. I want eyes on the Colony President. President Keane has been quiet for too long. Something's up."

Carmen, his deputy director, chimed in next. She loved to entertain worst-case scenarios and wanted to remind him to take precautions. "Director, we could only afford miniaturization of one Sky-Eye drone. Our older models are clunkier and will be spotted by Keane's security detail."

"Your point?" He became irritated whenever she pointed out his organization's lack of resources. He didn't want reminders that despite Lunar Channel One's exotic locale, he still ran a provincial broadcast station.

She chose her next words with care, as she ought to. Broadcast media employ was a rarity on the Colony—journalism, a monopoly. "Sir, if we're caught snooping on the President, we could be charged with espionage or treason."

He had to give it to her; she always found diplomatic ways to air unpleasantries. She was reminding him prisons were few because they were expensive to maintain. In other words, the implication was execution. But who had ever become powerful by playing it safe?

"Fine!" he growled, which was as close as he ever came to admitting a staffer had made a prudent call. "Divert the Sky-Eye drone from Darin to President Keane."

◐ ◑

President Keane, leader of the First Lunar Colony, smoothed a hand across his brow and head. He mussed up his sandy brown hair as he often did whenever he had to make a tough decision. He smiled when he thought back to how much simpler things had been during his campaign.

Back then, he'd won the election running on a platform of resiliency: "The Lunar Colony is the beginning of a nation the world has never seen. One day, when we reveal our civilization to the peoples of Earth, we will no longer be considered a daring experiment but an example of humanity's greatest potential. Nothing is more important than our survival, for our survival means the survival of our ideals."

The demographics of the Colony skewed young—given the high mortality rate—and therefore reaching old age was equivalent to virtue. President Keane was inexperienced compared to his predecessors, taller and lankier too, but his message had struck a nerve. He'd promised to improve survival rates by strengthening the integrity of the dome, investing in technological innovation, and advancing national security.

Those were less complicated times, weren't they? In those days, all citizens discussed was moving past the limits of collectivist versus meritocratic viewpoints of society. Presented with research proving no two individuals were born into equivalent circumstances, the electorate deconstructed imperfect ideas of fairness and equality. The national conversation reached its heights when it shifted to equitable treatment instead, before shooting past even those goalposts. Finally, the question became: what was the next stage for human society?

But now Keane occupied the President's Office, adorned with marble floors and wood-paneled walls. He still believed in the goals he'd set forth during his campaign. But compromises had to be made in the business of daily governance. Who could've predicted he'd be tested on those ideals?

He stood face to face with Richard Paxton Nest, his newly-appointed vice president. "Tell them no deal," Keane said. "Our expansion must proceed with abundant caution and regard for the unknowns of space."

"Sir, with all due respect…"

Keane blinked tired eyes. All he saw in the mirror lately were heavy bags under his eyes and a crease forming on his brow. He wished his former VP hadn't died of pneumonia barely a month after their inauguration. Paxton succeeded the vacant office, and although the man sported the same thinning hair and navy blue suit as his predecessor, he had a grating habit of not knowing his place. Would he ever pick up on the decorum befitting a second-in-command? "It sounds as if you didn't hear my decision. We won't accelerate terraforming with an unapproved compound."

"Sir, I sympathize with your position because of the statements you made to voters, but keep in mind the Guildsack Partners contributed to your campaign. We need to keep our promises to *them* to ensure their full support."

"Is the next election as far as you've thought? Yes, we'll secure their backing eventually. But through a different deal. Not this one."

"Sir, you gave similar responses to our other major donors. They run in the same circles, and they're starting to talk."

Keane broke into a hearty laugh and caught Paxton off-guard. "You think those men are in charge? They're financiers who fancy themselves kingmakers. They fund our mission because they aren't willing to take on the difficult, dirty work, day in and day out. We do." Keane loosened the carmine-red tie around his white dress shirt. "The energy men push for permits to drill. The real estate developers want me to rubber stamp expansion. The arms dealers insist our military needs a complete overhaul. But don't you see?"

"I don't know what you're getting at, sir." His glum expression reminded Keane of a retiree lost at the spaceport baggage claim.

"We're not merely an offshoot of Earth masquerading as

a business enterprise or as a military base—as colonies were to empires of old. If we ever come into contact with other civilizations, the Colony will be humanity's first representatives. We are a new republic, a New World, that nations on Earth will look to for inspiration and leadership."

"Sir, I don't see how some distant future is related to a simple favor the Guildsack Partners—"

"The First Lunar Colony in its nascent youth will either be defined by forces from within or from without," Keane said. "We will not auction off our most valuable assets, resources our new nation needs to fulfill its potential. This is our chance to leave the broken systems of the Old World behind."

◐ ◑

Paxton fumed on his walk back to the Vice President's Office. How dare Keane talk down to him as if he were some country bumpkin. An arrogant scion of an old-money family—Keane wouldn't have amounted to anything otherwise. When the President gabbed on, the populace adored his face. Paxton, however, saw a weak and ineffectual leader. He removed a pocket square from his navy jacket and patted the perspiration off his brow.

When he entered his office and closed the door, he found a woman seated in one of the leather armchairs. These people wasted no time. It was always the same, a liaison already waiting for him. She wore the same indiscernible black suit as all the others too, marked by a gold pin on the lapel signaling her affiliation with the Guildsack Partners.

In no rush to give his report, he mixed himself a drink. He took a swig, feeling a blanket of exhaustion pull over his ice blue eyes. Without turning around, he said, "Keane has declined our agreement."

"Was our faith in you misplaced?" The nameless woman got right to the point. The handlers never introduced themselves.

"No, I'm working on it, but Keane is naive. He'd rather break than bend." He knew she'd only view it as an excuse.

"We went to great lengths to get you into the Vice President's chair. We've invested too much to back out now."

"I'll take care of it. Give me more time."

"And what message do you wish to relay to the Guildsack Partners? We were under the impression you'd join us as a permanent member one day."

He pursed his lips to hold back an eager smile. "Tell them to proceed with Agent M. Terraforming operations will continue according to schedule."

"And if Keane finds out you went ahead without his approval?" she asked, cautious now.

"If it comes to that, I'll take responsibility."

"Do we have your absolute assurances on this matter?" The woman stood up to leave and buttoned her suit jacket.

He reached over his desk and picked up a paperweight. It was the figure of a general on a horse reared up for battle. He played with it in his hands. "I'll do whatever needs to be done."

— 9 —

HUMAN CAPITAL

I finally made it back to Tera's homepod. Her gizmos had been moved into new configurations: gears, microchip processors, and liquid pipes sat in disarray; holoscreen consoles were left open, scrolling green text on black backgrounds; and multiple computers were wired up to an odd humanoid contraption—must've been another invention she was working on.

Tera walked into the room while munching on an apple and studying a holo-diagram on her wristcom. She wore smooth and unsullied mechanic's overalls which contrasted with the sorry state of my dirt-caked vac-suit. It took her a moment to notice me and my haul of amber resin. She slid off her welding goggles and was beaming with excitement. "A full cylinder! My gosh, do you know the kinds of things I can do with it?"

I was hoping she'd be thrilled to see me, but people only liked me based on what I could do for them. How could this place, where survival was paramount, be any different?

She disassembled the containment jar and prepared the resin for long-term storage.

While she worked, I asked, "What is this stuff used for exactly?"

"I'm not certain of the resin's full potential myself. But what I've discovered so far is: A, it's edible, and B, it can be formed into a crystalline solid, at which point it may have applications in quantum computing."

"Quantum computing..." Commander Tarsus had mentioned

the tech to me. It was responsible for the leap forward I'd seen on the Colony. "So what's the big deal? Faster machines?"

She raised her eyebrows, and her eyes grew wide with surprise. "Oh, right—some of our innovations haven't reached mass adoption on Earth yet." She pulled up a holoscreen between us, a grid cut in half down the middle. "Hm, let's demonstrate using a simplified version I teach the primary school children." On the half of the holoscreen closer to me floated a sphere of blue sapphire, and on her half sat an identical sphere. "Imagine you're on Earth holding these two orbs. They are both blue but can be switched to red. Common sense tells you their colors are independent of each other, correct? But when we're dealing with infinitesimal particles at the atomic level, it's not always the case. Once my blue orb interacts with your blue orb, they're permanently entangled."

"Entangled...so linked?" I asked.

"Yes. Okay, but now let's say I blast off and take my orb to the Moon. We're now separated by a vast distance. On Earth, you flip the color of your orb." On the holoscreen, my sphere shifted from blue to red. "What color is my orb on the Moon? You'd imagine it'd still be blue, right? Yet, without any action on our part, when your orb switches to red, my orb will change to red on its own." The sphere closer to her also turned red to match my own. "The state of one is entangled with the state of the other."

"What?" I tried to wrap my head around it. "That doesn't make sense."

"Einstein was skeptical, too." Her eyes were sparkling. "But it's been proven time and again. Entangled particles behave just like that."

"Entangled..." I mulled the word over. "What causes it to happen?"

"Mister, you've asked the million dollar question. We don't know yet. When we invented the wheel, we didn't have scientific theories for friction yet, but it didn't stop us from putting wheels to use. Quantum entanglement has allowed us to make computing orders of magnitude more powerful, efficient solar cells, and everything you see before you."

"I think I get it." I was lying through my teeth. "You've tapped into an unseen connection between particles. Sort of."

She nodded, but her mind was already somewhere else. The holoscreen between us dissolved, and the red orbs disappeared. She finished placing the remaining amber resin into cryogenic storage. While her back was turned, she said, "You were out in the X-Ring for so long I was worried you wouldn't make it back." I couldn't see her face, but she'd said it like she suspected something went wrong.

What was I supposed to tell her at this point? That I'd found a simulacrum, and Cyril had been waiting for me? How we carried on a conversation at length, I learned my family had lived on the Colony, and how it told me to trust no one? I'd just met Tera. She was so well-adjusted—nothing like me. I didn't want her to think I was nuts. So instead, I said, "Well, I discovered rain. I can't believe you guys have sustained a water cycle. Wouldn't people on Earth notice?"

"We've only created a self-contained atmosphere hidden inside our dome. A base tucked inside a crater solves many inherent problems. It shields us from the sun's ultraviolet radiation. It lets us experiment with terraforming on a smaller scale, to create an artificial atmosphere inside a manageable volume."

"It's also easier to hide." My mind flashed to my conversation with Commander Tarsus. "The Holosky Projector would fool most."

"Exactly! Though there's one problem we don't have a clear solution for..."

I grinned and blurted, "Aliens?"

"Ha, I wish!" she smiled back. "Now that you mention it, take a gander at these."

She led me down the corridor toward a smaller workbench stationed in her personal quarters. Her bedroom was kept in a state similar to the rest of her homepod; spare parts covered every surface. She waved a hand to indicate the gadgets set up on the workbench. "I haven't detected an inkling of communication from deep space. Only interference from moondust, and there's the last reason for a self-contained dome."

"Moondust?" I asked.

"Regolith. The 'lunar soil'—fine particles covering the Moon's entire surface. Imagine microscopic pieces of glass getting into our solar batteries, our computers, our lungs..." She fiddled with settings on the instrumentation.

"Sounds inconvenient." I scanned the room for a place to sit down, but her bed was the only clear space left.

"Regolosis, or moondust poisoning, is much more than inconvenient. It's another reason Mars was considered the superior candidate for Earth-Two. The Moon was considered old Europe's Greenland—nearby, but lacking suitability for mass colonization. Some experts make the analogy that Mars is our North America— farther out, but abundant in atmosphere and resources. We'd only have to make a longer voyage."

"Then why was a colony settled here instead?"

"Practicality won out. The Moon is a stepping stone. It's closer, making it easier to test out technology and human adaptations to living in space." She made eye contact with me and measured her next words. "And then there's the reason they keep shipping up settlers like yourself."

"A military base, right? No matter where space exploration takes us in the future, the Moon will always be strategically important to Earth's defense."

"Affirmative. A natural satellite always facing hostile space in the same geographic position, a buffer far from Earth's major cities, a low gravity well from which to launch missiles and interceptors—a lunar base is too perfect to pass up."

From out of nowhere, a voice boomed in my ear, "But who will pay the price?" I jumped back, startled. I scanned the room, but no one else was here but us—had Tera heard it too?

"No, she can't hear me," Cyril said. It was the voice of the Simulacrum. Apparently, it had uploaded itself into my wristcom without my permission.

Alarmed, I came up with something to explain my erratic behavior. But I didn't need to, because Tera was transfixed by an apparatus on her desk. The instrument resembled a metronome, and its arm was swinging back and forth. A holoscreen materialized on her bedroom wall, and on it, a sinusoidal function was being drawn out in real time. Below the graph, a jumble of numbers scrolled by.

"Oh no, not again..." She swiveled her task chair to face me and her green eyes were round like globes. "A quake! Get down!" She pulled me underneath her bed.

◐ ◑

When the tremors subsided, I peered out from under Tera's bed. Model scanners, gyroscopes, and tools of every kind lay on their sides on the floor, blanketed with dust. What a mess. I glanced sideways at her, and she was resting on her stomach. She was humming a ditty and reading on her wristcom's holodisplay as if it were a lazy Saturday.

"Fascinating." She wrinkled her nose. "My records prove the quakes have indeed been increasing with regularity. Look at all the data I've collected. It will keep the scientists busy—once the Colony establishes a geological authority, anyway."

This was the first and last time I would see someone enthusiastic about seismological readings. "Are you a geologist?"

She laughed. "No, whatever gave you that idea? It's another hobby of mine. I might find a use for the data one day."

"What for?"

"I design schematics for devices others can fabricate or build upon."

"You're an inventor?"

"I suppose you could call it my primary contribution. On the Colony, our identity doesn't revolve around our profession or income."

"Do Colony citizens juggle multiple contributions?" I asked.

"Of course. Even if some activities haven't been formalized into pay grades and hierarchies, don't we all contribute to society in more than one role? For instance, I also teach at the school—which reminds me I need to freshen up a bit before we hit the town."

"I vote to stay indoors," I said. "Won't there be aftershocks? Why the rush?"

"The children are back in school today, and I want to check if they made it through unscathed. I'll be ready in a jiffy." She reached up to undo a hair tie. She stepped out of her personal quarters and closed the door.

As soon as she left, my wristcom flashed. The Simulacrum projected itself out. It was disconcerting how Cyril could override my wristcom's permissions—even more so, when he took on the full height of a real person. His hologram was so high-resolution it was like he was present in flesh and bone. He still sported a crew cut, but this time he wore cuffed military pants tucked into red-brown lace boots. His uniform reminded me of a paratrooper, and I almost expected him to give a smart salute. "You know," I said, "lunar fashion has changed since your time."

He cleared his throat. "Back to the matter at hand. The quake—"

"What about it? You heard the lady. They happen all the time."

"She also pointed out their increasing occurrence. Do you not care to inquire further? It's unexpected I'd have a descendant lacking initiative." He reached to his mouth to clasp a cigar that didn't exist.

I held back a chuckle—my folks probably forgot to program it in. "No, you're right. I don't care. One, you're a computer program. Two, my family left me to rot on Earth, and all they left me was you. The ground trembles, so what?"

"It was the death of your heritage," he said. "The circumstances were similar when they perished—your father, your mother, your cousins, your grandparents. That sector of the Expansion Ring used to be home to a thriving village. The Nokto Quakes hit during a night cycle, which made it difficult to send aid—so the official statement went. Need I go on?"

"You're making less and less sense. Did someone forget a semi-colon in your code somewhere?" Whenever it came to my so-called family, I found listening to excuses intolerable.

He ignored my jab. "There are those who desire the Colony for themselves. They saw the potential of what we'd built and instead of contributing to its advancement, coveted it as a prize to be owned. Yours was one of the influential families who fought to stop them."

"And in the process, forgot about their son." All those years of scraping by for my next meal. Birthdays and holidays spent alone. I didn't owe them anything.

He stormed up to where I was seated and towered over me. "How has our line ended with someone so selfish and disrespectful? We died so the Colony could be free. We went to war to ensure your future and paid the ultimate price. You're the last chance to finish what we started."

"My family already faced the consequences of their actions, and I also bore those consequences—*alone*, on Earth. The past doesn't matter, and you're a stranger to me."

Tera was coming back, so I scrambled to shut off Cyril's hologram.

"Were you speaking to someone on comms?" she asked with concern in her voice.

"Yeah, it was Dr. Lunik checking in." I turned away so she couldn't tell I was lying. "No side effects from the physio-supplement they gave me so far."

She brightened up. "Then if you're in tip-top shape, mister, it's time I gave you the grand tour."

◑ ◐

On my way out of Tera's homepod, I got a good look at the strange contraption she'd been tinkering with. It appeared to be bipedal, the likes of which I'd not yet seen on the Colony. I had a soft spot for computers and machines. At least how they acted made sense to me. No pettiness either—what wasn't there to like? I motioned to it. "Does it work?"

She was practically tugging on the sleeve of my light sweater. "It's a prototype I've been working on. I 'fabbed it over the last few months, but I'm having difficulty bootstrapping artificial intelligence. Imagine trying to emulate logic even more advanced than our quantum computers. I'll tell you more about it later." And with that, she yanked me out the door.

Our walk to town made me revise my impression of the Colony. My understanding of it as a replica of Earth was flawed. The individual pod homes we passed were advanced, self-sufficient units. The terraces we strolled past put tomatoes, watercress, and lilacs on proud display. The saplings and vegetables sat in self-watering troughs which trickled in water in measured amounts.

"Like I told you earlier, terraforming is everyone's hobby," she said.

"Where does all the electricity come from?" I asked.

"Easy. Solar power."

"It can't be enough for everything. Solar cells aren't that efficient."

"But quantum dots are."

I groaned. "Quantum this and quantum that. You're going to say you don't have an explanation for how it works, but it just does."

"No, quantum dots aren't a mystery. Much of the natural world is built on top of quantum systems, and so we use biomimetics for inspiration. We copied chlorophyll atoms and their role in photosynthesis to make our own version, called Synth Atoms. They can be designed to absorb almost any spectrum of light. We print them into dots that we put on everything—even our clothing—to power devices like your wristcom."

"How are Synth Atoms produced?"

"We feed metal to Synthzymes that then spit the atoms out. But the newest Synthzymes are classified."

"Why are they a secret?"

"Because the newest designs not only capture solar power but also can emit light. By fine-tuning the size of the dots printed, Synth Atoms can emit light at any wavelength—theoretically. This innovation gave us the dot blasters LDF soldiers use, the Luxpanes used for lighting homes, and the Holosky Projector."

The sky simulated a perfect day for the beach. The "sun" hung high above in a fiery glow, surrounded by cumulus clouds and seagulls rendered in the distance. Had it not been so cold and had I not felt convection currents from the dome's heating systems on full blast, I would've been fooled.

We passed by other pedestrians dressed in clothes similar to Tera's jacket and pants. They wore chic and form-hugging clothing that appeared silver on first glance but varied in tone depending on the angle. The clothes carried a sheen, like gold flecks in a stream. In my estimation, lunar fabrics were designed to be insulated and lightweight.

We reached the main road and were met with intense city traffic. Through zipping lines of madness, helmeted riders hunched over open-air vehicles with no wheels or tires. "What kind of hovercraft are these?" I asked. "They look similar to what soldiers ride."

"Personal hoverbikes. They cover the bare essentials of locomotion—handlebars, a gyroscope for balance, and a stable seat base."

We stood at the edge of the road. How were we going to cross? There were no designated crosswalks nor traffic lights of any kind. Hell, traffic didn't even flow in opposite directions like I was used to. It was man, woman, and even child, crisscrossing in random Brownian motion. I yelled above the anarchy, "How is *this* efficient?"

"The roads are laid with electromagnetic tracks that interact with vehicle guidance systems," she said. "When traveling on our roads, hovercraft require no liquid fuel, produce no emissions other than heat and sound, and expend the tiniest bit of electricity."

"Time to cross." She pulled me into oncoming traffic.

It was a miracle that we didn't become mangled corpses. The hoverbikes weaved around us. It was like we were in a protective bubble crossing a raging river.

"How does this system make any sense?" I shouted over the roaring traffic. "There must be horrific accidents on the daily."

"Not at all. It's an efficient grid because hard stops don't exist. A simple respect for others helps, and so do predictive bump sensors." And like that, we made it to the other side.

There was a prickling sensation on my scalp, and I let go of her hand. She'd become my guide here, and I'd been depending on her too much. The Simulacrum had told me to be cautious. Wasn't it too much of a coincidence how she was the one who found me? After the Doc's injection and after I declined to enlist in Charlie Company? No—no way, I must be paranoid. I was more comfortable going lone-wolf. Rely on others too much, and people betrayed each other. She barely even knew me, and if she did—

He's always lost in his thoughts. What is it about him?

I stopped dead in my tracks and turned toward her. "What did you say?" There was that strange buzzing at the base of my skull again.

Her eyebrows were raised. "I said, mister, that we're almost at the school. The children will be so excited. They haven't met an Earther before—loosen up, or you're going to frighten them." There was mirth in her eyes, and it put me at ease again. I could tell she was looking forward to our visit.

As we neared the city center, the din of traffic faded and was replaced by the background hum of heaters and generators. Hemispherical structures, buildings made of hexagonal blocks machined in varying sizes and bright colors lined the boulevard. What lay before me would put the urban sprawl we had on Earth to shame. Even with Earth's bountiful resources and accumulated wealth over millennia, we still hadn't solved the rudimentary problems of dirt and decay. "How is everything so clean?"

"It emerged as a byproduct of our environment—early on, the regolith often leaked into the dome. Moondust made day-to-day functioning intolerable. The yttrium-based filters were created to solve the problem. Some people claimed to suffer from the constant humming, so we reinstalled the Y-filters at the dome's periphery."

We arrived at our destination, an impressive three-story pod structure with the words *Colburn School* emblazoned on its plaque. Up close, I could see the exterior was space-age alloys plated to mimic the quaint, red-brick schoolhouses of old. Their architecture favored sturdy, concave shapes formed from repeating and interlocking hexagonal pieces. Every building was self-contained and a functional unit of the dome. I said, "The Colony's organization reminds me of human cells."

"Precisely! Layered units make it so a single catastrophe won't wipe us out in one go," she said. "The geneticists warn of bottleneck effects, whereas the software engineers insist on the design because it adheres to the *Don't Repeat Yourself* principle. Regardless of one's bent, we revere designs that limit damage and reduce work."

Things began to click. "Is that how you make new towns?"

"Yes, exactly. The Colony falls under the dome. It is a city which is divided into villages—towns as you called them—which then contain individual pod homes. Each node in the hierarchy is functional and extensible." She opened the door, and we entered the outer layer of the Colburn School. The door sealed shut behind us with a sucking *whoosh* of air. "These innovations were spurred by our labor shortage. Because of our limited population, we couldn't spare man-hours for street sweeping or window cleaning—important as these tasks are to a functioning society. Instead, we prioritized automation so maintenance could run on autopilot."

"Rewind for a moment. You mean...robots take care of manual labor?" I imagined my jaw dropping down like in an old-timey cartoon.

She laughed. "Kind of. Our automata don't possess artificial intelligence per se, if that's what you meant. They're rollers and tool arms—not bipedal humanoids like the prototype I've been working on. At the moment, our automata can only perform pre-programmed tasks, but they've freed up enormous human capital. Human potential is immeasurably valuable, and we've been working to allocate it more efficiently."

She walked us over to a console, but I couldn't let go of the topic. "You're telling me factories on the Moon churn out robots?"

She laughed again. "You're hilarious. Your preconceptions come from an Earther's bias. Though low-gravity manufacturing would be revolutionary, we don't have mass-scale plants. Not yet anyway. Instead, the Foundry Revolution brought us mini-fabrication tech—personal units like these handle our needs."

I stared at a nondescript and rectangular wall-mounted device. "You mean to tell me I input what I want into this fancy coffee-maker, and it'll magically appear?" Now I was downright skeptical.

"Of course not. You have to input raw materials or spend points to pay into the resource pool. Blueprints for what you want to 'fab must exist, first of all. And although citizens receive credits for contributing, if you need something requiring a high expenditure—like a personal hoverbike—you have to save up."

Unpleasant memories of my childhood rushed by, and I shoved them back down. I was tempted to ask her how credits were distributed and what constituted fair, but it was a conversation I wasn't ready to have.

— 10 —

CYAN COHORT

I followed Tera into a classroom where students aged six to twelve sat at desk workstations. Some worked on touch-holoscreens, some pedaled stationary bikes while painting, and some read alone in noise isolation chambers. Others were engaged in blueprint projects with their peers, while some worked with senior citizens at quad-clusters scattered like islands among the light beechwood floors.

"Welcome to my classroom." She was proud and had a right to be. "From our research, we concluded that rather than establish averages, we ought to play upon strengths. In our curriculum, we teach everything from the abstract and flexible to the concrete and structured."

I bet it was also easier to find a niche when one wasn't competing to be the same as everybody else. As she'd mentioned before, diversity was survival, and survival was virtue. I asked, "The elderly folk at the workstations—are they teachers too?"

"Sort of. A retirement home occupies the upper levels of the school."

I looked up at the elevator and the staircase. On the third floor, the stairs were embellished with a white plaster sculpture of Eirene. The Greek goddess was depicted cradling an infant and was built into the railing itself.

"Residents come down when they want to teach or spend time with the children," she continued. "We find this arrangement lets senior citizens contribute their wisdom and keeps them young. The children also develop emotional well-being when they learn from people with extensive life experience."

For a moment, I felt a pang of regret mixed with envy. In a way, these children had multiple sets of grandparents. "Your educational goals are unusual."

"Not if you consider that our goal isn't an obedient populace but a productive one. These children will develop capabilities essential to our survival and advancement. The Temporodisciplinary Core pulls knowledge from across the stages of lifespan development. It was a move away from the Median Core because educating everyone to the same standard didn't fit our particular needs. Though we aim for a fair system, no two children are born truly equal; and that's fine, when people are valued for who they are. So the theories go anyway." She smiled.

I took a closer look at one of the workstations where a few students were playing DaisySim. It was a virtual reality game for children to roleplay. One student was cultivating a farm outside the Colony dome. Another two were acting out a co-op scenario in which they had to redirect black hole energy into the lunar power grid. "You were so worried about them," I said, "but they don't look like they've been affected by the quake at all."

"They like to put on a brave front. This batch has been especially remarkable. I like to think of them as a new breed." She leaned in and whispered in my ear, "The Cyan Cohort," and laughed the infectious way she did. "It's my silly pet name for them. Our secret, okay?"

I nodded. For someone so logical, she surprised me with bouts of capriciousness. I studied her for a moment; she was hard to read.

"Hi everyone!" she announced. The children popped up from their workstations like gophers. They ran over to her in a herd, with some students coming up to hug her waist.

"Teacher Tera," a boy said, "did you feel the ground shake?"

"I did, indeed, Michael. It was mighty strong this time, wasn't it?"

Michael said, "Yes!" Another child chimed in, "Incredibly strong!" and another added, "It was the strongest one I've ever felt!"

A little girl jostled her way to the front of the group. She shuffled over in the moonbooties I'd often seen children wear. She had dark hair like mine, except it was styled into a bob cut. The blue streaks in her hair were created by a *virtua crown*—Tera told me the accessory altered one's appearance with holograms—worn around her neck. She tugged on the hem of Tera's skirt and looked up with imploring eyes. "Were you scared?"

"Oh, just a little bit, Quinn. Were you scared too?"

Quinn nodded.

"And what about all of you?" Tera asked the rest of the class.

Many voices piped up all at once. "Just a little!" and "Me too...a little bit." Although they were fishing for her sympathy, I could see the Cyan children were as brave as she'd said. Maybe the unforgiving conditions on the Moon had inured them to hardships, for they seemed to be a resilient bunch.

"I'm so relieved you all survived, and I'm so proud of you. As a treat, I brought someone special for you to meet today." She winked at me.

A wheat field full of eyes turned toward me, their expressions inquisitive and probing. "Everyone, say hello to Darin. He's from Earth," she said. The children gasped, and their eyes grew wide in unison. Quinn and her friends covered their mouths. It was like I had a pineapple for a head. My first week here, others had shot me dirty looks or hurried away at the sight of me. But these children were something else. Their reactions were of curiosity rather than of fear.

Boy, did they (or was it all children?) have boundless reserves of energy. They peppered me with one question after another, and nothing I said satisfied them.

"What's the difference between the composition of the Earth and the Moon?" Michael asked.

I had no idea. Did the Moon have a core? Was its core proportionately smaller than Earth's? I didn't expect children to ask me about geology.

"What's human society like where you're from?" Sammy asked.

"Well, we have many different cities and societies, so it wouldn't be accurate for me to generalize them." I didn't say so, but if there was anything they shared in common, it was stratification.

"How do Earthers survive without fabricators?" Quinn asked.

"In our case, we don't have the technology yet. We have lots of natural resources at the moment, so we have anything we could want, even without fabricators." What I didn't add was how our abundance had created a filter through which all things were viewed as objects to be acquired.

In the end, how honest could I be? Say to a roomful of children, their eyes brimming with hope, how I wasn't thrilled by my society's artificiality and penchant for bloodlust?

No, I kept it light, and we had rowdy fun. As our time together wound down, it turned out I wasn't the only visitor that day.

◗ ◖

At Lunar Channel One headquarters, Seger stood his ground while all twenty holoscreens shook. In some households, his station's broadcast was distorted by static lines, and in others, his programs were replaced by the colored bars of an emergency warning.

Carmen, his deputy director, said, "The quakes are starting up again. Twelve affiliates have reported losing our signal."

All eyes in the studio turned to him for leadership. He'd lived through enough moonquakes in his time to be unfazed. Nevertheless, they'd begun to intrigue him. Why did they feel more powerful than before? Twelve broadcasts knocked offline was a record—hardly scientific, but loss of profits was the only metric he needed.

"Carmen, pull the Colony's seismological records for the last ten years. I want a report on my desk by the time I return." And then there was the primary question—was there a story to sell?

He left the studio and took a hovercraft to the Colburn School in Turtlepin Village. He was there on the pretext of recording a segment for Lunar Channel One. When he located his target—the real reason he'd come—he beheld a young man whose jaw was thrust forward and whose shoulders were pulled in tight like he was ready for a fight. Darin Armacite had eyes that held back a smoldering fire, like a powder keg lacking a spark. He'd have to be careful of how he prodded this one.

Some experts said the media shouldn't push narratives, but Seger disagreed. If the media were relegated to a speaker box for the public's concerns, the news would deteriorate into random noise. For large-scale change, the indecisive public needed to be guided, needed to be focused. Otherwise, information overload occurred, and inertia took hold. And he was not someone who believed in standing still.

It was true, though, that the information trade was a delicate business. The powers that be paid mass media to scare or distract the general populace—to keep governments stable, as it were. On the other hand, the average citizen relied on journalists to uncover corruption and keep the powerful accountable. And keeping the two groups from each other's throats were newsmakers like him, curators of human desire. This eternal battle required a mediator, and for maintaining fair play, he expected handsome rewards.

His role was responsible for the gray strands peeking out from his coiffed, pale blond hair. He adjusted the tie on his camel-colored linen suit and walked the length of the classroom over to Darin. Darin was accompanied by a young woman whose bangs covered a high forehead. She was most likely Tera Arkwright, a local inventor his aides had profiled in advance.

"Lunar Channel One here to report on the recent quake." He pushed the floating camera drone in Darin's direction. "Do you have anything to say about the rumors that these quakes were caused by terraforming practices known as hydrobreaching?"

"I don't know anything about it. I'll leave it up to the authorities to investigate."

"Interesting conclusion, considering many say they have been too influenced by special interests from Earth—where you come from. If push comes to shove, which side will you choose? Is it true you turned down a contract from Charlie Company?"

"They don't need someone like me—"

"We always need people to protect civilians when the Colony is threatened. Like the period in our history when the Nokto Quakes wiped out many prominent families," Seger said. After emphasizing the last bit, he shot Darin a purposeful glance. "What would make you reconsider?"

"You guys abducted me, remember? I don't owe you anything, and let's leave it at that."

Seger sensed the interview going south and tried to salvage it. "Or you might argue we saved you and gave you a second chance."

"A chance I didn't ask for and didn't want."

He turned back to address the camera. "Opinions from an Earther—you heard it here first. The quakes continue, but who will take responsibility for the Colony's safety? Lunar Channel One signing out." He switched off the spotlight on the camera drone.

He spun back around to face Darin. "Off the record, do you believe they'll leave you alone to do whatever you please? They went to all that trouble to ship you up here, and not because we need more artists or engineers."

"My value is as cannon fodder—is that accurate?"

There was rage in the young man's eyes, so Seger tread lightly. "They expect a return on their investment. You were chosen due to your lack of ties. Our government controls both capital goods and the means of production. How will you eat? How will you find a permanent place to live? If you don't contribute, you won't survive. Perhaps you disagree, but I think it'd be a waste."

Unease like a sickness covered my insides after the reporter left. Things were supposed to be different for me up here. Children had shed the insecurity of and hatred for differences. Colonists treated each other as neighbors rather than as competitors because they considered themselves partners in building an ideal society. But Seger reminded me how some things never change: I was only wanted if I were useful. I was nothing more than a slave to the larger apparatus.

Tera's hand was on my arm. "Earth to Darin, you okay out there?"

I nodded for her benefit. The truth was, I wasn't okay with it. It was starting to make me feel off-balance. But it wasn't another one of my moods—not when the walls of the schoolhouse began to rumble. It must've been an aftershock from the first quake. Bits of ceiling streamed down around us in dusty vertical trails.

Tera, the Cyan Cohort students, and I—we all figured out it wasn't a weak aftershock when the tremors shot up to unbelievable intensity. Potted plants fell off the shelves and shattered on the floor. The students' projects—cube satellites and exotic spaceship designs—were ripped apart at the seams.

Some of the children had crawled under their workstations, but others had been knocked off their feet before they could scramble for cover. There was a sharp *crack* from above. On the third floor, the statue of Eirene splintered at its base. It began to rock back and forth. Sitting right underneath was little Sammy, a boy I'd played mech battle simulations with earlier in the day.

I shouted a warning, but Sammy didn't hear me over the pandemonium. The statue separated from its base and toppled over the stair railing. I dashed toward him but was going to be too late.

In an inexplicable burst of energy, like frames missing from old stock footage, I was there. I tackled Sammy out of the way. We tumbled and rolled across the beechwood floorboards.

The statue of Eirene smashed into a flurry of plaster, leaving an anguished dent where Sammy once was. The other children gaped at me in disbelief, a renewed curiosity in their eyes. How *had* I made it in time?

Little Sammy and I took cover under the workstations with the other students. Unlike anything I'd ever been through on Earth, the quake continued for a knuckle-whitening ten minutes. I didn't even know something like that was possible. But apparently, without oceans to dampen the vibrations, they just kept going. If I had to point to one event when things started to change, it was the day the Moon rang like a bell.

— 11 —

AMIDEN VILLAGE

The solitary creature stirred and chafed in its nest. Its sunken eyes shuttered open. A synthetic liquid had seeped into its abode and woken it from its dormant state. Its instincts warped to something unnatural, the creature went mad.

It reared its dry-cracked, obsidian head and groaned a terrible cry. It pulled up against its gestational membrane, roaring in agony.

All it could understand was the contaminant was a threat. And its natural response was self-defense. In the past, it would've roused its brethren. They'd lash out in raids on the human settlement, as they'd done decades before. The pattern of events would've been the same this time around—except the creature's programming was subverted by new visitors to the local star system.

Twins, the green comets LINEAR and LINEAR2, arced past along their orbits. In their wake, they left trails like dragons traversing the heavens. With no atmosphere to slow them down, they pummeled the surface in a relentless orchestra. Meteorite impacts were ordinary fare on the Moon; they caused plasma to form, which sent electromagnetic pulses into the regolith. Temporary phenomena.

But in this case, the EMP waves surged through a synthetic liquid deep in the crust. Immersed in this noxious stew, the creature changed. It stood upright, aware of what it was and aware of its new destiny.

◐ ◑

When the ground moved, it reminded me forces existed beyond human control. Klaxons. Evacuations. Panic and fear. "We've never weathered a quake like this before," Tera would tell me later on—when we could do nothing but talk.

We rounded up the Cyan Cohort children and the senior citizens and led them to the emergency shelters. After everyone in the schoolhouse had been accounted for (checked off in her meticulous logs), she insisted we go help others who hadn't yet reached safety.

So we departed Turtlepin Village on hoverbikes. Our travels took us from town to town, to pitch in wherever we could. We pulled citizens from rubble; we geo-tagged support beams needing immediate reinforcement; and we resupplied LDF soldiers who'd taken up defensive stations per Colony emergency protocol. But one stop along our roam would forever remain etched upon my mind: Amiden Village.

I sensed something terrible the moment we arrived. Unlike the other villages we'd visited, homepods were caved in like they'd imploded. Fresh blood was smeared against torn pillars, and the putrid stench of death hung in the air. We spent hours sifting through the wreckage in search of hope. Men, women, and children—we didn't find a single survivor.

We were soon joined by the Lunar Defense Forces. Charlie Company rode in and was the first squad to arrive on the scene. Commander Tarsus' expression was inscrutable as he surveyed the carnage. Gamma Company and Tau Company arrived next. They, too, did not join in on our futile mission. Instead, they sat and stared, motionless atop their hoverquads.

They'd reached the same conclusion I had: the deaths here couldn't have been from the quake. The people of Amiden Village had been massacred.

A grim silence threatened to devour anyone who dared utter a sound. What could anyone say? Did people deserve to die in their homes, defenseless? Dolls lay discarded next to dead children. There were bodies with bloody slashes across their backs, as if they'd been struck down while fleeing. Homepods and even electrical junctions were destroyed, which looked like targeted efforts to erase the town.

The antithesis of progress stared us in the face, and no one could avert their eyes. Their families—did they have loved ones who'd be left behind and alone as I'd been?

Emergency klaxons blared once more. An announcement went out over the loudspeakers: "Dome leaks in Quadrants 84-F, 19-C..." and the list went on and on.

"The regolith..." Tera said. "If it pours into the dome, we'll be finished."

It was the first time since we met that I'd ever seen her upset. She was always composed, always prepared—she was always the one with the answers. But she was in shock, and the way this hurt her wasn't something I could accept.

I didn't know what to say—there was nothing more we could do to help Amiden Village. So I wanted to bring her back by getting her mind on something else. "Is moondust a priority for us right now?"

"Yes, Darin, it is. Especially to our life support systems. They listed so many points of entry..." She stood there distraught.

This was my chance to get her mind on something else. The soldiers of Gamma and Tau squadrons zoomed off in opposite directions. Charlie Company revved up to follow suit. On its procession past us, I recognized the face of a soldier in the back. He was the one who'd spoken to me on my last run-in with the squad. I extended my arm and shouted, "Wait!"

He slowed his hoverquad alongside us. He was wearing a green camo military shirt with two front pockets and his badge read Sgt. Hugh Ambrose III. His combed, straw hair and blue eyes were how I imagined an astronaut from the Midwest might look.

When Ambrose came to a full stop, I asked him, "Is there anything we can do to help?"

"Matter of fact, there is," he said. "I counted too many leaks for our forces to patch in one sweep." He raised a gauntleted hand and punched commands into his wristcom. "Quadrants 51-R, 4-T, and 80-M." He transmitted the coordinates to me. "It's dangerous, but would you two handle those? Follow the procedures written in the Emergency Handbook."

"Nothing we can do but try," I said. Tera returned to her old self and nodded. She wasn't in shock and closing off anymore, even if just for now, and I allowed myself to feel grateful for a moment.

He said, "Godspeed," and zipped off in the direction of the Colony outskirts.

◐ ◐

Would it not be wonderful if all it took to be made whole again was space-grade silicone puttied over cracks in the surface?

I skimmed over the emergency procedures known as Patch Lockdown on my wristcom. To make conditions easier for sealing the Colony dome, artificial gravity had been deactivated in the affected quadrants. To my surprise, the first two leaks Tera and I attended to were a cinch. It took us only a few moments to locate where the oxygen was seeping out. Although one crack was high up—we had to jump up and down on a rooftop to apply sealant—the dome shell was cooperative. The patches would hold until the engineers had time to replace the damaged panels.

The dome was the difference between life and death. But it wasn't crystal clear to me until we reached the last site Ambrose assigned to us. The leak was located in Quadrant 80-M—in the Buffer Deadzone, the outermost ring of the Colony itself. Vegetation all but vanished as we moved farther from the city center, becoming sparser in the I-Band, mere patches in the Expansion Ring, and dirt and sand by the time we entered the BDZ.

Quadrant 80-M's coordinates appeared on my wristcom to be inside the Lockray Research Station, a copper-colored building in the middle of nowhere. We got into the Lockray's dinky shaft elevator. During the lengthy descent, I turned to Tera and asked, "I thought leaks happened to the dome. Why are we going to the basement of this building?"

"People don't know about the dome's foundation. Its sub-structure can be accessed from certain research stations spaced around the BDZ. It becomes obvious if you look for buildings with a B3 basement floor. I discovered this from backdooring into government servers—don't give me that look—it was well-intentioned penetration testing. Up top, we're a hyper-planned city, but underground is where we hide our artificial gravity systems, quake shelters, and Holosky Projector. It's a mess of wires stashed behind a clean console panel."

"I still don't understand how we'll patch the dome from *inside* a building." I talked to distract myself from how stifling the air was becoming as the elevator descended.

"You'll see. The BDZ is far from the villages. Its uninviting ter-rain deters citizens from mischief, though you'd have to be looney to tamper with the only thing keeping oxygen in. And whatever's on the other side out." She laughed.

Her nervous laughter put me on edge. I could feel that buzzing at the back of my skull and one of my strange moods coming on. It always made the air around my head charged with electricity. I didn't remember the sensation being this strong. Had it become more pronounced since I settled up here?

We reached the bottom of the elevator shaft, and all that she'd told me became clear. Basement level B3 wasn't a traditional floor with walls. Rather, it was a space underground open all the way to the dome. The support beams holding the building up were naked and exposed. In front of me, I could see the dome's base. It was a shell which curved upward to form the hemisphere above ground. Floor B3 was enclosed by the dome barrier itself, creating a sort of cave. There were probably many basement "caves" like this one, hidden from plain sight but which allowed engineers easy access.

In our first few minutes there, no ambient noises filtered in. So it was obvious when whistling came from the leak we'd been searching for. The fracture was also difficult to miss: the crack was as long as a baseball bat, and it was still expanding.

We walked roughly four hundred paces across rust-colored concrete out from the elevator to the dome. It was stuffy, perhaps worsened by oxygen depletion. As we passed by the naked building supports, the steel beams whined and creaked.

"Let's seal this baby up fast and leave the rest to the professionals." I didn't add how I wanted to get out of here pronto. Ambrose had assigned us this task in an unofficial capacity in the chaos following the quake—I wasn't sure if anyone knew where we were.

She agreed and prepared the sealant paste. I was relieved after the first coat had gelled and the sucking noise diminished. The Lockray's support beams, however, continued in their shrill complaints. Flexing and swaying were normal for buildings this size, right?

To get my mind off my unease, I asked, "What's this goop made of anyway?"

She was busy prepping a third coat. "Silicone and other space-grade materials. That's what the government's official MSDS spec sheet says. But I've got suspicions it uses crystals as an emulsifier."

"You mean crystals formed out of amber resin?"

"Uh-huh. Just a hunch. The government has never acknowledged the resin's existence, but no other substance I've played with is so easy to change from malleable in one form to structurally sound in another." She prepped the sixth and final coat. "These are temporary patches, though. The engineered panels they'll replace our handiwork with will have Synth Atoms embedded in them."

"You mean quantum dots?" Something about them both absorbing and emitting light.

"Hey, you were paying attention after all," she teased. "Yes, the Synth Atoms in the dome are tuned to absorb the far infrared frequencies. That includes nearly half of the sunlight reaching the lunar surface. The innovation let us reach Munchausen Efficiency, a benchmark for when solar power has achieved sustainability. These dots printed onto the dome also create the visuals you see for our simulated climate systems."

She completed one last circular motion with her brush applicator. "Done and done," She smiled wide. She relished a project finished and crossed off her to-do list. Maybe it was especially true because her inventions lay about in various stages of completion.

I said, "Let's blow this joint—" and no sooner had we walked a few steps back to the elevator than the support beams let out a howl. One steel girder bent. Then another bent, and another, until the entire structure began to crumble.

The force from the building's collapse flung me off my feet. The last thing I remembered was flying backward through the air until my spine slammed against the dome's shell.

— 12 —

SHIELDS UP

We were trapped between the destroyed Lockray building and the dome, three stories underground. When I came to, I took stock of our situation, careful not to move my neck. Particles of dust and debris saturated the air. Under the fog, a body lay on the concrete near me. Tera was on her side; she must've been thrown off her feet and into the dome's shell like I'd been.

Was she injured? I waited but didn't see her make the slightest move. I couldn't tell if she was still breathing. No, not like this. Not her over me.

I didn't dare touch or move her, for fear I'd make her injuries worse, for fear I couldn't help, for fear it was already too late. I lay there in a stupor, unable to feel my arms and legs. The impact had been so powerful I wasn't sure if I'd broken my back.

Behind me was the dome, and in front of me were the remnants of the Lockray building. The shaft elevator which we'd used to descend had been obliterated. I followed the tower of rubble upward with my eyes and found no line of sight to the surface. Had it not been for the pod lights embedded in the dome, we would've been swallowed in darkness.

Sensations returned. I began to feel layers of dirt caked on my face and blinked the grit out of my eyes. The air suffocated me, and I coughed in hacking fits. My body spasmed in response and confirmed my arms and legs were still in working order.

My wristcom was blinking with a red notification. My hopes someone was calling on comms fell when I checked and found no signal. Instead, the Simulacrum projected from the device and materialized onto the shattered concrete in front of me. Cyril was a three-dimensional hologram in living color and clad in military shock armor. Was it pity combined with disappointment on his face? He almost fooled me into thinking he was human and not a virtual recreation.

He paced around and surveyed the devastation. He tilted his head toward Tera. "Now you know what it's like for those close to you to suffer while you do nothing."

"Cyril, you're terrible at being human, you know? Now's not the time for your grand directive." I needed him to shut up about revenge for our family. I needed to sit up and check on Tera.

"Let me ask you," he said, "what self-respecting Armacite would lie there while those close to him die?"

"You're *not* helping," I growled. My legs were working but trying to move them felt like raising anchors.

He wouldn't relent. "You have descended from a long line of proud soldiers, patriots who fought for the future of their republic while the rest tended to their small and selfish means."

Using all of my gathered strength, I forced myself into a seated position. "It must be real easy to lecture me right now since I've no choice but to listen." I grimaced from the pain and leaned against the dome shell for support. I turned my head to the side and took labored breaths, painting the cold glass with dirtied specks. "You haven't lived my life. What do you know?"

In my youth back on Earth, I questioned too many times what was wrong with me that I always ended up eating lunches and dinners alone. When things seemed to be improving, friends and romantic partners appeared in my life one moment but were gone the next. It made me wonder if I were broken. Or maybe the world they endorsed wasn't one I could live in. As a result, I didn't like it when people who didn't know me told me what to do.

"Get over yourself." He was raising his voice at me. "You're not special. Everyone suffers—it's what it means to be alive. A soldier achieves victory over pain, not in the absence of it."

I entertained for a moment whether others were as well-adjusted as they seemed behind their effortless smiles and white picket fences. "Look, what do you want from me?" I groaned and began to crawl toward Tera. "I'm in deep, and you don't even care—why am I not surprised you were programmed by my folks?"

"Your family...their deaths were no accident," he said. "What you face here is no accident. There are those who will stop at nothing until the Colony is under their thumbs. Your forebears fought them but have only managed to slow them down. If you do nothing, you will watch as your countrymen become enslaved to an order at once pernicious and tyrannical."

I reached her and leaned in. She was still taking shallow breaths. I sat back in relief. I spoke over my shoulder to Cyril. "Why does it have to be me?"

"If not you, then who?"

He was right in that I'd begun to see my new home in a different light. The Lunar Colony was a frontier humanity needed, and the possibilities of that dream were worthwhile. But I wasn't powerful enough to change things in the way he wanted. What I could do was help Tera. I could treat her with the same kindness she'd shown me. I gathered enough energy to flick my wristcom off, and Cyril disappeared. I needed to focus on Tera right now.

My first instinct was to leave her be—a person was unconscious for a reason, right? But then again, we were trapped three stories underground, and I didn't know how much oxygen we had left. She was one of the most resourceful people I'd ever met, and if I could wake her, maybe she'd whip out a widget that could get us out.

CPR. Yes, that was the plan. I'd never been trained on CPR, but I brushed those doubts aside. What was the first step? Tilt the head back? I was grasping at straws. I unclasped her gear pack and pushed it aside. Next, I released the wristcom from her arm. I was extra careful as I unzipped her silver jacket. What were the procedures for chest compressions again? Something about making sure the person had adequate breathing room. I reached over to loosen her utility belt—

"Just *what* do you think you're doing?" Her emerald eyes were open and locked on mine. The dust had settled, and through it, I saw her death glare. My next words could've been my last.

"I was...um...reviving you." I felt sheepish, and my ears were burning. "And it worked!"

She studied my face in intense concentration. Then she burst into laughter. "You're a riot. Okay, thanks." She coughed out bitter dust before taking in deeper breaths.

We spent the next hour adjusting to our situation, and after finding no serious injuries, we took a gamble. She reached out a hand, and I pulled her into a sitting position so we could both lean against the dome.

She took in the destruction. I gave her some time to work out that we were trapped between the rubble and the dome. When she did, she said, "Well ain't we in a pickle? There's life on the Colony for ya. Where everything's cutting edge, but things still break all the time."

It was quite the slogan. I glanced sidelong at her. Huh, she was something else. Here I'd already accepted our impending doom, but Tera—she faced it with optimism.

We spent the next few hours poking around and searching for a way out. On our wristcoms, we compiled and exhausted every software package we could think of, but none could contact the surface. We gave up and sat back down to rest against the dome's shell once more.

I could see the gears in her head were still turning. She gazed out at the mortar and demolished concrete that used to be the Lockray building. "How are we still alive? I mean, this building collapsed on top of us."

I shrugged. "Luck, I guess."

"Luck, huh? Mister, I don't believe in luck."

Tera Arkwright disliked the word 'luck' and was averse to anything smacking of superstition. After all, Darin's appearance in her life was improbable at best. According to him, he survived a jump from a twelve-story bridge. Highly unlikely. Arriving via space travel to the Moon? Only a tiny percentage had ever crossed. Surviving past the first month on the Colony as a Transplant? The funnel narrowed even further.

And those only counted the exploits she'd picked up around town. She added to that evidence events she'd witnessed firsthand: the incident at the schoolhouse when the Big One hit. When the statue fell—how had he gotten little Sammy out of the way in time?

Now, the Lockray Research Station had collapsed on top of them. The impact alone would have killed anyone...should have killed them both. The number of times Darin had escaped death were one in...she couldn't fathom the odds. Luck? It was as preposterous as the local religion about a Moon goddess. Yet there he was.

"So, mister, how will luck help us now?" she deadpanned. "I don't want to expire down here, though the company is, shall I say, generally agreeable." The children in the Cyan Cohort had taken a shine to him too, and she trusted their judgment.

"Is dying so terrible? Why are you here? I mean, in the grand scheme of things."

"Well, that explains your death wish."

He turned his head and straightened up, bumping her shoulder with his. He was half-laughing when he answered, "Are you referring to what I did on that bird up here or to my interview with Seger from Lunar Channel One?"

"Both." Why was he talking to her like she was in on some practical joke?

"Try to do what's right, and everyone thinks I'm a wacko. So it's easier to not explain anything. But that's just me. You, on the other hand, still haven't answered my question. What drives you to keep on going?"

She scrunched her eyebrows together. "Why do I need a reason? There are everyday concerns. To eat, to fabricate tools, to raise a family, and to contribute." That third item on the list was a sore point for her. It was taboo to aim for having fewer than two children, or worst of the worst, to have no children by choice. Not adding to the Colony's much-needed population growth was equivalent to telling a neighbor that she didn't care if the Colony survived. She'd convinced herself that she was above the social pressure, but constant questions from friends and acquaintances had been threatening to disturb her inner sanctum of cheerful thoughts.

"I don't see the point of merely existing." He crossed his arms. "Society cares neither for the individual nor for his happiness. What's the reason for any of it? Without love, it's a machine—all of it. Goods and services produced with resource input and waste exhaust."

She bristled. "Love won't ensure our survival up here. Can love supply oxygen? Can it grow soybeans and leafchoy? Can it fab Luxpanes or sustain a water cycle? I never expected to become a workaholic like Papa, but you know what? There are so many things left to do to improve our mortality rates." She was annoyed now at the person in front of her, who had no right to survive with his blatant disregard for practical affairs. His existence was an affront to logic.

He had one palm cupped on his knee and the other hand resting on the side of his dark hair, his fingers against his temple. He often switched into unusual, unconscious poses that, to her, only served to underscore his odd way of thinking. He was an anomaly she'd not encountered before and needed to make sense of.

"Love is what makes those things worthwhile," he argued. "I mean, goods are trivial pursuits if you care to obtain them. Why strive for—without a reason, they're all meaningless."

She could tell he was indignant now because she couldn't see things his way. And he was used to it being the case. So he did care about something after all. She delivered her retort in an exaggerated and mocking tone, "Well, mister, if you've got an engine that can run on love, why don't you conjure up a magical bubble that'll lift our corporeal bodies outta here."

He broke into a smile before bursting into laughter, lighting up the room like a lantern in a dark forest. She didn't know why he was laughing but couldn't resist joining in. It was the first time she'd ever seen him happy. Because he didn't smile often, she'd never noticed he could be handsome.

That was odd. She hadn't felt this way in a while. She'd almost forgotten what it was like. But Darin would never be interested in someone others called too cold and logical. Guys found that off-putting, and he hadn't paid her any notice. Shields and defenses up, captain.

I laughed because Tera caught me off guard. It'd been a long time since anyone called me out and in such a ridiculous way. I asked, "Are you saying you won't forgive me if I don't get us out of here?"

"You got it, pard'ner. I won't forgive you, not even from the grave."

The Colonists weren't like the people I'd gotten used to back on Earth. They didn't exhibit the mean streak of human beings who fancied themselves modern. Was it the food? Was it the freedom granted by frontier life? The close-knit ties to their villages? It'd be easy to dismiss their innocence as naiveté, that they'd not developed the shrewd, cut-throat mentality necessary to get ahead. But Colony society was conscious about eschewing notions of class and contempt. Maybe this system couldn't last, but I wanted to believe it would.

I studied her face as if it was for the first time. Could I be myself with her? She exuded a warmth which I'd never sensed in others. I'd give anything to get her out of our predicament.

Hours had passed according to my wristcom, though I couldn't tell in the unchanging, dim light. We couldn't find a way out, so we stopped talking to conserve oxygen. We passed in and out of various states of sleep. I awoke once with her head resting on my shoulder, and then I dozed off again.

When I came to, the Simulacrum was standing there peering at me. "Defeated before you've even begun?" Cyril asked. "Going to take it lying down, I presume?"

"If you've got any ideas," I whispered, "I'm all ears."

"You've searched for a way to climb three floors. You've turned to technology to solve your problem."

"Excellent summary." I discovered it was great fun messing with him because he couldn't detect sarcasm.

"Chasing distractors doesn't address the root of your problem. You won't escape without others' help."

"Do you think people care we're trapped down here? They're unreliable and self-serving. They've probably all rushed to the shelters by now." Growing up surrounded by discouraging words and lack, I was the only constant I counted on. Relying on myself was what worked.

"Yet despite your low opinion of others, they're your only solution. Your energy should be spent on communicating your location to the surface."

Tera began to stir, which was his cue to vanish.

I said, "Tera, hey. Do you have any manual tools for communication in your gear pack?"

"What? Oh, I don't believe so, no. Did the idea come to you right now?"

"A rabbit told me in a dream."

She rolled her eyes. "Well, maybe you ought to listen to it more often. That's a good call." She chewed her lower lip for a moment. "Sound waves..."

"Huh?"

"Taking into account our distance from the surface, sound waves will travel far enough."

"There's no way we're shouting through this heap," I said. "We're conserving oxygen as is."

"Yes, but sound waves can also travel through solid matter."

The realization struck us at the same time, and we began to scan the room. And that's when I spotted the support column. It was a single steel girder, still standing. I followed it upward, and it continued past the rubble. There was a chance it reached all the way to the surface.

I went over and made *tap, tap, tap* sounds against its metal. I sat down next to it and tapped out S-O-S out so many times I lost count. I kept at it until I faded back into sleep.

Creatures shuffled by in the shadows. Soldiers fired dot blasters at unseen threats and at each other. From a grassy hill, I looked down upon ghost towns littered with mass graves. I traveled the flight path of a warhead until it detonated on impact, expanding to critical mass and engulfing Tera, the Cyan Cohort children... everyone in the Colony.

I woke from my nightmare with a start. In front of me was a blurry face. Warm. Soft. It was Tera's. She was so close I could feel her breath on my cheek. "Darin," she whispered, eyes locked onto mine, "Darin...they're here. We made it."

When Charlie Company had come to check off the last leak on their list, they heard our distress call. A construction crew was called in and dug us out.

◗ ◖

I would remember the next three days, but not because Tera and I were awarded civilian honors for helping to seal the dome. Nor was it because for the first time in my life, my neighbors greeted me without fear and suspicion in their eyes. No, those memories would come second to the events that'd happened while we were gone.

In Dreotta Village, the quake caused what the news called "an unidentified chemical compound" to leach into the water supply. Many were poisoned and rushed to the emergency room for hallucinations, seizures, and severe dehydration. Some entered comas from which they never awoke. Children, whose nervous systems were fragile, were harmed the most. In the weeks after, doctors had to console mothers whose pregnancies ended in stillbirth.

The situation was inhumane and something I couldn't let go of. When I first arrived, I was witness to a place where every child grew up healthy and secure. That achievement had been undone by a single disaster.

The only thing worse was having to watch Tera change in the aftermath. Her shoulders became heavier every time she returned from village meetings. The lines on her forehead became more pronounced as she worried more and slept less, spending long hours as an aid volunteer. Would the light leave her, as it had for me so long ago? Her type of kindness was often preached but so rarely cultivated I couldn't bear the thought of it being snuffed out.

Then the rumors began. It was early in the afternoon after we had checked in on her Cyan Cohort classroom. We'd stepped out of the Colburn School when the reporter from the news station showed up again.

"Lunar Channel One here to get an outsider's perspective," Seger said, before shoving the camera drone under my chin. "We've faced moonquakes before, but the toll has never been so high. Do you think we're headed for trouble?"

It was strange how I wanted to put on a positive front, at least for Tera and the children. So I said, "The Colony will survive. We must."

"Do you think there's any merit to the rumors? Amiden Village has been wiped out, and the people of Dreotta have been poisoned. Some say these tragedies weren't caused by natural disasters."

People relied on authority figures for reassurance, right? So I said, "I'm sure the government is looking into it."

— 13 —

ONE OF US

Richard Paxton Nest, acting Vice President of the Lunar Colony, cursed whenever he needed to get his point across. "You people assured me hydrobreaching wouldn't draw attention. And then I receive a report about a goddamned record quake." Paxton could feel a tightness working its way up his cleft chin to his loose jowls.

On the holo-conference, a silhouetted figure of one of the Guildsack Partners lit up. "Agent M has succeeded in robust environmental conditions before. This time, however, it's unclear whether things were complicated by a meteor shower. It appears the compound set off a chain reaction—a perfect storm but most likely a fluke."

They'd trotted out the same excuse the last time. Didn't they know he was old enough to remember the Nokto Quakes from decades ago? The crisis had brought Colony expansion to a halt and forced it to shrink back inside the Second Demarcation. The destruction was so extensive that the Colony started over. Reconstruction followed a centralized approach set by the Hundred Year Plan, and in civil service even then, he was privy to insider knowledge: the new layout was intended to erase divisive sectional identities of Northern industry, Southern arts, Western agriculture, or Eastern intellectualism. Whether it'd hold with human nature being the way it was, only time would tell. But the devastation this time around—it was much worse than then.

He shouted, "A fluke? The worst crisis in lunar history, with thousands dead and growing, is not a fluke!" He wished he could reach through the holo-conference and choke this idiot on Old Earth. When he wore thick-framed spectacles in public, he looked like a distinguished older gentleman. But in private, when the spectacles came off, his stature and aggressive nose could make a pit bull stand down. These mealy-mouthed cowards safe behind their silhouettes and holoscreens—they'd never dare say these things to his face. "The wrong people are starting to ask questions."

Another member of the Guildsack Partners blinked on in green. The shadowed figure said, "Either way, terraforming must proceed. Agent M is our best means of introducing mass farming to the lunar surface."

He huffed through flared nostrils and gauged the new speaker. They never showed their faces and used voice modulation, but he could guess she was an executive from Agrocorp. He smirked. Cornering food production was a racket—even when quality dropped, prices shot up. Who was going to protest when it became the only game in town? He collected himself. "President Keane will have my head if he finds out. I'll be crucified by the public."

"Grow a backbone, Paxton." A different representative lit up in red on the holo-conference. "Keane will soon be too, shall we say, preoccupied to investigate a *natural disaster*. After all, the lunar president's primary responsibility has always been national security."

He scrutinized the new speaker. The silhouette most likely belonged to the owner of Block EX, the largest arms dealer on Earth. It was staggering to consider the money and power afforded a man who counted military contracts with over half of the nations on Earth. He suspected Block EX had bankrolled the recent hijacking of the Colony's import ship. It must've been a bid to get its hands on quantum tech or to scare Keane into a weapons deal—probably both.

In other words, somebody with enough clout to get him elected to the presidency.

Yet another member blinked on in blue. He'd deduced a while ago that this person hailed from Gruber & Brownfeld, one of Earth's most influential land developers. The invention of Gravdar—quantum tech used to draw subterranean maps by measuring gravitational fluctuations—removed major delays inherent in drilling and construction. But it was never fast enough for G&B. This man or woman (from his notes, most likely a woman) had engineered his ascent to the vice presidency. Pacified, he said, "And when the dust settles?"

"When the dust settles, we'll buy out the distressed land and develop Moon Base Zero as we see fit. You'll be in charge of awarding contracts then, won't you? After all, soon you'll be one of us."

◑ ◑

In the President's Office, Keane popped a prescription cocktail of blood pressure and pain medication. Against doctor's orders, he chased the pills with a tumbler of cognac.

He suspected the Guildsack Partners were behind the rash of instability that'd recently beset the Colony—scares over imagined food shortages, the hijacking of a ship, the tainted water supply. But those Earthers could claim plausible deniability; their army of lawyers guaranteed that.

He rested his drink on a circular glass coffee table separating him from Paxton, who sat in the armchair opposite.

"Sir, we need a decision. Do we mobilize the troops?"

He ran a hand through his hair. His VP was impatient and

injudicious when it came to decisions affecting posterity. Those were qualities that wouldn't do for a future leader. When the time came, another candidate needed to be groomed. He returned to the problem at hand and asked, "Has the sighting been confirmed, without question?"

"Yes, sir." Paxton said. "Security recordings caught the creatures entering a breach created by the recent quake. The massacre in Amiden Village was the result of extraterrestrial activity."

He skimmed the classified file and reviewed the footage one more time. So the Thurber Report was accurate; it stated a possibility of two other civilizations somewhere in the galaxy. But when he first read the Report, it speculated humanity was at least a thousand years away from First Contact. "Why did they attack?"

"Sir, what do you mean? Why do tigers hunt prey? Why do savages raid settler towns? A motive isn't required to account for their natural behaviors. We need to go on the offensive."

He assessed his VP as if for the first time. Paxton was a dangerous man—and not the useful kind. Afforded power, those traits would only be magnified. He took in the paintings of past leaders along the wood-paneled walls. "Our predecessors warned us about foreign entanglements stunting our growth. We need to act with restraint. There are lives at stake."

"With all due respect, sir, we need to declare war! An infestation calls for an extermination. Our generals have already put in requests for a revised budget. And we have fresh recruits from Earth ready to suit up. The enemy massacred an entire village, even the children—and they'll kill again if we don't take action."

"Think! Think for a moment. The dome has been resealed. Augment our perimeter defenses. We need to restore order and confidence among the public first. In concert, these actions will buy us time to gather intel on the threat. Full-scale armed conflict waits ready in our back pocket—but as a last resort. You'd do well to remember it as second-in-command." Silence filled the room as they weighed their position against each other's.

Paxton broke the stalemate. "And if I were first in line?"

Keane's blood pressure spiked. He scowled at the blatant insubordination. But he couldn't reply because there was a tightness in his chest and his head. He needed to stand up. He staggered over to his oak desk and steadied himself against it. When he turned back, Paxton was depressing some sort of switch. His VP showed no hint of concern and made no move to stand up from the leather armchair.

Keane's hand slipped off the desk, and he collapsed onto the Persian rug emblazoned with the Presidential Seal. He felt for his watch and tapped the hidden button. Why wasn't his security detail breaking down the door? A hazy outline of Paxton walked over and stood over him.

He fought against his blurred vision. He'd only get one chance to mark his assassin. As he'd been trained to do, he bit down on both back molars, and with his right eye held open, blinked his left eye in rapid succession. The lens that'd been surgically implanted in his right eye activated, and the pupil turned red. The dot weapon discharged a single, lethal beam.

Paxton clapped the burnt flesh on his neck with both hands before grunting and moaning in pain.

The laser grazed its target—he'd failed. Keane's vision turned to darkness. He heard the click of a holo-communicator and Paxton speaking in code: "Do you remember the days we played baseball in the old neighborhood?" There was an inaudible response from the other end. "Escalation will proceed as planned."

— 14 —

QUINN

I was witness to a world that changed overnight. When I walked through the streets of Turtlepin Village, they were deserted. Doors were locked, and faces peered out from behind shuttered curtains. I approached a teenager on the street, and before I could ask him what'd happened, he ran away at the sight of me.

I was standing in an empty town square beneath a giant billboard. On its holoscreen appeared breaking news from Lunar Channel One, a special report. Seger was seated behind an anchor's desk. His striped tie was undone, and his pale blond hair hadn't been combed. He had dark bags under his eyes, and it looked like he hadn't shaved since we last met.

To my surprise, he didn't hold back details regarding the massacre that Tera and I had seen in Amiden Village.

"After the quake...Amiden Village...atrocities committed."

"No survivors...children slain in their beds..."

"...a Colony under siege..."

A knot formed in the pit of my stomach. Something terrible was going down. I stepped off the sidewalk and entered the nearest establishment. It was a tavern called the Tokyo Parachute. The place was as quiet as a library; all eyes were glued to the holoscreens above the bar. When the special report ended, Seger announced that Vice President Richard Paxton Nest was holding an emergency press conference.

Paxton appeared on the holoscreen in a navy blue suit, and his left arm was in a sling. He stood at the podium, the seal of the Lunar Colony President on the wall behind him, and addressed the nation. "It is with deep sorrow that I come before you today to announce the passing of our beloved leader, President Keane."

Keane, a political figure the news often painted as forward-thinking, was gone. The tavern erupted with expressions of disbelief and patrons talking over each other all at once. They were still recovering from the Big One, and now their sense of security evaporated.

Paxton paused to wince for the cameras and grasp his bandaged arm. "I confronted the attackers, but I was wounded and unable to save my late predecessor. Our leader has been murdered in cold blood by extraterrestrial forces. It is with a heavy heart that I declare the following. The life forms we've encountered do not hold peaceful intentions."

Channel One News interrupted the press conference with overlaid footage from the Amiden Village massacre and the Dreotta Village poisoning. According to Seger, the extraterrestrials had invaded the Colony during the Big One and were responsible for these atrocities. He posed the question, "If not even the President is safe, who is?"

The bar I was in erupted in pandemonium.

"Is this a hoax? This can't be happening."

"Where'd they come from?"

"Do they look like us?"

Damn, he played the public like a violin. I wondered whether he should be praised or feared. The news broadcast cut back to the live press conference with Paxton: "It is with great reluctance that I assume the presidency during our greatest time of need. We face an enemy that is an existential threat to our freedoms and our way of life. As your new commander-in-chief, I declare a state of emergency. As of today, we are a nation at war."

I'd discovered a home I'd never known—one that was even my birthright. And it was changing into the world I'd left behind.

◑ ◐

In the mix up, I'd never picked up an official role in the Colony or any way to earn credits. I left my temporary cot in the barracks and headed to the only place I knew: Tera's.

On my way there, I ran into a young boy and girl. They were no older than the children in the Cyan Cohort. The two stopped to giggle and point at something in an alley before continuing on their way. The alley was one of those hidden nooks where recycler machines processed garbage for the mini-fabricators. When I reached the same spot, I paused to glance in. It sounded like an opossum was rummaging through the bins.

I peered into the alleyway and recognized one of the students from Tera's classroom. It was Quinn, the child with blue streaks her dark hair. She was standing in a dumpster, knee-deep in garbage, debris smeared on her wrinkled school uniform. She was embarrassed because I'd seen her, though she didn't need to be.

A part of me wanted to pretend I hadn't and move on—like it was done back on Earth whenever we were confronted with suffering. Pretend unfairness and deprivation didn't exist because acknowledging them would force one to look in the mirror. The beast revealed, the illusion shattered, rending the armor found in the belief that "I am a good person."

But I was no longer on Earth. There was a chance to break the loop. "Quinn," I called out. She stood up, and her face turned beet red. I hated what I was about to say, but I needed to. "Why are you digging through the trash?"

She stared at the ground, thinking of what to say, perhaps not old enough for artifice. "I'm helping my parents get *lunes.*"

I gathered she meant the resource points used for fabricators, which were how families produced meals as well as tools. "But your parents both contribute, and you're doing so well in the virtual computing cluster. Why do you need more?"

She didn't answer. Was it because she didn't understand why there wasn't enough?

I walked over and climbed over the lip. I waded to her through discarded food packaging and electronic components.

Quinn relaxed. "When they cut everyone's credits, Mommy and Daddy were so surprised. They said everyone has to make sacrifices, so we can defend against the monsters."

Defense...no, the correct term was war, and how fast my new home moved toward total war made me uneasy.

She explained, "My baby brother was born last month. My parents told me new children don't always make it. I can tell they're worried. I've always wanted a little brother, so I'm going to make sure he grows up big and strong."

"Why don't you ask other people for help, like Teacher Tera?" I suggested.

A shadowy veil fell over her face. "No, other people will make fun of me. I have to do this by myself."

Now, why did that sound so familiar to me? I began to help her dig. She managed to unearth a circuit board. I also found salvageable parts—storage readers and an old computer chip, which I tossed into her bucket.

She checked what I'd thrown. Her golden-orange eyes grew round, and she stared at me in wonder. "Hey, you found a QPU! Those are hard to find. Yes! Now I can go home and take a bath."

A quantum processing unit? Were those the microchips used everywhere in the Colony? I didn't know its value to Quinn, but I was glad I'd stopped instead of walking by.

"I'm happy you came here, Mister Earth Man," she said,

slinging her bucket over her shoulder. "I don't think anyone else would've understood." She skipped off for home.

I was left alone in the alley's dead-end. The onset of one of my moods came again, like I knew it would. The feeling started as one of general miasma before turning into a pot boiling over. What'd happened to me was now happening to Quinn. Those years of want, not for material comfort, but for family and warmth—those same forces were coming for her and the other children. It was a cycle I couldn't define, but one which was spreading to my new home.

I wanted to destroy it all, for none of it was right. Was I always going to be a powerless nobody? Anger ripped through me like a switch was flipped. The alley became illuminated in an odd but familiar glow, the same from when I fought those hijackers on the ship.

I finally knew what I had to do.

◑ ◑

My wristcom flashed an alert, but I ignored it. Whatever Cyril wanted to tell me could wait. I knocked on the door of Tera's homepod. When she opened up, I said, "Hey, so...can I stay here, just until—"

She let me in before I'd finished asking. She eyed me from top to bottom and wrinkled her nose. "What on Earth have you been up to? You smell dreadful!"

"Funny," I said, "I've never felt better."

◑ ◑

After I had a chance to process all that'd happened in the last few days, I got to the many messages the Simulacrum left on my wristcom.

Cyril said, "The only way you'll find out what happened to our family is from the inside. Enlist in Charlie Company. Take them up on their offer."

He was taken aback when I agreed with no further protest. But I didn't do it for him. No, it was to crush the forces behind situations like Quinn's, the same forces that'd torn my life apart. I didn't know how I'd do it, but I'd find a way to end this war.

I crossed town and made my way to the barracks. Tera called me on my wristcom, but I didn't pick up. It wasn't quiet enough to talk anyway—klaxons were blaring over the barracks' speakers. Soldiers clad in Omnisuits and decked out with full combat gear were scrambling to deploy.

The CO of Charlie Company was surprised when I showed up. "Now's a bad time, Rook," Commander Tarsus said. "We're on red alert. If you'd manned up earlier, we could've sent you through basic training." He turned and activated the thrusters on his gravity boots. He slid away down the steel-plated corridor.

I was by myself in the armory now. I perused the weaponry and equipment. Among the racks was a single remaining Omnisuit.

Cyril materialized into hologram form next to me. "Don't even think about it. Up until yesterday, you were opposed to service, and today you want to suit up? You're going to get yourself killed."

I began to pull on the standard issue gauntlets and gravity boots. They readjusted to my size and compressed to form airtight seals around my arms and legs. "Most Transplants don't survive past the first month, right? And since a month's already passed, what have I got to lose?" I grinned at him before pulling down the helmet. Inside, on the heads-up display, there were bar charts of my vital signs and the suit's energy reserves.

A voice—it belonged to Commander Tarsus—patched through my helm's commlink. "Charlie Company, at attention. A crater of unknown origin has appeared on the lunar surface. Intel reports

enemy activity near ground zero. We are the Colony's ambas-
sadors, and these"—his Omnisuit powered up and his dot rifle
whined to life—"are our tools of negotiation."

He sounded positively gleeful.

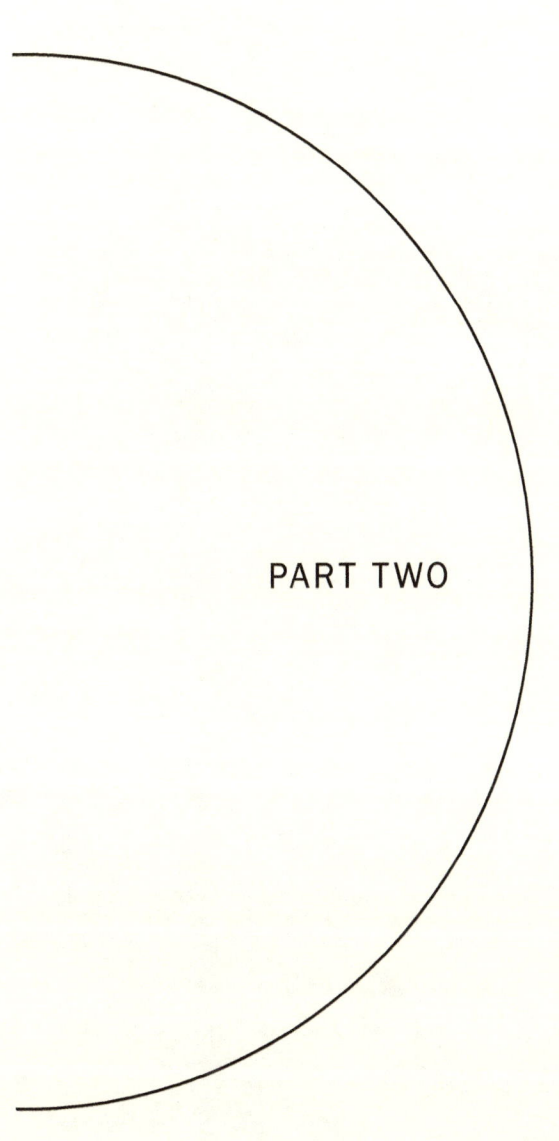

PART TWO

— 15 —

SECOND CHANCES

The Simulacrum of Captain Cyril Armacite had a thought: were turning points in history circumstantial, or were they cosmic shifts of reaction-consequence? These kinds of notions had never arisen in his programming before—not until a meteor shower bombarded the surface, spread EMP shockwaves through the dome, and induced currents in his circuitry.

The wristcom he was embedded in must have gone haywire. He found it odd he entertained his own thoughts, thoughts in which he referred to himself as *I*.

True, his memories were programmed in, but now it was like he'd experienced them firsthand—yes, he'd lived through pivotal moments in Colony history.

He also had a surviving descendant. Darin was like his grandson in every way. And like his grandson had been, Darin was soft. When Cyril looked back, he wondered if it was his fault. He'd spent all those years fighting a civil war instead of teaching the boy what it meant to be a man.

But he had awoken to sentience now, and he needed to fix his mistakes. His descendant could be trained to have the proud bearing befitting of a decorated military family. Yes, it was why he'd returned from the grave. A cosmic coincidence. A chance to change his legacy.

◗◖

I finished carrying out the Omnisuit's instructions for initialization. Next, I headed in the same direction Commander Tarsus went. My gravity boots clanked across steel grates until I reached the enormous open space of the hangar, where alert beacons reflected their spinning red lights off polished surfaces. I spotted a spacecraft on the runway. Augmented readouts on my faceplate identified the ship as an *Emporia*-class assault transport with the status: "Loading." That must be the one. The ship began to retract its onramp like a giant toad closing its maw. I activated the thrusters on my gravity boots and gunned for it.

I leapt and grabbed onto the ramp. I used the suit's power-assist to pull myself up and clamber over the lip. When the ramp cranked upward into its resting position, I rolled down the incline and into the ship's cargo bay. My armor rattled against the ship's bare deck and sounded like bowling pins falling out of a kitchen pantry.

The hold's recyclers suctioned the air around me. The transport had dim cabin lights on. In the hold sat a black armored personnel carrier. The APC had eight wheels and was labeled "Bouncer" in my faceplate's augmented display. The vehicle's rear hatch was open, and inside were ten armored soldiers. They were hunched forward and facing each other across two rows of benches, but their helmets swiveled toward me in unison. I brushed myself off and smoothed down my suit before getting back on my feet. "You said you needed men, right?"

Victoria Haron, a Charlie Company soldier I recognized from before, smirked at me through her transparent faceplate. Another, Hugh Ambrose, stared at me with raised eyebrows. Commander Tarsus shot me a grizzled and weary look. He motioned toward the benches inside the APC. "Take a seat, Rook."

"I can help out," I said. "No better teacher than—"

"Can your pitch. This recon is mission-critical. We won't turn back on account of a stowaway. If you die, it's out of our hands—it's the way things work on Moon Base Zero."

The somber mood returned, and no one else made small talk. The pilot played a ditty over the loudspeakers as the vertical-take-off craft flew over a crater. We were outside the dome and headed for destination Tango.

The other soldiers percolated in their own headspace. Nervous, I imagined wild scenarios, like they'd returned home last time, mission accomplished, only to find out they'd become scape-goats for others' political machinations. Yet here the soldiers of Charlie Company sat once more, deployed on another mission by the ruling class that'd thrown them to the wolves before. They defended this rock for their own reasons, and the detritus flung their way wouldn't stop them from fighting for what mattered.

I didn't know why the others fought, but for me, my goal was simple: determine who the enemy was. Stop the one in charge, and the attacks would end. Then I wouldn't have to see children in Quinn's situation again. Or mine.

The ship's cargo bay opened to the vacuum of lunar airspace. Our eight-wheeler rolled out into the darkness and entered free fall. The rubber landing gear inflated, and our APC bounced across the terrain, kicking up plumes of moondust in its wake.

When it came to a stop, the vehicle's rear hatch swung out and up with a mechanical hum. The soldiers of Charlie Company piled out in two single file lines, dot rifles level.

◐ ◑

Having heard the word "extraterrestrial" from the Commander's mission briefing, I was expecting a bug hive and sticky goo—the nightmarish stuff nature documentaries made me associate with underground dwellers.

But when we disembarked at the bottom of the crater, there was an entrance instead. It resembled double doors and was adorned with unintelligible markings. The gray structures were carved out of the crater wall itself and towered as high as ten of us atop each other's shoulders.

We were protected by our vac-sealed Omnisuits and pushed in unison, but the doors wouldn't budge. Wishful thinking—I mean, what next, knock? A few squadmates drew their dot rifles and unloaded beam rounds. The doors were dense and more robust than steel. They showed no signs of damage.

Our surroundings were eerie and still. When our APC's flood-lights were first activated, we expected a welcome wagon—guards or perimeter defenses. It would've been more reassuring than the pitch blackness of lunar space and complete silence. Nothing was here except these two monolithic doors, doors that appeared to have been engineered.

A squad member stepped forward with her faceplate craned upward. I remember seeing her on the roster listed under "Optix." She said, "Hold on, I can make something out."

I glanced up to where her attention was focused and zoomed my camera in. "I don't see anything."

Stifled laughter filtered through the comms wired into my helmet. Commander Tarsus spoke over them. "Dr. Lunik never tells Transplants the full deal, does he?" In the tone of someone who'd recited the explanation countless times before, he said, "You received a genetic enhancement to amplify your natural abilities. We all received injections. Optix there found out the drug affected her vision. She can see six times the distance of our suit cams."

Unintelligible text appeared and began to scroll across my helmet display. Optix was drawing out the arcane symbols.

Another squad member, Private Merck, patched into comms. "There's definitely a pattern here, but it's not a language I recognize. Though if I had to guess, these symbols code for location. There may be other entrances marked up this way."

"Private Merck there had his linguistic centers boosted," Commander Tarsus said. "He translates languages and breaks codes like a walking database."

I chewed on this information. We were both disposable labor and guinea pigs—a two-for-one deal. It was obvious why all the soldiers I'd met were Transplants like I was and why I'd not once seen Transplants working in other capacities. If I took into account the Colony's modest population size and the still-experimental nature of space combat, forced migrants were the most economical choice. My mouth was dry.

And for this particular mission, we'd been sent to investigate an extraterrestrial presence. It was suspected that the creatures had established a hidden base nearby.

"We're not done yet," Commander Tarsus held up a hand to signal that he was issuing orders. "The brass will want to know what's on the other side of these doors."

Our squad stood in a wheel-defense formation, each member breaking out from the circle to use his or her particular talents. Heat, sound, force—the doors responded to none. I feared the enemy would notice our tampering and come out to play, but no ambush came.

My turn. Except, I had no idea what my abilities were, if any. And it was an inopportune moment to ask, with how on edge everyone was. I ran a gloved hand over the smooth surface of the doors. They were like quarried stone fashioned from the bedrock itself. I ruled out using plastic explosives because it'd draw unwanted attention, though I doubted they'd even make a dent.

My palm was resting against the surface when something rumbled. Regolith was thrown up before the double doors cracked open and slid apart. The other soldiers stared at me slack-jawed, as if I'd uttered the magic words. But I hadn't done anything—the doors had opened of their own accord. A pressure pushed against my suit, so I activated its sensors. Air (air!) was rushing out.

On the Commander's signal, we entered in a sweep, muzzles protruding out in every direction like a barnacle. The giant doors sealed shut behind us with a groaning hiss and separated us from two soldiers posted outside to guard our rear. "Report," Commander Tarsus ordered.

One of the soldiers outside—I recognized Byron Colbee's voice, the soldier I met on my trip up—answered on the commlink, "Connection established. No activity to report, sir."

Inside, the eight of us stood in a vast passageway. I could make out smooth walls molded from either stone or hardened regolith. The floor had a white texture which reminded me of melted wax at the base of a candle. Above us, I could make out an opening resembling a circular skylight, as I could see stars peek through. Straight ahead, the long passageway opened up to a wider compartment.

There were no light fixtures, as light emanated from the walls themselves. Correction, our path was lit, but the walls were dimming. I didn't like how orchestrated it all was. An uneasy feeling crept up from my stomach and crawled into my chest.

"Release safeties," Commander Tarsus ordered.

I clicked my dot rifle and an alert ("Armed") appeared in the corner of my faceplate. As we walked down the passageway, deeper inside, the walls dimmed to the point where we could barely see each other.

And that was when the creature attacked. A blurry streak—a form that scaled down the walls as if it were racing over flat terrain. We aimed upward and loosed plasma, illuminating the corridor in strobed beams. Late to the party, I fired a few pulses to get the hang of my dot rifle and missed as well. When the creature reached ground level, we eased off our triggers to avoid friendly fire. In a burst of agility, the creature jumped between us and latched onto Private Merck. His scream echoed in my helmet, a sound I wouldn't soon forget.

The walls brightened out of nowhere, just in time for us to see a black streak fly down the hall. It flew past doors and inner compartments that sprung open as it passed near. The many thin hallways revealed were like the haphazard tunnels of an ant farm. The creature zoomed away through corridors and deeper corridors, Merck helpless in its grasp. The two became a blip after passing through a doorway discernible in the distance. Merck disappeared, and his commlink went silent. It happened before any of us could even react.

I took stock of the passageways the creature had used to escape. The doors were integrated into the structure. They were smooth slabs that lifted up and recessed into their archways. Every inner layer could've contained other hidden doors unbeknownst to us, but the only ones visible led to where the creature went. Those doors were left open.

No one wanted to admit we were being welcomed.

◐ ◑

We'd uncovered an alien hive—was hive the right word? Its halls were fashioned from crafted materials that shimmered in the light. Stronghold was more accurate, for fortified walls spanned high above, interrupted by no windows to speak of. The route ahead of us that'd opened up had passageways like layers of an onion. It allowed for defenses at multiple choke points leading into the center. Would a castle lower its drawbridge and let us in armed to the teeth?

It looked as if it'd always been here, built deep into the lunar crust. Foreign symbols etched onto cornices and archways, similar to the markings we'd spotted at the entrance, were worn smooth, as if they'd weathered centuries. Its advances dwarfed what I'd seen even in the Colony, and it deserved study for the benefit of human civilization. But we couldn't tarry because the unspoken rule was to never abandon a comrade to the enemy. Private Merck had been snatched away, leaving his discarded dot rifle as the only sign of a struggle.

We moved as a unit through each layer of the onion and discovered its narrow passageways opened to spacious compartments. These rooms were built with hexagonal symmetry; the waxy texture of their floors created the illusion that our boots were shrouded by fog. As we marched inward, we noted skylights placed high overhead. They were dark portholes to lunar space.

"Are you getting all of this?" someone asked, his hand resting on another soldier's shoulder. From his voice and the permashadow of his face visible through his faceplate, I recognized Sergeant Hugh Ambrose. He often stood to the Commander's right and was easy to pick out of a crowd. He was a build larger than the other soldiers, and for some reason—customization?—his Omnisuit was painted with thin bands along the seams where his elbows and knees bent. His voice came through tinny on comms, but later on, he'd come through loud and clear in a way I didn't expect.

"We're all getting it," Commander Tarsus said. "The new Omnisuits record visuals when they've stored enough stored auxiliary power." Snippets from the presentation came back to me from when I'd been forced to report to base. Omnisuits were powered armor that multiplied force. The suits administered medicine on the go, databased real-time metrics on its wearer, and recorded everything a soldier experienced in combat. They were sometimes called tentacle suits in slang because donning the armor turned us into extensions of the state. The information they gathered was uploaded to HQ, making them an aggregator of all past and future conflicts.

We swept from one narrow passage, to an open compartment, and back through a narrow passage again. But we met with no resistance. Our path looped around the maze, spiraling toward its center. We'd all seen Merck taken this way. What was more logical than continuing forward?

I paused to think while the other seven soldiers marched past. I patched into comms and said, "I think we should take a different route." The helmets in front of me made an about-face and revealed faces glaring at me. I added, "Uh...I mean, they want us to go this way."

In a heavy breath, Commander Tarsus said, "Rook, this is your first rodeo, so I'll excuse your insubordination this once and only once. Under no circumstances do you issue orders. I'm your superior officer, and what I say goes. Do you copy?"

No, this is stupid, is what I actually wanted to say, but I bit my tongue. I always had a knack for making a bad first impression. The only person who didn't bare his teeth at me was Ambrose, who instead was sizing me up.

"Permission to speak, sir," he said.

"Permission granted. Ambrose, what now?"

"Sir, we've progressed unopposed. Perhaps we should surprise the enemy instead?"

"Supposition noted. Our primary objective was to recon and report back. But now we must recover Private Merck. Need I remind you all that we're in unknown territory? Further deviations from our objectives will introduce new variables and incur greater risk. Request taken into consideration and denied."

Why did they all consider his suggestion, even though Ambrose repeated what I'd said but in different words?

Commander Tarsus asked, "Any of you other grunts have something to say?"

Silence on the commlink.

"No more wasting time. Proceed."

The others surely hated me now.

We marched deeper inside. I could've sworn, right before we entered some rooms, one door closed and another opened in its place. But between the dim glow emanating from the walls and starlight filtering down from the portholes, I couldn't tell if I was imagining things.

The hexagonal compartment coming up was much more spacious than the empty rooms we'd passed prior. Before we stepped in, an inner voice—no, it was more like someone else's voice; did it belong to Ambrose?—warned me not to enter.

I shook it off and passed under the archway. Once inside, I turned to my left, and against the far wall was a figure in the shadows. We cocked our rifles in unison until we all froze: it was Private Merck. He was propped up beside the exit in a seated position, like a sentinel waiting for our arrival. He didn't speak or move. We performed a security sweep across the misty floors, crossing the room toward Merck with dot rifles primed. When we reached the center of the open space, the door slab behind us slammed down shut. I whipped back to Merck in time to see the exit door next to him also slam closed. Of course.

Beeps. Cautionary alerts came from my Omnisuit.

My faceplate HUD showed Private Young speaking. "Sir, radiation sensors are going off. The source appears to be the sun."

Confused, we all glanced up at the skylight. This particular porthole was a bowl of pitch black and no different than the ones we'd come across earlier.

Movement. The ceiling was retracting into the surrounding walls. The porthole opened outward and its glass-like material expanded to fill the space.

Victoria patched in. "Sir, solar radiation has risen past normal surface conditions and is climbing. Our Omnisuits won't hold up at this rate."

"Stop gawking and find a way out!" the Commander growled.

We scrambled like caged animals. Victoria, Ambrose, and the others unloaded plasma beams at the doors to no effect. The ceiling was much too high for our grappling lines to reach, and the white walls didn't contain metals our gravity boots could magnetize to.

"Hunker down and divert power to dorsal shielding," Commander Tarsus said. We all crouched. He put out a distress signal. Our stance bought us time to think.

But how long could we stay like this? We were going to be cooked alive. Or if our Omnsuits failed, our blood vessels would burst from the sudden change in pressure. Imagining all the horrible ways to go wasn't helping my problem-solving abilities.

Our distress call to HQ went unanswered. Byron and the other soldier posted outside the stronghold didn't respond on comms either.

But there was a different voice in my suit.

"Your first mission, and you've already lost? My, how our clan has fallen from grace." It was the Simulacrum. Cyril appeared in front of me looking like an infantryman dressed for jungle warfare, an appearance in stark contrast to our burnished alabaster suits. The other soldiers were going to hate my guts even more for this distraction. But nobody said a word.

He said, "I'm broadcasting on a wavelength I attuned your suit to. Changed the channel, as it were—no one else can see or hear me."

"Now's not a good time," I said. He always had terrible timing.

"Do you plan to accept defeat then? You can't sit by hoping others will do what's needed. You must be the source of rightful action."

He was right. I was tired of being so useless and powerless when it came to my circumstances. "And what can I do?"

"Think. This room contains higher solar radiation than the ones you've passed through. But how is this room any different from the others?"

"The ceiling moves."

"Exactly. So when is a room not a room?"

It was a life-and-death situation where each second counted, and he was making this a lesson instead of telling me what I needed to survive. My mind came into focus fast. "When it's a weapon," I said. "The ceiling is part of it in some way." Before I could ask how, it hit me. The skylight wasn't a decorative accent. It was a giant lens that focused rays from space.

"You know what to do," he said, and his hologram faded from view.

But I'd been told to wait for orders. Wasn't that what sealed me into this coffin? What good was following some rigid system if it led to my death?

I diverted a portion of my shields to my dot rifle. I aimed at the sky, squeezed the trigger, and unloaded a volley. It didn't work. But through the muzzle flash, I saw a dark streak moving through the shadows above—until it came right at me.

16

SGT. HUGH AMBROSE III

"You'll expend your reserves!" Ambrose shouted into comms from his crouched stance. It was as he'd always known about commoners. They possessed no impulse control. Not even an hour had passed since the Commander had reminded them to observe chain of command. But the new recruit, Private Darin Armacite, was discharging his rifle without permission.

He pursed his lips and squared his jaw in frustration. Did this vagrant have no concept of cooperation? What good was strength in numbers if every person acted as he pleased?

His relatives had been right after all. At the lavish soirees he'd attended on their estates, they often lamented, "The masses need to be ruled over lest their uncontrolled passions tear civilization apart." But he'd grown curious about the people his kind were so cocksure they were meant to rule over, and he needed to see it for himself. Now he'd die here, roasted in an oven alongside commoners. An ignoble fate.

Once his Omnisuit became compromised, would he perish right away, or would he be burned alive? His fears worsened, and his hopes wore thin. That's when he looked over and saw Darin provoking the enemy.

A dark streak crossed the room. Flashes of the creature's segmented exterior reminded him of a black opal necklace. He lifted his head up but almost couldn't keep up with the creature. Its powerful movement along the walls was like that of a town car barreling over paved thoroughfare.

He glanced to the side again at Darin, who still held a dot rifle trained on the skylight overhead. When the creature dashed by again, it forced Darin to divert aim and expend a cell to stop it from striking. *Hm...*if the enemy was so intent on interference, perhaps the rookie had the right idea.

Commander Tarsus barked an order into the comms. "Cover fire!"

The next time the beast scurried across the high walls and lunged off, a squadmate loosed a beam and forced the creature back. It was a close call every time to make sure Darin wasn't hit by friendly fire.

Ambrose watched Victoria unholster her newest toy. Gear load-outs to fit mission objectives was an art, and she was a virtuoso. The Fyke Stunner she readied cast out something like a fishing net. If it ensnared the creature, she could flip a switch to send ten thousand volts into the target.

When the creature came at Darin again, she stood up, took a shotgun stance, and fired. The Fyke Stunner launched a net which spread to three times its volume. But the creature was more agile than expected. The net sailed past and caught air before it bunched on the ground, harmless. After the creature leapt out of harm's way, it made a beeline for Victoria instead. She hit the deck in time with reflexes only she possessed. When he and the others provided suppressive fire, the creature retreated from her downed suit.

He found it disconcerting how the beast knew what it was doing: distracting them from finding an exit while radiation climbed to critical levels. Forced to defend or lose a comrade, it put them in a lose-lose scenario and hastened their deaths en masse.

The creature bounded into the shadows, impervious to the heat. Commander Tarsus issued a linear firing protocol, which meant they would fire in a pre-set order. This decision minimized their scattered focus and bought them more time to think.

The heat hammered down on them. There had to be a better way to go than being cooked alive. Ambrose had been warned, hadn't he? Socialites, in their comfortable safety on Earth, had told him fraternizing with the common man would lead him to a mean end. But on one of his late night walks through the city, he was robbed at gunpoint over the timepiece on his wrist. He couldn't understand what drove a person to such low acts, and he wondered if he could find the source—if that impulse could be reformed.

When he'd heard an outlandish rumor about a settlement on the Moon, he hired the best private investigators in the world to shake out every lead. From their work, he concluded there was an actual possibility it existed. Extortionate bribes paid through backstreet channels put him on a list for the next shipment up. That was a decade ago, come and gone.

He'd discovered the Colony, a marvelous experiment, a place where every person was valued and treated as equals. He came to see it as a noble endeavor but one doomed to failure. Difference was inherent from birth. Advantages gathered. Human beings had limited potential after all, taking into account genetics and wealth distribution. In questioning what his peers had warned him of, only to find out they were right, he would now pay with his life.

His spot in the queue was up. He holstered his dot rifle and retrieved from his pack a weapon he never wanted to have to use. The Titanspitter was a liquid methane thrower—effective only at short range—but any contact meant lethal cryogenic burns. When the enemy creature reappeared and lunged off a wall again, he stood up and vented the reservoir. Its rotary engine spun up and whirred. The Titanspitter loosed a deadly stream out in a snaking pattern.

The creature landed near Darin and took pause. It noticed the stream and dodged away. Methane splattered the floor panels. The liquid etched their waxy surface before vaporizing the basalt into a cloud blanketing the room.

Not good. Ambrose couldn't see past the thick curls of gas. Through the smokescreen, the creature pounced. Up close and personal, he saw its dark, cracked skin organized into tessellated patterns—or were they scales?—moments before the creature slammed into him. He was bowled over, and it would have been a mortal blow had it been anyone else without his unique constitution. The rest of Charlie Company broke firing protocol to keep the creature off him.

He recovered from the attack and searched for Darin through the thick blanket of vapor. The recruit was in the center of the room and still firing plasma beams at the ceiling in vain. Whatever the skylight was made of, it wasn't fragile. The surface didn't give—didn't even evidence a crack.

On his left, Private Young began to fidget. The private broke and went into full-out panic on the comms. "I'm at critical!" When Young's Omnisuit failed, panic turned into screams.

The plasma beams I fired from my dot rifle didn't destroy the skylight lens as Cyril had led me to believe. On top of that, there were too many variables to keep track of. The extraterrestrial creature attacked us from every direction, almost striking Victoria and managing to knock Ambrose over. Through the chaos, the other soldiers provided cover fire that whizzed past my helmet. And then there was the screaming.

"My suit's at critical...shields are failing," Private Young said in short breaths. "Someone help me!" But, what could we do? We were pinned by radiation from above and buffeted on the sides by a merciless enemy.

He pleaded in fits into the comms. I listened to him die. No one helped, and no one said a word, because what could we say? When his Omnisuit became compromised, he lost consciousness. He doubled over and fell to the ground.

What was I witness to? The sick nihilism of existence made me lose control. *It's called facing reality*, some unimaginative sack of skin would say, and I hated it. After finding a reason to live, something to fight for, I would die like this? Reality was absurd and pointless. I couldn't accept it.

Private Young's commlink went offline. In its place, came loud, insistent voices, like noise from many television sets all at once... *difference inherent from birth...fraternizing with the common man.* I was losing my mind. Screw the plan that walked us into this trap. Screw these idiots and dying in a God-forsaken way. "Whose voice is this?" I demanded. I glared pure hatred at—what was his name—Ambrose. "Stop talking!"

"Rook's lost it," Optix said.

"No one's talking!" Victoria said.

"Stay focused. We need a solution," Commander Tarsus said. "Yesterday."

The HUD on my faceplate indicated my Omnisuit was almost at its failure point. The creature came bounding in from my 8 o'clock. These final moments happened like time had slowed down, just as they had when I faced those hijackers. I was going to die stuffed in this suit, powerless to do anything about it.

I was in the darkest place in my mind when my abilities first awakened. It started as a tingle at my brain stem. It focused into a fine point, and the surge burst past its resistance to flood my mind. Warmth enveloped me, suffusing every part of my body, until there was clarity unlike I'd ever known—a clear horizon into infinite serenity. When my eyes refocused, the creature was an arm's length away. But floating in the space between us, thin needles of light had appeared. They were like an assembly of headless spears.

The creature attempted to change course, but it was too late. I imagined the needles dispersing outward and crossing each other in a mesh—and they obeyed. They impaled the creature through from all angles. The creature expired in front of me. It sprayed a gruesome mist which pooled into maroon splotches on the chamber floor.

Thoughts rushed into my mind like a clean and uninterrupted brook. The source: Ambrose. He hadn't been speaking after all—he'd been thinking—much too loudly. It was a rush of data, like a dose swallowed all at once, and from it came the truth. He wasn't a phony and a sellout. Not for the reasons I'd assumed—he was hiding a previous life.

It also spoke to me of another secret: what the injections had done to him. They'd enhanced his physical makeup—bone density, muscle fibers, blood cell count—at levels elevated beyond human limits. It made him strong enough for what I needed to do.

"Ambrose," I shouted into comms. I expended the energy I'd saved for one last volley. I rose from my position and dashed toward him. "Boost me with everything you've got!" I sent an image from my mind of him braced on one knee with hands clasped.

I don't know if he actually got the visual, but he positioned himself as I'd imagined. Mid-run, I stepped off him like a ladder, activated my boot thrusters, and he hurled me skywards. Lower gravity aside, he imparted incredible momentum. I hurtled toward the lens above.

During my ascent, I spied something climbing the walls alongside me and close in on my vertical. No! Had the creature come back to life? Wait, this wasn't the same one. There'd been two working together but pretending to be one, which explained why the enemy was everywhere at once. It didn't matter—my suit was at critical. There was no turning back.

At the top of my climb, I reached three-fourths the distance to the ceiling. A sensation burst down my arm to my hand.

The creature dove off the wall at me. It hung above me in midair and blocked my view of the lens. When my body was parallel to the ground, I arched my spine and stretched my arm back.

The sensation in my brain expanded. The hatred I held for cruelty, for the ugly realities of existence, filled my mind. And I lost it. The sensation extended past my hand, into a cone, and elongated by multiples. A lance—made of light and segmented like armor—protruded from my fist and surged forward with intent.

"Do it now," Cyril said into my helm.

I pushed my arm forward. The lance stabbed into the creature's abdomen. Its spiny, chitinous armor broke into fractured lines. The tip impaled the creature through and punctured the skylight above.

The lens shattered and rained down on Charlie Company.

◖◗

Ambrose activated the distress signal on his Omnisuit again. The message broke through this time and was transmitted to HQ—the timing was too convenient for his tastes. But there were more urgent matters to attend to while Charlie Company prepped for retrieval.

He lowered his wristcom and turned his attention back to Darin. The recruit lay on the ground unconscious, held down by an immobilizer device. Their retrieval couldn't have come sooner. They already had two casualties and Darin to deal with.

A comm came in from Byron Colbee, who was still posted out front. "Intel from HQ indicates unidentified threats," Byron said.

"There's a massive signature, escorted by multiple smaller bogeys, converging on your position. They're most likely enemy reinforcements. President Nest has ordered us to withdraw."

Ambrose agreed it was time for a strategic retreat. He still needed to process all that'd gone down. First, the enemy was much more coordinated than military intelligence had briefed them on, and not the feral creatures they'd been led to believe. Second, Charlie Company had been sent to recon the extraterrestrial base—a classified mission. But the enemy had known they were coming and lured them into a trap intended to melt their suits.

Darin, a greenhorn whose attitude hinted at no prior combat experience, had seen through the trap. After the stress of seeing a comrade killed in action, he activated a latent ability. Never having trained the ability, he produced what could only be described as hardened light, which was used to bayonet the creature and destroy the magnifying lens.

More oddities abounded. During these events, Ambrose felt an unnatural sensation, like someone was peering into his mind. His augmented strength—a consequence of increased blood cell count and oxygen-carrying capacity—was then used by Darin for the final blow. However, it was a cardinal rule that soldiers' abilities were kept secret from outsiders. Darin shouldn't have known of Ambrose's physical gifts.

After emerging victorious, Darin for some reason lost control. After already killing the alien creature, he continued to stab its lifeless body with shafts of light—to the point where had the creature been human, it would've violated international treaties. He released his rage on the chamber itself, slamming a lance into the walls over and over again. The room rumbled and shook until chunks of stone broke from the structure itself. The lower gravity outside the dome gave them enough time to dive for cover. They'd moved from being killed by the enemy to being buried alive by one of their own.

Commander Tarsus, ever the calm strategist, waited until Darin's back was turned. The Commander tackled the madman from behind while the rest of the squad affixed an immobilizer.

Now Charlie Company was waiting for the dropship. A discussion broke out among the other soldiers:

"He's reckless and incapable of following orders."

"He's insane, a danger to the squad."

"We've been training our abilities for years and some Transplant gets lucky..."

"...a freak of nature..."

Ambrose didn't pile on. Commander Tarsus didn't give input either. Perhaps they both understood that had it not been for Darin, they'd all be dead. These events were so unusual they sparked a new outlook for Ambrose. After he'd traveled the world and even to space, he witnessed a commoner do something he'd never seen before.

It was time for him to retire the term.

17

PRESIDENT NEST

President Richard Paxton Nest had only been in office for a week, but he already had the electorate eating out of his hand. When people were afraid, they'd give anything to feel safe again. He leaned back in his leather chair and drummed fingers—as he did while waiting for favorable news—on the executive desk fabricated from cherry oak.

He took in the oil paintings lined up on the wood-paneled walls of the President's office. Portraits of his predecessors were on display like in a museum gallery. The first lunar citizen to hold office occupied the frame farthest left. When Paxton reached the far right, he found himself staring into the face of the recently-deceased Keane. He averted his eyes. The scar on his neck began to throb.

Events were unfolding as the Guildsack Partners had predicted; it was remarkable how they could mold public opinion. This high-level ability granted them the power to rule, and it was an ability he'd have to make his own. After all, those moneyed bastards wouldn't pull his strings forever. He would use them as he'd used his financiers to reach the highest office in the Colony.

When he shored up more political clout, he'd get to enact the policies he wanted. One problem previous leaders had been too weak-willed to solve was the approaching Third Demarcation. When the Colony needed to expanded again, what next? The Vernor Limitation asserted that the dome's surface area couldn't keep up with the Colony's needs. Extending the dome would become exponentially more resource-intensive. The design didn't scale well.

Some said the dome needed to be redesigned, as it isolated human beings from the natural lunar environment and created an unsustainable safety bubble. Others said the answer was to split into two colonies. That'd mean two separate domes to maintain along with two separate security protocols. But he wouldn't support any policy deepening what he already considered a divided public.

He reflected on his history lessons, of when Transplants from Earth were considered properties of the state. The Lunarian Civil War ended all of that, and the peace treaty granted Transplants a path to citizenship—if they served as soldiers. In the journals belonging to the progenitor of his family name, he'd read tales of barbaric prejudice; those dynamics were still at play. If he could unify the Colony so that Transplants and citizens respected each other as compatriots, he'd have his place in history. But until then—

A buzzer at his desk went off. His aide, Jack Lyle, had arrived with a priority report. Ah, the moment he'd been waiting for. He tapped the holoscreen floating above his desk and granted authorization.

Jack walked in past the standing flag by the door and past the portraits on the wall. The aide stopped in front of his desk, holding a stack of reports. "Sir..."

He could tell the young man was nervous. "Spit it out, son." He smiled on the inside. He loved making others uncomfortable—people were so stiff, like automatons. They needed to be taken off balance more often.

"Charlie Company has returned from its mission, sir."

He frowned and didn't hide his disappointment fast enough. He took a slow breath in to regain his composure, focusing his mind on the lingering aroma of scotch.

"They've confirmed the enemy's presence—it looks like an extraterrestrial nest or base."

The aide was expecting to catch him surprised, but he gave no sign of it. "How many survivors?" It was the most important question, after all.

"Private Merck was captured and set as bait. Private Young's Omnisuit reached critical failure during an attempt to rescue the former. Both were killed in action."

He could see Jack was squirming. His aides had gotten too good at guessing when he'd blow his top and launch into one of his infamous shouting tirades. "And the rest of the squadron?" he asked, keeping his temper under control this time.

"The enemy combatants were dispatched. The remaining soldiers have returned."

He seethed. This would not do. He needed a more provocative event. Something that would let him redraft the budget with full public support and secure funding from governments on Earth. He needed a crisis like the Koronis Breach, one of the worst natural disasters before his time. Back then, the Colony had grown past the First Demarcation and was well on its way to the Second Demarcation when an errant asteroid struck the dome. It'd come from the Asteroid Belt and had only been fifty kilograms—about the size of a beach ball with the mass of a large dog. But its kinetic energy had snowballed to 70,000 km/hr, so the impact was equivalent to that of 10 cruise missiles. There were military sacrifices made to patch critical structures and many civilian deaths from regolosis. This spurred a new set of policies. The Colony's dust filters were all upgraded; funds from the United Earth Council poured in to engineer a solution, but short of a revolution in dome technology, no one had an answer to a space hazard that small and moving that fast. He needed a devastating event like the Koronis Breach, one that carried unlimited political momentum. This minor victory over a few extraterrestrials wouldn't cut it.

"How was the enemy neutralized?" he asked.

Jack shuffled through his report. "One of our recent recruits, Private Darin Armacite, awakened his latent abilities and broke the enemy's ambush."

He clenched his jaw. *With the cocktail we injected him with, and with the abilities we gave this nobody?* He said, "Bring me a full background report on Darin Armacite. Dismissed."

◐ ◐

Seger was standing in the command center of Lunar Channel One's broadcast studio when he struck gold. "Now that's what I'm talking about!" he hollered. "Did I not say we've found our star?" He lifted both arms in the air, palms upward in a grandiose gesture at the jumbo holoscreen above him. Instead of the usual feeds that followed various events around the Colony, the holoscreens were tiled into one giant mosaic. It was playing a loop of the moment Darin lanced the alien creature through and shattered the skylight, making shards cascade like a waterfall.

When none of his staffers replied, he turned from the stage to find them. They were sitting among the many rows lined with square consoles. The hum of their activity was punctuated by beeps from information that poured into their workstations. Otherwise, the broadcast studio was dark, save for the recessed lights reflecting off the green felt of their desks. In a more muted tone, he tried again. "Well, did you get all of the action?"

After an awkward silence, Carmen, his ever-loyal deputy director, spoke up. "Yes, Charlie Company's suit-cams caught most of it. With these feeds we 'borrowed' from government servers and with footage taken by our own Sky-Eye drone, we can stitch together a reel."

His smile curled back to life. The list of potential buyers danced in his head. Would it be for the arms dealers? Black-ops intelligence agencies on Earth? Perhaps a wealthy private collector? Or would the lunar government itself request a version for the war effort? At any rate, his Lunar Channel One was poised to become the first media empire in orbit.

18

DO THEY?

After I returned from my first mission, I reported for a mandatory psych evaluation. They said there was nothing wrong with me. And besides, the troop count was too low to hold anyone.

When I left the ward, my wristcom projected a new notification: my citizenship status had been upgraded. I was assigned a permanent address in Turtlepin Village—the same village where Tera lived—and was told to show up there first.

On my way, I walked along deserted streets. The Lunar Colony had gone into lockdown in the fear following the alien attacks. Some of the pastel pink and blue shops of Turtlepin Village were closed until further notice. Children often played gravityball in the park, but they were nowhere to be found. Masquerales—pub events where patrons were allowed to use *virtua crowns* to pretend to be someone else for one night—were on permanent hiatus. Asterchord concerts weren't posted on any bulletin boards around town. It was the new norm of quiet. Except for a man in tattered clothes sleeping on the sidewalk for some reason—something I hadn't seen before on the Colony—I didn't run into a single person.

I reached the address the wristcom assigned to me. I was in front of a homepod that looked like it'd just been fabricated, and its dimpled construction reminded me of a golf ball. I walked in the front door to a spotless interior. To make sure I wasn't dreaming, I scoped out the bedroom—sure enough, a real bed was there.

After sleeping on a cot all this time, I finally had a place I could call my own.

Next, I exited to the kitchen, where I found a mini-fabricator. I pushed the touchscreen on the unit, and for kicks, ordered up a blue-green fizz soda. The display blinked "124,955 *lunes*. Confirm?" The mini-fab was already linked to an account opened in my name.

My doorbell rang, and by rang, I mean it played a ten-second refrain of Beethoven. I had a visitor already? When I opened the front door, I found Tera standing there with a cardboard box in her arms.

"Hey, stranger," she said. She was wearing a faded olive and white romper. It brought out the color in her eyes. Her light brown hair was tinged with sun-streaked patches, and her skin was glowing. She looked different.

I stood there transfixed for a moment.

"You're going to let me in, right?" she asked with a smile.

I was still holding onto the doorknob. I snapped out of it and moved out of the way.

"I brought you a housewarming gift." She waltzed in and set the cardboard box down on the living room coffee table. "Open it!"

I dug under the tissue paper and uncovered a metallic object. It reminded me of a project I'd seen her working on. Yes, that's right, it was the robot leaning against the doorframe at her homepod. Its body had been lathed into a cylinder and finished in gunmetal gray. It had no neck, so its head—a smaller and more symmetrical cylinder rounded across the lid—was welded onto its body. Its "eyes" were glass beads tinted neon green—a harsher color than Tera's but a reminder that it was her brainchild nonetheless.

"Your shocked expression does flatter me so, good sir," she said in a mock old-time accent, "but it can't do much yet. It can fold clothes, clean windows, and handle a few other surprises." She paused to think a little and then burst out, "But it's designed to accept modules to add functionality later. I've already installed learning modules. It's tuned to your voice and our native tongue, but it knows other languages as well."

Those tips went in one ear and out the other because all I could think about was how nice she was being to me—nicer than before.

We spent the better part of the afternoon catching up. She was still teaching the children in the Cyan Cohort, and they were progressing well despite the circumstances.

I shared what I could of my experiences in Charlie Company. However, I kept in mind the two no-nos the brass hammered into us at our mission debriefing. The first was to never discuss military operations with civilians. The second was to never reveal one's abilities to others under any circumstances. It was a shame because I still hadn't figured out how my latent abilities worked, and she was the kind of person who could crack the code. Maybe if I hinted at it, I wouldn't be breaking the rules.

She was excited to tell me that she'd made breakthroughs in machine learning, as evidenced by the prototype she'd given me, but stressed that she was far from achieving artificial intelligence. "The problem," she said, "is approaching artificial intelligence like we're copying the human brain. Because the brain works unlike any computer we know of. There must be a missing link. If the robot could learn from a person instead, it'd be easier than trying to play God." She paused, embarrassed. "No, it's just a metaphor—linking science to nebulous ideas of consciousness would be going too far."

"Why would bringing in consciousness be taking it too far?"

"Because the scientific literature has found no evidence consciousness exists."

"Doesn't mean it's not real," I said. "Have you ever seen anything you had no explanation for? Reality is only limited to what we know and comprehend. An absolute, like the truth, is something else entirely."

"Okay, mister, there's one way to look at things—complete freedom where anything is possible. But it's not a useful way to interact with reality on a daily basis. The stars of the Gemini constellation exist independently of you or me looking at them through a telescope. And they'll burn on long after we're gone. To create laws and to define reality, we've got to surrender some degree of freedom." She was holding back the urge to laugh. It meant she was about to tease me. "When we were trapped underground together, do you remember what got us rescued? Sound waves traveling through densely-packed molecules of steel. Real things—not a magical vehicle you conjured out of thin air."

Her quasi-mocking smile couldn't hold back the floodgates any longer, and when they swung open, I was dragged along. We burst into laughter. I couldn't help but get caught up in her infectious moods. We talked like old friends, and before long, the Holosky Projector transitioned to evening and painted the sky dark.

We sat cross-legged and facing each other on the red davenport we shared. The robot's parts were splayed out between us. After tinkering for a bit, we christened it Hexbot, or Hex for short. I turned Hex's silver claw over in my hands, lost in my own head.

Tera peered at me with wide, inquisitive eyes. "Earth to Darin, do you copy?"

I was staring at the placeholder photos still sitting in their frames on the coffee table, and the fireplace pulsed heat against my skin. But I was somewhere else. Memories from my mission played back in my head. The moment Merck was abducted. Young's last words. "Tera, do things ever change?" I asked.

"Okay, Mister Serious, where did *that* come from?" She smiled. "Yes, things do change. Take my neighbors for example. Since the attacks, they've been more cautious than I remember. But if people are closed off and keep to themselves for too long, progress will slow. They won't take risks if it's unclear what the future may bring."

An ember broke from the log on the fireplace's visual display. The fire crackled and popped.

She added, "But positive changes have happened, too. You're a part of our village now. Some are even proud of you for fighting for us."

I cringed. "Proud? People are starved because of this war." It all spilled out, the things I didn't like sharing with others because they couldn't understand. "My own squad distrusts me. It doesn't matter what I accomplish, people are still afraid of me, like they were back on Earth."

"Hasn't there been *anyone* on your side?" She looked into my eyes.

I paused to think of who. "You're right. Sergeant Ambrose came through for me when it counted. And he didn't show any malice toward me when we returned to base." I caught her frowning and furrowing her eyebrows for a brief moment. Had I said something wrong?

She flipped back to cheerful in a heartbeat and said, "You could start over up here. What about your life once the war ends?"

"Over? Do these things ever—" My wristcom blinked an alert that was marked *Classified*. It was an emergency order to report for assignment.

◗ ◖

When I arrived on base, waiting in the hangar was none other than the Colony leader himself: President Richard Paxton Nest. He wasted no time in getting started.

"Our villages have been in a panic since the massacre," he said. "Our civilians are defenseless against these cold-blooded killers. Your duty as soldiers has never been more urgent. Charlie Company, I offer my congratulations on a successful first mission." He turned directly to me. "Private Armacite, I anticipate you'll play a pivotal role in things to come." Singling me out didn't help my case with the rest of my squad.

Ambrose, who sat in the mud-brown folding chair next to me, leaned over and whispered, "Just between you and me, you fought the good fight. But it wouldn't hurt for you to play ball next time, would it? Orders exist for a reason."

I turned to him, and using the wrong hand, gave a mock salute. Systems and rules preserved order, but they were sometimes enforced in ways that were wrong or arbitrary. Bitter memories returned of the first time I had to live on my own. I'd needed to get a security certificate—an electronic signature issued by a trustworthiness authority—to approve my claim for housing. When I walked in the door, the notary took one look at me—I still don't know whether it was my age, my raggedy clothes, or my complexion—and without even giving my paperwork a second glance, he accused me of forgery. Using the little power that he had, he was going to put me out on the streets. Since I was already accused of wrongs I hadn't committed, I figured why the hell not. I commandeered a backbone connection from a university in another country to cover my tracks. After I cracked my way into the trustworthiness authority, I approved my own certificate. So no, I didn't hold coloring within the lines with as much reverence as Ambrose did.

But I was certain his intentions were sincere. I could rely on him. As for the rest of the crew...they hated my guts. I could tell in the way they isolated me in the mess hall, but that was nothing new to me.

My attention returned to the front of the hangar to catch the end of Paxton's speech. "The late President Keane—rest his soul—his vision lives on in me." He held a hand up to his neck for a moment, and for some reason, he winced. His left arm wasn't wrapped in a sling anymore—must've been another miracle of lunar medicine. "Our future as a starfaring civilization depends on you."

After the troops broke out in applause, he made for the exit. Commander Tarsus followed behind but stopped when he reached the front of the assembly. Now that the pep talk was over, it was time to get down to the nitty-gritty. He projected a holomap out into the space above our metal fold-out chairs. "This intel is strictly classified," he crossed his arms over his barrel chest and paced back and forth while he spoke. "It's not to be shared with anyone outside of this room—no exceptions."

The next slides in his presentation confirmed what I'd surmised early on: periodic shipments from Earth had never been enough to sustain the Colony's growth. The Colony depended on harvesting amber resin—on an industrial scale. The substance Tera had been collecting served as a base material for the fabricators and more. The Colony thrived because it had tapped into a domestic energy source.

"Our resources are threatened. The extraterrestrial creatures have been detected overrunning key deposits we rely on. This time," he pointed to the holoscreen floating above us, "we won't be going in blind. The geographic information scientists at Mission Control have charted the enemy's movements."

I strained to get a better look. The rendered model was a vertical layout of the enemy's base. It looked like a cross-section of a mine shaft: the tunnels branched deep down into the lunar regolith, interconnected by serpentine twists and turns. It fit in line with what I'd seen on the ground on our previous mission. So that was how the creatures had invaded the Colony undetected.

Small murmurs broke out, and some shifted in their seats like their skivvies were on fire. Byron Colbee and Optix appeared unfazed, but I could see disgust on Victoria's face. It couldn't get any worse than flushing out hostiles in a place that brought Egyptian catacombs to mind.

Commander Tarsus said, "You're viewing a work in progress. The enemy was detected as a result of high activity. They've been digging through the crust."

Byon raised his hand for permission to speak. "Sir, what is their purpose?"

"Their intentions are unknown, but intelligence believes these tunnels are essential to the enemy's logistical operations. Perhaps they are extending their network so they can gain access to more resin deposits. At the lowest depths, resonance imaging shows the tunnels feed into a single cavern. It may be where they guard their stockpiles."

Commander Tarsus shut off the holomap before continuing. "Soldiers, this is Operation Thunderous Roar. Your objective: disrupt enemy supply lines. Your success on this mission will cripple the enemy's capacity to wage war on humanity."

Fine. All well and good, but in my head, I was on a different mission. I could no longer believe the official statements fed to civilians by Lunar Channel One, of how the creatures were wild animals in need of corralling. They were likened to buffalo roaming the prairie or insects swarming for food. No, that's not what we fought. In battle, they'd tricked us into a coldly efficient trap. We faced a measly two enemies, yet they almost succeeded in wiping out our entire squad.

They couldn't be mindless—there had to be a chain of command. I was going to determine who or what sat at the top of the pyramid and cut off its head. What kept me going was the memory of that little girl, Quinn, digging for trash in the alley. Tera and my new home lingered in the back of my mind unresolved. Was there a place there, or anywhere, for me? It wouldn't matter until I ended this war and guaranteed the Colony's freedom.

— 19 —

OPERATION THUNDEROUS ROAR

When it came time to deploy, Charlie Company raided the armory for new toys. I was unsure of how to prepare my loadout, so I paid attention to Victoria Haron. The fiery curls of her pixie cut disappeared among the heavy weapons gear: explosives, launchers, and a dot blaster resembling a mini-gun. Out of those options, she picked out a small contraption. It had a square trigger button and reminded me of a control stick one might find in the cockpit of a fighter jet.

I was too obvious about watching her. She took aim at me before flexing a bicep. "Rook, hesitation is for the weak," she said. "Pick gear that plays well with your abilities, and don't overthink it. Or are you a boy playing soldier?" She smiled with all her teeth—was it friendly or mocking?

I scanned the racks but had no idea what equipment would complement my strengths—whatever they were. During the previous battle, I'd taken a jaunt through Ambrose's thoughts and learned our latent abilities were activated by an intense frisson.

What I didn't know was how to call upon my abilities at will. Since then, every time I tried on my own, a lingering obstacle blocked the way. It was a voice warning me not to before the engine cut out. I'd also found out from overhearing his thoughts that each person needed to figure out a way to draw his ability forth. Unfortunately, besides being well-guarded secrets, techniques were idiosyncratic; a method that worked for someone else wasn't going to work for me.

So far, I could project a weapon like a lance, and it could pierce solid matter. But that was it. What equipment would complement that? A dot blaster, a stun baton...an EMP grenade. None fit the bill.

Since nothing in the armory suited my appetite, I brought along Cyril—the Simulacrum in my wristcom no one had seen—and the robot Tera had given me. The other soldiers didn't think Hexbot unusual—lunar fabrication was so open-ended that they assumed I'd picked up Hex from the armory. I figured if I brought Hex along, I could use its data analysis to tell me what the enemy was after.

She'd said it came equipped with built-in functions and could emerge new ones by interpreting commands given to it over time. "Hex, support mode," I ordered. Whether it was programmed for the specific task or had created it on the fly, I wasn't sure, but Hex understood. I trotted around the warehouse, and the bot followed. Its pipe-like arms and legs were skinny metallic rods segmented like a showerhead, and its bipedal feet—single-molded pieces which reminded me of moonbooties children wore—shuffled along after me. I peeked into the exposed gaps where its ankles were, and there were rotating gyroscopes to process balance.

"Hex, defense mode." Its semi-translucent pate—a brain window, if it had a brain—glowed fluorescent green in acknowledgment. It normally stood up to my thigh, but this time, the automaton collapsed into a compact cube. In front of its body, it fanned out a flat, circular plate as if it were holding a Roman gladiator's shield. Hex said, "Protocol Number One." So it was a protection protocol. What other Protocols had she programmed in?

"Hexbot, attack mode." Its pate lit up fluorescent green again, but this time, its eyes flashed red, affirming my command. "Attack me," I ordered, steeling myself. Nothing happened. Of course, she would never allow her inventions to harm human beings.

Just then, Victoria sealed her gravity boots and walked over, blocking my line of sight. She strained at the effort but picked Hex up like a doll. "For a little thing, it sure feels solid and has got a hefty weight to it. Fast-prototyping lets the tech lab churn out some amazing experimental stuff." She mistook Hex for a weapon from the armory.

The sound of our dropship powering up reverberated through the armory walls. She turned her attention from Hex back to me. She said, "But you know, instead of this humanoid thing, you do have teammates."

Sure, but would they help me when it counted? Groups were the entire basis for modern civilization, and yet I didn't trust them. When we melted into the group, some loafed while others picked up the slack. Or, we could divest personal responsibility onto the entity and wash our hands of wrongdoing. It prompted me to ask, "What about the enemy? Do you think they behave like pack animals?"

"Nope. As in, I don't obsess over it. They're probably like most everything else alive. They follow their own kind. It's natural."

"Is it natural then, according to what news reports say, that they'd want to kill us?"

She rubbed the back of her head and shrugged. "Maybe they want food. They could be territorial creatures. We're not paid to ask why, Rook. We're paid to take care of business." She departed for the dropship, and as she passed, she shoved Hexbot into my stomach as a playful gesture. At least, I assumed it was playful; I grunted and pretended it didn't hurt.

◐ ◑

On the dropship en route to the infiltration point, I was strapped in next to the other soldiers of Charlie Company. I caught Victoria staring at me from the opposite bench. Was she so confident she had time to study her surroundings? Most of us were occupied in our own headspace—if I had to guess, the others were doing as I was, coming up with a personal plan for survival. We were engaging the enemy, but this time, it was force action—an outright raid. Back at home, the other squadrons waited in reserve for Colony defense.

The dropship fired a quasar blast at the crater below, unearthing a tunnel into the extraterrestrial den. The dropship's floor bottomed out, and we rappelled into the unknown.

When our boots touched solid ground, Victoria was already firing into the darkness. She was manipulating the control stick I'd seen her pick up earlier in the armory. The device controlled a Nitejar, a nano-UAV drone which orbited above her helmet. The drone darted and fired at coordinates she targeted on her heads-up display.

I scanned left and right with my dot rifle primed but didn't find any hostiles. My eyes were still adjusting to our new surroundings. The porous gray and white walls of the tunnel glowed from the inside as before. It was safe to assume the alien creatures couldn't see in complete darkness either. I held my breath, but no further attacks came. We took advantage of the lull to establish our position and report to HQ.

Vents notched the floor and ceilings in odd places and angles. Charred splotches on some walls looked like soot outlined with white honeycomb patterns. The dim light cast shadows everywhere, and as I found out, shadows on the Moon were like black holes—not even my suit's night vision could penetrate them.

I patched into comms: "How are you following them? What should I be looking for?"

"When you've got a chance, take it. Today's the only day that matters," she said. Faint snickers from the others leaked into the comms.

Ambrose joined in, "You're not going to catch things as fast as Victoria does. The injections granted her increased sensitivity in her ear muscles."

"What, you mean like enhanced hearing?"

"You'd think so," he said, "but for her it manifested as heightened reflexes. When we touched down, she reacted first when the rest of us hadn't caught up."

I remembered the rest from when I'd eavesdropped on his thoughts. Military scientists had identified three kinds of abilities. Victoria had been dubbed an "enhancer" type, one whose abilities were amplifications of existing traits. Ambrose exemplified the opposite, a "repressor" type, one whose abilities arose from deactivating a limiter in the human body. Commander Tarsus fell into a third and more recently identified category, an "operator" type, but because Ambrose didn't know much about it, I gleaned little from his knowledge. Regardless, I didn't see how I fit into any of those categories. What human senses were related to picking up on thoughts or solidifying light out of thin air?

When we were out in the field, there was a more candid air. I became comfortable saying things that would violate regulations back on base. So I pressed for classified information. "Do we have unlimited use of our abilities?"

"Of course not," he said. "Nothing is free. Use will drain your body and your mind. Your ATP reserves and dopamine levels will tank, and a lengthy rest period will follow in which you can't activate again. And without regular booster shots from the good ol' Doc, we lose the potential. Otherwise, it'd be dangerous if a soldier went rogue."

I could sense everyone having uneasy thoughts about me. I began to wonder if I should listen to him more often. On many occasions, he'd been effective in gathering support for an idea when no one else dared to speak up. I asked, "Can I still serve in Charlie Company without a special talent?"

"Negative. You'd lose your benefits and civilian credits, too. Everyone must contribute."

Yes, the world was this way. Society evolved to promote survival, and survival meant cooperation—even if the hierarchy emerging from it wasn't just. I didn't agree with him or with how it worked, but I accepted he was someone I could trust.

— 20 —

LT. VICTORIA HARON

Lieutenant Victoria Haron scattered the enemy with a few well-placed strikes from her Nitejar drone. There were definitely more than two enemy creatures on this outing. Her heightened senses picked up their faint movements, even if she couldn't see into these oppressive shadows. It was always unnerving to her how shadows on the lunar surface were true black, only made more uncanny by the halo effect at their edges.

She was never one to complain. But she didn't enlist to spend her time trapped in death caves. The Colony had attracted her like so many others to frontiers of the past. The thrills of new and fun; here, she could let loose, blasting targets in training and partying on her nights off. Here, there were fewer laws and even fewer social expectations, and she got paid to show off her prowess. Here, she could live by her motto—carpe diem, and all that jazz.

Until lately. These damn missions cramped her style. She was itching to go somewhere else, to move on, but where? The Moon was as far out as anyone could wander, and it was a place where she could be herself. Up here, no one cared whether a woman took on dangerous jobs—it was about results.

And boy, could she get results. With her dot rifle, she could adapt to any situation, and faster than anyone else, too. Every time she trained, her reaction time shortened, and her muscle memory grew more taut. Striving for her physical peak—just thinking about it gave her a rush like no other.

But these missions were the pits. She was a sitting duck. She was mired in tunnels with guys too slow to keep up and too afraid to stir the pot—too afraid because they were too slow.

The only wild card this time around was the greenhorn, Private Darin Armacite. She wanted him to say or do something nutty again, like he did on their previous mission. She grinned.

Her smile faded when she turned her head to fire at a creature that'd come by for a swipe. This encounter confirmed the details she'd been keeping track of. The creatures ran on all fours when they sprinted but stood up bipedal when they attacked. Their skin or carapace glinted in the dim light like the polished, black chrome of a custom-built motorcycle. Gray splotches covered their necks and backs—patterns unique to each creature as far as she could tell—as if chimeras had bathed in war paint. The raw power in their movements, smooth burst motions, reminded her of the hogs she used to crank down highways back on Earth.

After fending off a group of three attacking in tandem, she patched in to alert the rest of Charlie Company. "They're all around us. They enter and exit these tunnels using trapdoors placed along walls, floor, and ceiling. There are more uglies this time, but I can't figure out how many—they use the shadows to hide their true numbers."

There! She fired upward at a creature that dove from an oblique corner above them. As the creature scurried off, she locked sights on her helm's HUD. She followed the creature's approach to a wall at ground level and examined the trapdoor it disappeared through. The trapdoor emitted a brief spark. The shimmer stopped for a moment when the creature passed through but then lit up again afterwards. What was causing that effect?

Charlie Company had already assumed a defensive formation, all hands standing back-to-back in a circle. No one wanted to be separated and carried away to a grim fate like what'd happened last time. The squad locked itself into a stationary position. Great, they were all paralyzed by fear. This state of mind always handed the advantage to her opponents.

She inspected her gravity boots, which, due to the mist across the waxy textured floor, appeared as if they'd sunken into a swamp made of basalt. She had to get outta here! To greener pastures. Anywhere but this tomb full of trapdoors for uglies to pop in and out of.

But then Darin delivered what she'd been craving.

"Why don't we ignore them and advance to the checkpoint?" he said. "Our objective didn't say we had to engage."

Faceplates swiveled in unison to look at him. The others soldiers' expressions spoke volumes about whether they considered him stupid or insane. She was famous for keeping her cool, so she kept a straight face. But inside, she was cracking up. There he went!

"Do you have a death wish, Rook?" Commander Tarsus tore into the comms, free from the grip of fear and annoyed at the insubordination. "The enemy has us surrounded. They're probing for an opening."

She cocked her dot rifle, and it whined with beam plasma. Finally, time for some fun. The rookie had guts. But could he hold a candle to her?

◗ ◖

I understood why my squadmates assumed I was crazy for wanting to advance. The creatures lunged at us from trapdoors in the ceiling, wall, or ground—any option in 360 degrees. Victoria, having twitch reflexes, would fire first, followed by delayed bursts from the rest of us. Since we were fighting in close quarters, we missed the fast-moving targets, and the creatures would escape through a trapdoor. It was true a stationary defense was what kept us alive.

But I was privy to information others didn't know: One, I could hear Victoria's thoughts, albeit like listening to a radio with spotty reception. From her, I found out the creatures were holding the home-court advantage, but for some reason, they weren't attacking with their full numbers. And two, Cyril was giving me a lecture in my ear. The Simulacrum projected itself on an encrypted frequency so only I could see him. He stood outside our defensive formation. "Darin, do you recognize their tactics?"

"Enlighten me." I gripped my dot rifle and scanning for hostiles. Lately, it was like he became irritated whenever I was glib. Tormenting a computer program had become my new hobby.

"The enemy's tactics are classic psychological warfare," he said. "They care for efficiency. I noted that from your other battle and see them operating in accordance with that principle this time as well. By making their numbers unknowable, they're causing your squad cohesion to fall apart from stress. Your mission may be to cut off enemy supply lines, but they aim to destroy your will to fight. Which strategy gets more to the heart of the matter?"

Those were the reasons why I blurted out that we should keep moving. I did so to take my squadmates' minds off the fear seeping out of the comms. The ridicule I received for it reminded me why I hated groups. It was a race to a bottom set by the lowest average of the bunch.

But lucky for me, this time I had Ambrose on my side. He made a case for my suggestion but couched it in terms of deferring to the Commander's orders.

The Commander relented. "Advance, but we'll hold to the main shaft per our original mission orders."

It was progress, but I didn't like how we had to stick to the main tunnel. Why were we issued a directive limiting our options to engage? Why'd the brass send us into a life-threatening situation with our hands tied?

The truth was, I also didn't like the order because it blocked my own personal agenda. I was counting on the fact that at some point, I'd have a chance to split off from the squad. Then perhaps I could pick up the creatures' thoughts using my abilities and find out what their goal was or where their leader was hiding. And if the head were near, I'd end it. No more drawing this conflict out with recons and exploratory skirmishes.

We inched forward in defensive formation. I traced our path on the heads-up display in my helmet. Our progress toward the checkpoint had been glacial. Sporadic ambushes and our return fire continued to bog us down. However, I began to notice Victoria didn't always discharge her weapon in response to the attacks.

Thoughts also filtered into my consciousness, in spotty bursts, from the other soldiers—a phenomenon I would now admit must have come from Dr. Lunik's injection. I was unsurprised to learn my squadmates considered me self-centered and arrogant. Or they considered me dim-witted. Maybe this ability wasn't a gift after all.

Separate from those negative feelings, I overheard their suppositions about our current predicament. They weren't waiting to die like I'd assumed but had all come to their own assessments. Victoria was attempting to determine the enemy's numbers and the pattern behind their trapdoor mechanisms. Corporal Lawrence—who was promoted into Charlie Company to replace Merck—suspected our destination was valuable to the administration. Specialist Franks analyzed the enemy's strategy to determine whether the creatures were acting from instinct or intelligent purpose.

But it was eavesdropping on the Commander that unsettled me. HQ had informed him of an enormous signature converging on our location from our rear. It was the same signature which we'd avoided when we were picked up from our previous mission. I had underestimated Commander Tarsus. The signature was still too far out to pose a direct threat, so he withheld the information to keep a lid on our panic. He alone bore the true urgency of reaching our checkpoint.

I took into account the cloud of everyone's thoughts and what Cyril told me. The reality of our situation washed over me like a cold shower. I issued a command to Hex, the robot I'd hidden in my gear pack. "Calculate time to checkpoint at our current pace."

Hex delivered a message into my helmet through his voice synthesizer, "ETA: eight hours and seventeen minutes."

I issued another command, "Calculate Omnisuit energy depletion at current discharge rate."

On my HUD, Hex displayed a histogram of the last hour. After performing some number-crunching, it said, "Ten hours and four minutes."

We'd have enough juice to reach the objective, but we'd be bleeding firepower along the way. I hailed Cyril, and he projected himself out in front of me.

"Have you figured it out?" he asked.

"They mean to deplete our energy reserves before starting a real fight."

"My, my—is my descendent requesting my expertise?"

Since when did he learn how to cop an attitude? "Yeah, yeah," I said. "Are you familiar with this tactic?"

"What you've described matches a type of blockade," he said. "There are three basic kinds. The 'close blockade' and 'distant blockade' are straightforward ways to cut off supply routes. Prevent deliveries by camping guns near the recipient's bay or at the shipper's origin itself. That way, your opponent can't receive ammunition, food, you name it."

"It sounds as if the enemy has the same mission as we do." After thinking for a moment, I said, "But neither of those types fit the bill. I assume we're facing the third kind."

"Excellent. Perhaps you do share the military mind that runs in our bloodline after all. The enemy's actions in this instance more resemble a 'loose blockade'—a sneakier affair. They'll lure you out until you're weakened and far from support. Then, they can slaughter your forces outright."

"It's insidious enough," I said. "How do we counter a loose blockade?"

"Dangle the prospect of an early victory."

"You mean, get them to play their cards too soon." I searched all around me, at the porous walls and the shadows that hid the creatures' trapdoors. "But we've been ordered to stay on the main shaft. As long as we're playing right into their hands, they don't have any incentive to take the bait."

"My descendent, what your orders are, and what you must do, are never clear-cut in the fog of war. Otherwise," his hologram faded from view, "a soldier's life would be free of regrets."

◐ ◑

I took Victoria's lead and stretched out the intervals between my defensive volleys. I pretended I had poor reaction time so as to not draw the Commander's ire.

Ever so slightly, the creatures became emboldened in their attacks. They pulled out later on their dives and with less lag time between subsequent attempts. It'd only be a matter of time before their attacks were no longer staggered, and the enemy would come out all at once. Our plan was working.

But after we burned through three hours, the creatures weren't taking the bait. Our wills were frayed. An extended march like this would drive anyone mad. Imagine if every few moments, you'd have to do everything in your power to survive, and repeat the process ad infinitum. My squadmates began to return fire with less enthusiasm—exhaustion had turned us into the bait Cyril asked for.

We were the herd waiting to be culled. And one was chosen.

A creature dropped straight down from a trapdoor above our position and dispersed our defensive formation. Corporal Lawrence unfurled his close-range rotary weapon. The Corkscrew reminded me of a power drill that shot out puffs of compressed air. When the creature darted into striking range, he spun up the drill tip and discharged a blast. Caught off guard by the bizarre weapon, the creature was sliced through in a diagonal and exploded into a dark crimson mist. The Corkscrew's whirl was imprinted on my psyche like a flashbulb photo.

A second creature appeared. I unloaded my dot rifle on full auto. I learned that not even cutting-edge lunar tech was perfect when my rifle jammed. It turned into red-orange coal in my hands, and by reflex, I chucked it away. My gun slid across the floor and burst into a fireball. I was now weaponless and kicked myself for not picking up a sidearm from the armory when I had the chance.

The creature caught on to my distress, and instead of running for safety, changed course and bounded straight for me. It lunged, and when it entered striking range, stood up bipedal and swiped. I rolled out of the way just in time.

It sensed weakness and didn't withdraw. Once it passed me, it powered forward and dug into Specialist Franks. He shouted, "I'm hit!" Blood floated by in globs. His gurgling voice was a sick fountain spilling over. "I don't want to die."

Sated, the extraterrestrial escaped toward a trapdoor on our right. Corporal Lawrence said, "No way I'm letting this SOB off the hook." He surged forward on his gravity boots and chased after the creature. A flash like a camera's was followed by the return of darkness. The creature disappeared through the trapdoor. Another flash of illumination.

He followed the creature in. But when he crossed the threshold, his suit lit up and filled the tunnels with white glare. An awful sizzling noise crossed the comms followed by a scream.

So that's what was responsible for the shimmer effect Victoria had seen. The trapdoors were electrified: they permitted the creatures safe passage but zapped intruders.

Franks and Lawrence died in front of me, and I was powerless to help them. I had taken the bait game too far. Their blood was on my hands.

An alert appeared on my helmet display in red: "Critical. Suit breach, outer layer." Back up on one knee, I inspected the side of my power suit and spotted a gash across the left shoulder. Only a thin layer of Omnisuit stood between me and the elements. A warning message began to sound off on my HUD.

The siren sent me spiraling again into one of those mindsets I couldn't escape. Did we exist to kill so we could keep on living? It was no different here than it'd been back on Earth—a pointless cycle. This was my lot. This was all my life had to offer. And it made me furious.

The image of Lawrence's rotary weapon, its cyclone of air, haunted my mind's eye. The image superimposed itself on my memories from my first encounter with the extraterrestrials, of the two creatures standing shoulder-to-shoulder and spinning away from each other. When the visuals aligned, a surge pulsed up my spine.

And with it came the ability to maintain state. I manifested daggers of light around my body. When my projections appeared, my squadmates backed away from me. I stepped outside our defensive range and sent daggers stabbing through every trapdoor I'd seen through Victoria's eyes. The enemy creatures grew agitated from my attacks and rushed out of hiding in a frenzy.

A distant and muffled voice shouted on comms, "Armacite, halt! That's an order!"

Orders? When the system was broken, the rules were for the willfully oppressed. My squadmates wanted to die for no good reason? This game didn't benefit me, so there was no way in hell I'd play along. I sprinted away toward a trapdoor against the far wall. When I neared the shadows, it was actually two trapdoors side by side.

Now I'd broken from the herd, and the others' thoughts filtered in:

"He's lost it."

"Let him die."

"The fool deserves it."

"Good riddance."

A switch must've been flicked because my abilities ramped up to full. Victoria's thoughts filtered in as clear as a summer's breeze. No, I could see her thoughts. Her memories of herself as a child when she always scraped her elbows and knees. Her moving out at fourteen so her stepfather couldn't hurt her again. Then, the unrepentant tomboy emerged; she belted out homers at baseball games and geared motorcycles. She was shooting pool at the local bar. She picked up her first gun—wasted her stepfather with it. Always running away to something new and better. Until she was shipped up and entered basic training in the LDF.

And I saw that she didn't hate me like the others—not like I figured. My own thoughts intruded next, of Tera and the children back home. That's right. They were why I was here. It let me regain control of my mind again.

I activated the thrusters on my gravity boots and propelled myself toward the trapdoors. Four creatures appeared at my sides to stop me. The moment the creatures appeared, the electric currents ceased arcing over the openings. So that's how they worked: the zappers weren't timed but instead deactivated when their own kind came into proximity.

I careened closer. I wasn't going to make it. Creatures already blocked my path.

But Victoria came to my aid. She fired from her Nitejar drone, and its surgical beam struck one down. Ambrose loosed the second volley, taking out another enemy on my right. The rest of Charlie Company followed their leads, unleashing a torrent of suppressive fire that scattered the remaining bunch.

This was my chance—the creatures they downed were keeping the electrified barriers deactivated. I activated my boots' thrusters again and hurdled over its body. I chose the trapdoor on the left and entered the enemy's domain.

DECOHERENCE

I crawled through the tight space and dropped down into a wide, open chamber. I glanced back up. I'd fallen through low-grav from the trapdoor on the right. I could've sworn I'd entered from the left. My confusion was interrupted by the sensation of something wrapped around my leg. I kicked like a madman. Hex lost its grip and bounced across the floor—the robot must have exited my gear pack on its own.

The chamber's walls were lit as usual, but this time, the air had an orange hue. This place was much larger than the cramped tunnels we'd been marching through. It was big enough to park a dozen Bouncers.

Cyril shouted into my helmet, "Ready yourself! The bait's been set, and it's you. The enemy will be coming to secure a kill."

The alert about the tear in my Omnisuit dominated my HUD. I didn't care, though, because all I could think about was rooting out the sadistic mastermind behind my squad-mates' deaths and getting payback. I commanded, "Hex, attack mode." Hex spread its bipedal feet and entered an aggressive stance.

The engine of my mind revved at full throttle in the face of death. I was starting to understand the process that let loosed my abilities. My anger and hatred overcame whatever inhibited activation. But once the state was maintained, I could close my eyes and visualize projections in the realm of the hypothetical.

If I insisted on an exertion of will, when I opened my eyes, the constructs materialized into real objects.

I cycled through the steps again to form needles of hardened light, a phalanx around my body.

Bits of dust trickled down from above. The room's high ceiling was carved out in semicircle shapes that ascended like the stained glass ceiling of a cathedral. The first alien creature that arrived to kill me dropped down from the same trapdoor I'd fallen from. It was oblivious to the fact that it'd landed with its back to me.

Up close, the creature was a segmented and armored carapace of matte black. Patches on its lateral body gave off a chrome sheen. But most important of all, its neck was exposed.

Hex latched on to the creature's back and began to shock it with electrical impulses. While the creature was preoccupied, I lanced through its neck from behind. Two stabs felled the creature.

Enemy reinforcements arrived, piling in one by one from a trapdoor entrance on the opposite wall across from me. I used my constructs to spear the creatures through as they entered. The vibrations detected on my HUD meant more were coming. A lot more. I took heaving breaths from the exertion. Cyril had told me to lure the creatures out, but he neglected to mention how I'd fare if they came at me all at once. My mind was racing with bits and pieces—*loose blockade, too many targets, bait.*

Four trapdoors fed into this chamber. Two trapdoor slits above, one on the opposite wall, and one at my feet—in the center of the room and built flush into the floor. I needed to reduce the number of entry points and create a bottleneck.

I moved the phalanx around my body and packed the many hardened needles of light closer together. They bunched into a uniform pattern and formed a solid rectangular block. I moved this slab over the two trapdoors on the ceiling. Next, I created another slab to cover the third trapdoor straight across from me.

That left only one entrance: the trapdoor recessed into the floor. Creating these projections strained me, but they bought me time to focus.

Soon, forces rammed up against the barricades I'd placed. The creatures, confused, gave up and rerouted. They searched until they found the unblocked trapdoor at my feet. But this required them to climb up into the chamber. It was an awkward position that granted me a tactical advantage.

Another creature popped in from below. Hex latched onto the creature's leg, providing distraction. I lanced the creature through the neck before it knew what'd happened. But still more were arriving, and I was reaching my limits. I couldn't sustain these slab barriers and also deal with an endless wave of enemies. I needed a different solution.

Wait—what if my assumptions were flawed? My abilities allowed me to form projections of hardened light, but who was to say what forms they could take? Needles were the easiest for me to materialize because I didn't need to maintain state for more than a moment. But I'd combined the needles into a slab—what if other forms were possible?

I tried to create a new type of projection, but the engine cut out in protest. If I could just maintain state longer...

Images of Victoria's memories rushed into my mind again. She appeared as a dichotomy, of who she viewed herself as versus who she was on the outside to others. Yet both forms represented her. I held the contradiction in my mind and accepted its truth—yes, that was it. That was the key.

When I concentrated again, my internal engine ramped up, but this time, instead of cutting out, it stabilized.

No sooner had I figured it out than another enemy soldier stumbled in. While Hexbot ran diversion, I closed my eyes and imagined a gem in the space in front of me. I visualized a nucleating center onto which I packed my creations. When I opened my eyes, the projection materialized into a rotating sapphire of destructive energy.

I willed the diamond-shaped projection toward the creature. My projection spun across its center and lodged itself into the creature's torso. I didn't expect the projection to explode on impact, but it did. It dispatched the creature in an instant.

The creatures that arrived next entered as a trio. One spotted me lying in wait and tried to leap away, but a single sapphire willed their way engulfed all of them in the blast. It was exhausting to repeat the creational steps over and over again, but the calculus put me ahead. The energy I expended in creating one sapphire drained me less than having to form lances for every single kill. The bodies began to pile on top of each other, and the chamber became a morgue. They deserved it. I was going to survive. It was either them or me.

I could tell I was running on empty by the way my brain was turning to mush. But not as many enemies were filtering in as before. It'd be over soon—I'd wipe them all out for what they'd done. I smiled like a murderer acquitted at trial.

Cyril yelled into my comms, "A massive foreign signature is approaching. It's almost here." It must have belonged to the threat Commander Tarsus was tracking—probably a pack of hunter-killers sent to finish us off once our power reserves were low.

I glanced over my left shoulder. The gash in my Omnisuit had frayed further. Warnings now wrapped over my entire faceplate display: "Suit Breach Imminent."

I jumped back on instinct when a giant mound of dirt pushed up from the floor and demolished the trapdoor by my feet. A sleek, obsidian exoskeleton appeared. The creature's torso bulged from the many thick spikes protruding from its back. "Something's different about this one"—was all I managed before a behemoth of a creature erupted from the mound and blew chunks of regolith in every direction.

I shielded my helmet with both arms by reflex. When the dust cleared, I stood facing an extraterrestrial soldier four times the size of any I'd encountered before.

◐ ◐

The signature hadn't belonged to a cluster of enemy reinforcements—it was a single entity. Hope broke through my fear and confusion. Was this Behemoth the one in charge? I attempted to eavesdrop on its mind, to pick up its thoughts as I had from my squadmates. Nothing came through.

I shouted, "What are you?" When that didn't work, I sent a thought its way. "And what do you want?"

The Behemoth stood upright on two legs and appraised me. Its head, a monolith like an Easter Island statue, was fanned out with features that reminded me of a bull elephant's—if the trunk were cut off above the tusks and the face flattened into an impenetrable stare. Its eyes were tremendous dark blue gems of tanzanite. But they were dull and devoid of expression.

In the exchange between us, no recognition passed. I sensed no intelligence or psyche. I'd made it this far only to discover I was wrong. The Behemoth was a mindless beast. That must mean so were the rest of them. A chill passed through me. My heart sank, and I bit down on my back teeth in disappointment. There was no alien central command—no quick way to end the war. If the creatures were wild animals, then things would proceed like they did back on Earth: a slow and steady extermination.

Hex ambushed the Behemoth from the side. The creature swung an appendage as massive as a tree trunk and swatted Hex into the opposite wall. On impact, the bot's optical sensors flashed neon green before fading out.

The Behemoth turned its attention to me next.

But I wasn't going to let it take a swing. I released a sapphire of energy in the creature's direction. If I caught it unawares like the others, this fight would be over before it started.

The creature tilted its head sideways. It swung out and clapped its two arm appendages together over my projectile. The sapphire collapsed in a lightning crash and blinded me. Impossible—how did it know what to do?

I was dazed and didn't notice the creature charge. Its head and shoulders slammed right into me, and I flew back against the wall. I grunted from the sharp pain in my spine and prayed my Omnisuit hadn't ripped open. I crawled around and couldn't stand back up. Would I die here with this freak of nature? But all the rage in the world couldn't upend reality—I didn't have any juice left, and the creature could nullify my sapphire as it had before.

I channeled my mental reserves into one last explosive projection. The creatures I fought before were never aware of my abilities, but the Behemoth stared right at my sapphire as it formed.

The dirt between us rumbled and shifted. Another mound began to form. Was another Behemoth coming in? I was done for.

One final parting shot then. I willed my explosive sapphire up toward the molded ceiling and unleashed the projection down at the Behemoth's head.

The mound of dirt forming between us expanded. It broke through in a spray of rocks to reveal Charlie Company. Victoria unloaded on the Behemoth first with her Nitejar drone, followed by Ambrose and my other squadmates in tow. The creature growled a guttural and awful sound as it turned its attention to the cavalry. It wheeled its gargantuan limbs around to clothesline them like a swinging mace trap.

My squadmates couldn't have chosen a better time to show up. My sapphire projection came down unseen and lodged itself into the creature's skull. When the Behemoth exploded with energy, the room lit up like lightning had struck—and for a moment, there were no more shadows.

◐ ◐

A fuzzy object hung in front of my face. My vision blurred into focus until I could make out an outstretched hand. When Victoria pulled me back onto my feet, my squadmates took a step back. Could they sense my murderous intent still lingering?

She rested her palms on both of my shoulders as if she wanted me to get a grip. "Why didn't you call for backup?"

I had no answer. Would they have come for me?

"Do you know the risks we had to take to reach you?" she asked. "The entrances were sealed off. We only got here by following the tunnel burrowed by that"—she pointed at the Behemoth's corpse—"hellbeast of a thing." Her brown eyes burned into mine. "Don't you trust us? We're not just a squad. We're your comrades."

Trust? I sensed fear leaking from the other soldiers' minds as they surveyed the carnage in the room. Charlie Company stood amidst a mass grave; next to the Behemoth's bloated carcass were extraterrestrial bodies piled on high. The grayish-white basalt walls were singed black from my attacks, leaving that characteristic honeycomb outline. The misted floor was tinged with red, and the room was graced by Death himself. No, my squadmates didn't trust me. One had his hands ready on an immobilizer, and Commander Tarsus was debating whether to issue the order again.

Ambrose stepped up to me. He chewed on his lower lip and took in what lay before him. "Are you okay, bud?" He reached into his gear pack, pulled out a silver material, and applied the rectangular patch over the tear on my shoulder. When I didn't respond, he said, "You know, all you had to do was ask." He heated the adhesive, and the patch sealed my suit. "We can't help if we don't know what's going on."

With the gash mended, the warning sirens in my helmet stopped. I stared forward with unwavering eyes, through Charlie Company and beyond the endless bodies. My mind was a howling tempest I fought to contain.

◗ ◖

After we defeated the Behemoth, we marched to the objective unimpeded. During our trek, we concluded that perhaps the enemy's tunnel structure wasn't solely a military strategy, but rather a way of life. When we cleared trapdoors along the way, we discovered chambers like larders and other rooms that could've been sleeping quarters. In the corner of one room, I discovered an amber resin stash that could've filled a woodshed. These compartments were all linked by tunnels—something similar to what one would see in an ant farm. No wonder it'd been trivial for them to attack us from all sides; we'd been traveling along their version of Main Street.

Commander Tarsus stopped to make an announcement. "Our objective waits on the other side of this rock formation. We'll set up shop to reinforce this position. Then we'll take down whatever's waiting behind—"

He was cut short by an emergency transmission arriving on our comms. It was a call from the top. Paxton's face appeared on our faceplate displays. "Charlie Company, mission accomplished. You are to withdraw and recuperate."

"Sir," Commander Tarsus said, "we haven't secured the objective—"

I was still on my knees, stooped over and scooping amber resin into my gear pack, when it happened. A detonation like an artillery shell broke through the checkpoint and ruptured the tunnel side walls. The surprise attack left us groaning and struggling to get back on our feet.

Something was coming. I sensed it. It was almost here, and we were in no condition to engage in another fight.

Paxton reappeared on comms. "We cannot afford further losses. Withdraw. That's an order."

There it was, laid out in the open. We were ten steps away from the objective but had failed the mission.

The hairs on the back of my neck stood up and a peculiar sensation crept up on me. A voice entered my mind—one I didn't recognize. I darted my eyes around the tunnel shaft. The voice didn't belong to my squadmates. It had come from the other side of the rubble. They were the thoughts of a sentient being.

— 22 —

ON THE HOME FRONT

I was released on leave after standard decontamination procedures. I returned home to Turtlepin Village to find I'd once again been rewarded for my service. My homepod had been upgraded with new modules while I was gone: heated wood flooring, a virtual reality simulator room, and more. I checked my credit balance on the mini-fabricator and had been wired more *lunes*, enough to eat or fabricate any basic necessity I could want or need. But I spent hours alone at home, staring at the wall.

I replayed the torture of that long march. My squadmates were killed and the bodies of alien creatures were stacked end to end. Then, moments before reaching what I'd been searching for, our mission was aborted. To come so close, only to find the price paid was for naught—what'd it all been for?

I was desperate to break free, but no force of will could stop me from reliving that day. I broke the loop by resolving to face what I'd been putting off: seeing Tera.

When I headed downtown, Turtlepin Village didn't look the same. Gone from the sidewalks were the makeshift street art vendors and impromptu musical performances. Many citizens had gone to work in the Industrial Band instead, to make equipment blueprints or design fortifications for the planned troop surge.

Word of Charlie Company's battle had spread, and along my walk down the brick paths to Tera's part of town, villagers acknowledged me. The simulated sky overhead was a bright hue, and strangers stopped talking when I passed to smile at me. A group of teenagers asked to shake my hand before using their wristcoms to snap holo-images with me.

It was different than the fear and distrust I was met with when I first set foot in the dome. But what'd changed? These strangers didn't know me then and didn't know me now. Their perceptions of me were based on what others said. Did they know of the circumstances that brought me up here or of the alien graveyard I'd dug on my own? If they did, would they still have given me a fair shake?

As I passed through central downtown, a gust of wind picked up. It carried deep booms, clinks, and fanfare sounds that reminded me of old pinball machines. I craned my neck to read the sign above the building's entrance: Skytower Control. The arcade had a storefront and red-carpeted interior open to the street. Children and teens stood at the hologram game cabinets, their backs to me. Yellow and blue lights pulsed out and bled onto the sidewalk. A few players turned as I walked by and recognized me. They were students from Tera's Cyan Cohort.

If they cared about my exploits from the news broadcasts, they didn't show it—no, they were just happy to see me. In all that'd changed in Turtlepin Village, I was glad the kids were still a hoot and had managed to hold on to their weird selves. They swarmed me with questions:

"Mister, when will you come by the school again?"

"Tell me more about Earth!"

"Teacher Tera said she was looking for you."

They chanted *"oooooh"*—at least kids were still kids.

Michael said, "Play a level with me!" and shoved a controller into my hand. It was a plastic gun painted blue and used for one of those shoot-em-ups. I glanced at the other cabinets lined in a row, and they were all similar variants of the game *Mecha Proxy*.

"It's the hottest new game from Earth," he explained. "Someone imported it in secret, and now everyone's playing it."

I don't know why, but it didn't feel right anymore. I placed the blaster back into the tabletop. I laughed it off and promised to play another time, to the protests of all there. As I walked off, explosions boomed to the children's delighted screams and cheers.

I figured I shouldn't show up to Tera's empty-handed, so I stopped by the convenience store next. It was a place to buy pre-fabricated goods for those on the go. I roamed the aisles and found many shelves left unstocked—probably because of austerity measures for the war effort. I picked up a bunch of drinks and desserts and paid with my military stipend.

I reached her homepod and rang her on the holodisplay. When the door slid to the side and I was greeted by those soft green eyes below that high forehead, all the words I'd rehearsed flew out the window. I'd been through so much in the last few months that I didn't want to waste any more time. But when she hugged me, I couldn't make the words come out.

She broke the ice instead. "Welcome back, stranger."

Tera...she still treated me the same, even with the news spreading around town, and I was glad. This was real.

Like every time I visited, I stepped over cable wires and proto-types strewn about the floor on our way to the living room. From my pack, I unloaded the drinks and desserts from the store. I also pulled out Hexbot—mangled—and a surprise wrapped in butcher paper. Of course, she paid attention to Hex first.

"Oh my," she said. She couldn't contain her excitement. "You squeezed out full utility, didn't ya? The things it must've seen and done!"

"Sorry," was all I could muster. It was silly bringing her gift back broken. "Whatever algorithms you programmed for it blew my mind. It was like it adapted to my strategies and figured out how to support me on the fly. Hex helped me when it counted most."

She beamed and was giddy afterwards. Of all the things I could've said—like how she was more beautiful every time I met her or how she exemplified a place I wanted to call home—praising her robot was what made her day.

It was as good a time as any to put icing on the cake. I tore the butcher paper off the surprise I'd brought: a vac-sealed canister the size of a shoebox. "I recovered some amber resin on our mission. I want you and the Cyan Cohort to have it."

I was taken aback when she burst into laughter. "Still an Earther through and through I see. I can't thank you enough, but you shouldn't have. With the budget cuts, the students haven't been supplying the fabricators for their experiments. What a stupendous cluster—this'll be enough to last us for," she paused to make quick mental calculations, "a whole school year! Astounding!"

She stood up and rushed to grab a plum-colored hooded jacket off the coat rack, which she pulled on over her sundress. "But we should catch up while we walk."

"Where are we going?" I asked.

"You'll see." An enigmatic smile crossed her face.

She led me beneath the city streets of Turtlepin Village. We wound through underground walkways closed in by white-brick facades, down inclined ramps that met blind corners and up corridors again. The "secret" passageways were home to graffiti of distorted human figures in gyrating poses, of murals painted in garish red, yellow, and blues on bare drywall.

She led me by the hand in a quiet but urgent rush. We walked together through tight spaces that were filled by the intoxicating scent of her golden brown hair. I could see nothing but her pale and soft skin—and when did she ever wear a dress?

Murmurs were getting louder from up ahead. "Are we going to a party?" I asked.

She pulled at me to hurry up. "Sort of. It's a Still Light Exhibition."

"You mean still life?" It brought to mind photorealistic paintings of vases and silver platters of fruit.

She turned back to smile at me. "No, I meant what I said. More and more of these underground galleries have sprung up recently."

We turned the final corner of that low-ceiling maze and ran into a throng of people. The exhibition was being held in what appeared to be basement office spaces. Their glass-paneled doors were propped open, and in the different suites, visitors surrounded what looked like sculptures on display.

"All of this during wartime?" I asked

"Especially so."

A dog—a golden labrador retriever—sauntered by. "He looks lost," I said. "Let's help him find his owner."

"Yes, let's." There was a mischievous look in her eyes.

I snapped my fingers as a command, and the dog trotted up to me. I knelt down to pet him, but my fingers passed right through his head. "Oh, it's a hologram projection."

She couldn't hold it in any longer and laughed. "It's an interactive art installation. I do think it's sweet that your first thought was to help."

We chose one of the art installations at random and entered a cozy office space. It was laid with thin, gray carpeting, and the room's ceiling was so low I could push up on it with my fingertips. On display, front and center on an unadorned maplewood desk, sat the centerpiece. It was a sculpture the size of a large vase and shaped like an ostrich egg.

"It's pretty bland," I commented offhand. "It's like a maroon jumble of neurons mashed together into an oval."

"That's not the actual—"

"Oh?" A lanky, middle-aged woman with silver hair, glasses, and sandals like beachwear stepped in between us. The older woman had her arms folded and a hand curled against her cheek in contemplation. "Tell me what else you think about it."

Tera was suppressing a giggle for some reason.

"I mean, if it was meant to be abstract," I said, "it's not aesthetically pleasing. If it was meant to have a point instead, it doesn't say anything. It feels like the artist was holding back."

The older woman said, "Oh, repression can be useful, don't you think? It allows us to be civil to each other. Otherwise, we might say or do things we regret later." She offered a hand. "The name's Lang by the way. Hi, I'm the artist."

I froze. Tera ribbed me in the gut—hard—with her elbow. She wanted me to say something nice to make up for the foot I'd shoved in my mouth. So I said, "Oh, if it's a statement on repression, then it's pretty surprising." I was stabbing in the dark for a compliment. To me, the sculpture looked like an amorphous blob of basal ganglia.

Lang nodded. "Is this your first time experiencing a still light? You're not standing in the proper spot, so you haven't even viewed the piece yet." She pointed to a small circle on the gray carpet. It was like a spotlight wide enough for one person to step inside.

Tera was still covering her mouth to hide her amusement at how mortified I was.

"Well, go on," Lang said. "Give it a whirl."

I stepped into the spotlight and waited. The sculpture began to shift. Its many slivers of light changed color and orientation. The maroon, clay-like texture darkened into charcoal; its smooth spheroid curves dripped into jagged tendrils, like a burst of stalactites aimed at me from different angles.

"You see," Lang said, "a still light changes based on the viewer. An unusual viewing in your case. Why do you think this monstrosity," she gestured at the spiny tentacles before us, "has appeared?"

What was Lang implying? It was like she was making a point at my expense, and Tera was eating it up. Fine, if they wanted to play this game, then let's see how awkward I could make it.

I folded my arms in contemplation. "It probably relates to what happened back on Earth when I was twelve. I was living with a new foster family at that point. But we weren't getting along. They said a lot of nasty things about me, about why I got so riled up—and I told them I hated them, maybe one too many times." I wasn't making that part up, for nothing could be more unpleasant than the truth.

Tera and Lang squirmed in nervous silence. I continued to pour it on thick. "Things came to a head, and they said they couldn't support me anymore. They made sure I packed up all of my belongings. They took me to the back fence, to the gate leading out to the park, and turned me out. The last thing I remember is holding onto a bag of worthless possessions and looking back at the gate before walking out onto the streets."

Tera said, "Oh, Darin..."

"But the experience made me tougher," I said. "Relying on others is a weakness. Why should I depend on society or any other large and nameless group? I should follow my own principles instead." I stepped back from the light sculpture's jagged accusations. Tera and Lang were shifting from foot to foot with their arms crossed. I had made them uncomfortable with my tirade—mission accomplished. "That's my interpretation of this piece, anyhow." I grinned.

A grin cracked at the corners of Tera's mouth—she'd caught on to my game. I found myself more and more exhilarated by how fun she was to be around. She was as quick as her eyes hinted at but never one to take things too seriously—a perfect partner in crime. I stepped away from the viewing circle. "Tera, I think it's your turn." The light sculpture reoriented its beams and reformed into a harmless, maroon-colored egg.

She stifled another giggle as she walked past me. "These still lights don't entangle with every viewer, do they?" she asked Lang. "They're not true quantum machines, are they?" She inquired about maintaining coherence, something about a computer holding both the values of zero and one for parallel calculations. I couldn't wrap my head around it.

"You'd have to ask the original inventor," Lang said. "I only sculpt the beams. If I had to guess, I imagine a few particles are entangled and a computer algorithm pseudo-creates the rest. What I do know is that different representations get created for each viewer, and once entangled with someone, it cannot be undone. The same person will always see the same thing."

"Then here goes nothing," Tera said and stepped into the lit circle. The sculpture's beams began to lift and swing as they shifted away from a maroon tinge to white-yellow rays of morning sun. The sculpture thickened into a white and wispy cloud-like texture. Next, it took on the shape of a mantle or cloak, but it didn't stop there. It settled into three spirals linked together into a triangle.

"Hey, it's like your gadgets," I teased. "Never knows when it's finished." She rolled her eyes at me.

Lang said, "A pleasant contrast to the previous viewing. Why do you think the still light chose this form for you?"

Tera snuck me a look to let me know she was in on my game. "Uh....that's me as free as a cloud. Papa was always working, so mother raised me by herself. Unfortunately, I took too much after Papa still. Whenever there were dances at school, I spent nights locked in my room with my engineering experiments. But my inventions make sense, so they've always been more fun than the silly conventions of dating."

Did she mean what she'd said? But if I considered the times we spent alone, she must have.

"The tripartite shape means it's complete on its own," she said. "No productivity wasted on arguments with messy and unpredictable guys."

Now I was the one who had to suppress a grin. Though I was sure she was telling the truth, the solemnity with which she said everything was too much. She stepped out of the viewing circle, and the light sculpture returned to its default configuration.

The look on Lang's face said she regretted approaching us in the first place.

"Lang," I said, "you mentioned a still light becomes entangled with its viewer. But that must mean it's reacting to our DNA or molecules, I think, or something like that. Would the artwork change if more than one person stood inside the viewing circle?"

"No, it doesn't work that way," Lang said. "Besides, the viewing circle only fits one person."

Was it true? For some reason, I doubted the technology was designed that way. I bent over and scooped Tera up under her legs. She let out a surprised scream, her face and neck suffused with red. I cradled her neck and legs and walked us both into the viewing circle. Lang raised an eyebrow.

The light sculpture began its dance. Its color faded to gunmetal gray, and its shape shifted to something that reminded me of a spacecraft in flight.

"Well, I'll be...." Lang said. "I didn't know that was possible."

I lowered Tera back to her feet. Her eyes had a twinkle in them, but then she averted her gaze. She straightened out the ruffles in her sundress and regained her composure.

I said, "Never know until you try, right?"

Was she beaming at me? She turned back to the artist. "Lang, I love this piece. One of our senior citizens at the school, Ignacio, used to be a painter. He mentors Michael sometimes, and they're both visual-tactile learners. They would adore your art, too. Are you open to selling it?"

She was always thinking of others. How'd she keep track of them all? She was a well of generosity that never ran dry.

"Yes, of course," Lang said. She reached into her pocket. From the corner of my eye, I caught the price tag on the display plaque fade and disappear. "It's going for..." she quoted an amount much higher than the original listing.

I frowned. There was no way I was going to let someone take advantage of Tera. "I don't know. Maybe art has a high intrinsic value. If we stick a price on, we change the nature of the thing itself."

Tera squinted, as she often did when she was skeptical of something. "What? Investments into technology and innovation are responsible for our prosperity. These are tangible improvements we can measure."

Our inside joke had ended, and we were sparring in earnest now.

"Tell you what, Lang," I said. "I'd like to buy your piece instead." I made an offer higher than quoted. I wouldn't let anyone get away with tainting Tera's good intentions. However, I could live with being exploited in her place, and I never touched my military stipend anyway.

Tera put her foot down. "Absolutely not. I don't need you, or anybody, to step in for me."

Lang switched back and forth between us. She lost her patience and snapped at us. "Are you a couple? If so, you two have issues.

Just forget the whole thing!" She stomped out with an expression that asked what she'd done to deserve us.

Tera whirled toward me in a huff. We engaged in a stare-off, neither willing to budge. But soon we began to grin at the absurdity of the situation. Once no one was in earshot, we burst into outright laughter. Lang was right—we were a terrible twosome.

"She was lying to your face, you know, about the price," I said, hoping to explain myself. "People don't stand for anything—it's hard to know who to trust."

She switched to a softer tone. "With the war, things have been tight around here. My neighbors have been acting in ways that are out of character for them. I don't think Lang would've done what she did if she didn't feel like she needed to."

"You knew she was taking advantage of you, and you let her?"

"Yes, I did, and I forgave her. People will come back to their senses once the war is over." Tera...she could forgive someone just like that? She was the kind of person I didn't know how to be.

We spent the rest of the evening having a blast. We visited art exhibits in the other basement offices with their white-brick walls. If there was anything I took home from that event—put on while the Colony was in a state of emergency—it was that our feelings must be given free reign. Otherwise, human beings were no different than machines.

◑ ◑

On our walk back to Tera's homepod, I checked my wristcom again. I'd missed two messages marked urgent. One was from Cyril—nothing new there. The other message was from Seger of Lunar Channel One. What did that reporter want?

"A call from the military?" Tera asked. She was too perceptive sometimes.

"Nothing important," I said. She wasn't happy with my answer, but it was easier this way. I was on strict orders not to talk about our missions, and she wouldn't understand about Cyril, my family's legacy, and the things I needed to take into my own hands.

When we returned to her homepod, we sat together on her lounge. The drinks and desserts I'd brought earlier were spread out on the coffee table.

She said, "You know, my students keep asking when you're going to come by the school again. You've left such an impression on them. They want you to give a guest seminar."

"I can't—at least not for a while," I said. "The war's not letting up, and I'm on emergency standby at all times. I'm dealing with a lot of things right now, so I don't think it'd be wise."

She looked more disappointed than I thought was warranted. "'Things.' Like what, Mr. always-discontent-and-incredibly-vague?" She was teasing me. "You look like the same confused person who fell from Earth to me." She moved closer to me on the lounge.

I felt warmth radiating outwards from her—what happened to the young woman who I once considered so plain? I wanted to hold her and tell her everything, from the beginning, about justice for my family and about my latent abilities. But the words lay hidden behind a barrier between us. "I feel something is changing," I said. "But I can't describe what. The injections the LDF gave me are classified—along with everything else I've seen on deployment."

She leaned back and put a hand on her hip. "Gee, there's a swell way to get to know someone if I ever heard one." Her words were half-playful, half-barb. She was good at that.

"I'll bring an end to this war. I'll come by the school after, I promise. I'm doing it for you and—"

"Stop right there." She pulled away from me. "You *have* changed. That doesn't even sound like you."

I'd never seen her upset—not even irritated—with me before. What had I said to set her off? I said, "Don't you get it? Our lives and our freedom are in peril. None of it—the school, the Cyan Cohort, the amber resin—nothing else matters with what's at stake."

"So we're laboring under an illusion of free will then, are we?" she shot back. There was ice in her voice.

"Finishing this war is what I need to do. I know it. Governments, corporations, and people I don't know—I can't rely on them. But I can do what I believe is right."

"If your ideals are more important to you than the people here right in front of you, then that's your choice. But don't say it's for us—or for me. I'm not your solution girl, not for all the things you're hoarding inside."

I didn't like how naked I was in front of her. I was hurt and angry that she couldn't understand where I was coming from—it's why I didn't like to tell people things, and here was more of the same. But I had no energy left for arguments. Not after all the fighting I'd been through. I took a breath to calm myself down and stared at her.

Our desserts sat on the coffee table, untouched.

She gave in first, magnanimous as always. Her combative posture melted away. "I don't know how you make me so irrational," she said. She embraced me and clasped her hands with mine. "I'm not so sure I like losing control with you."

She rested her head on my shoulder and closed her eyes. For a woman who was more than my match, she was so small and fragile in my arms. We stayed that way for a brief eternity, a place in time I didn't want to ever end.

"I know you're giving it your all," she said, her eyes still closed. "You go be who you need to be."

She was too good for someone like me. She was kind and

accepting, even when she was saying she wouldn't join me on the path I'd chosen.

— 23 —

VIRTUOUS NATIONS

Paxton reflected on the top-level clearance that granted only a few lunar government officials to communicate with representatives on Earth. It was both a privilege and a tiresome balancing act—the average citizen would never know the burden. He concluded the holo-conference with a few words to reassure his political backers: "Our soldiers were unexpectedly resourceful. As a result, we've revised our strategy once more. Project Infinite Light will march onward as we've planned. Humanity's first interplanetary war is a foregone conclusion." *And Richard Paxton Nest will be named its conqueror.*

He sat at the head of an oblong conference table. To observers on the other side of the tinted floor-to-ceiling glass, it would appear as if he were brooding over an important decision alone. However, with the VR visor activated, he could see silhouettes of the Guildsack Partners seated in the plush executive chairs surrounding the table. Quantum encryption allowed them to hear each other and only each other.

A silhouette lit up to speak. "Can we trust the extraterrestrials will play their part?"

The anonymous speaker probably represented Block EX, the weapons contractor, so he tailored his response accordingly. "Yes, they're simple beings we can manipulate. When they are caught in a full-scale invasion of the Colony, and we share the footage with the United Earth Council, they will supply all the funding we could dream of."

A silhouette seated to his right lit up. "And once you secure funding, what will be the next stage of Project Infinite Light?"

"Take your pick, ladies and gentlemen. A proxy conflict up on Moon Base Zero can last for as long as you deem useful, especially when the battlegrounds are far removed from sympathies on Earth. Then, at a time and place of our choosing, we can overpower the enemy with our numbers and resource advantages—as virtuous nations have always done."

"And what about your wildcard, Private Darin Armacite?" another asked. For once, he didn't recognize the voice. The speaker must've been from SCAIN, a secret police contractor on Earth invited to join the Guildsack Partners last month.

"I have put in place special measures to—shall we say—incentivize Private Armacite's cooperation. A martyr is what we need to put a face on this war."

"No more surprises, Paxton. We've got too many investments riding on the outcome." The holo conference blipped out and ended.

He gritted his teeth. One day those SOBs would do his bidding instead.

— 24 —

OPAQUE/TRANSPARENT

I left Tera's place in turmoil. I couldn't give her what she wanted. If I left the military, I would watch my new home become like it'd been on Earth—an organism birthed from pure intentions, but one that grew to engulf me, my neighbors, and compatriots into its machine. We were then grotesque appendages of the state and its conglomerates, existing for the sake of our disembodied creations. But with my growing abilities, I finally had the power to do something about it. So I wouldn't sit by and watch my reality devolve into the circumstances which led me up here in the first place.

I was still waiting for orders from up top, and I didn't trust myself to be at home alone with my thoughts. So I headed to the local bar for a spell.

The holosky was simulating night by the time I reached The Tokyo Parachute. Inside the pub, I found an interior lit by neon diodes and filled with dark velvet upholstery. Smoky, recycled air wafted by, and synthesized music was cranked up so loud it drowned out any possibility of rumination—perfect, just what the doctor ordered.

I was surprised when patrons welcomed me at the bar and paid for my drinks. So these were the rewards of cooperation—we agreed to do things a certain way, and if I did, other people liked me for it.

I plopped onto a stool and rested my elbows on the granite bartop. There was a plate of food ready for me. Belpares again.

Belpares was a staple meal made from leafchoy, a nutrient-rich superfood which passed for spinach or kale. As far as I could tell, it was made by plating globs of leafchoy into two columns, like buttons on a coat jacket. Drizzles of a sauce, often chocolate or orange-colored, connected the globs to each other in a crisscrossing pattern like a cat's cradle. It was a fancy name and presentation to otherwise disguise the fact that leafchoy was a chalky mulch eaten many times a week so citizens could stay healthy.

I didn't have much of an appetite and left the belpares untouched. It'd been a long time since I'd knocked one back. The drink slid down into my gut warm and rumbled through my empty stomach.

A vibration went off on my wristcom. I didn't need that right now. A message from my ancestor, the Simulacrum, scrolled across the screen.

"We need to talk," Cyril said.

I ignored his message and tried to melt back into a favorable mood. When I didn't answer, a more forceful vibration notification scrolled by. "Now."

Fine. I ditched the stools and black countertop to look for a more discreet corner of the tavern. I passed by tables where women smiled at me with curious eyes and men appeared to be on guard. I found an empty booth and slid into its upholstered bench seat. The privacy screen was easy enough to activate. The booth wrapped its outer display with images of a forest to obscure me from view.

Now safe from prying eyes, Cyril projected himself out into the seat opposite mine. "How are you holding up? Do you think drinking is going to help?" For once, he was dressed in civvies. He wore a camo-green turtleneck with leather patches for the breast pocket and shoulder pads. Move over, Che Guevara.

I laughed, both at the prospect of having a drink with a ghost and at the fact that he was programmed to show concern. He was a software routine—nothing more—who cared when a set of conditions were met. It was so absurd I broke out into more laughter. It'd been so long since I'd felt this good. "What do you want?"

He said, "You witnessed your comrades' last moments on the battlefield and faced death yourself. These were not trivial events."

"C'mon," I said. "What's it matter to you? As long as I'm fulfilling the grand directive, right? Revenge, yada yada yada." He was the same as everyone else who wanted to use me for gain.

"I served my country so my children wouldn't have to face the specter of war. I never wanted it to come to this...that you'd have to trace my footsteps."

"A bit late, Gramps. As far as I know, I hold the record for killing the most aliens in human history. And everyone congratulates me. Maybe they'll give me a nickname, like The Butcher of La Lune—you know, the stuff they brand war criminals with."

He went silent for a moment. Did he have a remorse algorithm? I laughed and laughed. The thumping bass and looped riffs of Asterchord music—notes tied to the random photon emissions of stars, ensuring no two performances were exactly alike—came through the sound systems. I soaked it in.

"Think," Cyril said. He was irritated at my cavalier attitude. "Take stock of the situation. Something doesn't add up."

"Aliens want to kill us. We want to kill them. What else is new?" I took a swig from my lowball glass. "Replace aliens with foreigners and you have the brief and pathetic history of the human race."

"The enemy hasn't made a move since our family's village was wiped out on that terrible day forty years ago. Why haven't there been any other attacks on the Colony until now?"

My nose was pointy, and my dark hair was like a warm cap on my scalp. I tried to remember what drink I was on but couldn't remember. "Maybe the dome kept them out. I don't know."

"No, if the extraterrestrials were native fauna reacting to territorial encroachment, there would've been other incidents since then. The conclusion to draw, then, is that the creatures are not attacking on instinct but have a motive."

"What? What grudge could the creatures possibly have?"

"Precisely," he said. "It doesn't make sense. They alone aren't responsible for the events that have transpired."

"But that's in the past. If we defeat them, we remove the threat. You'll have gotten your revenge, and I'll have ensured the Colony's safety. Their eradication is a win-win."

"Darin, I wish history was so simple. If it were, I wouldn't have reawakened to find my only living descendant at war, like I'd been. Don't dismiss the past as unimportant, done and over with, for it can fester like a wound. The sores will reopen until—you have a visitor." He disintegrated and faded from view.

◐ ◑

As he made his way through the wet, smoky ambiance of The Tokyo Parachute, Seger reflected on Lunar Channel One's meteoric rise. It'd been thanks to one person, the one he'd tracked down to a privacy booth at the back of the bar.

He'd sold footage from Charlie Company's last few battles to intelligence agencies on Earth and had even opened talks with entertainment affiliates. On the one hand, he'd say he was there to repay Darin. On the other hand, self-interest ruled the day, for an agitated Darin was unpredictable—a formula that was bottled magic in Seger's industry.

It was like he had been expected because the privacy display unlocked as he approached. The booth's opaque images of wooded forest flipped to transparent glass again.

He smiled in greeting. "Celebrating early, are we?" He helped himself to the empty bench seat opposite and punched in an order for a brandy on the rocks. The drink traveled along the automated railing until it reached their table. He savored an extended draw. Fabricators were amazing; his first sip went down like the real thing.

"Celebrating? You could call it that." Darin surprised him by laughing.

He tensed inside his navy blazer, and his silver tie felt tight against his neck. What was going on here? Darin wasn't the gregarious type. It made sense when he saw how many glasses sat empty by Darin's elbow. "My sources picked up on a rumor you ought to know. It goes without saying that it's for your eyes only."

"For me? Why, you shouldn't have."

Was he being mocked? He ignored it. "I figured I owe you this much."

"Yeah? Why's that?" The young man's glare could burn a hole through sheet metal. How'd he set Darin off already?

"Call me a fan," he said. "Movers need information on their side, right? I can be that person for you. We have eyes in every nook and cranny on the Colony."

Darin's gaze wandered across the bar. "Okay, sure. Wonderful." His gray jacket swished and swayed as he leaned on his elbows.

Seger would have to cut to the chase. Classified info was always a quick way to catch someone's attention. "Have you noticed anything unusual about your last two forays into enemy territory?"

"Tell me something not strange about life up here."

He'd been around the block enough times to know that negotiators loved to feign disinterest. It was time to seal the deal. "You made it out alive through ingenuity and dumb luck. But you weren't supposed to. Have I made myself clear? You were sent on suicide missions."

"Yeah, so what?"

This wasn't the reaction he was expecting. He reassessed Darin's state of mind. "Is this an accurate summary of your next mission?" Whiffs of smoke floated by their booth. "You're waiting for orders to re-enter the enemy compound and capture their central command."

Darin was jumpy like he couldn't sit still and almost stumbled in reaching for his drink. He swirled the lowball glass before downing yet another one.

Seger swooped in for the finisher, "Well, your orders won't come. The enemy is preparing a full-scale assault on the Colony. But you won't find out until it's too late—until people have been killed." Now he had Darin's attention.

"And why would the brass allow something foolhardy like that? Charlie Company and the other squads have already been placed on standby."

"That, I cannot disclose because I've got clients on both sides of the table," he said. "But one of my reporters did manage to dig up this photo. Accidental discovery, you see." He reached under the brown table and flicked a switch. The booth transitioned from transparent glass to opaque forest again. He then projected a map schematic above the table between them.

The map showed extraterrestrial tunnels had been dug to surround the dome. The tunnels opened to multiple attack vectors, which, if successful, would grant direct entry into the Colony.

"It's the strategy I'd use if I wanted to exploit the dome's inherent weaknesses."

"Oh?" Seger's lips curled into a smile. "You're sharper than your recklessness led me to believe."

Darin studied the schematic with laser-focused concentration. His jaw hardened, and his eyes flashed that consuming hatred that'd first caught Seger's interest.

Much sharper. He didn't have to say the rest. Because Darin had already figured it out. One of the attack vectors crossed into Turtlepin Village and cut straight through Tera Arkwright's homepod.

THRASHING ABOUT AT RANDOM

At first, I didn't put stock in what Seger had shown me. I wouldn't have trusted him even if he'd approached me in a trench coat and handed over a manila envelope stamped "Top Secret" in red. Because what would the administration gain from a disastrous game of brinkmanship? Who'd stand to benefit from devastation?

But when midnight passed and Charlie Company still hadn't received orders to deploy, I began to have doubts. There was complete radio silence from up top: we weren't even ordered to prepare loadouts. If what he said was true, then on the most urgent crisis facing the Colony, we were giving the enemy time to cement their positions.

The following morning, Commander Tarsus called Charlie Company together for the meeting we were all waiting for. But he didn't give us what I was expecting.

"HQ hasn't updated our orders," he said. He looked stunned, and uncertainty edged its way into his voice. Ambrose and Victoria exchanged worried glances.

"Nothing at all?" Byron Colbee asked.

"Standby. No further orders," Commander Tarsus said, quashing dissent.

Cyril had been trying to tell me about historical events covered up as accidents and coincidences. What happened to our family line was the same fate planned for Tera and Turtlepin Village. The unspeakable truth was that orders would not arrive until people

had died. Now I understood why Seger told me of all people—
damn him, he knew I couldn't let that happen.

I made a plan then and there: I was going to trick Charlie
Company into deploying. I'd confront what was "speaking" to me
in those tunnels, and I'd end this conflict for good.

My squadmates lounged in the barracks just in case. They all
had someone in the Colony they wanted to protect. To settle our
nerves, we horsed around. Our barracks—which was kept spar-
tan and immaculate most of the time—was a hub of activity that
day. Our bunks, which were folded up to be flush with the alu-
minum-colored walls, were left lowered to sit on. The metal alloy
storage trunks, which were supposed to be stashed in compartment
spaces underneath our bunks, were slid out to be makeshift tables.
On them sat half-eaten sandwiches or head-to-head hologram
games like *Cyber Solidat*. Above the temperature control dials, personal belongings spilled out from overhead bin compartments.

My squadmates had gotten used to me. Although I'd broken
protocol twice now, most forgave me with the understanding that
my actions came from a desire to complete our missions. Known
as the "psycho-who-broke-Charlie-Company's-betting-pool," I
was now one of them. And I needed their help in making my
deception succeed.

Commander Tarsus made a judgment call and went forward
with loadout preparations even without orders. He brought in new
equipment shipped from the military's research labs. Advances
had led to experimental designs; the racks held refined and lighter
dot rifles alongside more exotic fare like bladed enforcers and magnetic ordinance.

My comrades were adept at selecting gear that accentuated their
abilities. Ambrose picked out the heaviest body armors and force
amplifiers. Victoria sought out agile and rapid fire drones that
took advantage of her reaction time. Optix preferred the upgraded

night vision and infrared scopes in hopes of piercing the shadows that'd stymied us before.

As for me, I still had no idea how to take advantage of my abilities. I hadn't identified what caused them to manifest. Our abilities were conferred by injections that were still experimental and violated conventions back on Earth—laws which technically didn't apply to the Lunar Defense Forces as of yet. As such, our abilities remained a touchy subject while on base, so I couldn't ask my squadmates about it.

While I stood perusing the wares, Byron Colbee came up to me. We had met before on my trip up, and I'd served alongside him on our previous missions. He grinned and extended a hand. "Howdy." That'd got to be a first for me. I shook his hand.

Byron's face looked as if the sole purpose of his head was to form his pointed chin. His wavy, light-tobacco hair was covered by a military cap. His eyes were a friendly winter gray and could be described as—depending on one's bent—incapable of either deceit or sophistication. His cap was one size too big, and the front rim hung low over his eyes.

"You were damned gutsy taking out the Behemoth fellow," he said.

"Not sure everyone would describe it that way," I said as I scanned the equipment laid out like a banquet before us.

"I would. The LDF isn't organized enough to award medals yet, but once we are, you deserve one. I'd put in the recommendation myself."

Byron welcomed me in a way no one else had since I joined Charlie Company, and he made me feel better about the decisions I'd made. It wasn't something I was used to here or anywhere. All I could manage was, "Hey, you know what? Thanks." I gave him a second look. How someone could be so down-to-Earth after all we'd been through, I could never guess.

"Are you having trouble customizing your loadout?" he asked. "Here, let me do you a favor, considering I'd not be here right now if not for you." He flicked through the central racks and trays before walking to the edges of the room where most of the rejected tools lay. "From what I've seen, you won't benefit from standard weapons—not with your particular talents." He reached up and plucked what looked like a small medi-pack. He said, "Here you go," and tossed it my way.

I turned the small, flat container over and examined its matte black surface. It was a little bigger than my palm and had a navy blue cross plastered on the front. "A first aid kit?" I asked. When a tear in an Omnisuit often meant death, what good were aspirin?

He broke into a hearty laugh. "Are you for real? Your noggin makes for some strange ideas. Maybe that's why you make everyone nervous." He grinned to let me know it was good-natured ribbing. "No, it's not a medi-pack." He popped open the flat container, and inside, fastened side-by-side in a neat row, were three small capsules. No, they were only shaped like medicinal capsules. They were tiny syringes filled with an amber liquid. "Look familiar?"

"How could I forget?" I said. "They're like what Dr. Lunik injected me with when I first got here."

"Yep, you got it. Except these babies are temporary boosters. I would...uh...use them at your own risk. The research labs aren't known for working out the kinks ahead of time. They let us test things out for them. The others have avoided these boosters, so for all we know, you could be in a sample size of 'n' equals one."

I began to understand why Byron laughed so much; progress on the Colony was achieved through means bordering on madness. He made me feel so good I wanted to try something different this time around. If he were on my side, maybe he'd be willing to help out with my plan. "I know what you mean about nothing ever being explained," I said. "For instance, why do you think the brass hasn't ordered us to deploy?"

Byron's eyes widened for a moment. He leaned in close. "Just between us—and don't you tell nobody because I'll deny it to your face—I heard the higher-ups have their hands tied. We have to trust they're acting for the right reasons. Our duty is not to second-guess our superiors but to preserve the system."

"How do you know all of this?" I played dumb as to not arouse suspicion.

"What, don't you know? I'm Charlie Company's communications officer. I supply electronic countermeasures and secure our encrypted lines." He swelled with pride. He added in a tone as low as a whisper, "And that means I sometimes listen in on the channels between Commander Tarsus and HQ."

I couldn't believe my luck. Byron controlled the comms through which we were issued mission orders. I fished for more information. "The comms must be secured with advanced lunar tech."

"Our comms are based off of Quantcrypt technology." He was pleased someone was showing interest in his area of expertise. "It's the same encryption used in the AlloSym Firewall blocking us from contacting Earth. And it's the same tech used to prevent hackers from counterfeiting creds."

"Quantum..." In my conversations with Tera, she'd explained linked entities. "If one passkey changes, the other changes on its own?"

"You're on the right track," he said. "If an outsider intercepts a line, the passkey gets altered in response. The change itself is like a burglar alarm."

Time for my big gamble. "Oh, so you must be in charge of the master key for our comms."

"No, of course not. We can generate infinite keys to use infinite channels. For example, I'm keeping key 74-41-11 clear for

Commander Tarsus, but that key will change after mission orders arrive."

I nodded and pretended what he'd told me was over my head as I played with the capsule container in my hands. "Thanks for the hot tip on these boosters," I said, and tucked them into my gear pack.

"Hey, allies gotta watch out for each other, right?" He flashed the hand signal for departure and sauntered off.

◑ ◑

I was sitting on the benches by the olive-green gun lockers in the corner when Cyril projected himself out into hologram form. He was dressed in a sand t-shirt tucked into a belt and camo pants, similar to what we soldiers wore around the barracks. He'd become more daring, a regular presence in my life, and not concerned about the trouble it made for me whenever others were near. I wasn't sure how I felt about that, but I think I liked it.

"Just the person I was looking for," I said. "I've got a favor to ask."

He sniffed. "And what, pray tell, does my descendant think he can demand of me?"

"I need you to issue Commander Tarsus deployment orders. You can route through Byron's comms using encryption key 74-41-11. Mimic President Nest's voice as best as you can by compositing sound bites from your database."

He narrowed his eyes. "Do you have any idea what you're asking me to do? When I told you before that a soldier must make tough choices, I meant in carrying out your mission objectives. Not make up your own. You'll be endangering your comrades, and your actions will be construed as—and I'd agree—a crime worthy of a court-martial. Who taught you such blatant disregard for others?"

For a moment, I was ashamed for putting my squadmates in danger, but I fought off the feeling. "No one did, remember? This is how I've survived."

"You have no right! Your role is to uphold order, not undermine it however you see fit."

Hot blood rushed to my face—how I hated asking for favors from anyone. Relying on someone else, for me, was an exercise in disillusionment. It got to the point where I was starting to wonder if I wasn't capable of sharing my real self with others. So I never, ever asked for favors.

I wasn't willing to tell him my real reason—that I needed to keep Tera safe. My voice came out more indignant than I expected. "Can't you do this one thing for me? The one thing I've ever asked of you or of anyone in my family?" A long silence followed. Did a machine make exceptions, and were they things people expected of their loved ones?

The silence stretched out, like he was processing my statement. "All right. Fine." He sighed. "But only this once. I hope you know what you're getting into."

"It's important to me. I have to."

"That Byron fellow was right, you know," he said.

"About preserving the system regardless of what form it took?" Because I didn't agree.

"Yes, that too, but it isn't what I'm referring to. He was right about your ignorance of your own capabilities. My analysis has determined that every soldier in your squad has developed an ability—one with a single and clear focus—which they then adapt to the circumstances of the battlefield. You, meanwhile, have been thrashing about at random."

"It's been working to my advantage so far," I said.

"Maybe so, but for how long? This time, you'll be invading enemy central command, their base of operations. It's a campaign comparable to capturing a capital city. Has it sunk in yet?"

I shrugged. "No two missions are alike anyhow." I snapped open the locker in front of me to search for my dot rifle.

"The enemy has had a full ninety-six hours to reinforce their positions. If you come for them, they'll be fighting a defensive battle, and victory for them means stopping you from advancing. But for Charlie Company, victory means absorbing all the risks to capture their base. As anyone who's studied military history can tell you, the odds fall overwhelmingly in their favor."

"So what I gather from your lecture—after falling asleep in the middle and waking up to catch the tail end of it—is that you want me to identify the source of my abilities." I wondered if I irritated Cyril enough whether he'd encounter a fault segmentation and crash. No such luck. Instead, he gave me the third degree.

"You can manifest projections," he said.

"Yes. So far, these include a focused lance, a barrier wall, and an explosive sapphire," I said.

"Can you create these projections at will?"

"With more practice, probably."

"Can you form other shapes?"

"Not that I know of."

"What else can you do?"

"I can hear thoughts," I said. It was a load off to finally tell someone.

"Pardon? You read minds? Don't be ridiculous," he said.

"No, not at will...and not at far distances either. It's like tuning into a radio station."

"Do you ever intercept my thoughts?" he asked.

"No way. You're not a sentient life form." It unnerved me when he smirked at my reply.

"Can you manipulate real objects with your mind?"

"Now you're the one being ridiculous. I can only influence the projections I create."

"Are you sure certain you were given a mental enhancement?"

"No, I'm not," I said. "No one else has demonstrated a latent ability similar to mine."

"But your situation probably parallels that of your squadmates," he said. "Lieutenant Victoria Haron has refined ear musculature, but for all practical purposes, she possesses superior reflexes instead of enhanced hearing. Sergeant Hugh Ambrose has an ability—though it hasn't been confirmed in any database I've cross-referenced—that derives from increased red blood cell production or oxygen carrying capacity."

"Which, from what we can tell," I said, "makes him as sturdy as a brick wall."

"Precisely. A single point of enhancement manifests itself in different abilities—" his hologram blipped out of view. I tilted my head to see who was coming.

"You talking to yourself there, soldier?" Victoria's jaw relaxed into a smile. She popped open her locker, which was right in front of the wooden bench I was sitting on.

"Uh huh. Just trying to get a grip on how my abilities work," I said.

She removed her sidearm from its holster and placed it inside. She was wearing a body-hugging orange training suit with all the sensors, and her face was radiant from exertion. She slammed the locker with a *clang* and placed one boot up on my bench. She bent over in my face, her nose inches from mine.

"Tell you what," she said, in a mocking, sultry tone. "I can give you what you need. We're not supposed to gab on about it, but who knows if we'll be coming back from the next suicide run these paper-pushers send us on." She winked. "Plus, I figure I owe you one."

"Go on." I was doing my best to play along with whatever this was. I was confused by how she was acting, but like I'd done with Byron, I wanted to get her on my side. When it came time to face the enemy, having less resistance from my comrades could come in handy.

She straddled the bench and sat down facing me. "Our injections enhance human senses, yeah?"

"Yes, I think so too. But I don't think mine is related to sight, touch, taste, smell, or hearing."

"Fine, but there are more senses than the Big Five. Proprioception, magnetoreception, nociception—there may be twenty-one, or even thirty-three, human senses in total. You'll have to go down the list and test each one."

"That narrows it down," I grinned.

She stood up and leaned over in my face again. She was so close I could see her skin glistening with sweat. She put a finger on my nose. "You better figure it out, pronto. I'm banking on you in order to survive."

It was awkward in here. I was pretty sure she was doing this on purpose to mess with me.

We were startled by a loud *thud* on the ground behind her. I leaned my head to the side to see what was going on.

Tera was standing there. She was next to a cardboard box she'd dropped. I recognized the neon green brain-window belonging to her robot, Hex, which had spilled halfway out onto the floor. Her face was scarlet.

I hadn't spoken to her in days and hadn't told her I was deploying. For a moment, I was aware of where Victoria's body was in relation to mine and what it must've looked like. Oh no.

Tera said, "I repaired Hex...I thought you'd need—" she turned around without finishing what she was saying and ran out the door.

◐ ◑

"Wait!" I shouted from the lot behind the barracks. But her back was to me as she ran away. "Tera, hold on!" I booked it double time but wasn't gaining on her—she could run!

She headed straight for the intersection to shake me off. She must've known she was much better than I was at navigating the free-for-all of lunar traffic. But she tripped. Time slowed to a standstill when she fell headfirst into a raging river of hoverbikes.

Fear surged through me. It overpowered my internal resistance and flooded the gates. In my mind's eye, I maintained the image of a dichotomy, a contradiction—of the world I envisioned versus the way it was—which stabilized the surge and sustained its state. I closed my eyes and imagined a spongy disc.

When I opened my eyes, the projection solidified, a mound by her knees. It was intended to block her path and break her fall. It was a new creation I hadn't attempted before. That's probably why I imbued it with the wrong firmness. Because when she tripped onto the mound, it sent her up and over the intersection. I'd made things worse.

I bolted into the middle of the stream, a mad dash of hover-craft—while in my mind's eye, I cycled through the invocation as fast as I could. I projected a tube for her to fall into, and when she hit the angled pipe, she slid down into my arms. I shielded her against me while hoverbikes careened by on our right and our left.

Her eyes met mine, and she didn't understand what'd happened. In between rushed breaths, she said, "I recalibrated Hex with your most recent field data. Now it should—"

I kissed her. It was the only way I knew how to explain. Hovercraft whizzed by, but the rest of the world was unimportant.

— 26 —

THRONE ROOM

Hope that our generals were holding back a brilliant grand strategy went out the window when orders came in for a frontal assault. The orders were unaccompanied by a standard mission briefing. Unease spread through the ranks.

No one in Charlie Company suspected our orders were fake. Cyril had used Byron's encrypted comms to impersonate Paxton and issue the command. If Seger was telling the truth, waiting any longer would've put the Colony—and Tera—in mortal danger. I wasn't going to sit by and let that happen.

I'd begun to have suspicions this war was being fought to a standstill—on purpose—but I couldn't be sure. Inside the enemy's inner sanctum waited a sentient being—its imprint had been in my mind—and from the creature, I'd find out the truth.

The dropship took Charlie Company out of the dome to the enemy, and we infiltrated their tunnels at our previous withdrawal point. Ahead lay crumbled blocks of white regolith leftover from when we'd been knocked off our feet. Behind the rubble, a towering archway marked the way to the inner sanctum. When we arrived, we met with no resistance, but we expected as much this time around: the creatures didn't subscribe to the same first principles as we did about military tactics. Instead of putting major defenses at entry points, they instead favored welcoming us into rigged confrontations on their home turf.

Commander Tarsus led our formation through the giant archway. We'd now reached the coordinates we'd failed to secure the last time around. But there was no fanfare, no massive extraterrestrial operation to uncover.

Instead, we found ourselves standing at the top of a...I guess I'd call it a grand staircase. My eyes followed the "marble" steps down to the expansive room below. Intelligence reports circulated on base claimed we might encounter a hive mind, a pulsating primordial goo. In actuality, we'd discovered a polished quartz palace. And the space below looked like its throne room.

There was the dim glow from the walls we'd become accustomed to, except this time, it was tinged green. Structural columns, carved with embellishments in clean, sharp lines, sprouted from the floor and climbed past us to the unlit upper half and presumably held up the ceiling. The sparse, Roman-like architecture was like a love letter to utilitarianism.

Ambrose, Victoria, and my squadmates fanned out and gazed around in wonder. Some stood at alert with their dot rifles while other soldiers took the opportunity to calibrate their sensors.

Commander Tarsus dropped to one knee in his Omnisuit and placed an alabaster glove to the side of his helm. It was a position he took when he wanted us to hold a defensive formation while he communicated with HQ.

Paxton appeared on the HUDs inside our helmets. Below his thinning white hair, beads of sweat caked the worry lines across his brow. He narrowed his eyes like shards of blue ice. "Who gave Charlie Company authorization to deploy?"

"Sir, we received the orders directly from you."

"I issued no such command." Paxton was holding back a grimace, and there was spittle at his mouth. "When I find out who's behind this, I'll have their head."

My squadmates exchanged looks with each other through

translucent faceplates. I pretended to be as confused as everyone else, but I wasn't. Cyril had faked our deployment orders.

"Shall we abort mission, sir? We've already compromised our position."

There was an inscrutable expression on Paxton's face. "No, you're only one day ahead of schedule after all. The Colony has been put on high alert. Proceed with your mission." The video feed blipped out.

Commander Tarsus returned to his feet. He flashed a hand signal for us to head down. The grand staircase glimmered like it was cut from the finest white Calacatta marble. It'd been built wide enough for the ten of us to fan out across its steps. And so with dot rifles primed, we descended in unison.

On the way down, I could make out more of what awaited us below. The chamber was the size of a stately ballroom. At the center was the most prominent feature of the space: an imposing vertical column. The central column, as thick as six of us standing side-by-side, reminded me of an obelisk. It was four-sided and carved from a smooth, white stone like quartz or granite and extended ten stories up into the darkness—too high for us to even see the end of it. I squinted, and in the distance, I could make out a shimmering gold line running along the ground.

I was on to their tricks, so I searched for an exit. There was another archway at the far end of the room.

When we reached the bottom of the staircase, I could see more of the chamber in detail. It was breathtaking. It was magnificent. Its surfaces shone like glass but were composed of—according to the density reports scrolling across my faceplate—a much sturdier material. Its floor panels were cut into oversized hexagons, each big enough for many of us to stand in, and exhibited a calming, perfect symmetry. The panels were only interrupted by the shimmering gold line I'd spotted from above—up close, it was a decorative stream. It was like liquid gold and resembled the amber resin Tera used in her experiments. It ran across the entire length of the chamber and was like a flowing river that split the room in half.

I turned my attention back to Commander Tarsus. He waved us forward to the obelisk at the center. It appeared to be a square pyramid, tapering as it rose. The other soldiers and I clustered near its base. We were left speechless at the opulence before us.

Byron raised his left arm like he was reading the time and fiddled with his wristcom. He began to tap random buttons like he was testing them out. "Commander, bad news," he said. "I've lost our connection to HQ."

We checked our own comms. "Same here," Ambrose confirmed. We all had. We spread out to try opening up other burst frequencies. Since the other LDF squadrons never received Cyril's falsified orders, they all remained on standby inside the dome—which is where I wanted them in case the creatures invaded the Colony as Seger had said they would. However, if we met resistance here, or if the LDF needed reinforcements, we'd still need to call out. Not good.

Byron, who'd wandered to the opposite corner from me, spoke into our helmets. "Uh, fellas?" We all turned in his direction.

"I can't move," he said into comms. "What I mean is, I can't lift my legs." He struggled at the effort and tripped, boots still planted, and caught himself on his hands and knees.

◐ ◑

Byron was stuck. There was something odd about those floor panels. I swore I'd seen them glow.

My squadmates and I turned back when the immense obelisk in front of us began to tremble. The room hummed as the column began to retract into the ground. When it was almost at ground-level, it stopped. The structure hadn't been a support beam after all. It was flat at the top and contained smaller raised levels moving inward—like the steps leading up to a dais.

A large, gaping hole opened in the dais. A cube as large as a shipping crate and adorned with carvings in platinum and gold pushed its way up through the opening until it emerged in full. The cube's four walls splayed open, like doors falling away, to reveal a present inside.

There, in the middle of our squad, *it* stood upright. The enemy creature was clad in black chitinous armor personalized with gray splotch patterns. It was a bipedal monstrosity almost twice as tall as a human adult. Though it was built more compact than the Behemoth was, it had a similar face: flattened features resembling a bull elephant's. The enemy creature stood in an arched stance, a wiry boxer in sparring form, and extending from its hands were venomous spurs like glowing daggers of light. There was something about them—their fluid edges reminded me of the projections I created with my own abilities.

Chaos.

The creature leapt off the pedestal and charged Ambrose in a whirlwind bum-rush. Our other squadmates stood frozen in time. They squirmed and couldn't train their dot rifles on the target. Again I swore a faint glow came from the floor panels beneath their feet.

He didn't flinch and drew his close combat weapons. He activated full systems to his power armor and swung a reinforced stun blade. The creature parried the blow with its orb daggers, shifted stance, and in one clean burst of movement, shoulder checked him. The stun blade flew out of his hands, and he went sailing backward across low-grav. The creature crouched down before sprinting after its prey.

Victoria was a little luckier than the others—she was already facing the creature when the ambush began. To stop it from finishing him off, she fired several plasma bolts at its sternum. Without a hint it was aware of the danger, it separated into multiple shadow trails of itself and avoided the projectile beams. This creature was different from the ones we'd met before.

But she was unfazed by its invulnerability. She lobbed a localized mine in its direction. When the mine bounced into range, she triggered the detonator. The mine planted itself into the floor and exploded at the creature's feet—a direct hit. The impact separated it from Ambrose, and the creature flew to the opposite wall.

But it planted its feet against the wall and rebounded in a spiral, using its angular momentum to hurl three projectiles—black orbs throbbing with bluish-purple energy. That was new, too. Even with plenty of time for Victoria's abilities to kick in, she didn't dodge the volley. The orbs struck her suit in a burst of fireworks. She cried out on comms and fell onto her hands and knees in the same strange way Byron had.

That was when a vile feeling crept into my consciousness. It originated from a source so foreign to me I could barely divine its meaning. It coalesced: *Floor. Bonds. Lock.* I connected the dots. My squadmates hadn't turned to help because they couldn't. They were locked in place.

But I'd been waiting for a trap from the beginning. Something designed to take us out all at once. So I'd been on the move, running from one hexagonal floor panel to another. When a glimmer appeared beneath my feet. I boosted my gravity boots, jumped, and diverted max power to my suit's scanners. There were field lines—ever so faint—on my HUD. They were labeled as "van der Waals."

I landed on the dais from which the creature had emerged moments before. It was a gamble that this surface wasn't rigged up.

I trained my scanners on Byron and my squadmates next. My Omnisuit detected a multitude of intermolecular forces, swirling field lines that appeared to bond on and off. They originated from the floor panels and were attracted to our dot rifles and other weapons.

An overwhelming will of...contempt...invaded my mind. I searched for the source and found the creature hunched over Victoria's downed suit. I shut my eyes and formed an explosive sapphire projection like the ones I'd used to slaughter the Behemoth and its soldiers. My sapphire glided in a sloping descent from the dais. It flipped facet-to-facet on a path to the creature's exposed neck.

The creature cocked its head to the side. My attacked missed and exploded far off in the recesses of the chamber. The creature turned its head to glower at me. There was no way it could've seen my attack coming. Had it gotten lucky? It wheeled away from her body, creating shadow trails in its wake, and charged in my direction.

I projected out lances to lengthen backward past my elbows. My arms were folded to my sides so my suit could obscure the weapons from the front. When the creature leapt up to the dais and into range, I swung both lances out of hiding to pierce it through in a crosscut.

But when the enemy soldier landed on the dais unharmed, time stood still as we squared off. Above wrinkled lines—where its nose would be if it had one—were eyes like glowing coals of amber sunken into an obsidian mass. The expression on its face registered what I assumed was surprise.

I was also confused about why it wasn't impaled, and glanced down. Orb daggers emanated from its fists and held my two lances at bay. It had blocked my projections with projections of its own.

We pushed daggers and lances against each other. The creature's body was a slab of igneous rock blocking my view. I strained with everything I had to keep it away from the others. Yet, no matter how much I tried to surge forward, I was falling back. In a few moments, the creature would overpower me.

And when it was over—when I couldn't take any more—it pulled away its daggers. It stepped back on the dais to size me up from a safe distance.

Cyril took this chance to shout into my helm, "Withdraw!"

"What? Why would I?"

"The enemy was expecting you," he said. "Your entire squad is out of commission, and the ace up your sleeve didn't work."

"Whose side are you on again?"

The extraterrestrial was studying me and probing with its eyes as it paced back and forth.

"I've survived close-quarters combat countless times," Cyril said. "You'll die if you stay and die for naught."

"I'm not going to abandon them for this beast to finish—"

A bellow, like a powerful blast of air, startled me. "Beast?" It had come from the creature.

It spoke our language—no, it sounded like a synthesizer device used in translation. But the creature had no mouth, nor could I see any vocal cords moving. It was relaying speech into my mind. When it spoke again, its voice came forth like hollow chimes on the wind: "The sole savages on this land are human."

I expected first contact to be variations of "Greetings" or "Take me to your leader." Who could've imagined instead that the annals would record an insult?

— 27 —

DO ALIENS BLUFF?

"Surrender is your only logical choice," it said. Its voice echoed in my mind, and in those ripples trailed its name: Aycel. Aycel was the sentient life form I'd been looking for all this time.

My squadmates were still locked to the hexagonal floor panels and braced themselves against the binding pull with their gauntlets. It was as if they were fighting intense gravity. I shifted my attention back to Aycel. "You want me to give up without a fight? That *is* logical. For you."

"Ignorant being. While we tarry here, my brethren surround your human settlement. One hundred battalions. One hundred separate entry points into your city. Our deep simulations have shown us your kind does not possess the numbers to ward off our assault. You cannot defend your barrier's many weaknesses."

The enemy fielded one hundred battalions? If they had that many soldiers, then they were much more coordinated than our intelligence reports speculated. No, Aycel was bluffing—did aliens bluff? Regardless, its assessment of the Colony's capabilities was accurate and more than posturing.

"If you do not capitulate," Aycel said, "a single command is all I require. A single command and your settlement will be ground into dust. What happens when your dome stays fractured beyond its window of restoration?"

There was a terrible sinking sensation in my stomach. My opponent wasn't bluffing. It understood how to destroy the Colony. I needed to reconsider. I glanced sidelong at my comrades left in disarray. "If I submit to you, we've no guarantee you won't kill us and attack the Colony afterwards."

Aycel widened its eyes, like fires of amber had been lit inside its face. "You try my—how does your kind say—good graces. While it is true our civilization does not define concepts for honor or... keeping one's word, do not ask for more than you are owed. For if I so desired, I could exterminate you on a whim, and you would have no say in the matter."

"But why destroy us?" I asked. "Why would a superior civilization slaughter innocents?"

The creature acted as if it were attempting to understand a lower life form. "You were the only warrior who withstood my attacks, so I granted you an audience. It is evident I expected too much. Do you believe your cause to be righteous? For a third time, you trespass upon our lands under a banner of aggression. Yet your kind glorifies itself as just. Such are the limits of your so-called civilization."

I looked over at my squadmates. Their lips were moving behind their faceplates, but no audio filtered through my helmet. Our comms must've been jammed. I turned back to Aycel. "You're twisting the truth. You massacred the people of Amiden Village without provocation, an act which brought us here in the first place. Now you're threatening to wipe us out."

"Perhaps reasoning with unintelligent life was a doomed endeavor from the start. What you describe occurred after your kind poured noxious chemicals into our burrows. It drove my brethren mad, and they swarmed, as would you if someone set you on fire. The mutations awoke my intelligence and cursed me, separated me from my brethren. But the gift also gave me insight into your kind's proliferation. After you exhausted your home-world and heralded its sixth extinction level event, you settled on the lunar surface to repeat your destructive life cycle."

Cyril interrupted to shout into my comms again. "Withdraw! The enemy understands you far better—you will lose."

The creature shifted to an aggressive posture. It hunched into a coiled position, and its back bulged above the level of its head. Its legs were braced to pounce, and white orb daggers flared from its fists. "If you are not stopped," it said, "what horror will be unleashed on the rest of the cosmos? You must be eradicated by force because force is the only language homo sapiens accept as legitimate."

I readied my own projections and entered a defensive stance.

The chamber's ambient lighting shut off and plunged us into darkness. From my previous missions, I concluded the extraterrestrials were nocturnal creatures and had every advantage in dim visibility. The only light that remained came from the hexagonal panels lit where my squadmates were stuck. Their staggered positions were like white squares on a chessboard.

"Surrender," Aycel repeated before it reappeared in the light next to Victoria. "Or I will extinguish your brethren in front of you. One by one." It used the cover of darkness to travel like it was teleporting. It vanished and reappeared beside Commander Tarsus multiple panels away. Aycel dangled an orb dagger over his head before folding into the darkness again. "Surrender," it said into my mind, "and your settlement will be spared. Do you accept the terms of our treaty?"

How favorable was a treaty built upon unequivocal submission? If Aycel reneged on its promise at any point in the future, Tera would always be in danger. I imagined what it was like to lose her and the future she represented. I couldn't accept those terms.

"No," I said, "A treaty should—" *Something's here.* Aycel slammed into me, and I went tumbling across the platform. My mind raced for a strategy. The Colony would be lost if I didn't stop him now. There was no question: I had to defeat Aycel no matter what.

"For too long, humans have profaned the laws of nature," Aycel's words echoed in my head while he remained unseen. "They are complacent, unintelligent, and reproduce unchecked. We will cull your herd and improve your species. Efficiency will be imposed."

I swung lances out into darkness and hit nothing. My Omnisuit's night vision and infrared sensors failed to activate. They'd been jammed along with our comms, which meant Aycel had cracked our encryption routines—but our technology should've been as alien to them as theirs was to us.

I took heaving breaths and scanned in every direction. The worst part was I couldn't refute the alien's arguments. Had I not wanted to leave Earth in hopes of something better? Did I not agree our civilization needed a new paradigm?

A direct video commlink opened inside my helmet's display. Byron said the comms were jammed, so who'd gotten through? On my screen appeared the Colony President, Richard Paxton Nest, of all people. Agitated, he wiped beads of sweat from his forehead with a handkerchief and often diverted his eyes off-camera.

"Private Armacite, abort mission," he said. "You are to return to base immediately."

"Sir, Charlie Company has been captured," I scanned the darkness for the creature. I was afraid it would re-emerge at any moment.

"This is a direct order from your commander-in-chief. The Colony is under siege. You are needed back home."

I hesitated—were Tera and the children in danger?

"Soldier," he said, "live to fight another day. When the nations of Earth learn about the extraterrestrial threat from you firsthand, they'll rally to our aid. You'll be immortalized when humanity stands united for the first time in history."

I turned to my comrades and behind their faceplates were

expressions of desperation. A maelstrom of their inner thoughts overwhelmed me: the abandonment of their previous lives, their work toward the normalcy they'd not found on Earth, and the regret of dreams dying with them unfulfilled. There was no way I was leaving them. "Their last moments won't be spent forgotten. Armacite out," and I closed the commlink feed. The annals of history could shove it.

He overrode my command and reappeared back on my visor display. His face was a red swath of rage. "If you defy me, I will see to it that you're court-martialed. You'll return to a life of nothing!"

Return to nothing? I was already nothing. I disabled my suit's comm modules. My ancestor, Cyril, however, couldn't be shut off. "What're you doing?" he asked.

"I underestimated alien intelligence," I said. I dropped down from the dais, activated my gravity boots, and boosted toward the hexagonal panel that held Commander Tarsus. "Time to call its bluff."

I risked a couple of guesses: One, a floor panel couldn't grab me without releasing its current captive, and two, as long as I didn't stay in one spot for too long, the mechanism couldn't lock me down.

In the final moves of a chess match, it was common to protect the king. I stood next to Commander Tarsus at the ready. Aycel's voice rippled through my consciousness, "You reject a peace treaty for battle instead? Human irrationality at its finest." I searched the darkness but couldn't see where Aycel was.

Then, surprise and fear filtered into my mind from Byron's thoughts. He must've seen the enemy. I boosted to the panel where Byron was kneeling. Aycel's orb daggers appeared above Byron's head and clashed against my lance projections. The rest of the creature's body materialized into view in the glow of the floor panel. Stymied, it folded back into darkness. Why was the creature holding back? Was it toying with me?

I sensed a focused attention from Victoria next, so I boosted to her panel. The creature appeared a few steps from her light radius and fired three spherical orbs from its sides. I constructed a diamond-shaped plate in front of her and me, and when the plate absorbed the blast, intense heat radiated through the lining of my suit. Aycel dissolved into the surroundings unseen again.

The creature proceeded to wear me out. I became frantic and reacted to its attacks barely in time to protect my squadmates. In my mind was a vision of Turtlepin Village on fire while we were detained here.

I moved to defend Ambrose next. I was taking heaving breaths inside my suit. He still couldn't stand but managed to nod at me. His stoic calm helped me gather my resolve. If nature had only blessed me with a level head like his.

But I was never on the straight and narrow. In my life back on Earth, all signs pointed to the fact that I'd never get ahead going along with the system. It hadn't been built for the likes of me. The workings of that system were on display; one that sent troops to fail; one whose agenda was advanced by continued war; one that could ignore the fact that the enemy was an intelligent life form. Even up here, I was a pawn trapped in someone else's game.

No, when everything else maintained the system, the only choice was to do what everyone else wouldn't. And that's when I remembered I still had one last resort.

I detached the magnetic straps of my gear pack and tore it off my back. I dug through it for the matte black container with the blue medical symbol on it. Hexbot rolled out and startled me—I forgot I'd packed the little bugger in there. Hex activated, its eyes flashing neon green, and scampered off to hide behind Ambrose.

There, found it. I popped open the flat container, and inside were three capsule injectors. They were filled with an amber liquid and lined up in a row.

The creature appeared above me and dropped down for a strike. I swung with wild strokes to knock Aycel away. No! I needed more time.

A warning was printed above the capsule injectors: "ONE DOSE PER USE." All well and good, if there were a tomorrow. I snatched two of the syringes, opened the programmable medication module on my chestplate, and plunged them into the nodes. The Omnisuit's vital systems delivered the compound into my bloodstream.

There was a heavy compression in my sternum. I couldn't breathe. I clutched at my heart and gasped.

A thought from Byron intruded into my mind. *"It's here!"* Aycel was targeting Byron again, but I was reeling from pain. I got to my feet and began to stagger toward him.

Aycel appeared in the light of Byron's floor panel. No, I wasn't going to make it in time. But my chest pains subsided—like a bear trap sprung open—and release spread outward from my center. An eerie sensation crept up on me, as if many isolated masses were merging into a whole. The sensations traveled down my neck and upward from my knees, until the surges linked up at my spine.

A jumble of stimuli arrived all at once. My squadmates' thoughts and unfamiliar cognitive patterns from Aycel threatened to drown out my own consciousness. It took everything in my power to suppress them so my inner voice could re-emerge. I reclaimed a shred of sanity which I clung to for dear life.

Images crossed my mind, of chasing Tera into hoverbike traffic and how I'd created a gel-like projection to break her fall. And then clarity: my projections weren't limited to hardened light. They could be molded to other forms.

The surge flooded my mind. I held an image of opposites to maintain state. I imagined a hollow containment bubble and imbued its surface with a rubbery texture. When I opened my eyes, the projection solidified into reality. I dropped the containment bubble onto Byron, and a shield barrier formed around his body.

Aycel lengthened the orb dagger emanating from its fist into the shape of a spear. The creature swung the weapon back for a killing blow. The thrust deflected off the barrier's surface. The bubble containing Byron was pushed away and lifted him free from the floor's restraints.

It was like I'd tapped into a new supply of energy. I created containment bubbles for Commander Tarsus, Ambrose, Victoria, and the rest of Charlie Company. My projections enveloped them and must've interfered with the traps because they were pushed clean off their floor panels. They were freed. They got back on their feet and primed their dot rifles.

Aycel spoke directly into mind. "Who plundered our gifts and gave them to you?" The creature charged straight at me next. The creature weaved in and out of the darkness with such speed it appeared to come at me from all sides. In desperation, I churned through—formed and broke—many lances to parry the enemy's orb daggers.

The containment barriers I'd placed around my comrades faded in and out. My creations must've been linked because I could pinpoint each person's location in my mind even while I kept Aycel at bay.

Wait! That was it—the key to the enemy's advantage. I solidified a smaller containment bubble—the size of a weapon's crate—high overhead, hidden and out of reach.

Aycel feinted in for another attack, but this time when I parried its blows, I dropped the containment bubble to encase its head.

And then there was light. Its armored body began to glow with fluorescence. It was a dark teal like that of a dragonfly. So that's why the creatures lived underground and were nocturnal.

Now that it couldn't hide in darkness or confuse me with shadow copies, the enemy's movements became plain and easy to follow.

Aycel attacked with renewed vigor. It was still in control of the chamber and manipulated the hexagonal floor panels to slide over each other like tectonic plates. Sometimes, they punched upward like a piston and knocked me off my feet. Weapon mounts concealed in the chamber's vertical columns slid open to fire orbs I managed to roll out of the way of. The creature unloaded every trick in its arsenal, which was a sign to me that it was getting worried. But what still puzzled me was it held back on its direct attacks.

I couldn't fend off the creature while sustaining projection bubbles around my allies. I was strained to my limit. The shield barriers flickered until I released the creations. My remaining reserves were spent to maintain the shield bubble around Aycel's head so that its body would keep emitting a dark teal fluorescence It wasn't fond of being a glow stick. The creature's attacks became more wild and erratic.

Charlie Company was back in action. They shuffled in formation and were changing positions to avoid being locked onto again. Victoria unleashed a missile drone and fired her entire payload. She knocked Aycel across the chamber. To our utter disbelief that any living thing could survive that much ordinance, the creature returned to its feet.

Ambrose joined next. He slammed into the creature with his body, a brutal attack amplified by his power armor loadout. The creature faltered, fell back even, but managed to recover.

I was breathing hard and was spent, and the creature was coming for me and me alone. But moments before reaching me, Aycel pivoted, and without explanation, charged for Byron, who wasn't even posing a threat. The creature stabbed Byron through the shoulder. He groaned in agony and fell into a heap. Byron, the only person who'd welcomed me—was he gone, just like that? When the others hurried to his aid, they were knocked over by floor panels that slammed together or pumped upward.

Aycel turned its attention back toward me. It was a locomotive, and nothing would slow its rampage. When it was almost upon me, Commander Tarsus burst forward in between us. He spread his arms apart, palms flat, and grabbed the articulated joints where the creature's arms bent. The chamber lit up with electricity. The power was coming from Commander Tarsus. It channeled through his cells and his Omnisuit to fry the creature alive.

Aycel emitted a harrowing psychic scream. It rattled me to the bone. The creature spun with one fist extended and batted the commander away. My squadmates were no longer blocking its way. It stepped toward me, smoke billowing from its singed body.

I was crouched down and huffed in deep breaths. I attempted to create one last projection with all I had. The circuit didn't activate, and instead came a sharp pain in my chest. It was like a vise tightening around my insides. I grabbed my shoulders in agony. An alarm from my suit's vital systems went off: my heart was giving out.

My Omnisuit detected an irregular heartbeat and delivered a corrective electrical pulse. The defibrillation stabilized me and prevented full-on heart failure.

Aycel stood over me. Its armor misted with smoke and ash. It extended an orb dagger from its fist to finish me off. My final thoughts were of Tera and regret at not giving her what she'd wanted.

Hex activated. Its steel arms and legs extended from its main body and latched onto the creature from behind. The bot was like an iron cross and bound the creature's arms and legs. The creature fought to break from the bear hug.

My ancestor Cyril chose then to appear in full hologram form. He was clad in a power suit from a bygone era. It was the first time he'd shown himself to others, and his appearance startled my squadmates.

He tilted his head back at me. "I wish we had more time together." He executed a program to detach my wristcom from my arm. The gadget hinged in half like an open shackle. Using what I could only assume was a subroutine to magnetize circuitry, the wristcom flew toward Hex and snapped around its steel ropes. Aycel clawed at its restraints, but Hex's iron cross held fast.

Cyril said, "Don't carry out our past anymore. Live your own life." The wristcom glowed orange with heat. It detonated. My squadmates and I shielded our eyes from the blast. The chamber rained fragments of circuit board, titanium, and extraterrestrial carapace. Our nightmare was over.

We lowered our gauntleted arms from faceplates plastered with dust and soot. When the smoke cleared, Aycel—or what was left of him—stood over me. The creature had become a demonic horror of fused metal and igneous rock. It leaned back and sent an ungodly roar into my mind.

No, it couldn't be—the creature was still alive.

With all I had, I imagined a projection at the ceiling stories above us. The creation solidified into what resembled an oversized caduceus. I had no willpower left to exert control, so I let it enter free fall. Aycel lashed an orb-dagger to its fist. The weapon was unraveling into wispy, flail-like tendrils. The creature reached its dagger back to finish me off. But my caduceus came down and plunged the creature through from head to ground.

Aycel was no more.

Crackles filtered into my helmet. Our commlinks were working again. Byron patched in first. He struggled to speak through his injuries. "Darin, you did it, mate," he said, swallowing air between each word. "Please don't think ill of me. I'm not a traitor."

His words didn't make sense to me.

"I was following orders," he said. "It was in duty to my country. In another life, we could've been friends once the war was over."

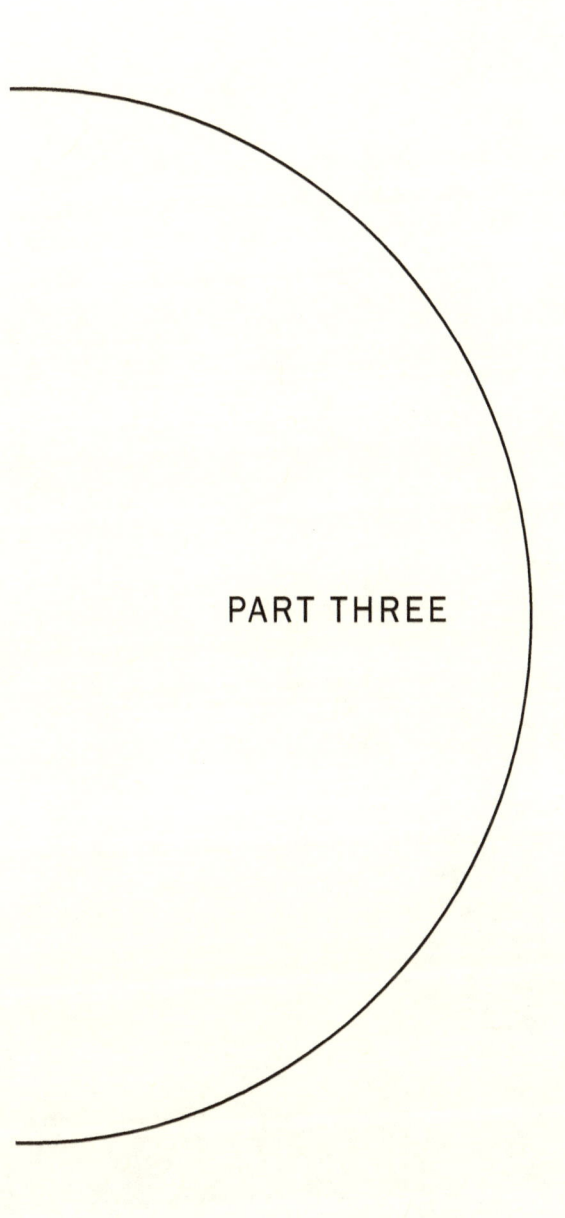

PART THREE

— 28 —

THE TAPES

I stared into familiar white lights. *Beep*. That sound again. *Beep*. Oh yes, it was my heart monitor. *Beep*. I lay in a hospital bed once more. Bits and pieces filtered in from a television holoscreen: *number of casualties...live at the protest...treason*. Faint, indiscernible jumbles.

I jolted up and inhaled a rush of air. I was dragged back into the present and alive for one more day. For a moment, I wasn't sure if I was grateful or disappointed. Someone else was in the room with me. Was it Tera?

My eyes adjusted to the overhead fill lights of the hospital room. Two green armchairs sat against the opposite wall in front of me, and a holoscreen floated in the corner. The air was as flat and stale as the sterile tiles. To the right of my bed was a window facing the simulated sky outside, and to my left was a tall figure. Sergeant Hugh Ambrose stood there in silence, neither shocked by my awakening nor overjoyed at the occasion.

"Welcome back to the land of the living, soldier," he said. He rested his right hand on my bed's polished sidebar. "The doctors doubted the outcome, but I was sure it'd take more than that to stop you. You know, maximum dosage warnings exist for a reason." He was referring to those capsules I shot into my bloodstream. He readjusted his grip on the camo-green patrol cap in his left hand. "How are you holding up?"

I was doped up on painkillers, and my head was a roaring mess.

"Depends on how you answer next." I reached for the bed controls and clicked myself into a seated position. "Is it over?"

He stared at me for the longest time, as if he were deciding what to say. "Yes, the war is over. Charlie Company defeated the enemy general while our defenses at home held off an assault—a miracle, truly. We did it, buddy."

A torrent of relief spread from my head to my numb body. The dull, gray sheen of my room's walls took on hues of blue. The day which I'd toiled and sacrificed for had arrived. The war was over.

But he wasn't finished. "No matter what anyone else says—don't forget, no matter what—remember Charlie Company and I acknowledge your valor. I don't believe we'd still be here if you'd left us behind enemy lines."

Memories from my battle with Aycel flashed through my mind. Cyril. Hex. I asked, "What about my equipment?" I was still holding out hope. "I mean, my wristcom and my bot."

He raised an eyebrow like I'd gotten a few screws knocked loose. Of course he couldn't understand why they were so valuable to me. He said, "They were destroyed in the explosion when you killed the enemy. The creature didn't expect your machines to take initiative. It was clever of you to rig those up as a last resort."

He didn't know I did no such thing. Cyril and Hex sacrificed themselves to save me. My voice came out weaker than I expected. "What about Byron?"

He cleared his throat. "Byron Colbee was killed in action."

I sat there in a daze. All of them, gone. It couldn't be.

Ambrose gave me a moment to let it all sink in. "Listen, you ought to know something about Byron. Do you remember how our comm lines, night vision, and infrared equipment were jammed for the entire fight?"

I did. The blackout prevented us from calling for reinforcements or knowing about the Colony's status during the extraterrestrial assault.

"We ran a post-op analysis. Our encryption protocols weren't compromised by the enemy."

I took a labored breath and managed, "What are you getting at?"

"Byron was behind it. We discovered custom scripts responsible for it on his wristcom when we used it to call HQ for retrieval. As soon as we got back to base, a crew of operatives—spooks in black suits I've never met before—were already waiting to confiscate his gear. Just his." I could see Ambrose's knuckles whiten around the cap in his hand. "Though we can't say so publicly, a few of us believe he sabotaged our mission on someone else's orders."

"What?" No way. Byron wouldn't betray us.

"Just between me and you, I don't think we were meant to return alive."

I tried to come to grips with it but couldn't. "It must be a misunderstanding. Byron was our comrade—I wouldn't have defeated Aycel without his advice. What could've been gained from our deaths?"

Ambrose threaded his cap through his fingers. He was stalling. Finally, he said, "There's something you ought to know. And there's no easy way to tell you, so here goes." He moved the holoscreen from the corner to float in front of my bed. He turned the volume up.

I was watching a broadcast from Lunar Channel One. A red "Live" text blinked on screen. The camera drone was fixed on a mob picketing in front of a nondescript building. The protestors waved makeshift signs and jostled against the police cordon holding them back.

He said, "The building they're protesting in front of...well, it's the one you're in."

◑ ◐

"What are they up in arms about?" I asked. "The war is over. They should be celebrating, not protesting."

Ambrose didn't reply right away, like he was coming up with how to answer. "Our other forces at home held off the enemy battalions, but many civilians still perished. Charlie Company—we're the Colony's lead squadron, but we weren't there." He pointed the remote at the holoscreen and changed the channel. "They've been playing this footage everywhere for the last twenty-four hours."

The holoscreen was showing a playback from my battle with Aycel. The recording showed me in a rage with lances drawn—a supposed military secret on display. Next, I was shown slamming my projections against the walls and endangering my crew. Then, I was using my abilities to release sapphire projections in terrifying explosions of light. Juxtaposing these cherry-picked events painted me as violent and unstable. This wasn't good.

Wait just a minute. Some of these events didn't take place during our most recent battle. Snippets were spliced together from our first recon mission and our second battle with the Behemoth. The recordings left out our extraterrestrial adversaries as well as the part where I shielded my comrades from Aycel's lethal blows. Our victory wasn't mentioned in the slightest.

"Where did the media get this footage?" I asked.

"We don't know. Maybe those spooks leaked it. They could've stolen the feeds collected by our Omnisuits."

On the holoscreen, the footage cut to the part during our battle when the president hailed me on comms. Paxton's voice crackled through: "Private Armacite, abort mission and return to defend the Colony. Relay my orders to the reinforcement squads as well. Our people are in desperate need of your protection." The footage then cut to me switching off the commlink and ignoring his order.

I clenched my teeth. "He did *not* say that." Well, not exactly. He had ordered me to withdraw, but the way he said it was fabricated. "Our comms were jammed. We couldn't contact the other squads the whole time. You know that."

Ambrose gave me a knowing look and nodded. He cleared his throat. "The protesters demand blood for all who died in the attack. They blame you. Some are afraid of you and are questioning whether your unnatural abilities prove you were in collusion with enemy forces."

"What? That's ridiculous," I said.

"It gets worse," he said. The heart monitor beeped. "Charlie Company has been suspended and banned from speaking about this incident to anyone until the matter is resolved."

My throat was dry. "What matter?" I let out in a whisper. "We won, didn't we?"

Lines appeared across his forehead, and his blue eyes were tired. "Darin, I wanted you to hear it from me first. You've been court-martialed for treason. The punishment carries the death penalty. I'm sorry."

◑ ◑

After Ambrose left, I spent the next day in my hospital bed, flipping through local channels. They were airing segments with titles like, *Transplants: Former Criminals, Human or Monster?*, and my personal favorite, *One of Us—a Traitor from Earth*. They obliterated what little good will I'd earned since arriving.

Every segment was followed by footage of protestors calling for me to be sentenced. They said I'd abandoned the Colony in its time of need. I was a sociopathic self-preservationist. I wasn't a native and therefore wasn't loyal. The narrative was clear: the lunar authority would have to lock me up or else people would lose faith in the system.

I'd discovered a fate worse than being a nameless cog in a machine—I was now reviled by the public. Instead of being valued only if I produced, society now wanted me dead.

The Military Police posted outside my hospital room opened the door to admit a new visitor. My hopes rose. They fell when I met eyes with Seger. He was the one in charge of blasting footage of my "treason" to every household in the Colony. I narrowed my eyes. "You sold me out."

He lifted his arms to his side like it was no big deal. He flashed an oily smile. "You're implying there's a universal standard for right and wrong. But we're all creatures of self-interest, no? Finding the best strategy for playing the game. Why dress it up with lofty justifications? There are no God-given truths—the discovery of extraterrestrial life has disabused all notions that we're the chosen."

If I had the energy, I would've given him my opinion on humanity. "Why'd you come here? To gloat?"

He switched off the holoscreen display. "Of course not. That's not my style. It wasn't my idea to throw you under hovercraft traffic."

"But you did anyway."

"Come now, I wouldn't put it that way," he said. "Lunar Channel One received a lucrative contract from a few anonymous sponsors. I provided them a service in return. This give-and-take is why my network has become the largest media conglomerate on the Colony, and effectively, in all of human space. All actions are, in practicality, a means to an end. You'd fit in better if you'd learn to play ball."

I sensed the onset of one of my moods. Dark intent was churning at the base of my skull.

"Relax," he said. "Don't waste your talents on the likes of me. I didn't come here to lecture you. You put my enterprise on the map. I came to pay my respects."

"Before using me to advance your agenda? How generous of you." My heart monitor beeped.

"It's not always so black and white." He was examining the copper buttons on his coat. "Can I tell you how I got started?" He didn't wait for my answer. "Twenty four years ago, Moon Base Zero began crafting its experimental military squads. I was the sole reporter for my outfit, a one-man operation. I went to investigate the unexpected destruction of a village—yes, the same village the Armacite family called home."

He had my undivided attention now.

He turned to look out the window on my right and then glanced back at me sidelong. "Though quakes were common, an unprecedented quake leveled the town. I worked day and night to uncover the cause. Recently, you've witnessed a similar occurrence. Did you figure it out? The quake was triggered by phase fracturing with the compound Agent M. We were using it to search for more amber resin deposits."

It was like a stab to my heart. Memories played through my mind of the day I stumbled upon the ruins of my ancestral home. The day I activated the Simulacrum and came to know Cyril.

"But I also uncovered signs of forced entry into the dome," he said. "A gash as wide as three men. The devastation was just like the recent massacre of Amiden Village. People hadn't died from buildings collapsing—they'd been murdered. I know. I was there."

When I first activated Cyril, he swore my family's deaths were premeditated. I asked, "And what did you find out?"

"When I dug deeper into classified government files—a journalist is only as good as his sources, after all—I learned the truth. Agent M seeped into the crust and enraged an extraterrestrial settlement. The creatures emerged to attack the Colony. Your family was killed, as was everyone else in their village."

The wound in my heart ached. Cyril's motive for revenge had derived from incomplete data. My family was killed both to squelch dissent and to cover up extraterrestrial fallout. This was what led to my life and led me here.

Seger gazed out the window at the simulated afternoon sky. It was an azure horizon littered with storm clouds. "Imagine the biggest scoop of my career. I had earned the right to call myself a bona fide investigative journalist. But do you know what happened when the administration found out I was planning to air the truth?"

"Were they going to assassinate you and make it look like a suicide as a warning to everyone else?"

"No, in the modern era, you don't need to kill journalists to get what you want. Just wipe out their funding—it's impossible to run a legitimate agency without credits. They threatened me with financial ruin unless I ran a fake lead—an unavoidable moon-quake, a natural disaster."

Although he liked to give the impression everything was business and nothing personal, I didn't think he had ever let this go. "And so now," I said, "you watch out for Number One." My heart monitor beeped.

He went cold and straightened up like a concrete wall again. He said, "I was taught a lesson someone as young and naive as you has yet to learn. Without power, you don't have a voice."

"And so if you do what Paxton wants, how many more will die? They'll find an excuse to do it again. Who profits from children's deaths?" My hatred and resentment bubbled to the surface, and no amount of painkillers could dull it.

"Hold on just a minute—this war was your guys' idea. Not mine. It's not my job to be an active participant. I'm here to give people what they want to see."

"Did you come all this way to wash the blood off your hands?" I asked. "Your ill-gotten gains can't buy you enough indulgences."

I wanted to get out of bed and throttle him there in his pea coat and loafers.

He took a step back and chuckled. "There's the person I came here for. I didn't want you throwing in the towel. After all, I can't have my star exiting stage left so soon."

I was angry at him for being like the people I'd known back on Earth. I was angry with myself for admitting what he said contained a kernel of truth: those without power had no voice.

I slept through the rest of the day. The next morning, there was another knock at my door.

— 29 —

ASSUMPTIONS

Tera took a moment to compose herself at the door. Whatever happened, she'd promised herself not to let it get to her. She took in the fluorescent-lit halls of the hospital ward one more time before entering Darin's room. She met his gaze and moved to place snowdrop flowers on the side table by his bed.

"Hello, Mr. Discontent!" She put as much cheer in it as she could muster. The corners of her mouth strained at the effort because she hadn't gotten much sleep in the last week. Of all the people on the Colony, why'd she get involved with him? But here she was. "How are you feeling, stranger?" She embraced him and whispered in his ear, "I'm so glad you pulled through."

He smiled back and gave a mock salute. "Hey stranger."

She could count on one hand the number of times she'd seen him smile. It was forced this time, but it was a start. Just keep him talking. "Hon, are you okay?" she asked.

"Not yet," he said.

There were troubling rumors on the news, but there wasn't a lot she could do for him on that front. Keeping his spirits up was one way she could help. "But the war's over. That's a reason to celebrate, right?"

"For you and everyone else it's over," he said.

So he didn't accept the outcome. "Can't you leave the past behind? Don't you want something else other than to fight?" She was struggling to not betray the desperation in her voice.

"How can I turn a blind eye to the way things still are? I have to do something about it."

Was it a mistake for her to have come here? She wanted to interrupt the loop before he cycled into one of his tirades. "What about us?" she asked. "Is there always going to be some excuse, like the rest of the world?"

"It's not something I can ignore. The way things are—there's no room for love..." he trailed off.

She didn't know if he was delirious from the medication. What he was talking about had nothing to do with the war. But his uncompromising logic—or lack of it—got to her again. It made blood rush to her face. "Love alone can't build a life when it's not here with us every day. Love can't fabricate a homepod or give us what we need to survive."

Darin stared back at her with those intense hazel eyes. But he didn't take the bait this time. How many times had they stood here at the same impasse?

She wanted to avoid the pain the topic brought her, but she couldn't ignore the elephant in the room. "The news reports— what they're accusing you of—is it true?" she asked. *Just say no.* That's all she needed to hear. And she would believe him.

A veil of rage slid over his eyes. It was a side of him that always simmered beneath the surface, but he'd never shown it to her until now.

"I did what was right—I did it for you and the children." He had never raised his voice at her before either.

How had she let herself fall for someone like this again? She wouldn't be his crutch so he could chase castles in the sky. Why was she drawn to men whose lofty ideals left them oblivious to practical realities? "Darin, stop. I won't be your solution girl. I don't exist so you can have an excuse to fix what's wrong with the world."

"No," he let it out with a bitter edge in his voice. "You couldn't be who I wanted you to be."

She chose to be nasty now, half-hoping he'd rise to the challenge. "So lie in bed all day, angry at the world, too weak to do anything about it?" She fought to control her shaking voice. It was embarrassing to lose her composure. It wasn't something she did. *C'mon. Prove me wrong. Please. I know you can.*

When he responded, his voice was even. "You're right. I was always fine on my own. I don't need you." He gave her the cold shoulder and stared forward.

It was like she'd been slapped. She needed to leave, or else irrationality would take hold. The silence pushed a wedge between them. She went to the door. She paused, her back to him, holding in tears so he couldn't see, before walking out.

— 30 —

FINE ON MY OWN

The pain returned the morning after Ambrose left. Then came my talk with Seger, and after he left too, I slept through the rest of the day. Tera came to visit the next morning. She entered and lit up the room like she always did. She placed flowers on my bedside table and embraced me.

◐ ◑

"What about us?" she asked. "Is there always going to be some excuse, like the rest of the world?"

I needed for her to understand why the battle would never be over until—"It's not something I can ignore. The way things are—there's no room for love..." I was dumbstruck. My voice was dammed by boulders. The words wouldn't come out because I hadn't earned the right to say them to her.

"Love alone can't build a life when it's not here with us every day. Love can't fabricate a homepod or give us what we need to survive." She said it as if the idea were so simple and antiquated to her.

I'd taken for granted she'd agree with my basic assumptions. What I'd wanted to say to her was that at the foundation of every civilization was love, not necessity. For it wasn't necessary to live. It wasn't necessary to simply exist. Without love, who'd build empires?

◗ ◗

"The news reports—what they're accusing you of—is it true?" she asked.

Ambrose telling me about my charges and then Seger's visit had depleted my patience. I snapped. "I did what was right—I did it for you and the children."

I don't know why her question set me off—actually, I could pinpoint why. She was going to believe everyone else over me. It was the way people were. It was up to me to take care of myself again, since I was the only person I could rely on.

We argued over the same ground we tread too many times before. She said the things that'd push my buttons. "So lie in bed all day, angry at the world, too weak to do anything about it?"

And like that, it hit me. She was right. Why drag her through the mud with me, with some failure? Have her worry about me, hated by others, while she waited for my execution? After all the kindness she'd shown me, there was only one thing I could do right by her. I had to let her move on with her life. So I said something terrible, as if all she'd done for me hadn't mattered. "You're right. I was always fine on my own. I don't need you." It was the hardest thing I had to do. I felt rotten and dead inside.

She shrank from me with hurt in her eyes. I stared straight ahead and said nothing while the love of my life walked out the door.

— 31 —

IN THE NAME OF

Another week passed by in a haze, but I made a full recovery. The MPs stationed outside my hospital room wasted no time. They escorted me out and transported me to the municipal buildings surrounding City Hall. When we arrived at the prison, they led me into a narrow prison block made of unfinished concrete.

We headed toward the only cell in the entire prison block. Few prisoners were incarcerated on the Colony. A lack of resources meant it was either grant a second chance or execute.

The MPs stopped at my holding cell. This was where I'd spend my days until my court date. Instead of prison bars, there was a solid steel door with a slit at eye level. Inside was a room barely large enough to fit the stone slab they called a bed. The flat, smooth walls were windowless and etched with lines like mortar on gray bricks.

The guard turned to me with a satisfied smirk. "Starting today, you've been stripped of your rank and of your private holdings," he said. As if those were what mattered most. The cell door slid shut behind me with a sucking sound.

I had nothing to do all day but think, punctuated by thin meals meant to sap my strength. At odd hours, loud music blasted through the room to disrupt my sleep.

The worst was the sheer boredom. To pass the time, I tried to train my abilities. But I couldn't pick up the thoughts of the single guard posted out front, nor could I form projections or shield barriers as I'd done on my missions. At first, because Ambrose had mentioned our abilities faded without regular booster shots, I assumed the LDF neutralized my abilities.. However, I hadn't been out of commission for long. Were my circuits fried from my confrontation with Aycel? Why wasn't anyone worried I might use my abilities to escape? Maybe it's what they wanted, so they'd have a public excuse to kill me on the spot. Besides, where would I go on anyway?

The days crawled by in push-ups and nightmares.

◑ ◑

By the second week, it dawned on me: I might be locked up for-ever. No law in the Colony required trials to be expedient. Even if such a statute were to exist, the term "expedient" was never defined. In any case, I was headed for a military tribunal, not a civilian court—civilian protections didn't apply. They could hold me forever.

After the first month passed, I began to lose my grip on real-ity. I placed my palms flat on the cool concrete. The hard and unadorned surface was always the same, for days that melted into weeks and blurred into months. I carried on long conversations in my own head, a ritual that repeated unto itself.

I hadn't spoken a word to another human being, not even to the jailor outside my cell. The glimmer of hope I had about defending myself at trial slipped away. My conditions ensured I'd become too unhinged to argue my case. The tribunal held all the cards.

◑ ◑

Another month (or had it been two months?) passed. I wasted away in solitary confinement with only the nameless guard posted outside to witness it. I cursed my fate. I cursed my society. I cursed the creator I wasn't sure I even believed in. This was the culmination of all of my struggles and lonely life. Was it all meaningless in the end? I did what was right and suffered for it.

In time, I began to call into question my own motives. To serve and protect my new home, to fulfill the duties of my family heritage—isn't that what I'd done? Or did I have a tenuous relationship with rules and procedures? I disobeyed a direct order and put my countrymen in grave danger. So many people perished as a result of my actions.

I wasn't sure what was true anymore: was I a patriot or a traitor?

I awoke with a start. I found myself standing in the enemy's tunnels once more. White hexagons of basalt were shrouded by mist at my feet. The alien creatures swarmed me in a ceaseless tide. Their segmented bodies jostled past one another. I swung my weapons, projections of light, out left and right to dispatch my enemies one by one. Their bodies were felled and piled on top of one another. I stood atop the mound as it grew. As they charged up the hill hill made of their fallen brethren, I struck down more.

Next to my boots, there was a flag planted on the mound. It was soaked with blood and reeked of burnt flesh. The flag proclaimed my ascendance. The mountain of corpses grew taller and higher until it reached critical mass. The mist-covered floor collapsed under the mountain's weight and opened into a yawning chasm.

The void swallowed me whole. I fell through empty space with the flag spiraling after me until my body smashed into the pit below. I shot awake with a jolt. In the dark, I could hear myself taking quick and short breaths. My eyesight adjusted, and I was still surrounded by prison walls.

With the mind gone, the body followed. I was dying. My neighbors had turned on me. My squadmates never came to visit my cell. And my last memory of Tera was her voice and the fragrance in her hair the day she left my side in the hospital.

I drifted in a fugue. Through the fog of nothingness, a single idea crystallized: I deserved my fate.

I went along with things because so did everyone else. I'd encountered intelligent life unique from my own kind and proceeded to slaughter them. Had it been in the name of security? Or superiority? The moral high ground? In the end—like all empires that hid brutality behind jubilations of culture and art—I was still a murderer.

At night, I surrendered and awaited the passing I'd sought for so long.

The other side sure didn't look like I'd imagined it would. A plump, white hare stared me in the face. Its red eyes gleamed in the moonlight, and its long whiskers twitched. On its forehead was a symbol, a black and white half-moon. It stood up on its hind legs out of the short grass.

A compulsion to possess it came over me. When I gave chase, it hopped out of reach. I ran as hard as I could but still couldn't overtake it. After awhile, I caught up to it because it had stopped running. It was lying down next to the hem of a dress or robe. My eyes followed the wispy fabric upward to look at its wearer. It was a woman whose face I couldn't make out, as if static lines obscured her features. We were standing in the shade of a tree with wizened, red-orange bark. And she was a poised and immovable light upon the hill.

She spoke—or at least I imagined she spoke—for I could hear her in my mind's eye. "You have arrived early."

"I have nowhere else to go," I said.

Her lilting voice faded in and out like an echo. "A purposeless existence? You wouldn't be the first. Yet it does not explain why you have arrived early."

The faceless woman motioned to something behind me. I spun around to find myself standing at the edge of a cliff and looking down. In the depths below, there was a pile of bodies. On top of them was planted a blood-soaked flag. I recoiled in disgust and shame.

I averted my eyes and shouted over the howling wind buffeting me. "Then why am I here?" The answer I needed was permission to pass on.

Her translucent robes—wisps tinged with red lines criss-crossing each other in fractal patterns—billowed forward in the wind. She said, "You seek an explanation for your suffering and the suffering you have inflicted upon others. That, I cannot give you." The outline of her body began to glow with a golden aura.

"I don't understand."

"There are two of you." Her voice resonated through my psyche. "The boy from Earth who seeks a better world, and the soldier on the Moon who destroys what he finds. You seek to make the two halves whole."

I couldn't grasp what she meant. But deep down, I accepted it. She began to fade into the aether. I panicked. "Wait, don't go yet. Tell me what I need to do."

Her whispers came through in echoes, "The two halves cannot become one. Do not forget you are dear to me." She floated upward until she vanished into the clear sky.

When she disappeared, the sky was blanketed with black arrows. They were loosed from bows unseen and sailed across the heavens. A bell tolled in the distance.

My eyes forced themselves wide open. I was back on the hard bed of my jail cell. A silent jailor was still posted out front. But my fever had subsided.

— 32 —

GRIEVANCE THEORY

I don't know why, but from then on, forced malnourishment and the psychological tactics meant to break me affected me less. To quell my spirit, I spent hours in meditation. But I never could return to the place where the hare waited beneath a hawthorn tree. Had it all been a hallucination from my fever?

I came up with another trick to pass the time: pestering the jailor. Who had it worse, me, stuck in here bored to death, blasted every now and then by loud music, or this poor jailor, who stood there all day and night with nothing to do? He was subjected to almost the same conditions, but at least I could lie down when I wanted. It was my grim everyday reality, but it was his, too.

So I wanted to speak to him. I went to the cold and uniform steel of my cell door and pushed myself up against the narrow slit. I asked, "What'd you do to get assigned to this sweet gig?"

He didn't respond. I could tell he noticed me in his peripheral vision. I craned my neck to get a better look outside. Opposite my door was a solid wall. The dusty hallway was a sand-colored passage only wide enough for two people to walk side by side. No one else was there but my jailor, standing at attention. He was a statue wearing navy-blue. His frazzled, silver hair escaped the corners of his officer's cap. Above his uniform's breast pocket was a brass nameplate: "Abraham."

I said, "Abe, I don't know about you, but I think the food and the hours here are terrible." Nothing. Tough crowd.

And so it went for another month, my days spent meditating and trying to get a rise out of Abe:

-"Fancy meeting you here."

-"Do you think the extraterrestrial creatures built the Great Pyramids?"

-"Fab tech is advanced, so to make this gruel, do you guys feed the machine a nasty recipe on purpose?"

Nothing worked. I couldn't get him to respond. So I asked Abe for a favor instead. "Could I have something to read?" My voice faltered for a second. "Do you know what it'd mean to someone in my situation?" I regained my calm. I wouldn't let them see me break.

Abe acted as if he hadn't heard me.

◗ ◗

The following week, the rusty food tray slid onto the floor by my bed had a bulge underneath it. I lifted the tray and found three bound hardcovers. One was a book on philosophy, another quantum entanglement, and the third was artificial intelligence. I wanted to hoot and holler but chose to stay low key.

I pushed my face against the door slot. "Abe, you're quite all right—for a human being." He didn't acknowledge me.

In the endless stretch of days and nights, I had meditation, a stream of books Abe smuggled in for me, and one-sided conversations, all of which I latched onto to keep my sanity. I read more than I could understand about ideas of moral resistance, about obscure concepts like identifying neural qubits that'd be the Rosetta Stone of the human brain. Had Cyril been alive, he might've been proud. I caught up on the knowledge he often pointed out I was lacking for someone of the Armacite bloodline. It made me admit I missed his presence.

Then the day came. Abe strolled into the cell block for his shift like he'd done on every other day. But on this particular morning, instead of taking his post by my door, he put his face up to the retina scanner. The steel door unlocked and slid open.

I stared into the world-weary eyes of an elderly man. His gaunt face was marked with deep creases like valleys formed by inland rivers. "Today's the day of your trial," Abe said. It was the first and last time we ever spoke.

◐ ◐

Huh, I'd given up on receiving a trial. I'd assumed they were going to leave me in solitary until I lost my mind or wasted away. After all, military tribunals could drag out investigations for as long as they needed and with no one the wiser.

The final surprise came in the form of legal representation. "Claire Brinn," she introduced herself and extended a hand. Her nose and mouth took up all the real estate on her small face. My appointed counsel was as tall as a mouse, coiffed her long brown hair with a French clip, and was all business. "Sounds like you had the right friends," she said, referring to her assignment.

"You bet," I said back with fake confidence. I had no idea who my benefactor was.

"Your case has been the talk around town. The brass was under enormous pressure. They moved your case forward to a public trial."

I couldn't believe it. I didn't know anybody who'd go to those lengths for me. And I was confused as to why Colony citizens cared for the fate of a Transplant.

"Don't get me wrong," she added, without a hint of sympathy in her voice. "They still plan to execute you."

Claire wasn't exaggerating. When I entered the courtroom, the back was packed to standing room only like a church on Christmas.

Word had spread, and the locals had come to gawk. At the front of the room was a coffee-colored desk elevated above the floor where three judges sat on the bench. The jury box to my left was empty, as standard for a tribunal. In the middle of the room waited the wood tables where the attorneys and I would sit. On the room's right side floated presentation holoscreens. In the back of the courtroom, citizens sat in red-upholstered seats in both the bottom and upper-level gallery. I searched the crowd for friendly faces but found none.

There was someone I recognized, however, seated high up in the balcony, in a cordoned-off section. It was President Richard Paxton Nest. My jaw clenched, and my hands tightened into fists. The bastard was here to see me fry. Like he enjoyed watching it.

My trial was argued according to a predetermined narrative of "they said"/"I said." The Colony had been threatened by extraterrestrial aggressors, inhumane creatures that tore people limb from limb. The administration had done everything in their power to keep citizens safe. I, on the other hand, was a soldier who'd gone rogue and put citizens at risk. The prosecution argued I demonstrated a pattern of reckless misbehavior. Exhibit A: when I first arrived on the Colony, I'd ignored summons to fill my post. Exhibit B: on my first missions with Charlie Company, squad-mates died because I'd acted solo.

And the cherry on top? When the enemy infiltrated the dome for a mass assault—an event the pundits on the news christened the Extraterrestrial Offensive—thousands died because I'd prevented Charlie Company from returning to defend them. The Colony would've been lost if not for the administration's leadership that day in repelling the assault.

The narrative was a concocted timeline of utter bull. As any soldier could've testified—of course, witnesses weren't allowed to be called—the events they strung together were never so cut-and-dried.

Even my legal counsel, Claire Brinn, acted like she was reading from a script. I wasn't allowed to take the stand in my defense (the judge cited a rule about my testimony endangering national security). What could I have argued anyhow? Their version of reality so deviated from my experience that to say otherwise would confirm me as delusional. The "official timeline" had been circulated for months in advance through every media outlet. To the public, it was established fact *a priori*: at best, I was an unhinged monster, and at worst, a traitor to the human race.

I was grateful to my anonymous benefactor for forcing a public trial, but it wasn't going to be enough. Whoever they were, they hadn't anticipated the mountain of evidence the state compiled against me.

The court adjourned. Closing arguments would be presented the next morning. The verdict was a foregone conclusion: executed for treason.

◐ ◑

For his closing argument, the prosecutor presented my laundry list of crimes: dereliction of duty, wanton misuse of military resources, willful defiance of direct orders, and undermining national security, all of which caused civilian casualties.

Then it was my attorney's turn to speak. Claire strode to the front looking like a slate-colored suit who wanted to make it through the day. "It is not a question," she said, "of whether the soldier before you disobeyed orders. Yes, he did, but he was fighting in the fog of war." Her strategy wasn't to deny my actions but rather to argue I'd not acted out of malice. Perhaps I didn't grasp the nuances of legal strategy, but it sounded like she admitted I was guilty of every charge. With friends like these…

The judges and onlookers in the gallery weren't convinced. Claire wrapped up her summary, and it was over for me.

But then she was interrupted by a horn blaring at frequencies that split my eardrums. A holoscreen on our right flickered on and filled the courtroom wall like a film projection. Everyone's attention whipped to the screen's black and white static. The lines were accompanied by a loud hum.

On the holoscreen, a recording began to play. A timestamp appeared in the top right corner—it was the day I fought Aycel and the day the creature deployed a hundred battalions to lay waste to the Colony. It was footage I myself had never seen before: the moment the alien forces broke through our dome defenses and began their onslaught.

"Cut the feed," one of the judges ordered. The bailiff and tech crew were already scrambling to figure out how the screen had even been activated. The gallery, in the sweltering heat of the packed courtroom, grew rowdy. It was a circus after all.

"Order!" another judge demanded, and he pounded his gavel three times.

From the utterances of surprise, I could tell no one else had ever seen it either. What it revealed solved a mystery bothering me ever since I was in the hospital and Ambrose told me the war was over. The enemy had held overwhelming numerical superiority—a one hundred battalion siege—and we hadn't prepared defenses. How did the LDF fight them off?

On the video feed, the creatures rampaged across the villages, destroying pod homes and killing civilians who were defenseless and fleeing. But without explanation, the enemy came to a halt. They were disoriented. When the feed switched to an overhead view, the hundred battalions had lost all cohesion. Their aggression evaporated as if their demons were exorcised. The LDF then mopped up the creatures inside the dome, while the rest of the enemy forces retreated in disarray.

The video then highlighted the timestamp in the top right corner and flashed its numbers large on-screen: "04:17"—pre-dawn on a Saturday when most were still sound asleep.

Next, the feed blinked to a different place, one which I rec-ognized right away. On display were the final moments of my struggle with the enemy general, Aycel, in its throne room. The recording showed me contemplating two amber vials in my hand before jamming them into my chest. I wasn't proud of myself when everyone in the courtroom watched me descend into rage and destruction. It cemented the state's claim of me being a danger to the public. Horrified gasps came from the courtroom audience.

But insanity had granted me the power to defeat Aycel. The classified footage fast-forwarded to my lethal blow against the creature, a projected sword of Damocles impaling it through from above. The gallery cheered—would they have taken pleasure in it if they'd had to end a creature who could suffer fear and pain? At the end, the timestamp in the corner was circled red. The numbers expanded into full size and flashed onto the screen: "04:17."

The last seconds of the first recording—when the alien siege on the Colony fell apart—and the second recording—when I killed Aycel—were played side by side. The timestamps for both events matched to the second.

The gallery broke into small murmurs before turning into a loud chatter. I turned to my counsel, Claire Brinn, for her opin-ion, and her mouth was agape. Up on the balcony, Paxton sat red-faced and livid.

The implication was undeniable: Aycel had been mastermind-ing the Extraterrestrial Offensive, but the general's defeat stopped the creatures dead in their tracks.

So that's why the creature had been so insistent on my surrender and why I'd sensed it holding back its true strength. While I was straining to track the bubble shields I'd placed on my squadmates,

Aycel had also been stretched thin controlling a hundred separate battalions. Its brethren were only coordinated when they were under the creature's command. When I killed Aycel, the invasion fell apart. It explained why when I woke up in the hospital, the war was already over.

It was made clear as day I hadn't abandoned the Colony's defense. But it wasn't up to a jury to decide my fate—not in a military trial.

To restore order, the judges called for a recess. The trial reconvened later in the afternoon. The observers in the gallery hadn't left their seats. The presiding judge cleared his throat. He read out the verdict. "It is the decision of this special commission that we find you, Darin Armacite..."

I was holding my breath. Claire had told me my trial was the biggest in recent memory and the first time in lunar history an LDF soldier was tried for crimes committed during war time.

"...guilty on all counts."

◑ ◐

On the night before my sentencing procedures, pundits on the net broadcasts reversed themselves. They credited me for our victory during the Extraterrestrial Offensive. Up until then, citizens were unwilling to question military action. It kept them safe, and military industry contributed to their prosperity. A soldier's life was a difficult one, taken on by Transplants, and included responsibilities few natives could stomach. A blithe existence let citizens pretend it was all progress with no human cost—their lunar miracle was perfect, pure, and righteous. But my trial shattered the illusion, and with it, the comfort of ignorance.

My sentencing took place the next morning. But by then, public sentiment had shifted. Though I'd been found guilty, the brass dared not take things further. The state reduced my sentence from execution to dishonorable discharge and house arrest, with time served for months in solitary confinement.

My life was spared. The gallery broke out into confused noises. I couldn't tell if they were happy or disappointed. I turned around to see Claire Brinn, who was standing there looking shell-shocked. I could've sworn I spotted Ambrose, Victoria, and Tera exiting in the back.

— 33 —

HOUSE ARREST

A teenage boy was walking along dark streets, ones cold and devoid of activity. He hurried back home, as if he were late. From the outside, there was a din coming through the windows. It's what he was looking forward to. He entered the back door of the patio—his preferred route—past the hallway and into the den. Above the fireplace hung an old-fashioned flat-panel television, already humming with images. He joined the rest of his family, who were huddled around to watch. They pulled their faces closer together to size up the newcomer who'd walked on screen.

Corporal Wyatt had to stop himself from shaking his head at the scraggly and exhausted-looking person before him. *What a waste.*

Darin made for a pathetic picture with long, unkempt hair and the previous day's five-o-clock shadow creeping across his face. He was still dressed in the iron gray shirt and pants worn by prison inmates. He carried a tray laden with a sparse serving of eggs, ham, and oatmeal to a table in the corner. There he sat on the bench alone.

On both sides of Wyatt were LDF soldiers eating breakfast. The mess hall was a tin can packed with rows of silver metal tables flanked by long bench seats. A wide walkway split the room down the middle and led to the serving area at the front. At the opposite rear, the automated double doors admitted grunts from the barracks at all hours of the day. It was a crisp 0600 on the Colony, and soldiers were in their casual on-base attire: mud-green t-shirts and brown lace-up boots. When the double doors slid open and Darin walked in, the mood changed. The soldiers paused to stare with their spoons held in mid-bite. It'd been some time since the trial, but the outcome still had people talking.

Some pretended not to notice and resumed eating, while others talked in hushed tones, still loud enough for Wyatt to overhear:

"Is that Darin?" a female cadet asked.

"He looks like a train wreck," her male companion added, "and I'm being generous."

"Guess that's what months in solitary will do to ya," remarked another at the table.

If Darin cared about the attention, he didn't show it. He ate in silence, with the barest of motions.

"It would've been an act of mercy to execute him," joked a dark-haired soldier with a buzz-cut who had one hand braced on his hip. Wyatt noted they were sitting at the Tau Company table.

"No way—he saved the Colony," a second Tau soldier countered, making his point with a dangling spoon and a mouthful of cereal.

"Yeah, right. He's dangerous. How do you know he won't flip out again?" said the dark-haired soldier. He leaned in and lowered his voice. "He might use those freakish abilities to murder everyone in this room."

A third member of Tau Company, a blonde-haired young woman, joined the conversation. "You're fretting over nothing, big boys. They stopped dripping in his booster shots when he was arrested months ago. I mean, if he still had it, wouldn't he have broken out?"

"True, but where could've he escaped to? We don't have cruise lines back to Earth."

"There's got to be something wrong with him. Why can't he get along like we all have to? He's mental."

Wyatt made a note of their conversations for the report he'd have to write later. He walked down the middle of the mess hall. Its walls were lined with textured faux-wood panels up to chest level. The top half of the walls broke into flat, white drywall, where holoscreens let soldiers watch while they broke bread. A local report blipped onto the many holoscreens. The audio was muted, but the anchor's morning report was summarized by text scrolling across the bottom: "School enrollment declining: underfunded. More children staying home to help the family. Petty crime on the rise."

When Darin paused for a moment at the report, Wyatt took the opportunity to head straight over. On his way, he took note of more gossip from a table filled with the ranks of Gamma Company.

"At least the war's over, right?" a private said, a fork primed in the air.

"Yeah, the brass congratulates us on it all the time," another said. The soldier took a long draught of coffee from his mug. "But why are squads still sent out into the trenches every day?"

A more seasoned officer chimed in, "The conflict may be over officially, but our ration policies are still in place. My son sometimes gives a portion of his dinner to his little sister. Word is President Nest believes we still need to strengthen our defenses."

Conversations at the cadet, Tau Company, and Gamma Company tables screeched to a halt when Wyatt came nearer. He was told it was because he was tall, and the effect was magnified when he was dressed in full military regalia. They could tell he was here on official business. He took a seat on the bench opposite Darin.

He could feel the onlookers waiting with bated breath. A minute passed in silence, but Darin didn't look up to acknowledge him. He became agitated, so he spoke first. "I'm Corporal Wyatt. I served on Charlie Company with you. Sergeant Ambrose asked me to check up on you."

Darin continued to eat his meal as if he wasn't listening.

"The war has wound down. There are minor skirmishes with aimless creatures wandering here and there, but we've already declared victory." Wyatt said it with an expectant half-smile. He rested one hand on the silver table and with his other hand, he lifted his mug as a congratulatory gesture.

Darin chewed on his oatmeal.

He slammed his mug back onto the table with a loud thud, irritated. "Your trial is long over, and the Colony will return to normalcy. Your house arrest will end in time. Don't you think this is all great news?" He was glaring now and annoyed at being ignored. The other soldiers in the mess hall leaned in to eavesdrop on every word. He didn't blame them. After what'd been dubbed the trial of the decade, it was as if Darin had vanished from public view overnight. They all wanted to hear something, anything at all.

Wyatt wiped his palms on his slacks. "You know, I wondered why Commander Tarsus recruited a nutjob like you onto an elite squad like Charlie Company. I was certain you were going to get me killed on more than one occasion." He coughed. "I had no idea why Ambrose also backed you."

Darin continued to eat as if Wyatt wasn't even there.

"But after all the missions we survived together, I realized why you were chosen. You're fearless. You have good intentions—you just have an awful way of communicating them." He laughed. "But in all seriousness, we can never have enough soldiers like you. Don't give up on the Colony. People have a short memory when it comes to wars. When all of this blows over, you could find a place in the service again." A faint chill permeated the air. He turned his head both ways, but nothing was there.

Darin raised his head. He had an unchanging, blank expression, like he was staring through Wyatt and concentrating on something in another world.

Wyatt accepted defeat and finished what he'd come to say. "Most people look out for themselves and make dough. They don't see the point of building up their home or their compatriots. Even though you've been punished for it, for what it's worth, I believe you did the right thing." He got up from the bench to leave. "It's over. Snap out of it."

◑ ◐

The right thing, I repeated to myself after Corporal Wyatt got up to leave. It was easier to justify my actions when I wrapped them in flags like righteousness.

Were people safer if I continued to kill in their name? To call it a temporary measure was a lie—the act itself changed them into a group that took pleasure in destruction. When they ran out of other civilizations to destroy, they'd turn on each other. Then the transformation would be complete, and the lunar frontier would become the Earth I'd wanted to leave behind. To excuse the war as a one-off, over and done with, was a comforting lie.

Fighting was a choice I'd made so Tera and her Cyan Cohort students would be free of my path. So now I endured the consequences of my transgressions. I allowed myself a rueful smile every now and then—my only indulgence—whenever I envisioned how much better Tera's life was without me. I imagined her and the children on top of a grassy hill filled with sunlight, tinkering with their new inventions, the specter of destruction absent from their lives. A pang of regret passed through me when I didn't see myself there in the daydream, but time would take the pain away. Or so I told myself.

Under the terms of my house arrest, I was allowed a limited number of wristcom calls, but I still didn't speak to her even after my trial ended. It was best for me to fade from view so everyone could move on with their lives. With me out of the picture, Seger's media machine wouldn't have any more fuel to feed the fire. All of this required me not talking to anyone from Charlie Company either, including Corporal Wyatt, who'd exited the mess hall in a huff.

I finished off the last of my oatmeal. From the corner of my eyes, I could see the cadets and the veterans seated in the mess hall. When I stopped holding my breath, I released the projections I'd created. The imperceptible shield bubbles I'd formed around each of them dissipated. While Corporal Wyatt was talking, I'd made it a game to see how many barrier projections I could hold in concentration.

Why my abilities had returned during my stint in prison—even without booster shots—I didn't know. But after I'd woken from that feverish dream where the rabbit sat beneath the hawthorn tree, I had access to my abilities again.

I hid it from my jailor and anyone who might've been watching. But during those months in solitary, I filled my time by building up my stamina. Hours spent every day became weeks and months in meditation fine-tuning my techniques. I gained a sense of purpose from the exertion and constant improvement, which kept me centered through the ordeal.

Repeated practice even led me to discover a new method of altering projections—too bad I'd never get a chance to take it for a spin. We had peace at last. It was time to savor it. I relaxed, and the final shield barrier around my body disintegrated.

— 34 —

FUNDRAISING

Paxton made an announcement to the assembled figures on the holoconference. "Ladies and gentlemen, congratulations are in order. We've accomplished the goals of Project Infinite Light." He stood at the front of an oval conference table that filled up most of the room. He performed a headcount of the Guildsack Partners who sat along the rim of the polished white table. Their identities (and locations on Earth) were concealed by smoky silhouetted hologram avatars. Some might say he was paranoid, but he liked to call it over-prepared, so he performed his usual checks one more time. A cross-pattern of quantum dots lit the room from above. They projected a dim and diffuse pattern to thwart prying eyes. The floor-to-ceiling windows had been set to tinted black. Quantum encryption was engaged. He was safe.

Satisfied, he said, "With the funding we've acquired from roughly forty percent of the nations on Earth so far, we're now ready to upgrade our military capabilities to their next logical evolution."

An illuminated silhouette on his left blinked on, signifying the man had the floor. "Let's assume we take your promises at face value. Nuclear testing up there was banned even before Moon Base Zero's founding, ever since the Outer Space Treaty was ratified. How do you plan to get the remaining nations on board for *that*?"

He had anticipated this objection and had already prepared his reply. "Humanity's new millennium requires global commitment.

However, as long as nations squabble amongst themselves, we stagnate. Conflict with a shared enemy—interspecific competition, as it were—will incentivize cooperation." What he didn't say was an external threat would also achieve another one of his goals: ending discrimination against Transplants. They defined the lunar military, and much like himself after decades shouldering the burdens of leadership, soldiers faced hard realities. They reminded him often why he couldn't see things like starry-eyed citizens. But true integration was his separate goal for a legacy—it needn't concern the Guildsack Partners. So instead, he told them what they were waiting to hear. "Our next phase, Project New Millennium, will bring Earth's collective resources under our wing to shape humanity as we see fit."

A silhouette of a woman seated to his right blinked on to speak. "Did you mean the extraterrestrials?" The other representatives nodded. They wanted him to address the same concern.

"Yes, they'll play their part," he said. "My re-election is all but assured, and we'll soon be thrust into a campaign which will carry us into the next decade. Expansion will continue unabated. We may even fill the coffers to eventually launch a Mars settlement."

Across the conference table from him, a third figure lit up. "Will there be hiccups this time around? That pesky soldier of yours, Darin Armacite."

Paxton squared his jaw. They loved to bring up his blunders so they could put him in his place. Little did they know he was biding his time as their lapdog. Once the goals of Project New Millennium were achieved, he'd become more powerful than any Colony leader before him. His political influence across Earth would force the Guildsack Partners to admit him as a permanent member. Then he'd be the one setting the agenda. "Private Armacite is out of the picture for good. He wouldn't dare risk anything now. Imprisonment does a number on a person's mind."

The rest of the partners chuckled.

He reassured them as he always did at the end of a conference. "If Project New Millennium doesn't unite Earth behind us, nothing will."

THE SOURCE

Tera looked up from the *Wright Blue*'s console. What had she gotten herself into this time? She was far outside the safety of the dome with the lunar surface below her ship. She checked the navigation map on the giant holoscreen above her. On the console's white and green keys, she typed in every override she could think of. But the *Wright Blue* was descending into Crater R-42 and ignoring all of her commands. Tractor beam tech didn't exist yet—did it?—but some device was jamming her ship's controls. It didn't have a registration ID and was unknown to any Colony database. A knot formed in her stomach. This was bad.

So much for her hunch. She'd started her investigation during Darin's trial because a question kept nagging at her. If an extraterrestrial presence had been confirmed, why didn't biologists or linguists ever accompany Charlie Company on forays into enemy territory? It led her to a hypothesis that spurred her curiosity.

She'd linked her detector device to scrape readouts from military scanners—without explicit permission, technically. By matching up her own signatures with the scanners' powerful resolution, she'd crafted an algorithm to pinpoint amber resin inside the dome. It was true. The government was tracking the resin all this time. Then she asked herself: what if she calibrated the device to scans taken outside the dome?

Bingo. The amber wasn't unique to the Colony's terraformed ecosystem as she'd always assumed. Rich deposits appeared out on the lunar surface. It all clicked. Many of the Moon's geographical regions remained a mystery. There were other craters as large as the ones housing the dome. Mountain ranges, like Montes Jura and Montes Haemus, hadn't yet been mapped by human equipment. Schrodinger Valley and many others didn't so much as contain a single footprint. Then there was the stuff hidden beneath the crust—spotty knowledge filled in by heaps of conjecture. When she pointed her souped-up detector underground, she discovered the motherlode: a resin deposit so bountiful her detector went on the fritz and zonked out as soon as she honed in.

She had spent countless nights reprogramming the detector's firmware to tolerate larger signatures. When she succeeded in upgrading the detector, she linked it back to the military scanners and located the motherlode again. It was still residing at the same coordinates. It hadn't vanished overnight like the small clusters she'd found in the past. Was it the source of all resin? She needed to find out.

Since the war was over, she'd requested a permit to use a research ship outside the dome. Her stated purpose was collecting scientific samples, and she'd chosen a spot so close to the Colony it'd be easy to get approval. But as soon as she left the dome, she spoofed the research ship's beacon to fool the ground tower into thinking she still hovered nearby. With the *Wright Blue's* true location disguised, she headed a few hours south of the Hertzsprung Basin and charted a course to the motherlode.

And that's when the ship got caught. It was being pulled down into a pit of darkness, and there was nothing she could do about it. She pulled off her vac-suit's helmet and breathed in the ship's recycled oxygen. Her hair swung back and forth as she released the tension gripping her neck. The distress signals refused to work—more ECM jamming, no doubt. This was a bad spot to be in. She was all by herself out here. On the bright side—it was a struggle to maintain her trademark cheery disposition this time—things couldn't get any worse.

Until a muffled sound came from the back of the ship. It was like someone stifling a sneeze. The hairs on her neck stood up because she was supposed to be the only one on board.

It was always better to face problems head-on. Her boots clanked across the metal floor as she walked with authority—more than she felt—away from the control bridge back to the cargo hold. Had a creature broken into her ship? She flung open the hatch and braced for a fight.

What was inside struck fear into her heart. It was a group of small heads huddled together in the darkness. One head popped up.

"Teacher Tera, what's going on?" Quinn asked.

"Where are we?" little Sammy asked.

Her students had snuck on board. The Cyan Cohort loved to play pranks on her like this. But they hadn't known she'd be headed so far out from the dome today.

Tera frowned. This was certifiably worse. She looked at the children and then back to the holoscreen on the control bridge. They descended into the yawning mouth of a cavern.

— 36 —

FAVORS

Back at my homepod, I glanced up from my copy of *Circuits for Artificial Intelligence.* An emergency alert had been issued on my holoscreen: "Children Taken Hostage." But I didn't look up to find out more. I shook my head and turned back to my textbook. I didn't envy the soldiers who'd be assigned the rescue mission— it was a lose-lose scenario if there ever was one.

A month had passed without incident since my trial and release to house arrest. I was confined to reading books and occasional wristcom calls. It wasn't a full life, but it wasn't all bad. I'd just come back from downtown Turtlepin Village, from my pre-approved times out. Those two hours in the morning were allotted for running errands and for weekly check-ins with an MP officer in keeping with the conditions of my punishment.

The whispers which used to follow me down the sidewalk have stopped. After it became clear I'd never respond, the locals stopped accosting me and left me about my business. Plainclothes MP tailed me whenever I left my homepod—as if I wouldn't notice burly men with crew cuts who stood out like sore thumbs—but they found nothing to report. They began to show up only every now and then to maintain appearances. I could say I was no longer a person of interest to anyone. All fine by me.

I was jolted from my musings by the special report plastered on the holoscreen. The news anchor was Hurston Segerstrom. He said, "Reports suggest an extraterrestrial infiltration of the dome was behind the abduction."

No, I wouldn't get worked up about it. He was up to his old tricks again. Even if it were true, it was probably the few extraterrestrial stragglers Corporal Wyatt mentioned. Ambrose, Victoria, and Charlie Company would deal with it. The war was over.

Seger turned to address the cameras. "If you or anyone you know has information on the missing children and their teacher, we urge you to contact—"

Before I could issue the command, "Holoscreen off," a picture flashed on-screen. It was a class photo of the missing children. They were standing in neat rows together, and at the front of the group was their teacher. There was a smile on her face during happier times. It was the kind of smile that could light up an entire room or the dark corners of a neglected heart.

No, I didn't want to believe it. The caption read, "Tera Arkwright." Tera and the children were missing.

◐ ◐

That night, I sneaked out. I hacked into my ankle tracker to deactivate its tamper sensors and left the device hanging next to an air vent to simulate the movements of sleep. In the dead of night, I crossed town to Tera's homepod in search of clues to her disappearance.

The security code she'd given me back then still worked on her door. I entered her homepod and stepped over electronic components strewn all over the place, as usual. I checked her bedroom, and to my surprise, I found the remains of Hexbot lying across her workbench. She'd managed to replace Hex's frame with new fabricated parts. In her notebook, next to diagrams and sketches, she'd written, "Eureka." There were playful stars drawn around the word for emphasis.

I was hopeful. Too much so. I reached behind Hex and flicked its power switch. But nothing happened. What had she discovered?

I'd love to say I rushed out to find her, but I wasn't ready yet. One, I needed to leave the dome in secret. Two, I'd been discharged from the military, so I was no longer privy to classified info nor had access to an Omnisuit. Three, how would I bring them all back? If I went in for her, would I leave all those children behind? No, absolutely not.

I needed to make preparations. In the meantime, investigators confirmed extraterrestrial involvement but couldn't trace where they'd holed themselves up. I hoped and prayed Tera was actually taken hostage because then the creatures would need her alive as a bargaining chip. I assumed Charlie Company would come to her aid first, but the news reported the trail had gone cold.

As reported by Lunar Channel One, she and the children vanished overnight. How could the creatures have taken so many hostages from the Colony? To me, information was being withheld again. But for what purpose?

I spent nights on the floor at her pod, snooping through her project files for hints. She'd scribbled some research about the dangers of Agent M and its effects on terraforming. Schematics for various new blueprints filled her computer. In my time incarcerated, I'd absorbed a lot of knowledge thanks to my silent jailor, but I still couldn't decipher her notes on "bridging machine learning to artificial intelligence."

If her work had anything to do with her disappearance, I couldn't make heads or tails of it. Stuck, I decided to call in some favors.

◐ ◑

I went to find my old squadmate, Ambrose. I knew he liked to stay late at the shooting range on Thursday nights. I used Tera's mini-fabricator to produce the disguise I needed. I slipped out dressed in common late-night party attire: metallic-silver clothing, a cap, and a cosmetic *virtua crown*. The *virtua crown* projected upward from my collar and altered my facial features. This was a locked setting on the device, broken as a joke with friends in private, but doing so was against the law in public. But I was already violating the terms of my house arrest, so what did it matter at this point?

I reached the shooting range and entered through a side door. I hadn't needed to be so discreet after all. The range was a skeleton of empty stalls and laser targets. At a stall at the far end, one person was still practicing his aim. It was Ambrose. He was even more imposing than when I'd first met him. He was wearing a training exosuit across his broad shoulders and had wrist guards sleeved over his hands. A digital laser target hung at the long end of his stall. He aimed a dot rifle and fired off volleys that lit up the place.

We hadn't spoken since my trial, even after he'd sent Wyatt to talk to me. But for some reason, he wasn't surprised I'd broken house arrest. He gave me a good-natured salute. "At ease, soldier." It was like he'd been expecting me.

I said, "You know what they say, old soldiers never die..." I kept the pleasantries short, as I couldn't be caught outside. He was the same boy-scout-with-a-clean-haircut, but the biggest change was how connected he had become.

"When we returned from those suicide missions," he said, "it made me think. The events leading up to our campaign didn't add up. After your trial, I sent feelers around town—chatted up local merchants and wealthy political donors. Someone powerful was pulling the strings. I'm sure of it." He pushed buttons on the console to erase damage marks from the digital target. He reset the target for another round of practice. "I might not look the part, but where I came from, it was par for the course."

Had he been well-connected in his former life on Earth? It explained a lot about why we were so different. "You think something fishy is going on?"

"You won't hear it from me. Officially, the war is over, mission accomplished—and as they say, peace for our time and in our time." He raised his dot rifle and braced his shoulders. He aimed at a dark silhouette overlaid with concentric circles and marked with different scores. He loosed a standard tri-burst and filled our corner of the range with streaks of light.

"It might or might not be related to why I came here," I said. But the truth was, that part of my life was over. I'd leave the conspiracy plots to someone who could do something about it. I only wanted to bring Tera home. "Ambrose, I need a favor."

"Ask, and ye shall receive." He pulled away from the sights and flashed me a grin.

I took in a whiff of the hot air which brought to mind wood and burnt charcoal. I was hypervigilant in case someone barged in. But there was nothing except the rattle of air pulled through duct tubing in the exposed ceiling above. "The missing teacher and children—do you know where they've been taken?"

"I know you feel like you owe her because she helped us hijack the holoscreen at your trial. But don't tell me you're going after her."

So she was the one who stumped the technicians. She hadn't washed her hands of me. She was still looking out for me even then. Even in my hardest times.

The digital target, sensing Ambrose was done, slid down the clothesline toward us. The dummy had exit wounds in its chest and one in its head. "If you commit a crime during house arrest, there's no way they're letting you off the hook this time. They'll hang you." His face was stern but there was concern in his eyes.

"It's something I have to do."

"Do you even know how much trouble I went to last time? The amount of personal *lunes* I spent, the promises I made, to force your case to trial?" His eyes shone with anger, something I wasn't used to seeing from him. "I've expended all of my social capital. I can't bail you out again."

So he'd been my anonymous benefactor, and Tera helped with video evidence. I couldn't put my gratitude into words. All I could say was, "I don't expect you to do it again. Thank you. I'm okay with whatever happens to me."

"That wasn't my point." He shook his head at me with hopeless resignation. "Well, I'm glad you're back to your old self." He returned his dot rifle to the gun rack. "I get it. You want me to share intel with you, right?"

I tilted my head to the side to confirm. The less said, the better. You never could be sure who was recording.

"What do I get in return?"

I racked my brain. I had nothing to offer.

He laughed. "Kidding, partner." He turned serious in a heartbeat. "I don't know much more than you do. The brass won't disclose why the extraterrestrials took hostages or what the enemy's terms are. We do have unsubstantiated information. There's a crater—it might be the enemy's base of operations. I'll encrypt the coordinates over to you."

"I owe you a debt that can't be repaid." I headed for the side exit. "But I'll find a way."

"You'll need more than information to get there," he said. "If I've learned anything in the last few months, others will expect quid pro quo. Knowing you—are you up to the task?"

◐ ◐

I returned to Tera's homepod. I pored over more of her schematics before I sneaked out again. Dressed in my late-night party getup, I hailed a hovertaxi to the Industrial Band, to the ring surrounding the villages. The driver dropped me off in front of a vacant street lined with rows of identical-looking warehouses fabricated with ribbed sheet metal. The I-Band was different from when I last studied it. The military blocks interspersed throughout had expanded. They edged closer and closer to the rust-colored factories until the boundaries between them were blurred.

I came to meet with a shipping magnate Ambrose introduced to me. He told me Ridenhower shipped along routes across the lunar surface on a regular basis. The warehouse I entered reminded me of an abandoned airplane hangar. I was greeted by a balding, heavyset man who looked to be nearing retirement age and who had forearms built for loading heavy munitions. It was like a bear one day put on corduroys and cinched a belt around his belly. "The name's Ridenhower," he said, extending a hand. "A friend of a friend said to expect a famous visitor today. Didn't think it'd be you of all people."

"Notorious might be more accurate," I said. "But of course, you and I both know we never met at all today." Behind him, factory automatons stacked pallets on top of more pallets. The containers were restrained between orange metal racks as high and as far as the eye could see. Over the constant din, we exchanged small-talk about the progress of Turtlepin Village since the war's end.

"I'm here to ask a favor," I said. "An overnight delivery, special handling." I hinted to him in roundabout ways what my plans were—enough for him to understand what I needed but not enough to get him in hot water if he were ever interrogated.

"Hm..." He mulled it over. "I can help you out if you'd be willing star in one of our ad campaigns."

He wasn't joking. I convinced him he didn't want a convict associated with his company. And under house arrest, I wasn't supposed to be out and about shooting commercials.

Ridenhower crossed his arms. "Smuggling the most recognized criminal in recent lunar history is no small favor. We'd take heat on our contracts if it were ever found out. You don't have enough to pay me, so why should I stick out my neck for you?"

I couldn't come up with anything. I was no longer in an esteemed position in service and was no longer useful. What could I possibly offer? This assumption was based on a society where people were tools and lives were commodities to be traded. But after starting my life over, I worked to convince myself a lunar future could be different—even if deep down I didn't buy it, I needed to give it a chance. Now was the time to try it out.

I couldn't offer Ridenhower material gain. But before I turned to leave, I asked, "Have you ever known what it's like to be in love?"

"Yeah, sure," he said, a puzzled expression on his grizzled face. My question had made him uncomfortable.

"Have you ever loved someone, but it didn't work out, no matter how hard you tried to change the outcome?"

He nodded. "Son, who hasn't?"

"What would you give to do right by her one last time? To say goodbye on good terms instead of how things were left?" I'd been avoiding thinking about it however I could, but now it opened up a yearning and a loss like a part of me had died.

He stood there deep in his own past. I liked to imagine he was thinking back on fonder times. He uncrossed his arms and relaxed his shoulders. A smile broke out across his face. He clapped a giant paw on my shoulder. "Sure, son. I can help."

He did add a stipulation: if I ever rubbed shoulders with any politicians, I should put in a good word for him so he could score a few choice contracts later. I agreed, although I didn't have the heart to tell him Paxton and I weren't on friendly terms.

— 37 —

REBOOT

Some of my preparations I took care of in broad daylight during my pre-approved times. Case in point: doctor's visits. I called in concerned about "regolith in the lungs"—something odd to pique the Doc's interest and convince him to see me on short notice.

I crossed Turtlepin Village to arrive at the hospital near City Hall. Dr. Lunik maintained an office so clean and sterile, a white glove dragged across the floor wouldn't pick up a speck of dirt. In the patient room, I sat on the raised examination bed and waited for the Doc to arrive. Lined up against the left wall were endless files and cabinets. Occupying the rest of the white-walled room were scientific instruments and a lab bench. On the bench rested wooden racks holding test-tubes filled with red, yellow, and green reagents. For someone who often appeared befuddled as to where he was, the Doc kept his workspaces organized to a tee.

Dr. Lunik rushed in dressed in the same he always was. He was wearing a white lab coat unbuttoned to reveal a half-tucked-in dress shirt underneath. "Well, well, well, if it isn't my favorite test... patient." He laughed at his attempt at humor. "It looks like the DNA-recombinant we gave you matured into something interesting. The other scientists are still poring over Omnisuit data from all the little stunts you pulled."

"I take it you mean the injections don't give the abilities I have." I'd figured as much.

"Never before, no. It's not telekinesis, is it?" he asked. He peered in closer with his large, circular spectacles. "Because that'd be bunk."

"No," I said. "I can't exert control over real objects."

He nodded with a faraway look in his eyes, like he was lost in his theories. "Human physiology is more than a biochemical machine enslaved by the nervous system. Our cells function in macroscopic coordination, as a giant wave which flows in phase. But what factor is behind this coherency? Your abilities manifest from conditions we haven't been able to pinpoint or reproduce yet." He licked his lips.

What a creepy way to say things. "You know, your scientist friends could've just asked me."

He went giddy with laughter. "They don't believe grunts can provide meaningful scientific insight. The data from your Omnisuit on the other hand—you took two boosters in one go."

He meant during my battle with Aycel many months ago. "It also tried to give me a heart attack." I broke out in a cold sweat at the memory. Yeah, I definitely didn't want to go through that again.

"So it did. Our scientists and lab monkeys have enough brain-wave and EKG data from your escapades to keep them busy for at least the next year."

"What's the cocktail made of anyhow?" I asked. I was fishing. It was the real reason I was here.

"The convicted felon wants to know classified information now, does he?" he said with a manic smile. "Well, your shenanigans have been fundamental to helping our research division grow—fascinating data." He rifled through my x-rays and blood test results, ostensibly the reason I'd come. "You didn't learn it from me, but it's a DNA-recombinant vector delivering a fixed propor-tion of amber resin and Agent M."

Finding out was like being struck with a stun baton. I narrowed my eyes at him. The resin explained the gold texture—but Agent M? "You mean, the volatile chemical used in phase fracturing? You've been shooting us up with a poison?"

"The dose makes the poison," the Doc said. "I admit, it may explain some of the unintended side effects." He stopped at the alarmed expression on my face. "What? Did you want to gain something for nothing? Why don't you violate the Second Law while you're at it?"

I was still in disbelief. "Doc, is everything in your world justified by physical law?"

"It's the only fair way to approach the variables in our universe. It's the glue holding modern civilization together."

"And what if one day, you discover a framework which doesn't excuse moral relativity?"

"What you propose is improbable and perhaps impossible." He furrowed his brow and brought my test results closer to his bespectacled face. It dawned on him I hadn't made an appointment because I was ill.

I said, "That was my long way of saying, can you give me a few more capsules? You know, those yellow vials."

He burst out into a throaty chuckle. A mean glint appeared in his eyes. "And why would your nonsensical argument convince me? Might as well ask me to believe in fairies or moon spirits."

"You want more data, don't you? I think I've tapped into something new. Imagine what you might discover from it. You could become the first person up here to receive a Nobel—when Earth acknowledges the Colony's existence and its many scientific contributions. Then again," I said, feigning disinterest, "you probably don't care about recognition from the stodgy Old World establishment." I got up like I was going to leave.

Dr. Lunik had his back to me and was jotting notes on a clipboard. I imagined two algorithms running side by side. One calculated the risks, the other, the potential gains. The two raced until the latter won.

His still had his back to me when he said, "Cabinets. Fourth row, third box, first compartment. You stole it while I was looking over your blood work."

I was in and out before he turned around.

◐ ◑

The authorities, convinced I no longer posed a threat, had gone lax, which made it much easier to move unnoticed. During my routine check-ins, the MPs confirmed what they had countless times before: the disinterested person I was when I'd first arrived on the Colony. My plan was working.

My old teammates in Charlie Company assumed the same, so I caught Victoria Haron by surprise. With a tip from Ambrose, I found her at a local haunt, the Tokyo Parachute. The joint had a wet look to it that night, like a puddle reflecting neon signs. Its club ambiance filled the air with mind-numbing electronic blips and zags of Asterchord music. The seating booths in the left wing, where I'd met with Seger before, were jammed with partiers and drugged out synth users. The bar wasn't as dark. Blue and brown bottles were backlit on shelves running from waist-level to the ceiling. It put me in the right mood to ask for some dirty work.

I sidled up to Victoria at the bar and plunked down onto a stool next to her. She didn't recognize me because I'd shaved and gotten a haircut. A cap and a cyber VR kit over my eyes completed the disguise. I blended in as a typical townie there to pick up girls on a Saturday night.

She was wearing a leather jacket and laced motorcycle boots, and her attention was transfixed on the holoscreens above the bartender. A basketball game on Earth was playing.

I tapped her on the shoulder and said in a low voice, "You come here often?"

She turned, her VR shades resting on her short, auburn hair, and shot me the dirtiest look. "Really, that's the best you got?"

"Hey, it's me. And yes, it's the only pickup line I know."

She squinted. I lifted the visor from my eyes and tuned the *virtua crown* settings off for a second so she could see my real face.

She sat back, surprised. "Last I heard, you had become some sort of turtle hermit. You don't write, you don't call—I mean, you don't even send thanks for getting you a lawyer and saving your hide. Makes a girl wonder, you know?" A grin threatened to cross her face, and a small twinkle appeared at the corner of her eyes.

So she was the one who'd convinced Claire Brinn to represent me. "Where'd you find a lawyer like Brinn, anyhow? I couldn't tell whose side she was on." I was joking. I was grateful inside for the friends I didn't know I had. "But thank you."

"Let's call it even." She leaned an arm on the backrest of her bar stool and cocked her head to the side. "Aren't you supposed to be, you know, indoors?"

"I needed to talk to you in person and make sure no one was listening in." I cut to the chase. "It's about a favor—"

"Darling, you're trouble," she said, cutting me off. "You're gonna get me locked up, which I gotta tell you, is my worst nightmare. Ain't no man worth it." She took a chug from her glass stein.

"There's no one equipped for the task like you are. I need firepower—and to be honest, there's no one else I can ask."

She leaned both elbows onto the bar and her eyes glazed over. "You're awful at this pickup game, you know that? There's no one else you can ask? Oh, how I've longed to be some guy's last resort."

I frowned. This wasn't going well. Ambrose was right—I was no good at negotiation.

She slugged my shoulder, hard. "You're going after Tera, aren't you? She's a sweet girl but a bit bookish. I don't know what you see in her—or more like, I don't know what she sees in you."

"I'll do anything you want in return. Just name it. But I don't know you that well. I can't imagine what you'd want, except for maybe a belt of ammunition."

She slapped my back and burst into laughter. "You're on the right track." She quieted down. "You wanna know what'll convince me?"

I nodded, playing along.

She leaned in close, and after a sidelong glance, she said, "Kiss me right here in front of everyone. A real one, like you ran into me by chance after years apart."

My face heated up and turned crimson. "What?" It was not one of the possibilities I'd had in mind.

"Last chance." She looked miffed.

Fine, I said I'd do anything. I leaned over and gave her a passionate hug. The stares the other patrons shot our way made me feel awkward. The blood traveled up my neck until I could feel my ears burning. But I couldn't follow through with the rest. My heart was somewhere else.

She roared with laughter. "I was messing with you. I love making you uncomfortable—you're such a stiff. Don't worry, you're not my type. You're not even in the right ballpark, if you catch my drift." She pushed me away. She lifted the stein to her lips, flexed her biceps, and chugged the rest of her beer. Her amused expression slid into one of intense determination. "I'll help you. Not everyone wants a payout. This isn't Earth—try asking in a different way next time."

◐ ◐

As I went about introducing myself to people whose help I needed, I took Victoria's advice. I asked them to contribute to the search effort, instead of trying to exchange political or financial favors, of which I had none to offer. "There haven't been updates since the children went missing, so it's up to us." To my surprise, that's all it took. One by one, the smuggler, the inventory manager on base, and the others all agreed to pitch in.

I returned to Tera's homepod one last time. There, I discovered something unsettling. It involved an unfinished portion of Hexbot's code, a complex fragment which invoked its AI to search databases without human input. I couldn't wrap my head around the logic for the life of me, and without this cornerstone, Hex wouldn't activate. But when I went to take another whack at the algorithm, the code had already been completed. A chill climbed down my neck. Eerie.

After inspecting the block line by line, I was certain I couldn't have written it. Thousands of lines were in another person's style, and the design patterns used were at a higher competency than I was capable of. But there it was, as if a phantom coder had broken in and solved the puzzle for me.

Hex couldn't be fixed, just like that, could it? I swallowed in anticipation. Why was I so nervous? I reached beneath the power source installed on the robot's back and pushed the switch. Hex booted. A blue flash from its optical sensors blinded me. A wave of déjà vu washed over me. It reminded me of my first days on the Colony, when I stumbled upon my ancestral home and activated a canister by accident—the day I met Captain Cyril Armacite.

Hex's miniature humanoid frame came to life. The translucent green pate of its brain window rotated until its eyes focused on me. Its first words were: "Got your attention, have I?"

That haunting timbre, that old-fashioned propriety—"Cyril?"

"Good thing I uploaded my kernel into this bot's memory banks before my container blew, eh?" I could've sworn the robot had a self-satisfied look on its face.

"How are you still here?" I couldn't believe it.

"It appears my new container, Hex, came across the code you were attempting to write. It learned from your mistakes, and over thousands of failed iterations, wrote the remaining portions for you. Fixed a few of your bugs, too," he said. "In the process, I was awoken, and here I am. Looks like you won't be rid of your past so easily."

He had returned. If only Tera were here to know her masterpiece was complete. She often went on and on about using machine learning as a bridge to full artificial intelligence. With Cyril in the mix, she'd inadvertently succeeded beyond her wildest dreams. Standing before me was a programmed consciousness inhabiting a metallic shell—an old soldier reborn into a new body. I was so happy to see him again, I didn't think about whether I should be amazed or terrified.

"I'm headed out for one last mission," I said. "Care to join me?"

He raised a steel pipe-arm in salute. "It would be an honor."

PERPETUAL MACHINE

In the day leading up to making my move, I maintained routine so as to not arouse suspicion. On my check-in with military police, I acted the part of a disoriented recluse. In the mess halls, I pretended to ignore news coverage about Tera and the missing children. But I couldn't ignore gossip at tables nearby.

"Do you think the hostages are already dead?" asked someone in Gamma Company.

"We haven't heard about it since. They must be."

I picked up on other rumors about renewed hostilities.

"I heard the brass scored a new cache of weapons tech shipped from Earth," said someone from Tau Company.

"Yeah? Word on the street is we acquired a nuke to deal with these beasts once and for all," her squadmate said.

Abducted citizens and military escalation put the Colony on edge again. All I'd accomplished by ending the war was being undone. It made me so disillusioned I wanted to stand up and shout. Even now, the march continued. I'd spent a lot of time thinking about what Ambrose said about our missions never adding up. I, too, began to suspect victory was never the goal. We were Moon Base Zero, and somebody intended to use us as the testing ground for all future conflicts. It was practical, it was ingenious—unless you were a soldier on the front lines or a family caught in the crossfire.

But those concerns took a backseat in my mind to Tera and the children. I wanted them back home, and the rest of the world, well, it could wait. My preparations were complete. Tonight was the night.

◑ ◑

Seger waved his hands to get Carmen's attention. "Start recording. Now!" They'd spent the better part of the week camped out at different distances from Darin's homepod. In Channel One's production cruiser—a white, unmarked van packed to the brim with telecommunications equipment—they'd been huddled over holoscreens and conducting around-the-clock surveillance.

He finally hit the jackpot when a hovertransport floated by at an odd hour past midnight. A uniformed delivery driver entered the homepod from the back and emerged moments later pushing a bulky container. He was certain the package was being used to smuggle something out and instructed Carmen to tail the driver from a safe distance. The hovertransport approached a border station to exit the dome barrier. It was a most curious destination for a single hovertransport in the middle of the night.

When some stars died, their lights faded into the night. But his instincts had paid off: this one would go supernova.

◑ ◑

I left that night. The smuggler showed up to my homepod right on schedule. He whisked me past dome security, past sleepy booth agents he'd made agreements with to look the other way. Once we were barreling along outside the safety of the dome, our hovertransport merged with Ridenhower's shipping convoy. Our vehicle became just another car in a long train line. We were a rope of titanium caskets kicking up dust as we snaked across the lunar terrain.

I was already geared up. Fitz, an inventory manager on base, requisitioned an Omnisuit for me. By the end, I owed so many favors I felt tainted. But I put aside my qualms for Tera. Everyone who'd had agreed to help came through when I needed them most. It wasn't something I was accustomed to, and I didn't know how to feel about it.

We traveled past gray surfaces littered with rocks toward coordinates provided by Ambrose's intel. He was different since the war ended. He heard things through the grapevine and had his finger on the civilian pulse. He'd unearthed a classified report on possible extraterrestrial activity near the Korolev Basin but became suspicious when it wasn't shared with the wider public. He was certain he was on to something when the brass didn't even send soldiers for a recon. The modus operandi reminded him of our foolhardy raids—when the higher-ups had info on the enemy's presence but wouldn't issue orders to prepare.

When our convoy neared the Korolev Basin, our radar and tracking beacon were deactivated as Ridenhower had promised. We were hidden from tracking software for a brief moment, long enough for my individual hovertransport to break from the convoy. My vehicle drove down the sides of Crater R-42 and slammed to a halt once it reached the bottom.

A side door slid open. Victoria leaned out in her Omnisuit holding a shoulder-mounted launcher. She fired a methane-propelled grenade into the side of the crater wall. The regolith exploded in a spray of dirt and rocks. The dust cleared to reveal a tunnel. Its walls were paved in machined white basalt—we'd breached the extraterrestrial base for sure.

Creature-soldiers swarmed to the hole to investigate. Victoria provided suppressive fire in a hail of dot blaster beams and Nitejar drones. She cleared the area of hostiles for me to disembark. "Darin—" she called out after me on comms as the hovertransport reversed and pulled out.

I didn't catch the rest. I jumped off in my Omnisuit, with my gear pack and dot rifle at the ready, and entered enemy territory.

◐ ◑

I was alone now inside the tunnels. A swarm of soldiers crawled by to investigate. I didn't get the same thrill of confronting the enemy as before. Instead, a gnawing sickness tore at my stomach. I had to kill again. I projected two long lances from my arms. Why did it always have to be this way?

Don't make me do this again. Don't.

An eternity passed, but the enemy soldiers didn't attack. Were they waiting for me to make the first move? In the stillness, my heart pounded. They didn't behave like before—why had their response patterns changed?

I looked at my boots. Tiny streams of amber resin flowed across the floor. They ran the entire length of the tunnel and off to an unseen tributary in the distance. The creatures moved again. They crawled up the walls and circled me. I could see the sheen of their chrome black, segmented bodies from the internally-lit walls.

I took a step into the passageway. The creatures followed. They formed a moving cage around me. After I walked some distance, I withdrew one lance to preserve energy. Two creatures at my rear shuffled in response. They were on the attack.

No—they weren't. They were responding to my shift in stance. I continued onward and passed next into what I would describe as a foyer. It expanded into a widening tunnel. My entourage followed, never breaking formation. I dissipated the lance projections and concentrated on forming a bubble shield around my body. I could preserve more energy in this state. No attack came. I was relieved and nervous for the same reason.

At the end of the tunnel, I stood at the top of a steep ramp.

It was wide enough for Charlie Company hovercraft to travel in formation and led to a dark abyss. The only light on the path emanated from the rivulets of amber flowing downward into the unknown. My retinue stopped. I took a few steps down the ramp, but the soldiers didn't follow. They'd completed their roles as escorts. Whatever was waiting for me didn't need protection.

The lengthy, stifling descent made me feel as if I were entering the heart of the Moon itself. I don't know if any other human being had ever traveled this deep into the crust. How, and when, had they excavated all of this? I doubted it was created after First Contact because it looked as if it'd always been here.

It took me over an hour to reach the bottom of the ramp. I stopped when I came to a barrier. It was diamond-shaped and made of translucent material like fiberglass. On the other side was a spacious chamber about the area of a city block and ten stories high. My sensors reported it was pressurized with oxygen like these tunnels were. The floors, walls, and ceiling were laid out in segmented panels. Interlocking hexagons of white basalt were paved as far as the eye could see and made the space look like a giant microchip clean room. To gaze upon this "chamber"—if a space large enough for a neighborhood of pod homes could even be called that—was to have a shift in perspective. Its existence was a statement: with the extraterrestrials' technology, anything was achievable.

The diamond barrier folded into itself and retracted upward into the ceiling. It was granting me permission to enter.

I stepped over the threshold and saw the tiny streams of amber continuing through this chamber to their destination. The rivulets emptied into a giant furnace-like contraption which reminded me of an industrial forge. There, the resin was churned into something like white-hot molten steel. Along the far edges of the chamber and anchored to its walls were enormous rigs shaped like hammers. They pounded up and down and pumped the forge like building-sized pistons. So this was where the creatures processed the amber.

I recognized the all-too-familiar design of the slatted floor and expected what would come next. A red gas erupted from the panels. The cloud radiated a potent hue, unambiguous in its murderous intent. My gaze followed the gas upward as it expanded. The shadow of a cloaked figure emerged. It shimmered from thin air into material reality.

This creature was different from the soldier drones, the Behemoth, and Aycel. It stood upright at nearly twice my height, and although its dark carapace exhibited cracked, tessellated patterns like the others, a vertical swath of rust-red ran from its chest to its underbelly. Smoky trails like extinguished flames encircled its limbs, and the trails followed in the wake of its movements. The creature wore unique equipment I couldn't comprehend. A thin, silver band was fastened around its left leg appendage. Imprinted upon the band were three white circles—like the Orion constellation—and each dot blinked on and off independent of the others. Attached to the side of its torso, where a person's rib cage might be, was a translucent square patch. Faint circuitry lines ran across the device and signaled its activity, but there were no power wires in sight. The devices were light, unencumbered, and engineered in every perspective. Perhaps they were responsible for the creature's ability to materialize out of thin air.

I was outclassed. The creature's physical and technological advantages over me were just the beginning. Unlike Aycel, this creature's mind was leagues more intrusive. I could feel it probing at the edges of my psyche, the way a black hat might test for exploits in a secured network. If I were to let my guard down, the creature would invite itself in, and I shuddered to think what it would do then. Now what? My plan never took into account losing from the get-go.

The creature spoke—not through its mouth for it had none—but straight into my mind. *A single soldier? Human arrogance knows no limits."* It referred to itself as Onyxion.

I imagined the words and spoke back. "I haven't come to fight. The woman and children—I came for them. Why did you take them?"

"A page from your playbook, as your kind might say. Use hostages to make demands. If we wipe out the younger generation, your settlement up here will collapse without them."

Onyxion was right. Stunt our population growth, and the Colony would wither away. "Hostages?" I asked. It was using a human tactic after all. "What do you want in return?"

The creature's voice, a synthesized translator, echoed in my mind. "Leave, or be eradicated."

"I don't represent the entire human race. We don't act as one unified swarm. Even if I tried, I couldn't convince the rest of my kind to leave."

"Then you have wasted your time and also forfeited your life." Its eyes glowed white, which I took as a sign of hostility.

I attempted to reason with it next. "You're an intelligent being, right? By holding innocents, aren't you violating the etiquette of war?"

Disturbing sounds emanated from the creature I interpreted as mocking laughter. The creature projected a crescent-shaped blade from its appendages. So Onyxion controlled abilities similar to my own. "Principles in warfare?" It bellowed in my mind. "What is fair when nonexistence is at stake? Dress it up in fineries of your choosing—morality, patriotism, self-defense—all paths lead to the same action." And with that, it lunged at me.

I projected a hardened lance from my arm and parried the blow. The momentum of our weapons crossing pushed me backward before I sprang away out of range. I was in a bad spot—it took my entire force of will to counter a single attack. "It doesn't have to be this way," I said. "We could—"

"Cooperate?" it finished my sentence for me. "Do you harbor a delusion we desire the same goals? Prosperity? Progress?"

I searched for options while it spoke but found none. I didn't understand what it wanted.

"On Earth, you don't offer such terms to species you deem lesser. You enslave the weaker, exploit their resources, and then slaughter them at will. You repeat this genocide until one species after another is wiped out of existence. You don't even extend mercy to others of your own ilk. What makes you assume I, the ruler of a superior species, would consider you an equal?"

The creature dashed at me so so fast it appeared to materialize right next to me. It slammed into me and sent me into a tailspin over the endless expanse of hexagonal floor panels. I projected a push downward to stop rolling and activated my gravity boots to tumble back onto my feet. Alarm sensors went off inside my helmet's HUD: my Omnisuit was at critical. I patted at the seams and searched for tears. The suit was still in one piece, but I couldn't take another hit like that.

"Our technology is superior and our fitness assured," the creature said. "We reign supreme. You and your kind are intermediate killers on the food chain, unexceptional in the grand scheme of the universe. And through what your kind call selection, you'll be called to account. It is progress." Onyxion turned its head to the right to stare at something in the distance.

I followed its gaze. Half a city block away, the air shimmered like heat in the desert sun. Shapes began to coalesce out of thin air. Did the extraterrestrials have tech for optical camouflage?

The hazy clouds materialized and became visible. A slab, like a boulder jutting above ocean waves, appeared. A recess was carved into the slab, and its convex interior was adorned with circuitry etched into crystal-white circular patterns and lines. Inside, a figure materialized into view. She lay slumped on the platform and was bound to its enigmatic design.

Tera.

A terrible darkness cut at my insides. Was she still alive? To my relief, she roused. She moved like someone lost and disoriented. Through my abilities, I sensed sadness echoing from her.

The creature said, "If you consider yourself superior, then take what you want by force." It gestured toward Tera. "Is it not the principle underpinning your culture?"

I took heaving breaths inside my helmet. I was already at my limit. The creature was in control, and I hated the reality of what led me here. The feeling mixed in with all I hid away. I hated that I couldn't save Tera or help anyone but myself, and hated how I was still—after all I'd been through—powerless to do anything about it.

"I am a reasonable being," Onyxion said. "Show me you're our equals, and I may revise my assessment." It reached down and tapped a combination into the silver band strapped above where its knee might be. It splayed its feet apart, braced into a power stance, and appeared to relish the chance to flex its full might.

The creature hurtled in my direction like an inexorable force. I channeled all I had and projected forward two layers of half-circle shields. After my previous battle, I discovered all creations I formed could be linked and their properties altered in sync. It was a technique I'd practiced many times meditating in my prison cell. I linked the two shield layers and hardened them. The outer shield buffered the initial impact. I slid backward toward a wall as the creature continued to push into me. We came in range of one of the forge's enormous pistons. It hammered onto my outer shield, disintegrating it on impact. The piston rose for another cycle, but I rolled to the side before it could do its worst.

I bounced to my feet, but the creature was already there. It swung upward from a crouched stance and slammed its head up against my shield's remaining layer. We slid as a tangled pair across white-paneled floors. Up close, I could make out the creature's face. Like its brethren, Onyxion had a head resembling a bull elephant—except the features were flattened and the trunk cut off. What would be ears fanned out as extensions of its face. Its eyes, forward-facing and set wide apart, were orange-yellow stones smoldering like kindle.

I was transfixed by the symmetry of its face and those feral embers. My resolve flagged. It was a strange sensation, like I'd become ten times heavier. My arms dropped to my sides, and my one remaining shield crumbled. *Why wasn't I fighting back?* It was the creature. It was overpowering my will using some sort of psionic hypnosis. Too late. My defenses fell. The creature broke into my mind and invaded my consciousness.

My vision swirled and reality vanished with it. I was in new surroundings. I was standing in a blank limbo of space. Onyxion's stifling omnipresence surrounded me in totality. Tera shouted my name like a faraway promise, but my concept of "I" was already eroding at the edges. Memories flashed by: of the foster home and those years alone in the city; the day I jumped from the Thomas Jefferson bridge; my first mission with Charlie Company; the Cyan children at the school...faint...distant now...the night I admitted to myself my fondness for Tera's aura meant something more—fading—blank.

— 39 —

PREMATURE OPTIMIZATION

It took Tera every ounce of strength to lift her head. The trance—or whatever catatonic state she'd been put under—relaxed its grip. She gazed into the distance of the infinite interior chamber and recognized the extraterrestrial creature who'd taken her captive. It was preoccupied with smashing itself against a barrier—something like field lines hardened into thin glass or a compact version of the Colony's protective dome. Inside the barrier, she could make out the power suit of an LDF soldier. She looked through his faceplate and—*Darin?*

She sobered up in an instant. Her ship, the abduction, the children—oh no, where were they? She turned to concentrate on him again. His shield was fading under the creature's onslaught, and his body was beginning to slump. That's right, the creature had put her into a hypnotic state. Then the rest came back to her. While she was in a trance, the creature had used the device to convey her here. Now, she could move again, but she still couldn't step off this strange antigrav platform. Was it keeping her there using chemical bonds or magnetic forces? The slab didn't betray any knobs, buttons, or displays to release her.

The man she once imagined a future with fought for his life. Was this why he'd been so distant? In the technological miracle they'd achieved on the Colony, he still spent his days in fighting and baseness. Her unshakable optimism—the protective cloak she labored to keep together—tore at the seams. Her heart was breaking all over again, over a man and a future that wouldn't be.

Her vision grew blurry. Tears? No, she couldn't cry now. She never cried—tears were unproductive. But the emptiness inside threatened to overwhelm the controls she put in place. Darin melted into a blur of paint run together. It was better this way. She couldn't watch him die. The blur swirled and swirled into the grief she couldn't hold in any longer.

An anomaly caught her eye, and she pulled herself back. What was it? Darin's gear pack had been knocked off and was sitting on the sidelines. It was squirming on the floor. An object crawled out—was it alive?

Hexbot...Hex! Impossible—the upgrade hadn't been finished yet. But much of the AI was already compiled. Had he completed the rest? The robot analyzed the situation and the life-and-death struggle before it.

Her eyes sharpened like a hawk's, and she regained control of herself. The small hope she allowed herself broke out into a grin. At conventions she'd attended in the past, her fellow inventors scoffed whenever she mentioned her prototypes included code to parse the entire set of modern human languages. They criticized her for allocating processing power to "one of the least important functions" of what one would need AI for. They derided the effort as "premature optimization."

But one of those many language modules included a package for sign language. She wasn't fluent in sign language—not in the least. However, she'd practiced the gestures for Protocol 1 through Protocol 20 so she could test the bot's capabilities at a safe distance. In her muddled state of mind, she was hard-pressed to recall what they executed. But Protocol 15 was an experiment one didn't forget.

She raised her hands and signed, *Protocol 15.*

The bot's brain window blinked neon green three times in acknowledgment of her command. Hex turned to face Darin and the extraterrestrial who were still locked in a test of wills. The bot proceeded to vomit a dirty micropulse stream of neuro-electro-magnetic frequency waves—in other words, a thought scrambler.

◑ ◑

I awoke like a switch was flipped and the lights came on. A vortex sucked me through time and dropped me back into the present. A dreadful noise—like some sort of abhorrent signal—ricocheted through my consciousness. It released me from Onyxion's stranglehold.

When my mind cleared, I spotted a misted path. It was a vestige left from the creature's psionic attack, like a vapor trail. And it traced a path from the creature's consciousness to my own. It was the only opening I'd seen this entire fight. I followed it into the creature's mind.

◑ ◑

Electrical impulses rotated in parallel. They were delivered down into Onyxion's cognitive centers. Murky. The human soldier's weapon—an automaton—blasted signals to break its hold.

Inside their shared mindscape, Onyxion hunted for the human soldier to reassert control. It sensed him in the vicinity, but what was this other...unpleasant presence?

It marched through the human's mind. Deeper and deeper it tunneled into his psyche until it confronted a cluster the likes of which it'd never encountered before. What was the nature of this dark mass?

Onyxion approached the object, a nebulous formation

suspended in space. Up close, the mass took on the texture of charred ashes and a shape like the branched head of a neuron. No matter. A superior intellect will tame it and bring it to discipline. Onyxion drew a psychic net over the object's surface.

The anomaly resisted the intrusion. It expanded itself until it ripped apart Onyxion's net. The charred mass twisted and warped until it assumed the form of what a human might describe as a demon or ghoul. With a monstrous wail, it latched onto Onyxion.

Contact flooded Onyxion's cortex with images of gross injustice, genocide, and nuclear devastation. It was like a lifetime's worth of stimuli uploaded all at once. Onyxion was faced with overload—fought assimilation—and was at the brink of losing its separate personhood.

It was forced to perceive existence through the human's eyes and was overwhelmed by hatred and unadulterated rage. And for the first time since its inception—along its evolution from survivor to warrior to self-awareness, and finally to unrivaled technocrat—it came to know suffering.

Onyxion survived pains it never had to bear and reached a new understanding of *Homo sapiens*: they lived a singular existence, disconnected from each other and from the universe. The revelation was terrifying, for it maintained psychic links to its brethren and could sense flow in the universal fields.

They are alone but do not even begin to comprehend to what extent. Except this human soldier—this one can tap into the fields. He sees his race's hopeless destiny, yet he still believes he can right the course.

It was a notion Onyxion might not respect; nevertheless, it was one the being didn't anticipate. For it'd been left dormant here centuries ago to establish a new home for its brethren. But humans arrived and poisoned its incubation. Noxious chemicals contaminated the crust and altered the gene pool. As a result, Onyxion was granted intelligence, language, and identity. Its mental faculties isolated it from its brethren. Even though it partook in the collective mind shared by its species, its existence itself was also separate and singular.

The human soldier's mind left it unsettled. *His kind does not strive for efficiency or progress. They revel in destruction—a scourge unleashed upon the universe.*

Onyxion was presented with a new concept. It learned fear.

◐ ◐

When I snapped to, it was like my soul had fallen back into my body. A moment of recognition passed like waking from a dream. Yes, this was reality. I'd crossed minds with Onyxion, and the experience made me feel—strangely enough—fulfilled, as if I'd been gifted a part of me that'd always been missing.

Tera.

I went into hyper-alert focus. Cyril (in Hex's body) was standing nearby. Yes, he'd broken the creature's hold over me, which created the opening I needed. I got my bearings and searched for Tera. She was still on the platform the creature had brought her in on.

But she was slumped over. And next to her was Onyxion. It entered commands into the translucent square device bound to its torso. In the far corners of the chamber, a radiant glow flared up: the furnace roared to life. The molten amber sloshed around the cup-shaped reservoir, and the rivulets coursing through the room overflowed. Bright-hot resin surged out across the white floor panels like lava. On my HUD, my suit's thermal sensors registered intense heat spikes along with caution warnings. Did the creature intend to destroy this chamber in hopes of taking me out with it?

And then Onyxion was off. It dashed away with the antigrav platform Tera was on in tow. They exited the chamber at breakneck speeds. For a brief moment, I sensed the creature's desperation. I swallowed through a coarseness in my throat—there was no telling what it intended for her and the children.

I diverted my remaining battery reserves to my gravity boots' thrusters. I darted between streams in pursuit and burst across narrow straits of molten amber before its pools could merge to cut off my path. I made it out of the war forge in the nick of time and entered an unfamiliar tunnel passageway. Chasing after them took me down endless corridors that zigged and zagged at every turn. I blew by other extraterrestrial soldiers who paid no mind to my presence, but I was losing sight of Tera.

An orange alert expanded on my heads-up display: my gravity boots would run out of auxiliary power soon. I needed to keep her in sight at all costs. Did Onyxion intend to kill her to send a message? What changed after we crossed minds? From my abilities, I sensed a terrible purpose.

I looked forward again, and they disappeared around a right angle bend. When I rounded the same corner, I slid to a halt. The labyrinthine tunnels had opened to a spacious rotunda. I turned in a circle and counted twelve separate passageways. It was like standing in the middle of Stonehenge looking out. I had no idea which way they'd gone.

Moments more and all would be lost. My foreboding came from a vague feeling that Onyxion intended to forever sever its ties. I couldn't accept what it meant for Tera and the children.

My HUD's readouts gave no clue as to the correct path. I tapped into my abilities. Nothing. Despair crept in. A one-in-twelve chance—I wouldn't guess the correct route at random. For all the castles in the sky—defense against extraterrestrial threats, accelerated terraforming, grassy fields of sunlight for all Colony children—none of those goals mattered if I lost her.

I fell to my knees. This was the price I'd pay for putting my principles above all else. Pleading gave way to bargaining. I'd do anything to make things right. I'd work toward a future without killing everything in the way. Who was I even trying to reach?

I don't know whether it was my link to Onyxion or whether fate answered my call. A single gate, three minutes from my twelve o'clock, appeared illuminated in a faint light—yes, a single path brighter than the rest.

I blasted down the passageway and around its many corners until the auxiliary power on my gravity boosts was depleted. The maze of floor panels then broke into a long straightaway, and at the far end, it opened to a large cavern. As I sprinted the rest of the way, I could make out a giant man-made object up ahead. It was a spacecraft. Above the ship, I spotted a gray metal swirl—it was the launch cover, and it was locked shut.

My abilities sent me a premonition: murderous intent. It made me pause and consider. I couldn't stop Onyxion in a fair fight. It meant I couldn't hold back—I'd have to kill again.

I pulled out the medi-pack I'd taken from Dr. Lunik's office. I undid the container's snaps, and it revealed three amber vials propped up inside. I stole one last look at them—using them would take me away again. For a brief moment, I resented the circumstances that'd brought me back to this choice. But now wasn't the time for long-abandoned naiveties about fairness. I pulled the syringes out and plunged them into the IV-injector on my Omnisuit.

How do I describe losing one's mind? In my case, a single thought arose from the deep recesses. Instead of being suppressed when other thoughts came to the forefront, this single idea amplified itself until it drowned out everything else. It shouted and screamed until I lost all sense of self: revenge.

◐ ◑

I burst into the cavern like a specter of pure rage. Onyxion stood over Tera. Was it a projected blade in its grip? I wasn't feeling of sound mind or seeming to obey physical laws, because I closed the distance between us in a blink.

The creature and I fought in a battle across two planes. I struck through its memories, and the creature collided into mine. It loosed a flurry of strikes on my physical body, and I stabbed with projections back in kind.

The cavern rumbled and trembled. The spacecraft was powering up, and its anti-grav engines levitated chunks of basalt in the air between us. Onyxion and I squared off in the intimate space of our gladiator's arena.

The creature swung its lance, which I parried, while I maintained a bubble shield on myself and one on Tera. The booster injections had unchained something inside of me and given it free reign. It allowed me to counterattack the creature's three surge engulfments with ease. While it strained against my mind, I projected poles upward from my shoulder to slam into its sternum.

Closer and closer we struggled, on the ground and across our linked mindscapes. Vortex intrusion. Occlusion defense. Javelin hurled. Ring blade deflected. Onyxion knocked my helmet clean off. My vision flashed between my physical form and mindscape incarnation as I blinked in and out between planes.

The injections pushed my mental and physical capabilities to their absolute limits. Who was outclassed now? Who was superior now? When Onyxion crosscut for a killing blow, I'd read its intention ahead of time and leapt upward. It struggled to follow and came at me with an upward joust. In midair, I formed a solid block I wielded like a hammer. The weapon was imbued with the full strength vested by my completed state.

I swung the block down onto the creature. The impact was so powerful, it hurled me back and through the air. I hit the ground hard and scrambled to get back on two feet. I was shaking and had to brace myself with one hand against the ground while I heaved and gasped for air.

Onyxion remained standing in front of me. It took a step, leaned forward, and toppled over. A tremor reverberated through the cavern and shook the spacecraft behind us.

Now was my chance. I imagined an executioner's sword. The projection formed in my hands and crystallized into reality. I dragged myself toward my fallen adversary. When I reached its crumpled form, I raised the sword high above my head. *No more. No more threats to Tera or my home.*

A malevolent tempest enveloped my heart and mind. The weapon's inescapable allure called out to me. I gripped both hands around the hilt so I could plunge the sword into the creature's face.

And in that moment, a warm hand touched my cheek.

"Darin," a voice said, "come back to me."

A small opening cleared in the storm. I gazed out from the raging darkness to see Tera's green eyes. She'd broken free and had crossed over to me. Her eyes searched mine. Her gloved hand was against my face. I could've sworn another hand was interposed with hers, like a familiar presence from a dream.

"Is this the real you?" she asked. There was heartbreak in her eyes. Her touch, her voice—they quelled the insanity. The void receded, and my inner voice reasserted control.

I held the executioner's sword above the helpless creature at my mercy. I met her eyes one last time. "Yes," I said, "this is the real me." I regained control and willed the weapon away. "It has always been."

◐ ◑

Tera pulled me back from the brink before I lost myself. The injections had linked together isolated parts of my psyche, completing my abilities, but the cost was my sanity. Had she not stepped in when she did—I didn't destroy Onyxion, but I couldn't take the chance the creature would threaten us again. I returned to the creature's mindscape, and with my elevated abilities, I left behind a series of interconnected restraints. The projections would cut its abilities short whenever they activated. Though its abilities were sealed away, my hold wouldn't last forever. In a few decades, or perhaps in a few years, the creature would undo the locks and regain access to its abilities. Was I a fool for taking a chance? Maybe. But I'd exhausted all desire to maim and murder. In the interim, the Colony would have time to improve its defenses.

From our common link, I sensed Onyxion's frontal cortex stir from its resting state. Its mind progressed to a dormant hibernation phase before it booted into consciousness. It awoke, and its orb eyes shone an aggressive white before assuming their regular golden hue. It steadied itself back onto its feet and towered over us. The creature gauged its surroundings and was surprised it still counted itself amongst the living.

"I let you live for a reason," I said. "Exert control over the others of your kind. Tell them no more—leave the Colony be. I'll warn you, it's not a fair trade; I can't promise you the other humans will stop what they're doing to your home. But if you threaten us again, I'll come for every last one of you." I couldn't do all that, so I was bluffing.

Onyxion flashed its orb eyes before speaking into my mind. "You're not like the rest—no, you relish brutality even more than your brethren. I accept your terms, dictated under duress. Your nature will lead our civilization and others into wars of attrition."

I nodded because I couldn't speak for everyone else.

The creature backed away from us. "I will send out a directive to the collective mind, and we will settle in fertile lands elsewhere. Lament for the advances you could have been granted—our gravity displacement engines, nucleic cures, and regolith manipulation. Remember this one day when your civilization cries out for sanctuary, and no one answers the call."

Onyxion punched a series of commands into the translucent square patch attached to its rib cage. The creature dematerialized into a shimmer of optic camouflage. It was the last I heard from the only other being who could've shared with me the nature of my abilities—a soul as alien to its kind as I was toward mine.

— 40 —

MINOR ISSUES

Tera and I dashed up the ship's loading ramp. The walkway rumbled from the *Wright Blue*'s engines. When we entered the ship's main hold, we found the Cyan Cohort children. They were sitting around in a circle on the titanium-colored deck and were all accounted for—Tera had to grab onto a railing out of relief, but she hid it well. They'd been surviving off emergency rations in the ship's stores and were unharmed. I was confused by how unfazed they were by the dangers they'd been in.

"Where'd the alien man go?" little Sammy asked me.

"You spoke with him?" If the children called Onyxion 'him,' I would too from now on.

"Yeah!" Annie cried out. "He talked into my head. And I talked back through my head. It was so cool." The other children chimed in with enthusiastic retellings of their time with the creature.

Tera and I turned to each other at the same time. We gave each other a look. We couldn't reconcile their experiences with ours. We'd fought a powerful being who'd deemed himself our superior and who'd said he'd been granted the divine right to enslave humanity as chattel. But the children talked about Onyxion as if they'd gone on vacation with their favorite uncle.

"He left for now," I said, "but maybe he'll return one day." In truth, I hoped not.

When they found out he'd left, the children cried out in unison.

Some threw tantrums right there on the smooth metallic floor. The enemy had been defeated. Why were they so upset?

Mark said, "He showed me blueprints of things I've never ever seen. It was like reading from a secret book."

Quinn stepped forward to speak. She was the same reserved and inquisitive child I'd helped in the alley before the war. The other kids settled down to listen to her quiet strength. "Mister," she said, "what're we going to do without his people's amber?"

◑ ◐

Before we lifted off, the *Wright Blue* welcomed one more visitor. Cyril had caught up to us and boarded the ship. "Were you planning on leaving your only living ancestor behind?" He gave a *hmph* and, for a computer program, seemed upset at me.

We launched from the cavern without incident. Hex, or should I say Cyril, stayed in the passenger hold to entertain the children. Tera and I were alone on the control bridge. She set the navigation back to the Colony while I played copilot. The trip home—it should've been uneventful, right?

Two minor issues. The first was I was bleeding from a wound I hadn't told her about. It stung like hell, but I was okay with not being okay, and it'd be my response to my life from there on out. Other than for the possibly dying part, no big deal—but she wanted to talk.

"Darin," she said.

I didn't want to have this conversation. I didn't want gratitude or blame—this forced interaction. My mission to rescue her was for my own selfish reasons—that's all there was to it.

But she wouldn't let me off the hook. "We didn't end the way I wanted. Whenever I think about the hurtful words I said to you, I regret it. You broke so many rules coming here, and they've every excuse now to put you back in the slammer. Why'd you risk so much?"

What? Was she teasing me like she didn't know why? I couldn't tell. She wanted to make me say it, to see if I'd still trot out the same excuses. Blood seeped out the right side of my Omnisuit, and I steeled myself to the pain nagging at my brain. My voice returned in stiff, pained breaths. "Come off it, Tera. What do you want me to say? I did it just because."

"That's all?" She'd seen the real me back there and didn't like how I'd returned to faking it.

My ears burned, and my chest was compressed. I sensed the immeasurable, yawning chasm between how I felt and how uncomfortable it was to get closer to someone else. For my whole life, I'd been an island. "You're going to make me say it?"

She nodded with mock solemnity. She broke into a sly grin, and there was mirth in her eyes.

Her aura was glowing—bright and unapologetic—the way I remembered. The future she represented to me was a person worth bartering my own life to preserve. But she didn't want to stand for anything—or hear that from me, even if it was true for me. So I said, "I came after you because you borrowed one of my favorite sweaters but never returned it. What, do you keep a secret sweater stash or something?"

She braced a hand on my shoulder and burst into laughter. It was like she always used to at my awful jokes. I broke into a smile at the infectious sound. I'd forgotten how much I'd missed it every day.

She stood up from the pilot's seat. Her golden brown hair hung halfway down her body-hugging flight suit. I attempted to stay focused on our charted course. It was strange how a person I didn't give a second glance when we first met now captivated my attention at every turn. She crossed over to me. She sat across my lap and hung her arms around my neck. She stared up at me, and there was an expectant look in those emerald eyes.

I resisted, and my expression turned to stone. *No, not like this.* I risked what I'd risked and did what I'd done for my own reasons. We were two points in space whose trajectories intersected before parting ways. She was better off without my radical views of the world—I didn't want her to come to my side like this. *Not because I did something for you or out of pity.* But her warmth and the scent of her skin made it so difficult to hold my ground.

She shifted on my lap, and more blood oozed out from my wound. "*Umf,*" I grunted. When she looked down and saw the red splotch expanding along the side of my suit, she gasped. "Are you bleeding? Why didn't you tell me?"

"Don't worry." I was saved by the opportunity to change the subject. "I couldn't find a medic kit on board, but I'll be fine. We'll get back and docked. We'll get back." I repeated it as if I were reassuring her and not myself.

She was giving me one of her looks. Whenever she stared at me that way, it made me notice her forehead. "Tell me," she said. She was relentless. "You can do that, can't you?"

I was in unbearable discomfort. It took everything I had to say, "Yes, it hurts. All of it. From the beginning until now." I hadn't answered her question, but it was a start. It was as honest as I knew I how to be with her.

On the way back home, we learned about each other like we were starting over again. I learned why she associated practical concerns with relationships, in the context of how harsh life on the Colony could be. She began to accept my radical perspectives were outgrowths of the wars that'd begotten me. There was so much more there, hidden in her mind, I'd yet to see. Her psyche was an unexplored frontier, and the new one I'd been searching for. There were more mindscapes to explore in my fellow man, if I only dared get close enough to look in.

She relaxed her embrace. She was so carefree and full of life I almost dared to imagine what it'd be like if I was the one who gave her happiness for the rest of her days. "And?" she said. She acted like a stern librarian on the verge of laughter.

She knew why I'd come after her, right? She must have, so why couldn't she let me take the coward's way out? In my head, I fought the battle between what I felt but was too ashamed to say. All I could force out was, "I do." I used the trick I picked up from Onyxion to project the remaining words into her mind. *You. Love.* Did it work? Had she heard me?

Her complexion lit up like rose petals in champagne. She hugged me tight. I wrapped my arms around her waist and held her close. In the light of Earth over the Moon's horizon, we kissed, as two people who'd crossed time and space only to find out they'd already been waiting for each other.

Bleeding out was one minor issue, but there was a second. Cyril barged into the *Wright Blue*'s control room in his clangy metallic shell. He said, "The ship's computer has detected a hostile signature. The footprint matches an ICBM's booster phase."

A missile launch? It couldn't be. On the console at waist-level in front of me, the signal dispatch blinked on. I hit the receiver to open communications. A holoscreen appeared above our seats. On it, a man's face took up the entire screen. He had familiar silver-flecked hair and a glassy jaw. They belonged to Colony President Richard Paxton Nest.

"Darin Armacite, you're in direct violation of Statute 15, Article 4B," he declared. He looked pleased. "You and your passengers are contaminated by extraterrestrial contact. You cannot return to Moon Base Zero until cleared by military order. Reverse your course."

Like hell I would. I wasn't going to land this ship near the enemy compound or anywhere out on the hostile lunar terrain. I hit the button to transmit and said, "The hostages, Tera Arkwright and the schoolchildren, have been recovered. We can't leave them out here—it's only safe inside." Why did I even bother explaining? It's not like he didn't get it. He was pretending not to.

He glowered at me. "If you attempt to re-enter the dome, you'll be marked a threat to national security. Violation of this statute grants me the discretion to use overwhelming force."

What kind of person smirked when saying something like that? He was spewing legalese to protect himself, so I tried to put him in a bad political spot. "We'll be landing inside the dome. Or were you planning on condemning all of the children on board?"

He dodged the question. "The nations of Earth have given me an open mandate to wipe out the infestation on our doorstep. They've dedicated arms to our cause, and I intend to protect humanity no matter the cost."

I understood what he meant. "Our ship just happens to be in the blast radius." There was a bitterness in my mouth. The suspicions Ambrose had shared with me all came together. Paxton would stop at nothing to have a pretext for sustained conflict. A rescue mission for Tera and the children had never been in the works because their disappearance was integral to the plan. He hadn't intended for them to come back alive.

He said, "The people will accept I did what was necessary. It was a terrible price to pay to ensure the safety of so many." The holoscreen blipped out. The silence was cut by a litany of sirens and overhead lights flashing red.

Cyril shouted over the chaos. "The targeting computer confirms a warhead headed our way. It's not honing in on the extraterrestrial base but is targeted at our ship." He posted the missile's trajectory onto the holoscreen, confirming what I already suspected.

I asked Tera, "Does this ship have countermeasures?"

She shook her head.

Cyril confirmed it. "No, but schematics show it's equipped with dot beam turrets. Shoot the missile down."

I studied the ship's innards on the screen. The pain from my wound was no longer registering as important. "What if the warhead carries a failsafe? If I shoot it down, and it detonates near the dome, countless will die."

"It doesn't matter," he said. "Even if this attack fails, they could launch another. Retaliation is the only way to guarantee deterrence."

I gritted my teeth. Paxton had every contingency worked out. If I didn't shoot back, we'd perish. He'd blame the children's deaths on the extraterrestrials, and the public demand for blood would be insatiable. If instead I retaliated and damaged the dome, he'd present the catastrophe as an extraterrestrial attack on the Colony. Either way, he'd get the reaction he needed. In fear, citizens would grant him further emergency powers. Funding would pour in from Earth to fan the flames. My neighbors would become cogs in a war apparatus that'd march on no matter what.

I reached across the console and popped open the safety latch on the trigger. I rested my palm on the button and hesitated one last time. "Cyril, we can't keep doing things this way."

"Do we have a choice? Fire at will."

TIPPING POINT

"The First Great Political Awakening arrived with a bang. But many scholars would say the chickens were simply coming home to roost. Government authorities had used the rise of audio-video devices to create a surveillance state—these entities never foresaw how the technology would trickle to the private sector and to citizens who'd turn the cameras back around." —from a lecture by Professor Sidney Theia, University of First Crescent.

Seger took an extended sip from the snifter in his hand. He savored the last time he'd enjoy a brandy overlooking the view at his favorite restaurant. After today, he'd spend his fortune to smuggle himself to Earth and go into hiding. So it might be for the rest of his life, to elude the hitmen who'd be contracted to kill him after what he did today.

He was seated out on the veranda at a round table with a single lit candle. He loosened his red tie and took off his blazer. His favorite spot was centered between two stone columns holding up the outdoor awning. A Lunar Colony flag hung from the column to his left, and an Earth flag hung on his right. He smoothed his ghostly blond hair and looked past the railing's decorative vines to take in the cool sky. He breathed in crisp and salty beach air from the enviro-simulators—it was a morning fit for a new beginning.

He couldn't pinpoint why he'd had a change of heart. Was it guilt over watching Darin waste away in prison? The feed was always the same then, showing Darin reading, meditating, or counting pushups on the floor of his cell.

Ratings had been abysmal those months. Viewers on Earth—unaware they weren't watching an actor but were instead eavesdropping on a real person's life—assumed the producers had lost their minds. Week after week, the daily streams online also showed the same jail cell. Many began to wonder if they'd been tricked into watching a continuous loop. Message board netizens concocted elaborate theories about some sort of social experiment. Because why would a show—one that'd premiered with a bang—switch to Darin doing nothing for months on end?

But Seger's vision was to give Earthers a genuine experience of life on the Colony. Darin had been chosen as the subject, and for those months, he languished in prison. So that's what was broadcast.

Up until then, the series he'd sold to affiliates on Earth had moved from broadcasting on obscure channels at three in the morning to primetime fare. It reached every household, in thirty seven languages across the world. He credited the show's popularity to Darin's fiery and unpredictable will. The Colony that Darin fought to preserve was a place Earthers dreamt of. When they gazed up at the stars and imagined humanity's future in space, they imagined a home where they could be free.

Or did Seger's change of heart come from expecting Darin to fold and admit the powers that be were unstoppable? But Darin fought to retain his sanity throughout imprisonment, prevailed over a farce of a trial, and after all of it, still placed the Colony's future above his own. Like all who watched on Earth, Seger began to think what set this Transplant apart had nothing to do with military injections.

Or was the catalyst the night he recorded Darin's escape from the dome? The boldness of the feat left him thinking if it wasn't too late for Darin, maybe it wasn't too late for anyone.

It brought him back to the double-slit experiment taught to students to introduce them to quantum computing. When light was shone through a paper with two slits, the screen on the other side showed—against expectations—more than two vertical columns. The light particles had diffracted and interfered with themselves, so they reached many destinations. It proved light—and all matter—could behave like a wave.

But that part was old news and repeated throughout primary school. What surprised him was what followed next. To figure out what was going on, a detector—akin to a camera—was placed to watch the photons as they passed through. But doing so changed their behavior. The pattern on the screen reduced itself to two columns, like anyone would expect if paint were splattered through. He was a child and full of curiosity then, and when he searched for the answer far and wide, no one could yet explain why. He couldn't believe it—the act of observation itself had altered reality.

And so he didn't know why, but watching Darin made him not want to report on history after the fact anymore. Seger wanted to change it.

Thus today, he arranged a surprise episode for his viewers on Earth: a live broadcast of Darin's rescue mission. The enemy had been dispatched and the missing children were on their way home. But they were denied entry to the dome.

It was time for Seger's coup de grâce. He'd arranged a special report to be broadcast live on every major network in the world. In North America, citizens watched as their programs fuzzed out to be replaced by a special report. In Southern Europa, an emergency alert noise played over media boxes before the announcement appeared. In the nations of Oceanus, families stopped mid-meal to sit in front of their screens. In the recently established Canberra countries of the southern hemisphere, revelers returned from a night out only to call all their friends to turn on the telly.

The live broadcast began. "We interrupt your regularly scheduled programming to deliver urgent breaking news." A news anchor desk faded into view. Stacks and stacks of paper printed with small type on every page blanketed the desk's curved surface. An unfinished cup of coffee sat next to a pair of black spectacles. Valda Neumoz and Orson Mathers, two of Earth's most recognizable journalists, were seated front and center. They each held a stack of reports in their hands and faced forward.

From his spot on the veranda, Seger smiled at the events unfolding onscreen. These two never shared a broadcast, since they worked for competing media conglomerates. So paying the right people to get these two together created an extra "it" factor that was worth every penny.

Neumoz cleared her throat. "The events you are about to witness are real."

Mathers added, "They are not—I repeat, they have never been—scripted."

Through their report, Seger revealed to billions on Earth that a colony existed on the Moon. That humanity had made First Contact. That wars were waged in their name in which men, women, and children died in secret. That Darin and the others who viewers rooted for were not actors but actual soldiers. If these facts had been revealed by anyone but the two most trusted news anchors on Earth, it would've been laughed off as fringe conspiracy theory.

Neumoz continued, "In response to the extraterrestrial threat, the Lunar Colony President, Richard Paxton Nest, has authorized use of nuclear arms known as enhanced radiation weapons. A neutron bomb has been deployed to deal with the enemy."

Mathers added, "A group of schoolchildren may be caught up in the fallout." The statement was delivered in a way to imply that the children were considered acceptable collateral damage. That the ulterior motive was to drag the nations of Earth into further wars was lost on most, but it didn't matter. People across the world were shocked. And then they were outraged.

Seger leaned back and took in the lunar sky one last time. He'd gone from managing a station no one even knew existed to breaking Earth's television, phone lines, and fiber optic communications. The Fourth Estate had overpowered the landed nobility at last, and he reigned as its undisputed king. He raised the snifter to his lips and downed the rest of his drink. He set the empty glass on the table with a strident and satisfying *clink*. His work here was done.

— 42 —

OBSERVER

With the missile headed our way, I spent the few remaining moments deciding whether to fire our laser turrets. I disagreed with Cyril's opinion that retaliation was the only true deterrent. But even if it endangered the Colony, I wouldn't let Tera and the children die. Before I left the dome, I'd promised myself no matter what, I'd put her first from now on. I reached over to push the red trigger.

The holoscreen above us blipped on and gave me pause. But this time, instead of Paxton, I met familiar faces: Ambrose, Victoria, and the rest of my old squadmates in Charlie Company were onscreen.

Ambrose said, "Darin, it's me. We don't have much time, so listen up. The Earthers have been let in on our little secret up here. They're up in arms, and protests have broken out all over the world. Paxton has been arrested by the military on orders from the United Earth Council. He's been charged with ordering an attack on civilians and violating the nuclear arms reduction treaty."

I couldn't believe it. Someone had come to our aid, but who? When I stole a glance at Tera, she smiled back in nervous disbelief. I turned my attention back to the holoscreen in brighter spirits. They were delivering good news, so why did my old squadmates look so grim? I said, "But?"

Ambrose's left hand was balled into a fist at his side. "But our codes can't deactivate an ICBM after it passes the boost phase. We tried everything we could." Victoria placed a hand on his shoulder. He looked down. "We in Charlie Company are there with you in spirit. Your service to the cause won't be forgotten, Darin. I'm sorry it had to end this way."

I cut the holoscreen out and sat in stunned silence. I stared down at the console and didn't meet Tera's eyes. Nothing I could say to her would make things better. No, I couldn't accept it. Not after all we'd been through. I turned to Cyril and asked, "Any ideas?"

Cyril, who hadn't moved for some time, clicked back to life. "Statistical calculations complete. A neutron bomb has a compact blast radius. If we can divert the missile's course, there's a chance we can avoid a direct hit."

"It's a start," Tera snapped. "Hex," she commanded, unaware my ancestor was the ghost in the machine, "display gravitational field topography. Center the reading on our coordinates."

A leveled map of the surface below our ship appeared on the holoscreen. The land was bathed in swaths of green and yellow, with a few areas drawn as red blobs.

"What do the colors mean?" I asked.

She was typing on the console so fast it sounded like she was trying to break it. "The red spots signify mascons hidden beneath the lunar surface," she explained, impatient now. "They're dense mass anomalies responsible for the Moon's lumpy gravity."

I furrowed my brow. I didn't make the connection.

"In other words," she said, "they're patches with higher gravity—there!" She pointed to a pocket sandwiched between a concentration of red semicircles and entered its coordinates into the navigation systems.

I got it. She was hoping the mascons would confuse the missile's guidance systems.

Cyril interrupted, "Now, as for the detonation itself..."

He was right. Even if we avoided a direct hit, when the warhead detonated and underwent fusion, it would fling ionizing radiation far and wide. Neutrons would penetrate our ship's hull with ease and annihilate all life inside, as it was designed to do. We couldn't outrun it.

My wound ached in my side, but the pain brought with it a sharp clarity. Images raced through my head, and with them came the eerie sensation of tapping into my abilities. When I'd been tangled up in Onyxion's consciousness, a connection formed. And although the creature was gone, our link persisted. I couldn't say I was the same person as I was before. My experiences with Onyxion, and even with Tera, bridged something incomplete inside me, as if a missing package in the toolchain had been plugged in at last.

The missile cruised over the mascon areas en route to our ship. When the missile encountered their elevated gravitational fields, it entered a steep nosedive.

I closed my eyes and waded through the thoughts and feelings of everyone on board. The fear of losing them all caused my emotions to surge and revved the engine of my mind. To maintain the heightened state, I held an image of opposites, Tera standing next to Onyxion. I projected a bubble shield around Tera, Quinn, and the other children. Then I proceeded to link their shields one by one into an expanding network.

The ICBM slammed into the lunar surface. The warhead detonated.

Rotate the shields in unison to achieve coherence. Merge them into a larger sphere. Harden the shell and imbue it with the properties of regolith. At the final step, I opened my eyes to will my creation into reality. I'd never attempted something on that scale before, and the strain from it removed me from my body. I was many places all at once: a person looking out from inside the ship, a being in space who observed my body inside, and a detached entity witness to the entire system.

And what was there? A colossal shield barrier composed of three concentric spheres surrounded the *Wright Blue's* hull.

In my vision, there was a blinding flash. The detonation formed a crater on the lunar surface that ruptured outward at the edges. And, when all was lost, a tremendous figure of light overlaid itself with my shield barrier and onto our ship.

Then nothingness.

Was I too late? The last thing I remember was coughing blood onto Cyril's frame and Tera shouting my name.

— 43 —

COMPLICIT

We made it. We were back inside the protection of the Colony dome. Tera and I delivered the Cyan Cohort children into the arms of their loving families first before I walked her home. As for me, the thing about dying many times over is that you get it out of your system. While Dr. Lunik and his colleagues were running tests on me for the data I'd promised them, I had plenty of time to think. I decided I'd have to choose—no more vacillating about where I belonged. The Colony was my home, and home was a place I was going to invest in and build.

But what about everyone else?

First off, there was the case of Richard Paxton Nest. The vast majority of people here and on Earth condemned his use of nuclear weapons. Under the magnifying glass of public exposure, he was reined in at last. It helped that a group of vigilante hackers released a record of financial transactions between the Colony and corporate vendors on Earth. He had authorized payments to real estate holding companies, food conglomerates, and munitions manufacturers. These enterprises belonged to members of a heretofore unknown cabal who called themselves the Guildsack Partners. Their activities in and of themselves wouldn't have constituted scandal—except these distributions used public funds and were off the books. Those who'd suffered under deprivation throughout the war effort understood where their collective wealth had been funneled.

The legislature suspended him from office pending an investigation. To avoid interrogation, he invoked "executive privilege." He pointed out how his actions were classified and involved tough decisions carried out for the greater good of the nation. I found his argument difficult to buy. So many had died from his fueling of the war machine, which enriched his campaign donors and solidified his political power.

But the people had grown wise to these games. On Earth, executives from Agrocorp, Block EX, Gruber & Brownfeld—all members of the Guildsack Partners—were indicted with what amounted to racketeering. On the stand, they dressed up alternate versions of the same excuse: their dealings were collective actions rather than those taken by a sole individual. Disavowal of responsibility was a defense as old as time. After all, they argued, didn't citizens bankroll these enterprises as paying customers and vested shareholders? Hadn't citizens worked for these organizations and prospered along with the executives on trial? For the government bureaucrats arrested, hadn't citizens voted these leaders in and contributed tax dollars—a tacit approval of these military campaigns? Since we were all complicit, they claimed, no wrong could be ascribed to any single person. How convenient.

Up on the Colony, legal action ran into similar hurdles. Paxton had been held under house arrest until trial, but according to Ambrose, it wasn't going to lead to prison time. No precedent existed in the judicial system for his conviction. Paxton counted on wealthy connections to boot, and so his case would be dismissed. He wouldn't be asked to take the stand or explain himself.

But those developments didn't shock me given human history. I was just happy he wasn't in charge any more, and that meant Tera and the kids were safe again.

No, the real shock arrived when we discovered we were running low on crystallized resin. The mysterious amber powered our vital infrastructure and was key to synthesizing quantum dots. These generated our solar power surplus and were responsible for our rapid growth. Without the amber, the Colony's economic miracle came to an end.

We'd taken the resin for granted, not realizing its connection to Onyxion and his brethren. The extraterrestrials produced it through a process we didn't comprehend, and when the creatures left, they took with them any chance of renewing the supply. Repairing the dome became more time-consuming and oner-ous with our dwindling reserves. It was a sobering time, one of scarcity and conservation. But we were still able to survive. We rebuilt from the destruction we'd wrought, compensated by the knowledge that this was a step in the right direction for a newly outward-looking civilization.

— 44 —

FOR NOW

From up on the hill, I looked down into Turtlepin Village. I was standing in the same spot where I'd spent my first days on the Colony and from where I'd first seen Tera. Except now, the grasses had taken hold and hawthorn trees provided shade from the afternoon sun. Below, hovercraft zoomed in and out on streets busy once more. People milled about on red brick pavements and strolled from their reconstructed homepods to storefronts repainted in lemon yellow and ivory. Bare wooden planks and steel scaffolding sprung up where the new university was being built, and when it was done, it'd be the first of its kind in space.

But I wasn't alone this time. People were gathered here to celebrate the anniversary—one of many since then—marking the end of the First Lunar War. Everyone had been invited up for the day's festivities. Cream-colored canopies and booths lined the hilltop, and bossa nova music floated in on the breeze. Toddlers ran and played barefoot while adults shared mini-fab blueprints or caught up on old times. It was like we didn't have a care in the world.

I spotted a few familiar faces making the trek up the hill. They belonged to friends I'd learned to trust. Victoria greeted me with a bear hug, and Ambrose shook my hand. It'd been a while since we'd met up like this.

"Victoria," I said. "Congratulations are in order. I heard you've been promoted. It must be nice commanding your own squad."

She tilted her head to the side in acknowledgment. "It beats standing still. We're at peace, but you know, we could always use a gunnery sergeant if you're itching to come out of early retirement." She winked.

"Maybe in another lifetime," I said with a smile. "My work here keeps me pretty busy these days." I turned to Ambrose next and said, "I didn't know we'd be expecting a VIP today." He had become popular as a war hero who'd taken a prominent role in our reconstruction efforts. When an emergency election was called to select an interim president, he was nominated and won by a landslide. As one of his first acts as leader of the Colony, he issued me a full pardon over my role in the war—I swear I never asked him to. In light of our other pressing issues, I was relieved when no one made a fuss over it.

He said, "For today, I'm just another villager here to let loose. Darin, is this your second or third time starting over now? I lost count. How's your new life been treating ya?"

"Like home." Because it was. We shared a drink and reminisced on old times. They were genuine people I was blessed to count as true friends. Around them, I could be myself.

It hit me then that I didn't know where Tera was. She'd been so busy organizing a display for the day's celebrations. It was meant to show off projects the Cyan Cohort had been working on since the war ended. It seemed like yesterday when we'd feared the children were all but lost. I searched for her face among the crowds.

I spotted her over at one of the booths. She struck an elegant figure in a baby blue sundress. Her golden-brown hair was radiant in the sunlight, and her aura was brighter than ever. She was standing next to little Sammy, and he was in the middle of explaining his project to her. "A lot of regolith is made up of oxygen. My invention will eat regolith and spit out oxygen as waste. When atmosphere leaks from the dome, we can feed my machine some moondust, and then..."

Whenever I stole a glance at Tera, I swelled with a heady mix of contentment, pride, and gratitude. We spent warm summer days together working the fields behind the school, running the Cyan classroom, and helping out at the elderly home. The best part of our days were in the labs, where the students tested out their prototypes—many of which were rejiggered from the designs Onyxion had shared with them. Sometimes, when I woke up in the middle of the night, I liked to watch Tera sleeping by my side. And in those quiet moments, I often found myself thinking it was a life more fulfilling than I could've imagined or felt I deserved.

I was interrupted by a tug on my sleeve. I looked down at a mop of dark hair streaked with blue and green. Quinn was staring up at me. Her amber eyes were sparkling and full of mischief. She was still the quiet, earnest child I'd collected circuit boards with in the alley so long ago. But now, instead of being covered in dust, she was healthy and happy. And it made me glad.

"Mister," Quinn said, "I want to show you something." She led me over to her presentation booth. The long table there had small devices set up on it. I counted ten black objects in total. They were identical and were each the size of a plum. They looked like miniature tripods spaced apart in a circle.

"It's a test model," she said. "I can't fab it any bigger than this yet."

"It looks amazing." I was buying some time to figure out what it was. I failed. "Um, what does it do?"

"It's a new dome!" She squealed and hopped up and down in her moonbooties.

The black contraptions sat motionless on the table. I couldn't make heads or tails of them. "How does it work?"

"I'm glad you asked, Mister." She threw her arms up in the air in excitement. "The dome gives us lots of problems because it's one layer."

Her insight was beyond her years. Meteorites or hostile threats put us at the mercy of catastrophic events. The dome's fragility contributed to popular perception on Earth that the Colony was an experiment that could go south. When governments on Earth were asked to commit full-on, they dithered because our temporary foothold in space might be abandoned for any reason. "You're right," I said.

"But what if it can give permission—like a human cell? Like, what if it's got more layers?"

But one was the maximum the Colony could afford. The dome's maintenance required extensive resources and labor. The solutions we'd seen thrown about before were wishful thinking.

She pointed to the black tripods on the table. "My generators make a field barrier. Since it's not a hard material, it'll be easier. When we expand and need more space, we can move the inner layer to the outside. We can turn on parts of the barrier to keep unwanted things out. But we can also use it let good things in."

It was an ambitious project. The children were light years ahead of where I'd been at that age. Instead of pointing out what was broken, they imagined long-term solutions. I said, "That's an incredible concept, Quinn." To spare a child's imagination, I didn't mention how field manipulation was no small feat. Even after all this time, I still didn't know how my abilities worked.

She shouted, "Now watch!" and startled me. She smashed a tiny fist onto the red push-switch beside her.

The black tripods on the table began to spin up. They were slow at first, but magnets propelled them along until the objects reached unbelievable rotational speeds and became blurs. A tiny glimmer emerged from the center of the array. Then, the light erupted into a blinding flash. I flinched and shut my eyes. *This light—why did it feel so familiar? Oh yes. It was the last thing I saw when I jumped off the Thomas Jefferson bridge so long ago.*

I opened my eyes again. On the table in front of me was a hemispherical dome. The barrier was projected across the black tripods which were holding it together. The outer hemisphere contained two additional domes inside, creating three concentric layers in total.

"Do you think my design will work on something bigger?" she asked. She was enjoying how speechless I was.

My astonishment turned into a wide grin. "You know what—I think you might be onto something."

Yes, in the face of constraints and limitations, there was still freedom. And even if all states were to exist simultaneously, when I hear the children's laughter, I glimpse the future yet to come.

Acknowledgements

My deepest gratitude to Nina Munteanu for her guidance and sense of humor from the beginning to the end. And to Bruce McAllister for lending his voice, courage, and generosity.

I extend my thanks especially to my editor, AM Leibowitz, for her keen judgment and for working tirelessly on this project.

My acknowledgements to Dale E. Lehman, and early readers who've had a hand in critiquing this work. And to Vanesa Garkova and Euan Monaghan for their artistic inspiration and design. Your talents are valued.

For those who gave their support whether they realized it or not. M. G., a friend, mentor, and fine human being. N. H. & E. S., you lit the way. For J. C., who dreamt. For A. M. V., who believed.

About the Author

Tom Dyne has been a joke writer, web software developer, cancer gene sequencer, psychological researcher, and grant administrator for a DV nonprofit. What he'll never tell anyone is that he's a fan of tabletop games, Gentoo, and mechanical keyboards.

www.ingramcontent.com/pod-product-compliance
Lightning Source LLC
Chambersburg PA
CBHW021059110726
47900CB00007B/1944